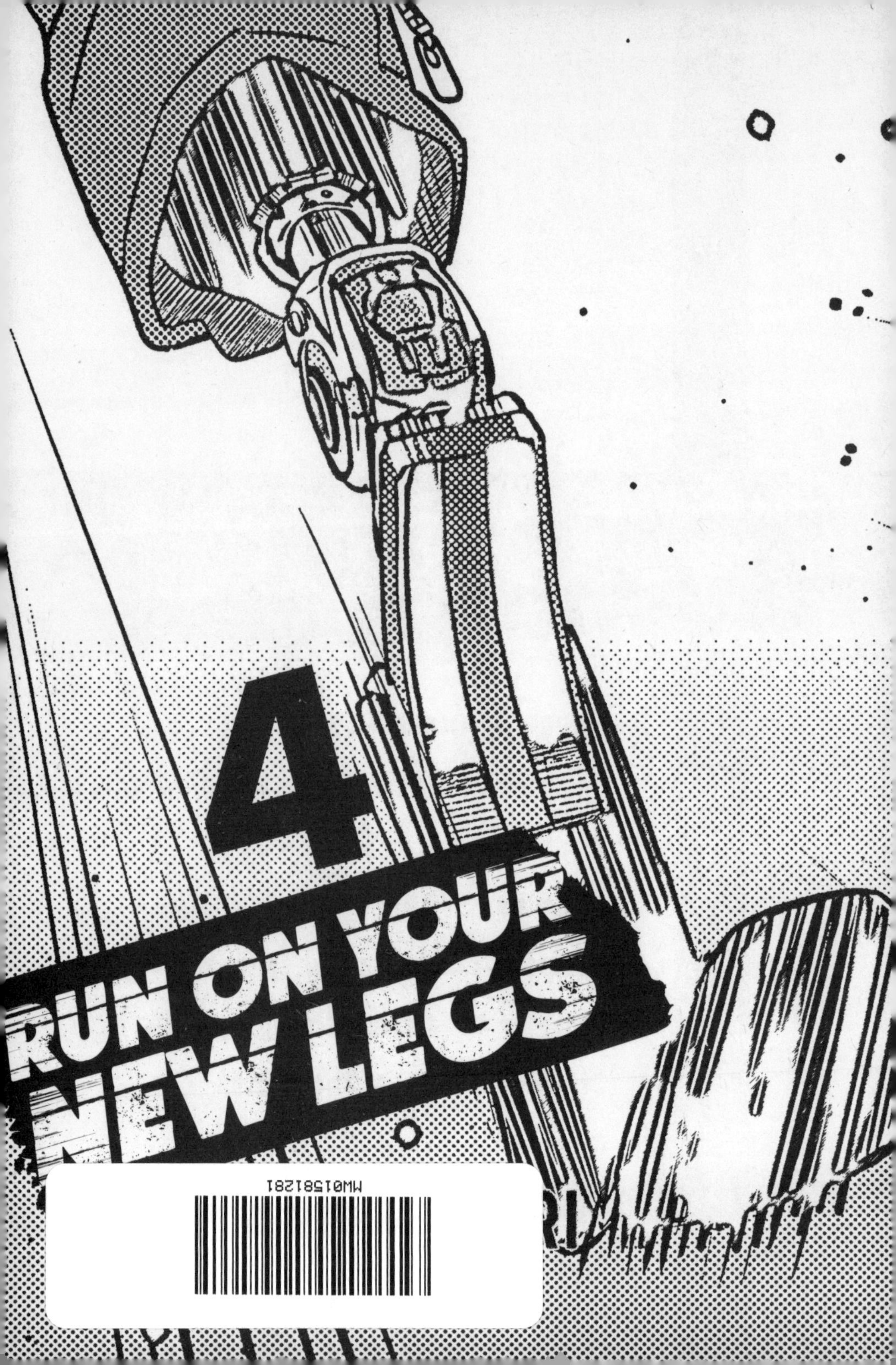
4
RUN ON YOUR NEW LEGS

TABLE OF CONTENTS

Chapter 23: Inter-High Canceled 003

Chapter 24: If It Were Me 021

Chapter 25: This Feeling 039

Chapter 26: I'll Be Cheering for You 057

Chapter 27: I Ain't Giving Up 079

Chapter 28: Back Then 097

Chapter 29: That Same Sky 115

Chapter 30: Check Me Out Then 135

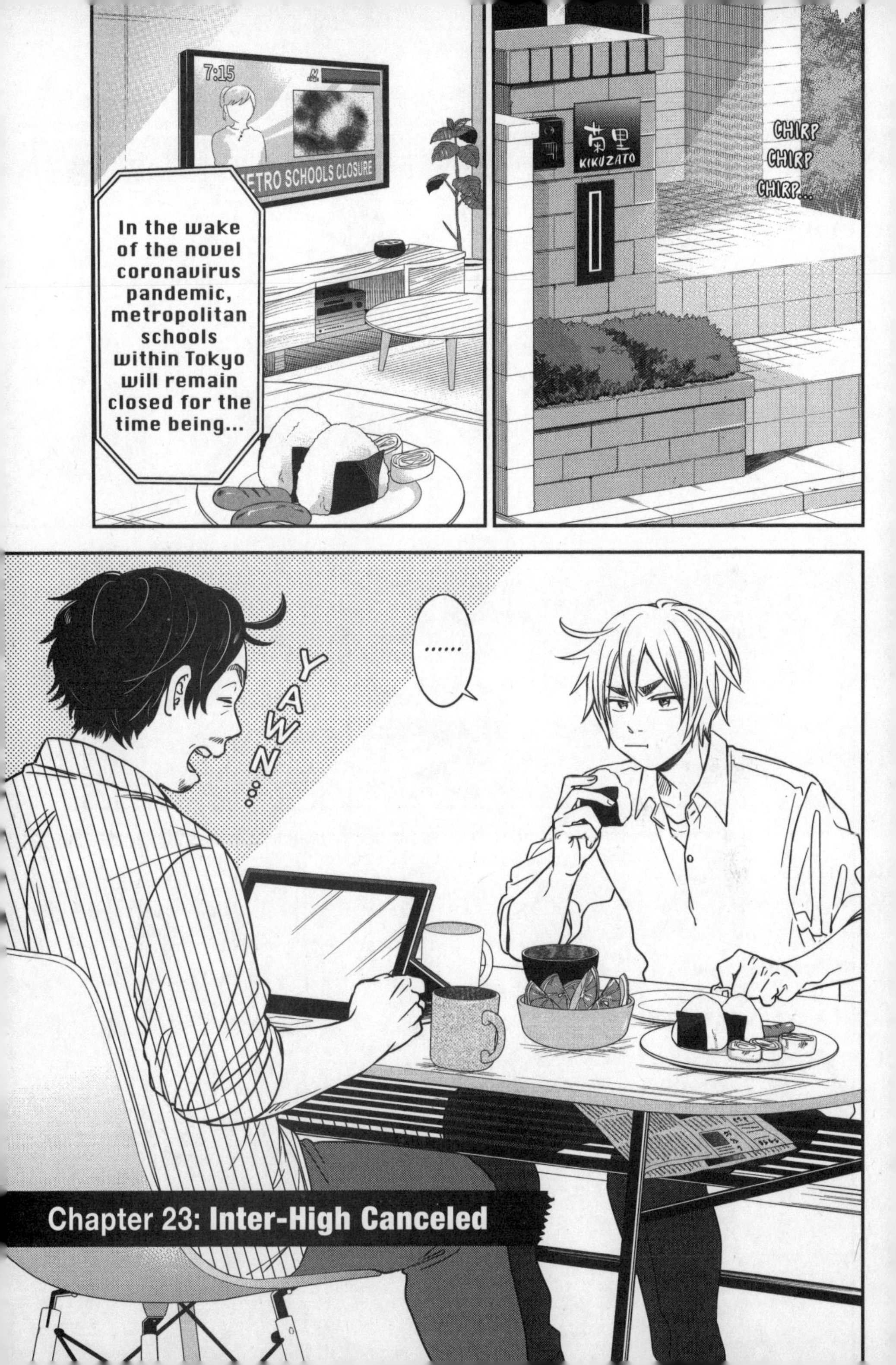
菊里
KIKUZATO
CHIRP
CHIRP
CHIRP...
7:15
ETRO SCHOOLS CLOSURE
In the wake of the novel coronavirus pandemic, metropolitan schools within Tokyo will remain closed for the time being...
......
YAWN...
Chapter 23: Inter-High Canceled

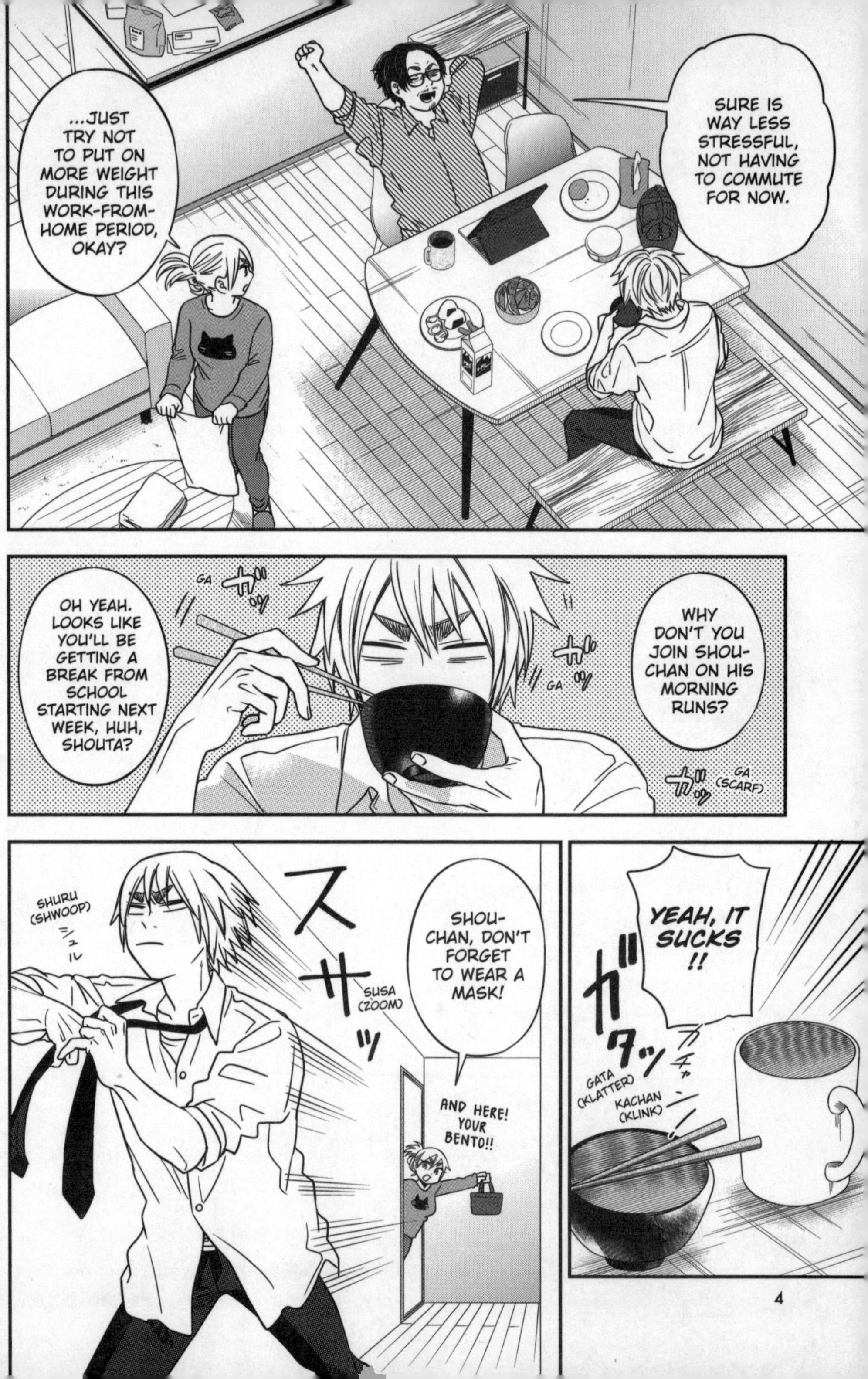

SURE IS WAY LESS STRESSFUL, NOT HAVING TO COMMUTE FOR NOW.
...JUST TRY NOT TO PUT ON MORE WEIGHT DURING THIS WORK-FROM-HOME PERIOD, OKAY?
WHY DON'T YOU JOIN SHOU-CHAN ON HIS MORNING RUNS?
GA (SCARF)
GA
GA
OH YEAH. LOOKS LIKE YOU'LL BE GETTING A BREAK FROM SCHOOL STARTING NEXT WEEK, HUH, SHOUTA?
YEAH, IT SUCKS!!
GATA (KLATTER)
KACHAN (KLINK)
SHOU-CHAN, DON'T FORGET TO WEAR A MASK!
AND HERE! YOUR BENTO!!
SUSA (ZOOM)
SHURU (SHWOOP)

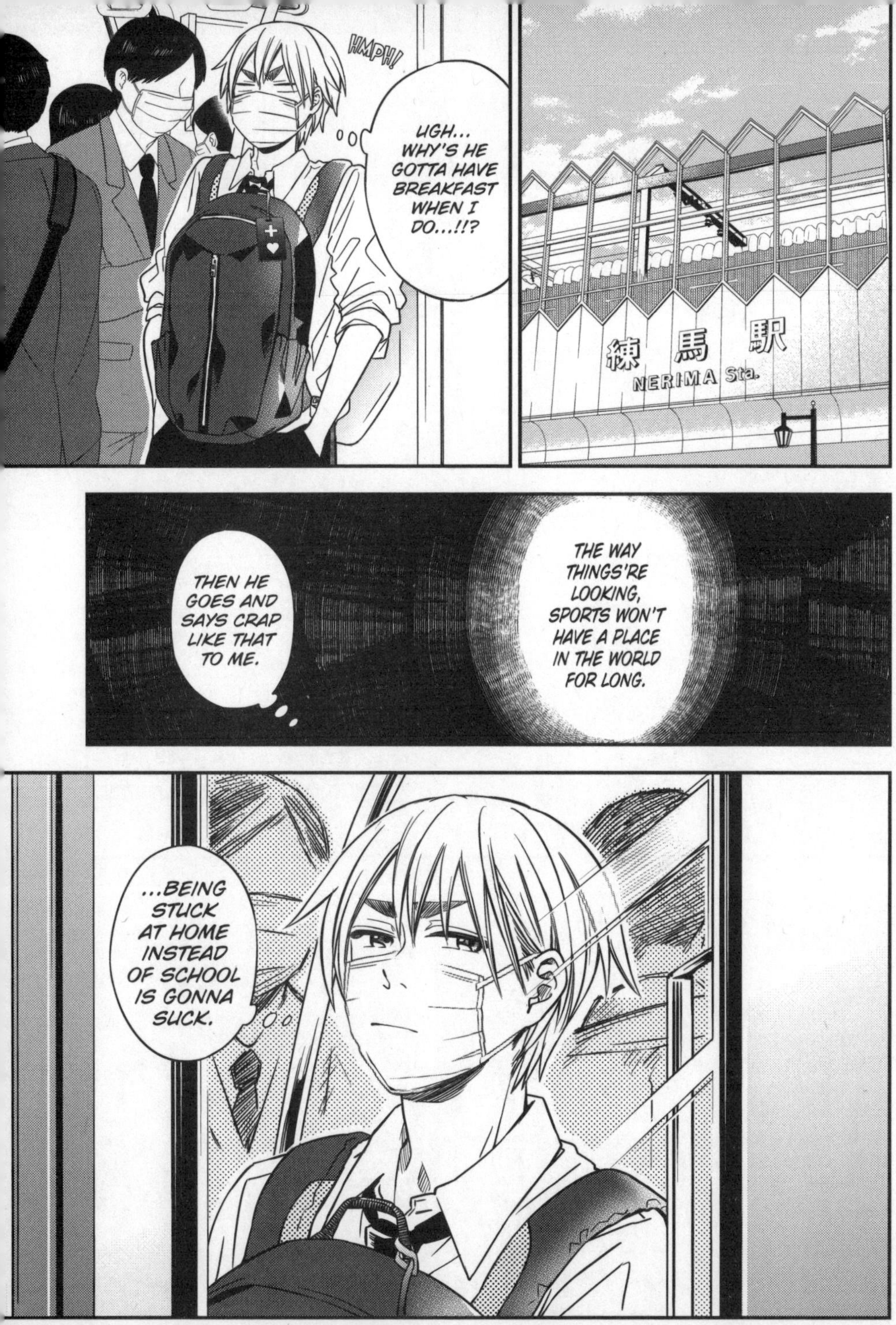
練馬駅
NERIMA Sta.
HMPH!
UGH... WHY'S HE GOTTA HAVE BREAKFAST WHEN I DO...!!?
THE WAY THINGS'RE LOOKING, SPORTS WON'T HAVE A PLACE IN THE WORLD FOR LONG.
THEN HE GOES AND SAYS CRAP LIKE THAT TO ME.
...BEING STUCK AT HOME INSTEAD OF SCHOOL IS GONNA SUCK.

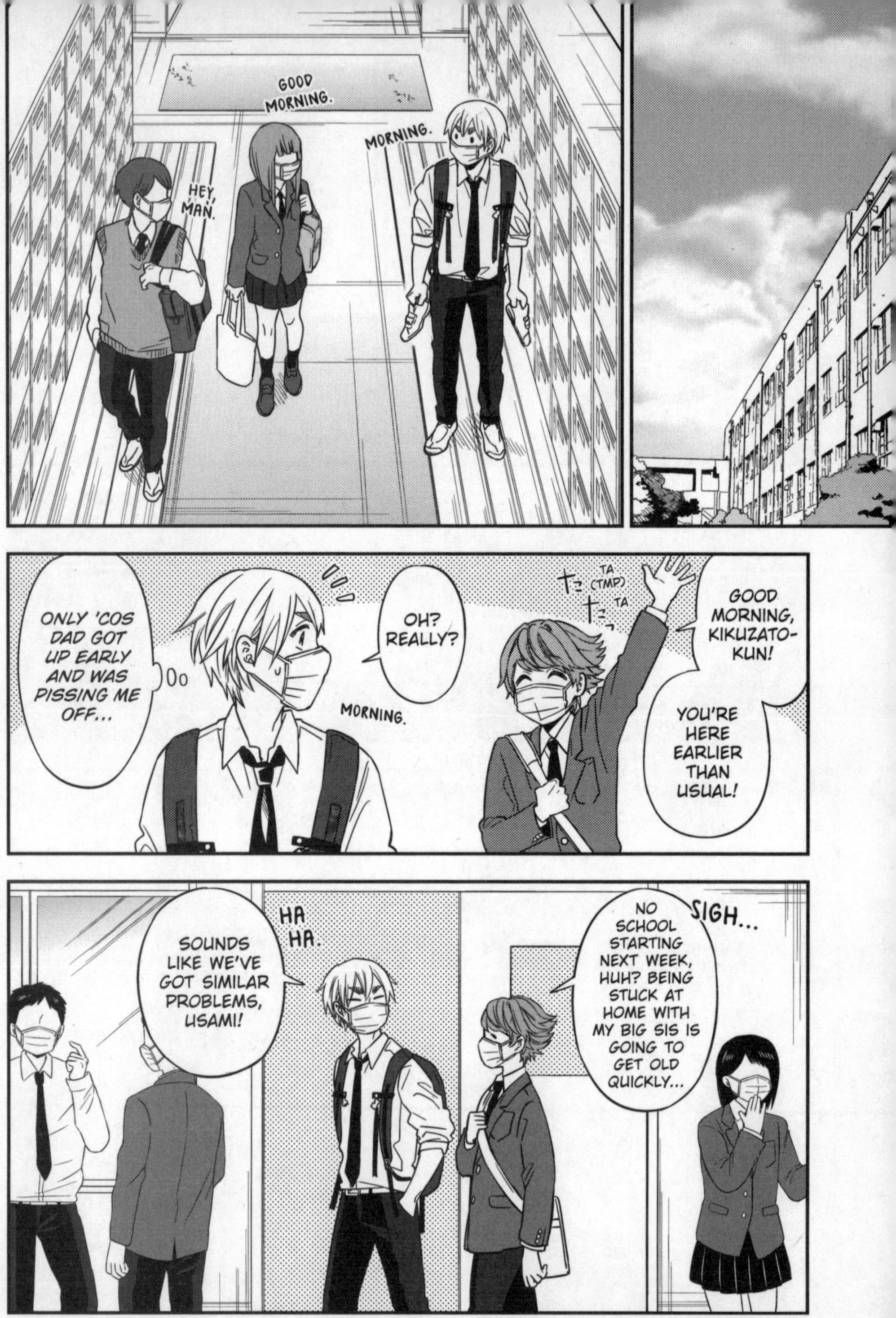
MORNING.
GOOD MORNING.
HEY, MAN.
GOOD MORNING, KIKUZATO-KUN!
YOU'RE HERE EARLIER THAN USUAL!
TA (TMP) TA
OH? REALLY?
MORNING.
ONLY 'COS DAD GOT UP EARLY AND WAS PISSING ME OFF...
SIGH...
NO SCHOOL STARTING NEXT WEEK, HUH? BEING STUCK AT HOME WITH MY BIG SIS IS GOING TO GET OLD QUICKLY...
HA HA.
SOUNDS LIKE WE'VE GOT SIMILAR PROBLEMS, USAMI!

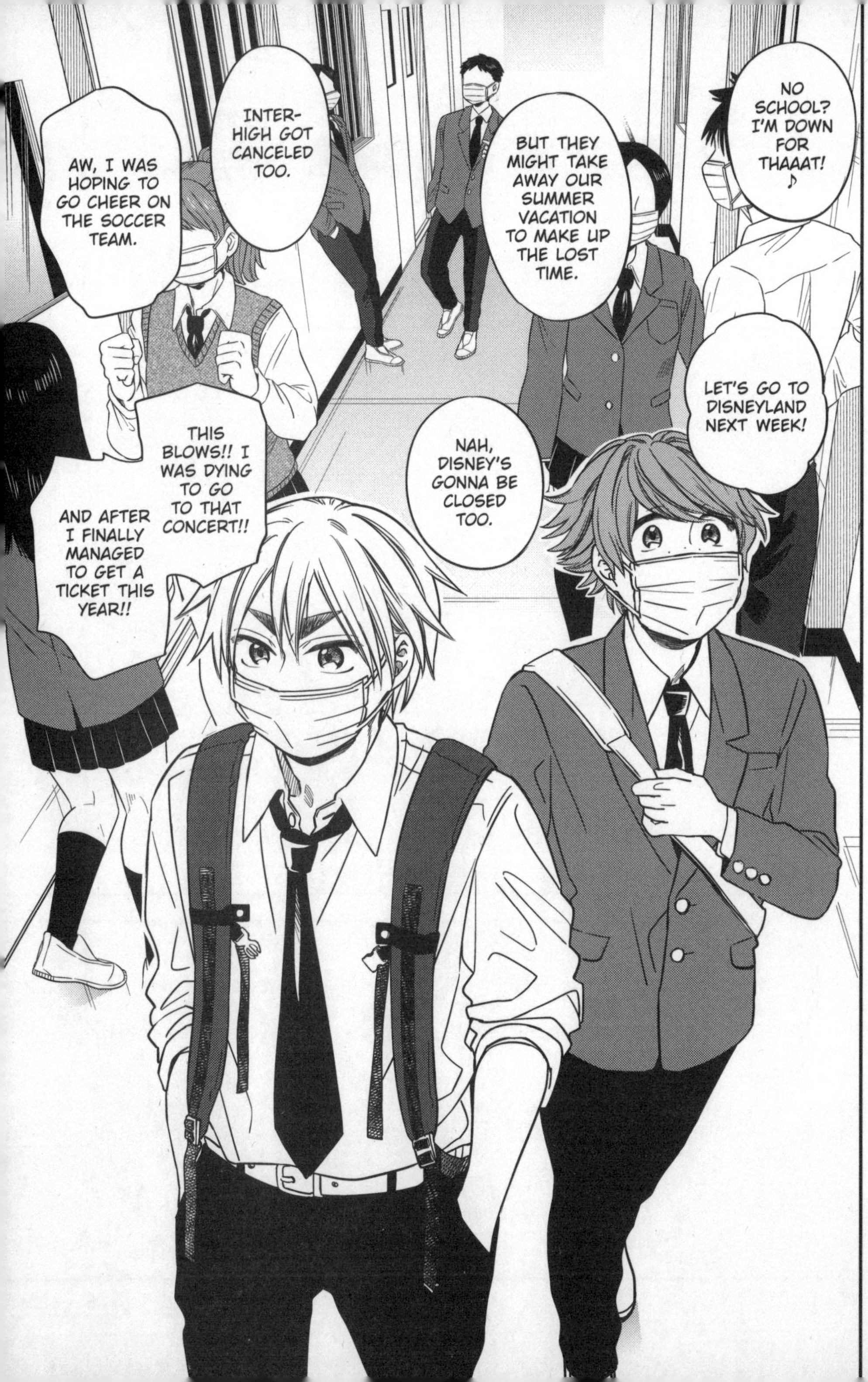
NO SCHOOL? I'M DOWN FOR THAAAT! ♪
BUT THEY MIGHT TAKE AWAY OUR SUMMER VACATION TO MAKE UP THE LOST TIME.
INTER-HIGH GOT CANCELED TOO.
AW, I WAS HOPING TO GO CHEER ON THE SOCCER TEAM.
LET'S GO TO DISNEYLAND NEXT WEEK!
NAH, DISNEY'S GONNA BE CLOSED TOO.
THIS BLOWS!! I WAS DYING TO GO TO THAT CONCERT!!
AND AFTER I FINALLY MANAGED TO GET A TICKET THIS YEAR!!

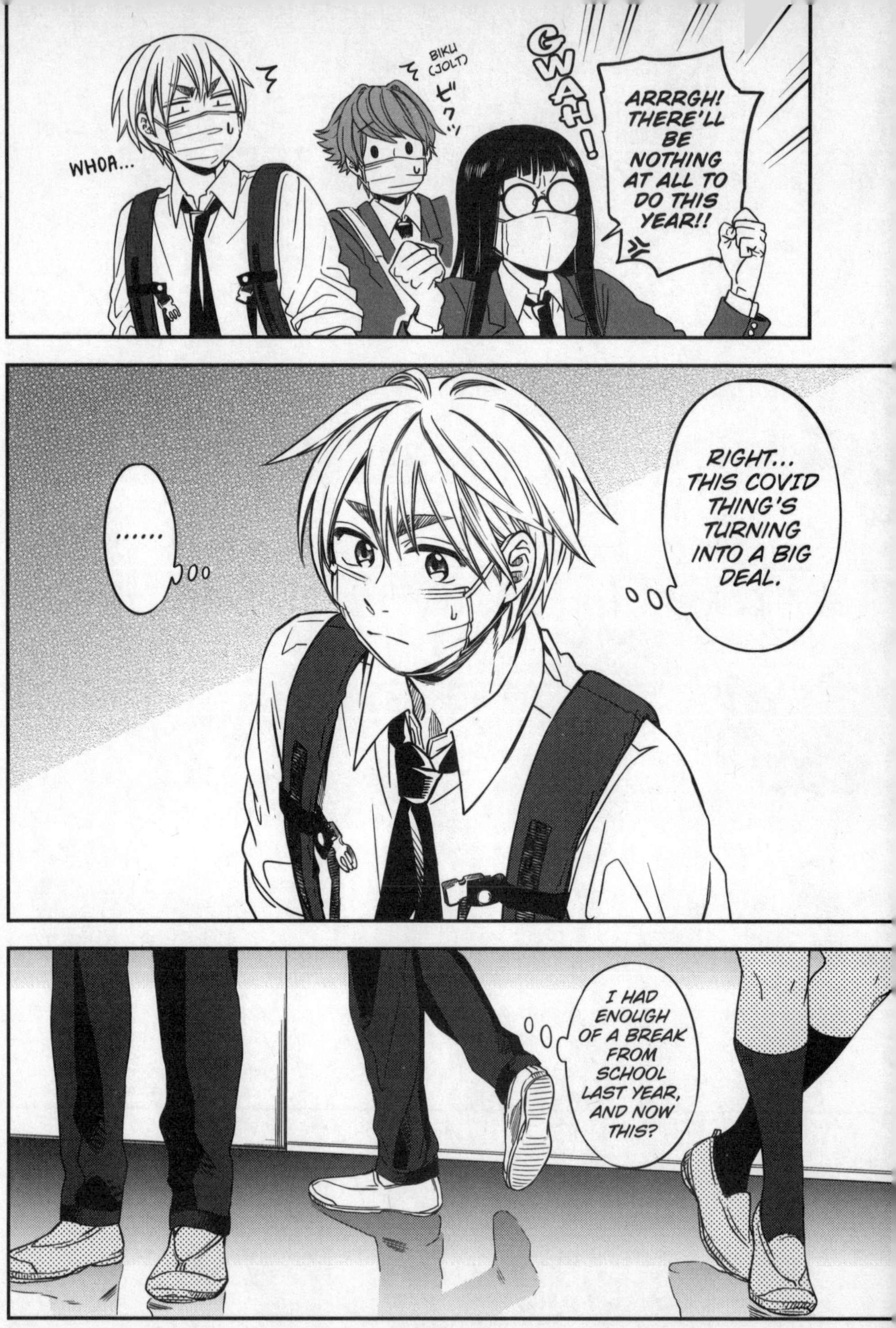
GWAH!
ARRRGH! THERE'LL BE NOTHING AT ALL TO DO THIS YEAR!!
BIKU (JOLT)
ビクッ
WHOA...
RIGHT... THIS COVID THING'S TURNING INTO A BIG DEAL.
......
I HAD ENOUGH OF A BREAK FROM SCHOOL LAST YEAR, AND NOW THIS?

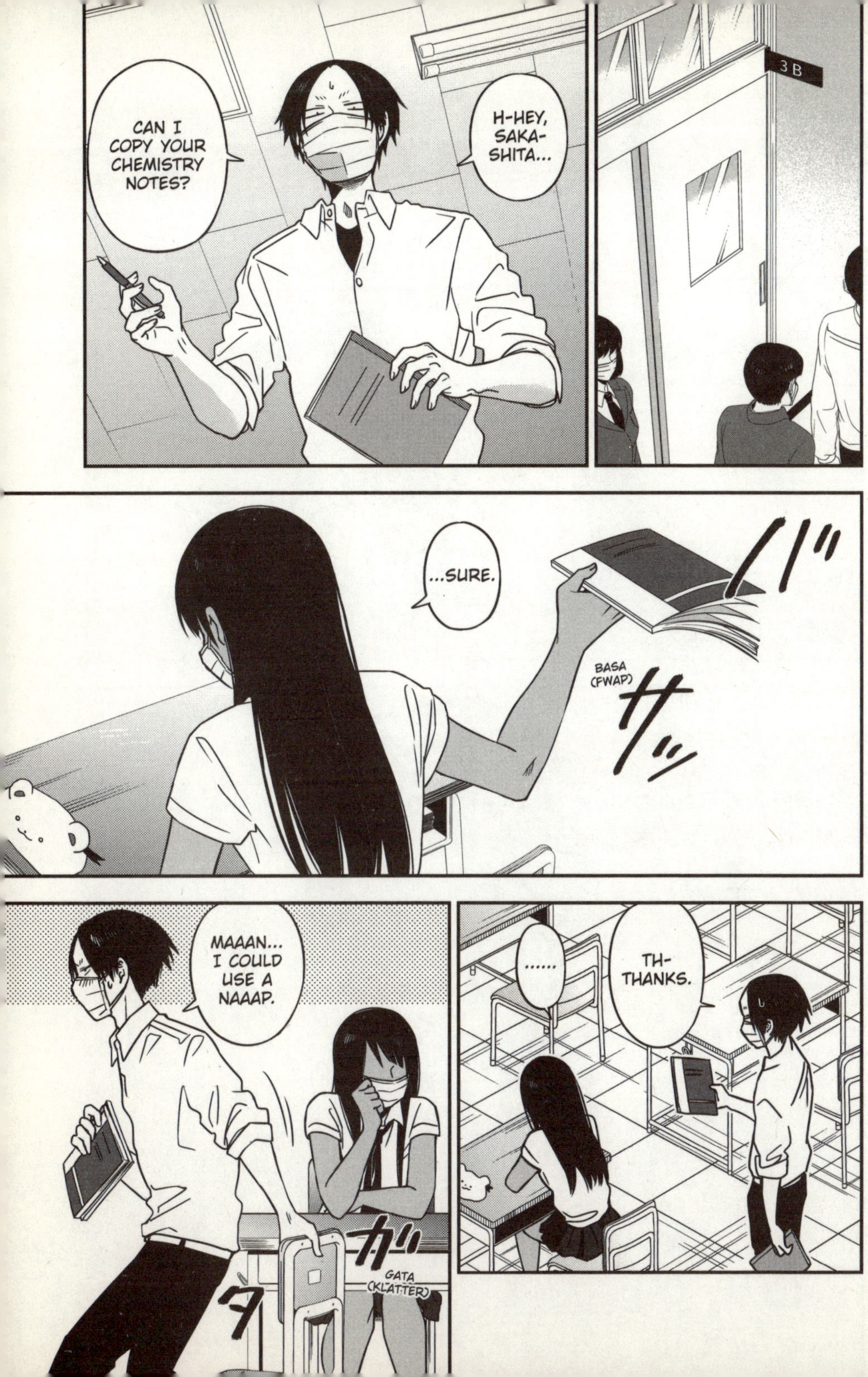
3 B
H-HEY, SAKA-SHITA...
CAN I COPY YOUR CHEMISTRY NOTES?
...SURE.
BASA (FWAP)
TH-THANKS.
......
MAAAN... I COULD USE A NAAAP.
GATA (KLATTER)

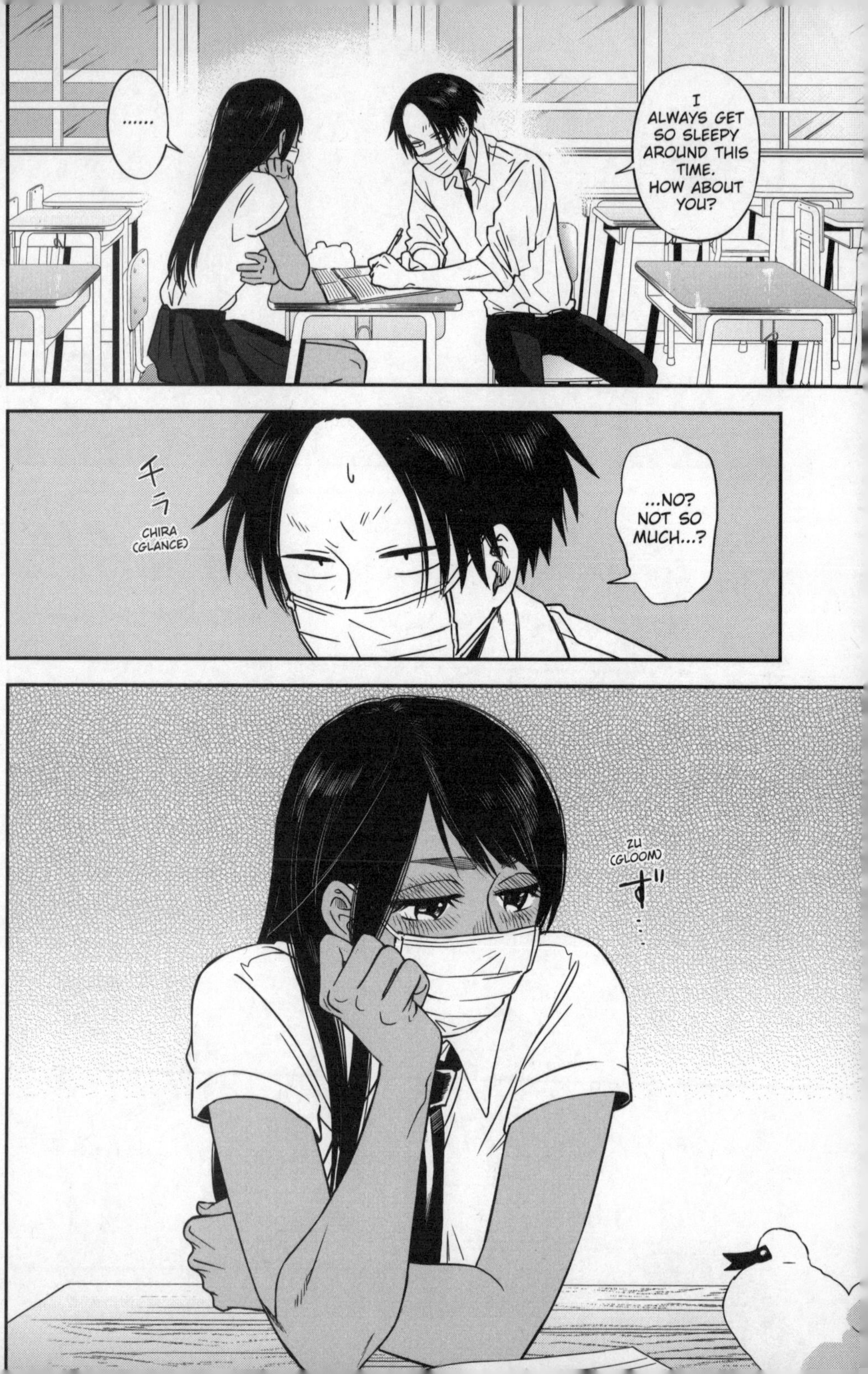
I ALWAYS GET SO SLEEPY AROUND THIS TIME. HOW ABOUT YOU?
......
...NO? NOT SO MUCH...?
チラ
CHIRA (GLANCE)
ZU (GLOOM)
ず…

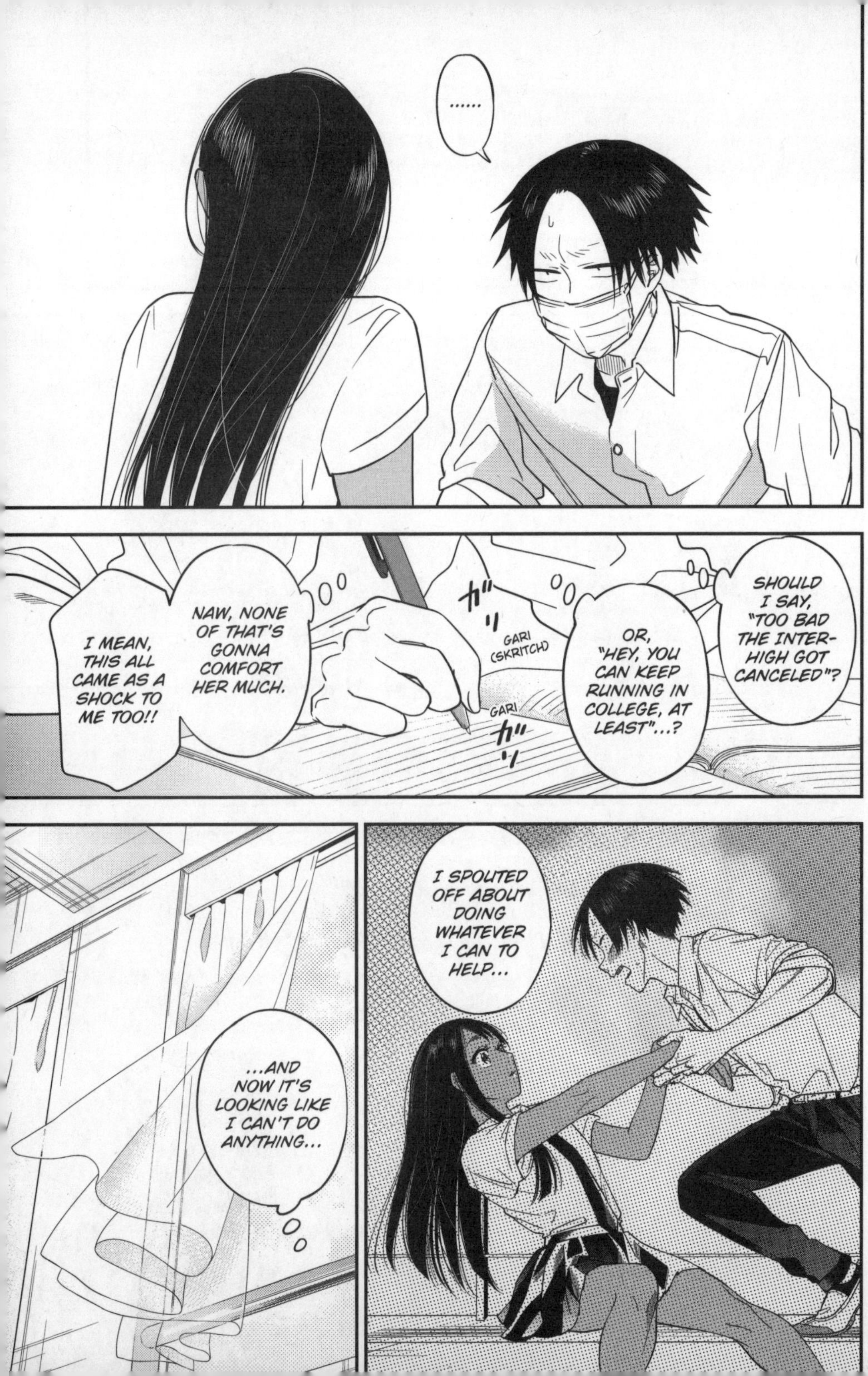
......
SHOULD I SAY, "TOO BAD THE INTER-HIGH GOT CANCELED"?
OR, "HEY, YOU CAN KEEP RUNNING IN COLLEGE, AT LEAST"...?
ガリ
GARI (SKRITCH)
ガリ
GARI
NAW, NONE OF THAT'S GONNA COMFORT HER MUCH.
I MEAN, THIS ALL CAME AS A SHOCK TO ME TOO!!
I SPOUTED OFF ABOUT DOING WHATEVER I CAN TO HELP...
...AND NOW IT'S LOOKING LIKE I CAN'T DO ANYTHING...

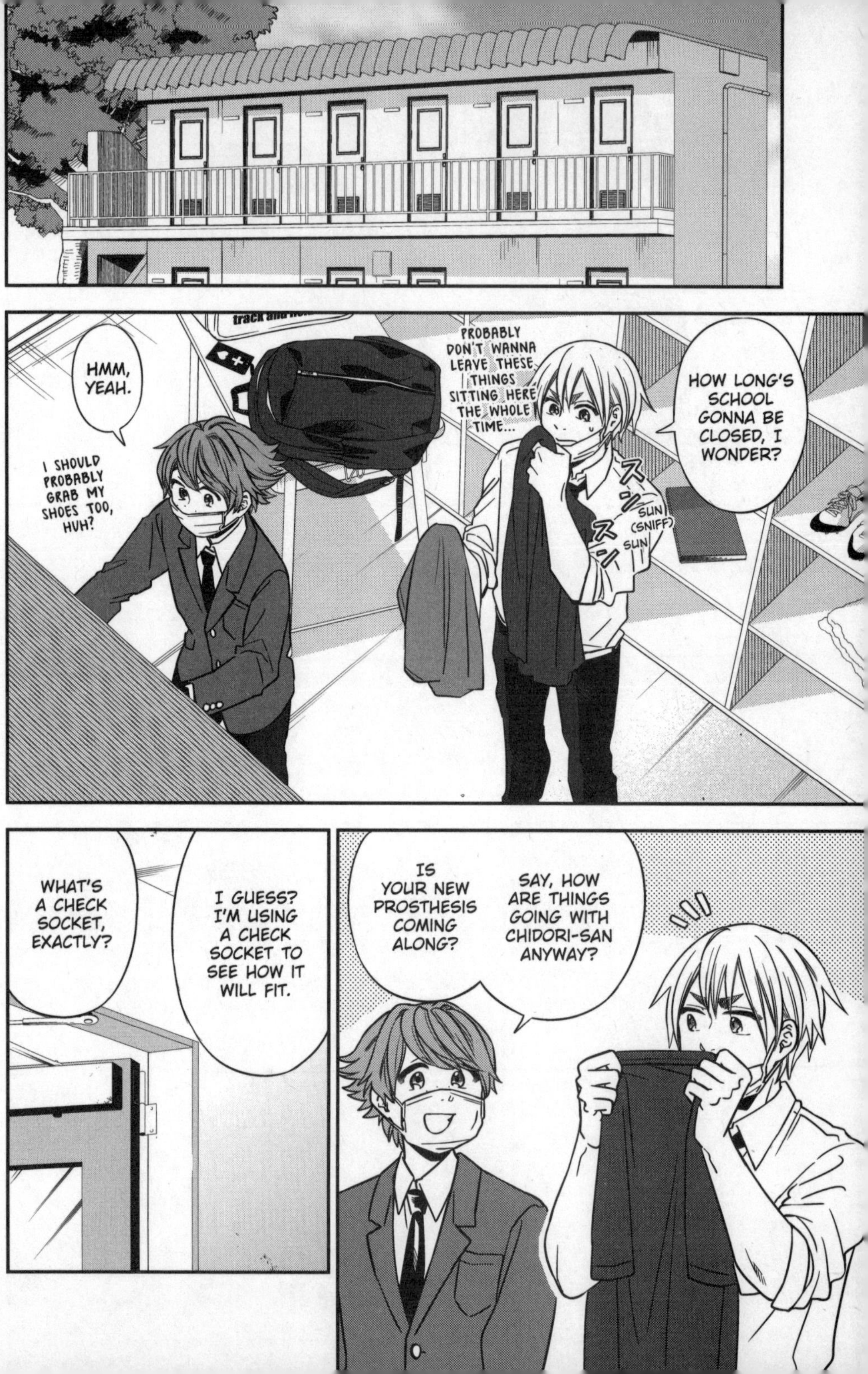
HOW LONG'S SCHOOL GONNA BE CLOSED, I WONDER?
SUN (SNIFF) SUN
PROBABLY DON'T WANNA LEAVE THESE THINGS SITTING HERE THE WHOLE TIME...
HMM, YEAH.
I SHOULD PROBABLY GRAB MY SHOES TOO, HUH?
SAY, HOW ARE THINGS GOING WITH CHIDORI-SAN ANYWAY?
IS YOUR NEW PROSTHESIS COMING ALONG?
I GUESS? I'M USING A CHECK SOCKET TO SEE HOW IT WILL FIT.
WHAT'S A CHECK SOCKET, EXACTLY?

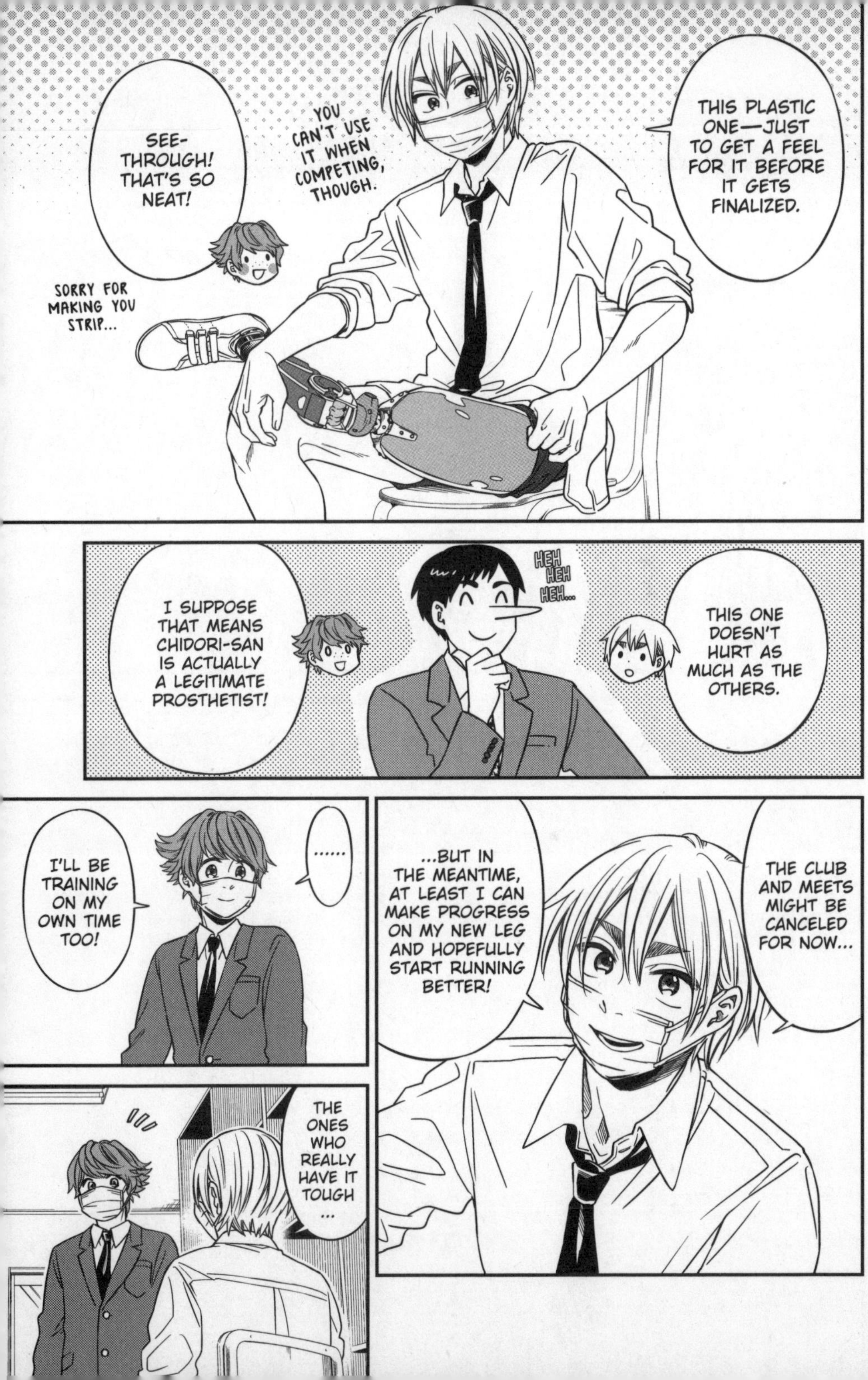

THIS PLASTIC ONE—JUST TO GET A FEEL FOR IT BEFORE IT GETS FINALIZED.
YOU CAN'T USE IT WHEN COMPETING, THOUGH.
SEE-THROUGH! THAT'S SO NEAT!
SORRY FOR MAKING YOU STRIP...
THIS ONE DOESN'T HURT AS MUCH AS THE OTHERS.
HEH HEH HEH...
I SUPPOSE THAT MEANS CHIDORI-SAN IS ACTUALLY A LEGITIMATE PROSTHETIST!
THE CLUB AND MEETS MIGHT BE CANCELED FOR NOW...
...BUT IN THE MEANTIME, AT LEAST I CAN MAKE PROGRESS ON MY NEW LEG AND HOPEFULLY START RUNNING BETTER!
......
I'LL BE TRAINING ON MY OWN TIME TOO!
THE ONES WHO REALLY HAVE IT TOUGH...

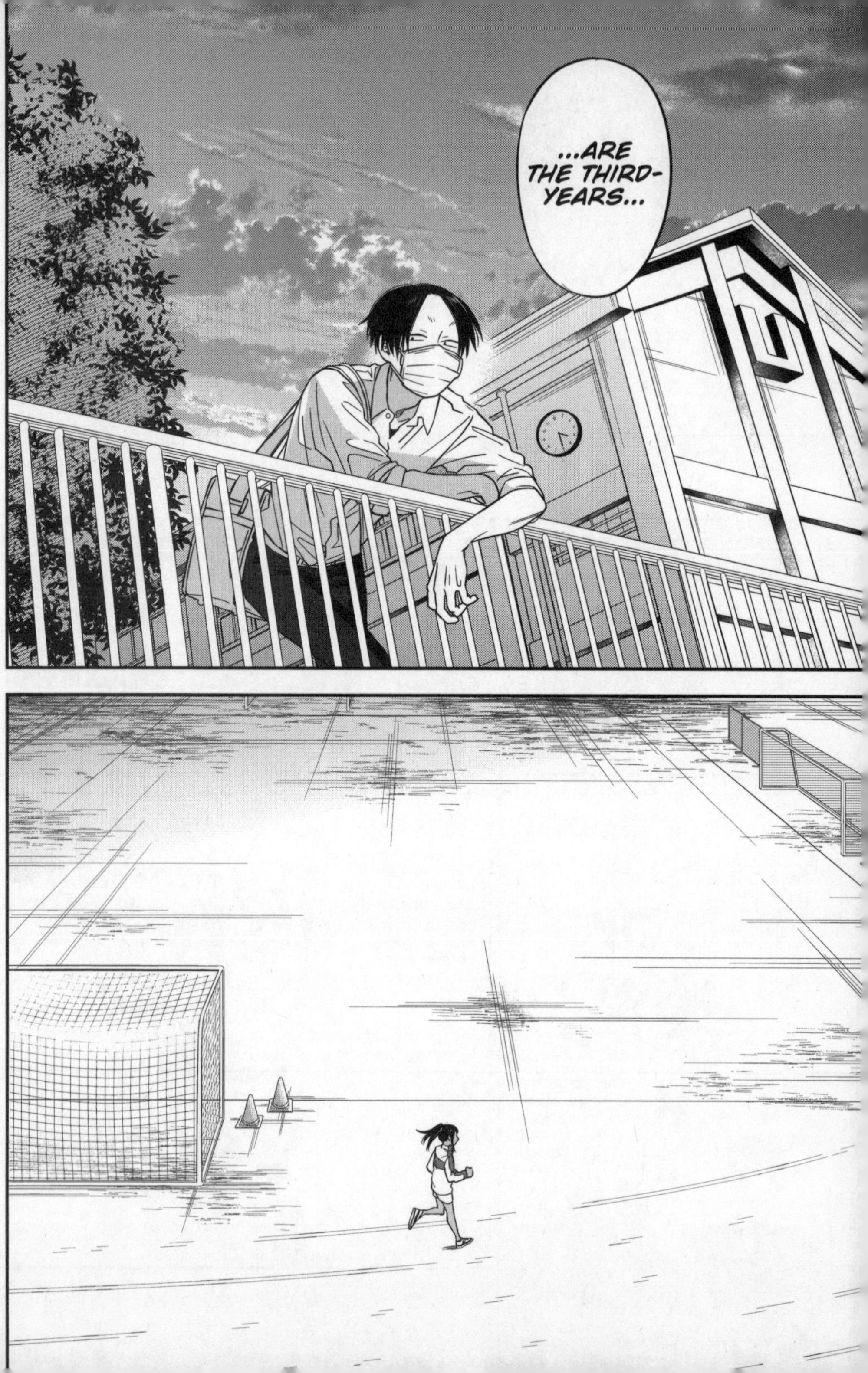
...ARE THE THIRD-YEARS...

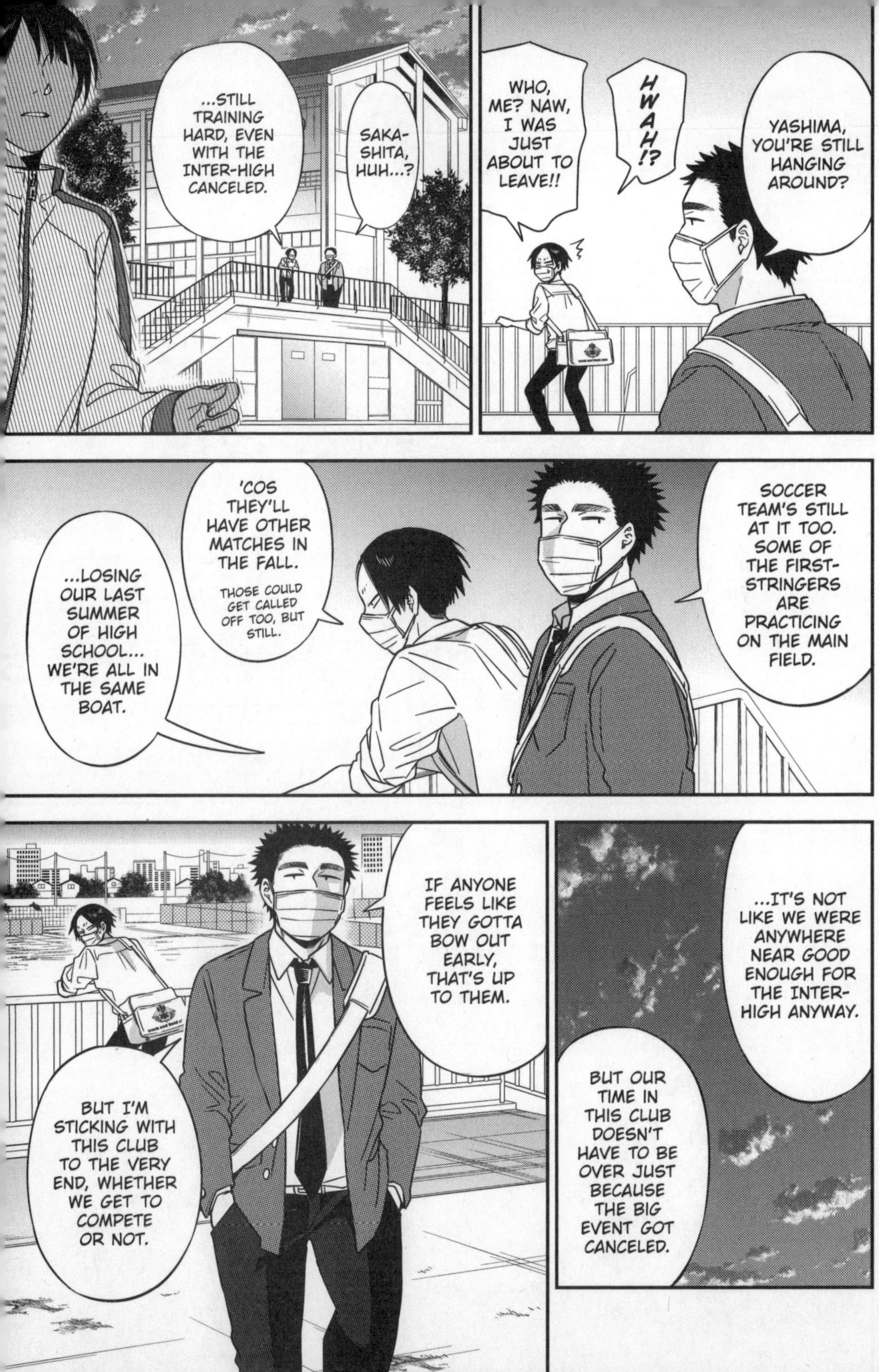
YASHIMA, YOU'RE STILL HANGING AROUND?
HWAH!?
WHO, ME? NAW, I WAS JUST ABOUT TO LEAVE!!
SAKA-SHITA, HUH...?
...STILL TRAINING HARD, EVEN WITH THE INTER-HIGH CANCELED.
SOCCER TEAM'S STILL AT IT TOO. SOME OF THE FIRST-STRINGERS ARE PRACTICING ON THE MAIN FIELD.
'COS THEY'LL HAVE OTHER MATCHES IN THE FALL.
THOSE COULD GET CALLED OFF TOO, BUT STILL.
...LOSING OUR LAST SUMMER OF HIGH SCHOOL... WE'RE ALL IN THE SAME BOAT.
...IT'S NOT LIKE WE WERE ANYWHERE NEAR GOOD ENOUGH FOR THE INTER-HIGH ANYWAY.
BUT OUR TIME IN THIS CLUB DOESN'T HAVE TO BE OVER JUST BECAUSE THE BIG EVENT GOT CANCELED.
IF ANYONE FEELS LIKE THEY GOTTA BOW OUT EARLY, THAT'S UP TO THEM.
BUT I'M STICKING WITH THIS CLUB TO THE VERY END, WHETHER WE GET TO COMPETE OR NOT.

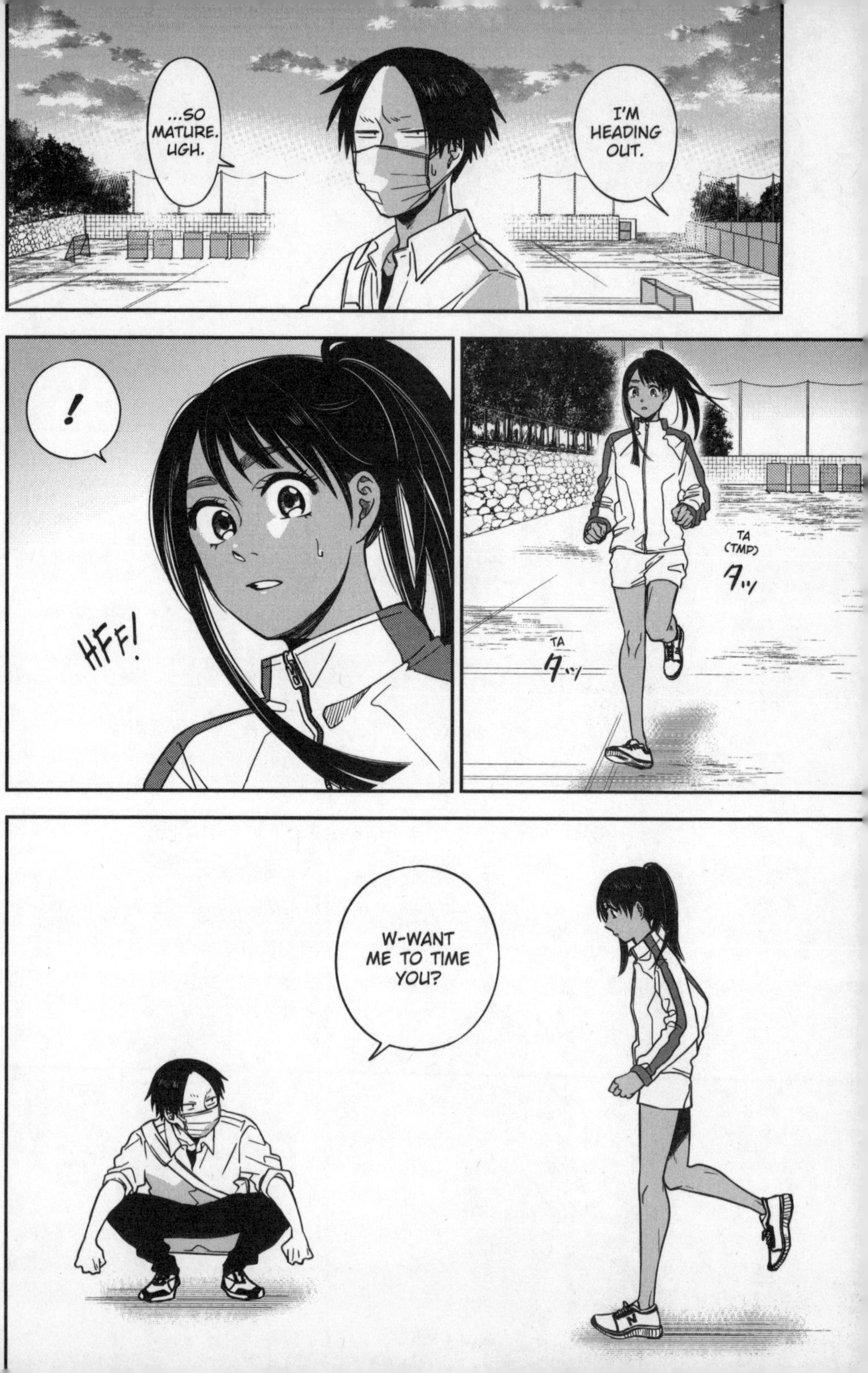
I'M HEADING OUT.
...SO MATURE. UGH.
TA (TMP)
タッ
TA
タッ
!
HFF!
W-WANT ME TO TIME YOU?

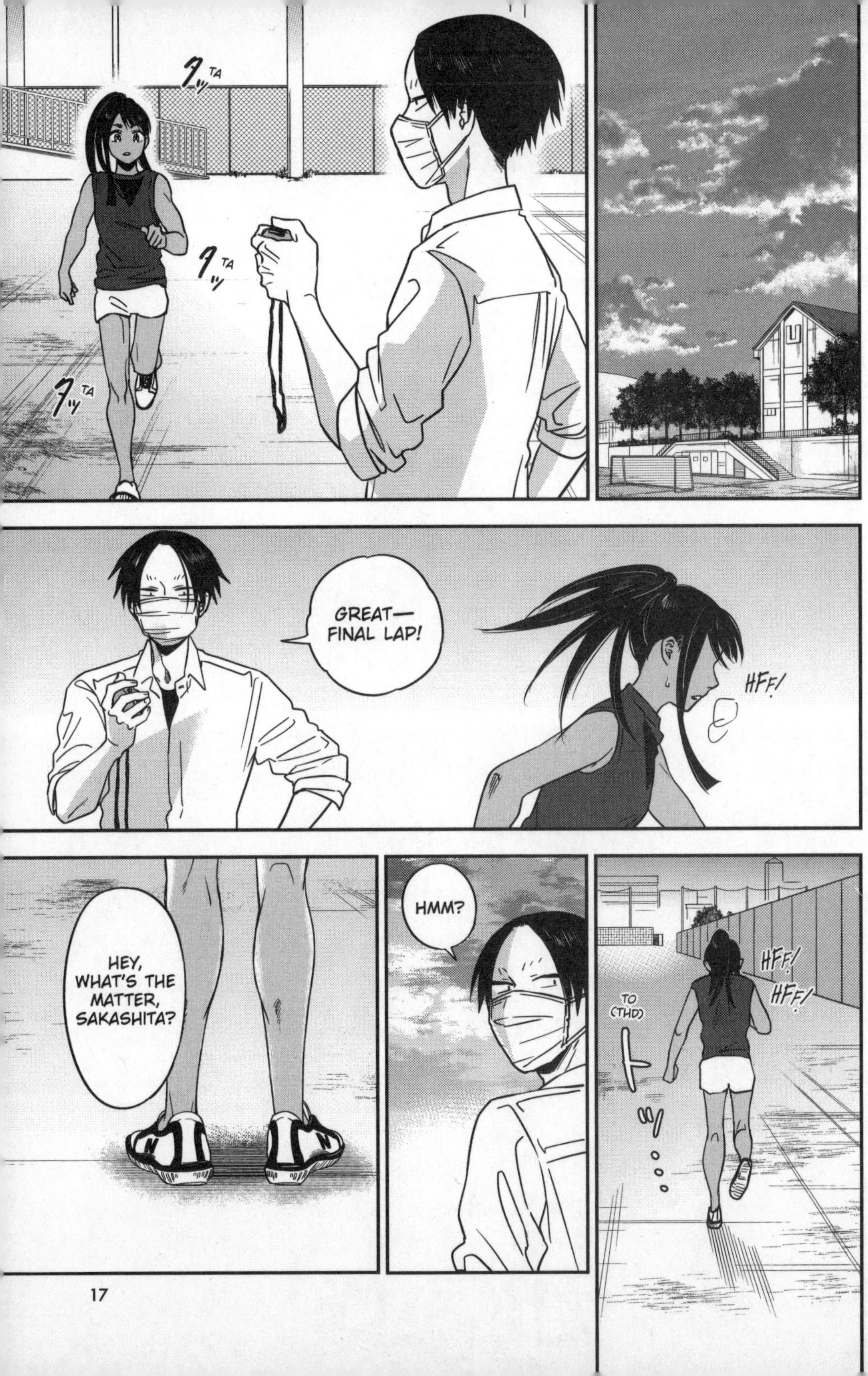

タッ TA
タッ TA
タッ TA
HFF!
GREAT—FINAL LAP!
HFF!
HFF!
TO (THD)
トッ
HMM?
HEY, WHAT'S THE MATTER, SAKASHITA?

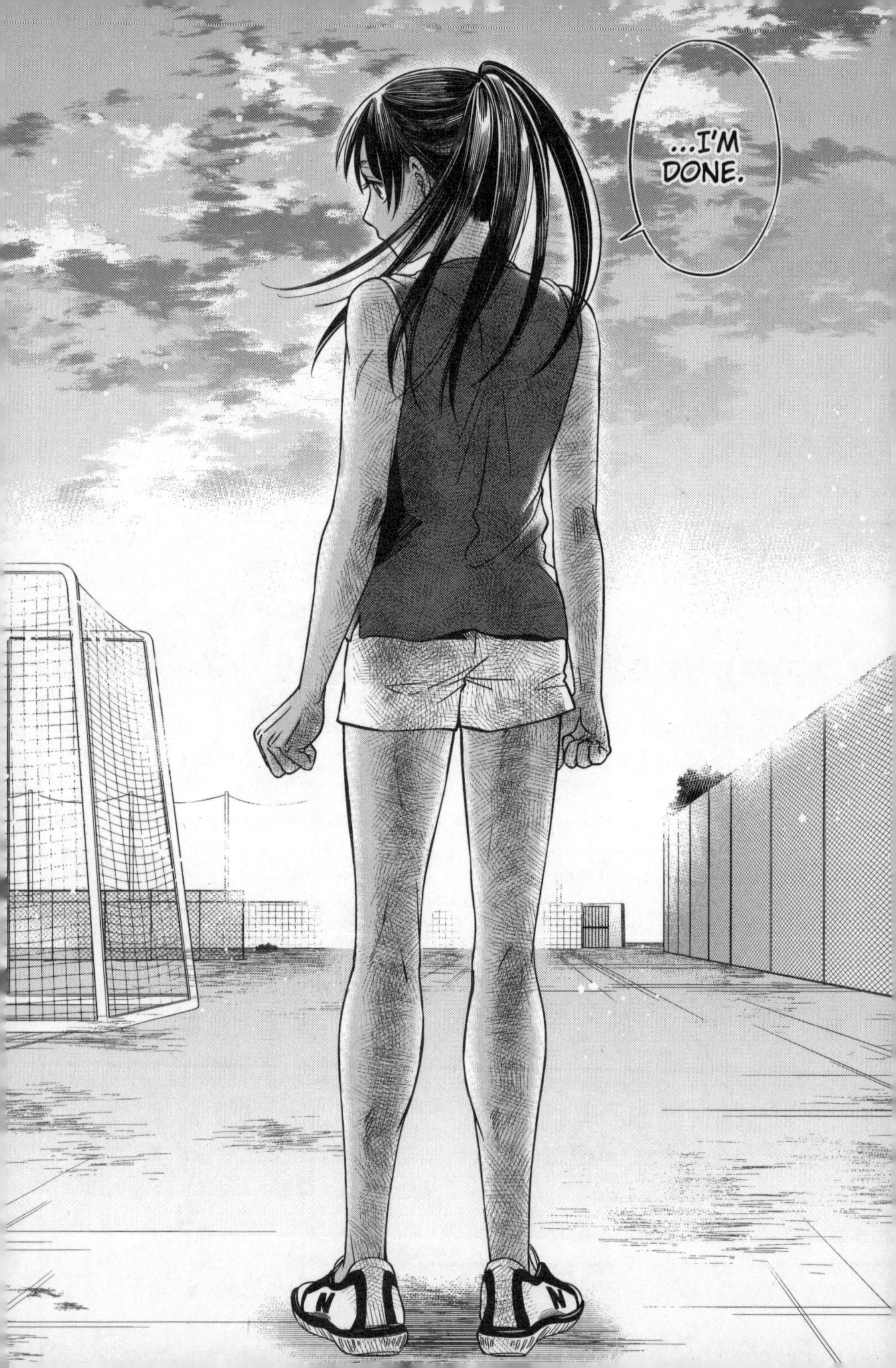
...I'M DONE.

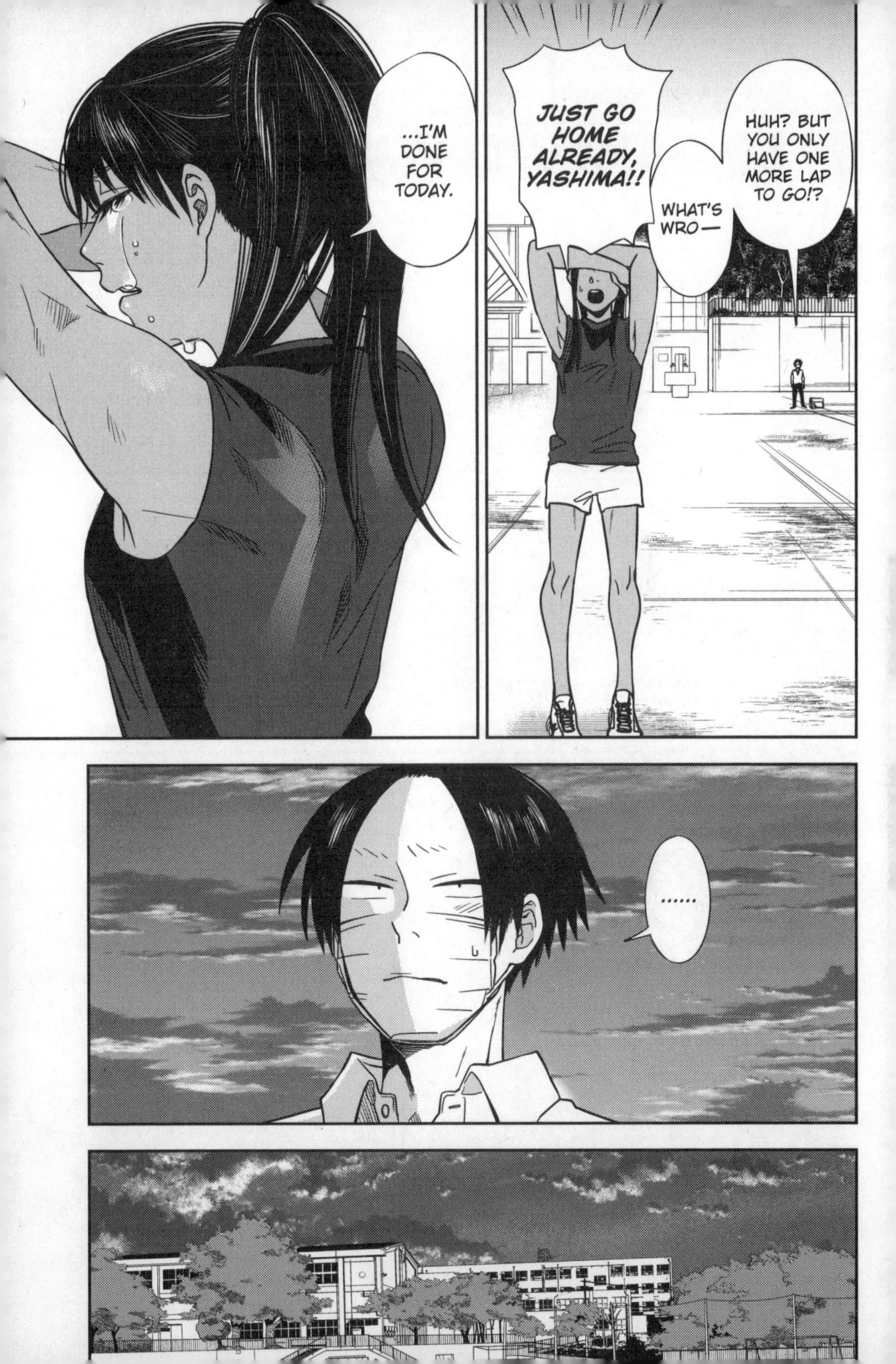
HUH? BUT YOU ONLY HAVE ONE MORE LAP TO GO!?
WHAT'S WRO—
JUST GO HOME ALREADY, YASHIMA!!
...I'M DONE FOR TODAY.
......

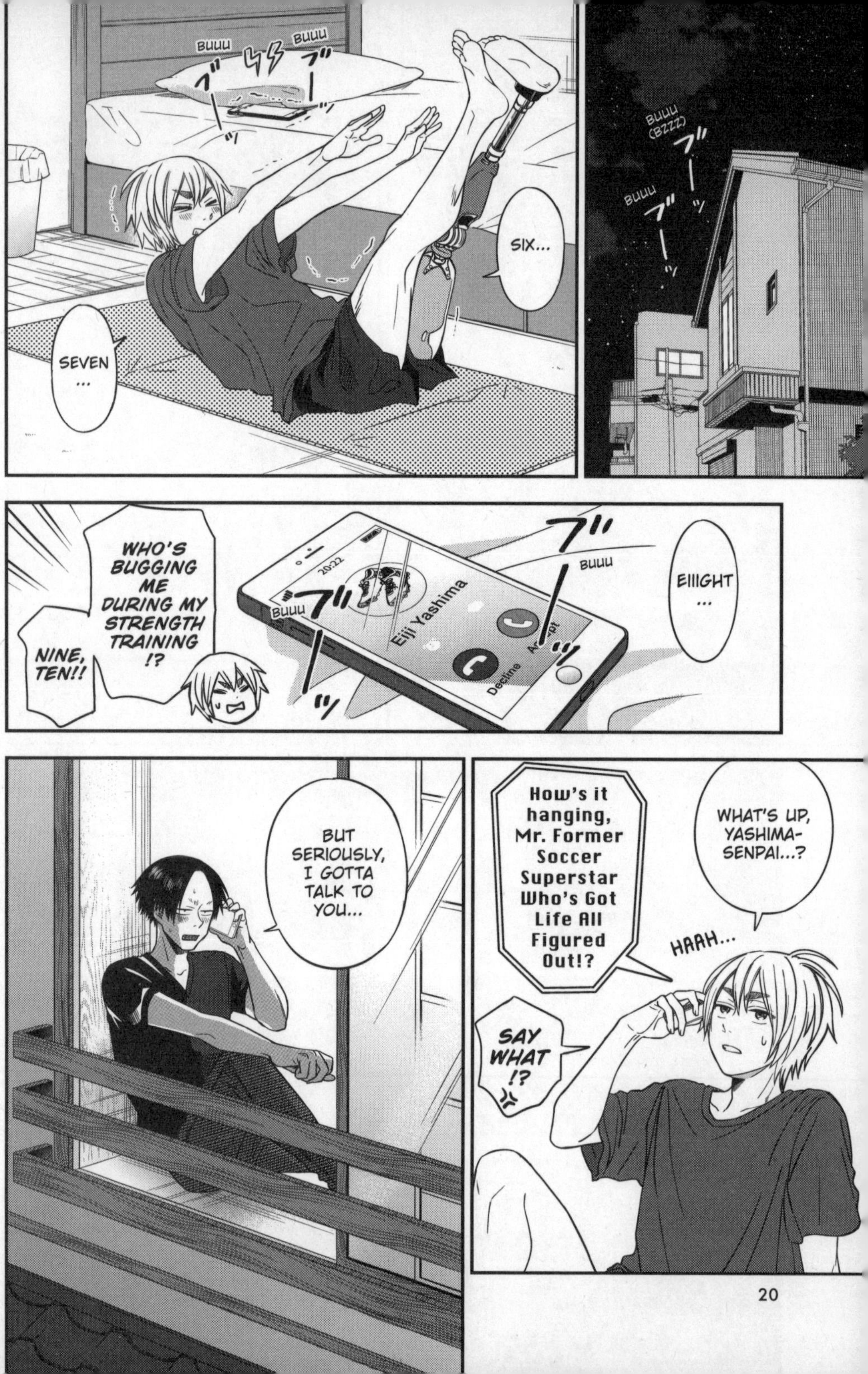
BUUU (BZZZ)
BUUU
BUUU
BUUU
SIX...
SEVEN ...
EIIIGHT ...
BUUU
20:22
Eiji Yashima
Accept
Decline
BUUU
WHO'S BUGGING ME DURING MY STRENGTH TRAINING !?
NINE, TEN!!
WHAT'S UP, YASHIMA-SENPAI...?
How's it hanging, Mr. Former Soccer Superstar Who's Got Life All Figured Out!?
HAAH...
SAY WHAT !?
BUT SERIOUSLY, I GOTTA TALK TO YOU...

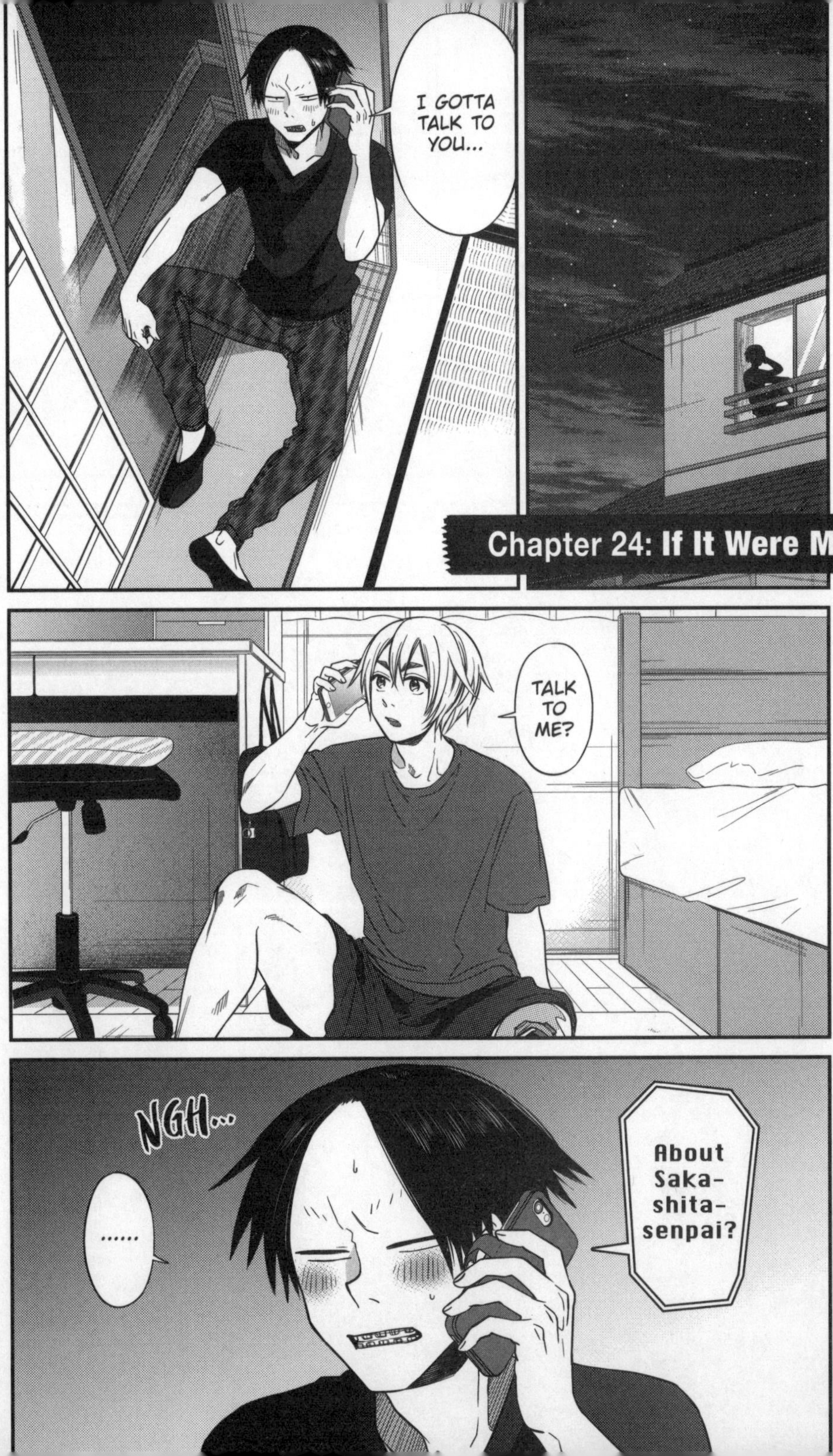
Chapter 24: If It Were Me
I GOTTA TALK TO YOU...
TALK TO ME?
About Saka-shita-senpai?
NGH...
......

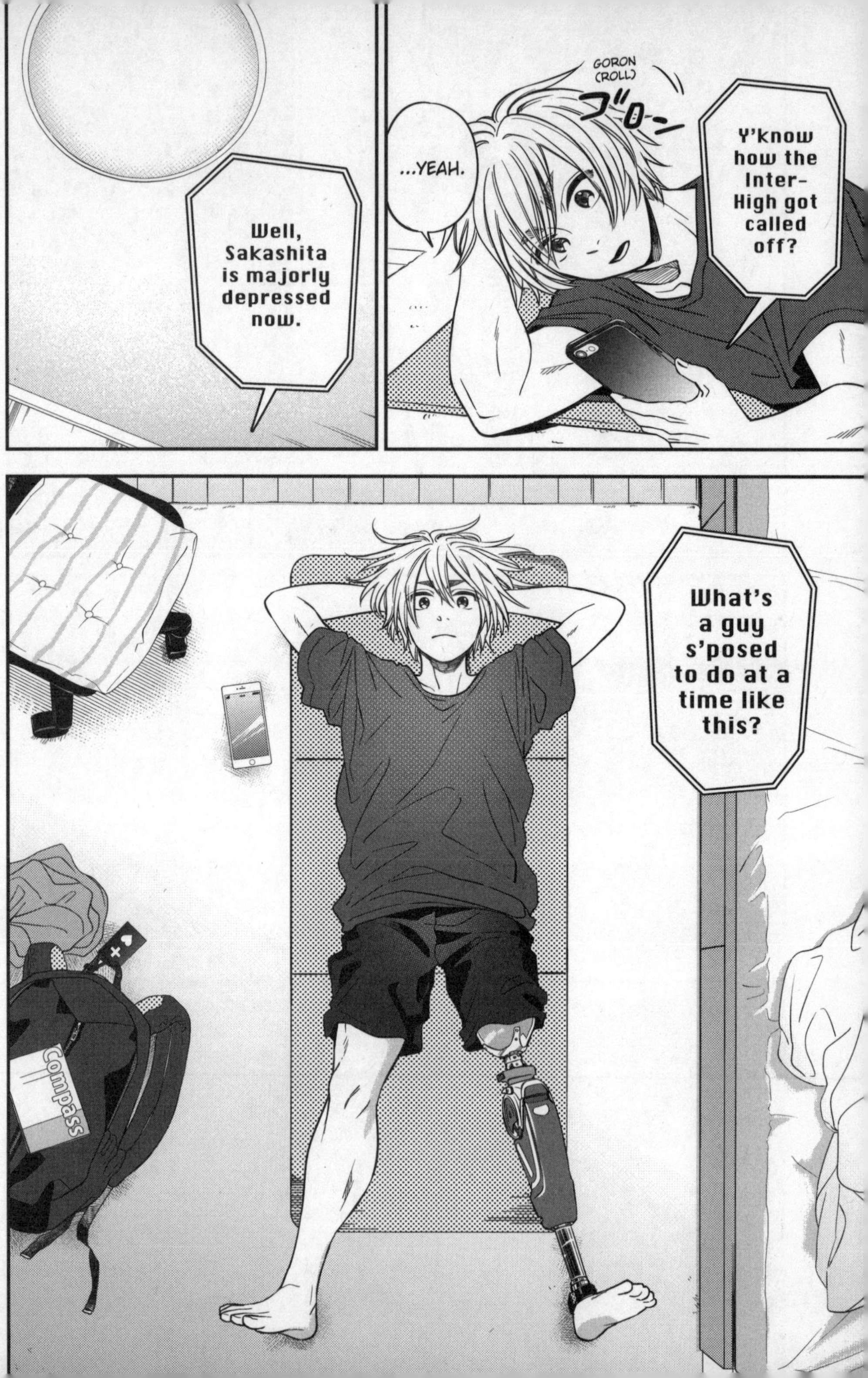
Y'know how the Inter-High got called off?
GORON (ROLL)
...YEAH.
Well, Sakashita is majorly depressed now.
What's a guy s'posed to do at a time like this?

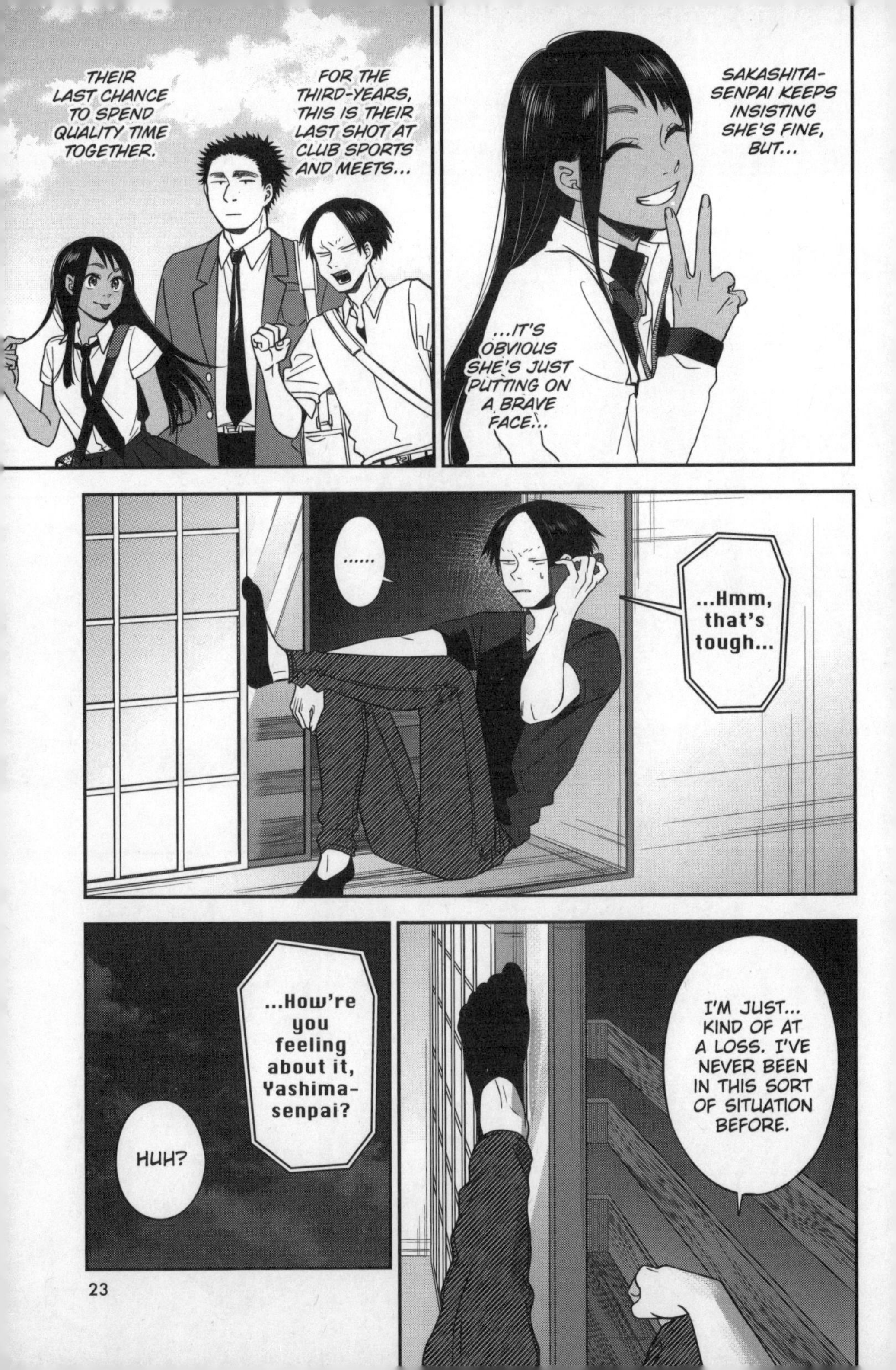
SAKASHITA-SENPAI KEEPS INSISTING SHE'S FINE, BUT...
...IT'S OBVIOUS SHE'S JUST PUTTING ON A BRAVE FACE...
FOR THE THIRD-YEARS, THIS IS THEIR LAST SHOT AT CLUB SPORTS AND MEETS...
THEIR LAST CHANCE TO SPEND QUALITY TIME TOGETHER.
...Hmm, that's tough...
......
I'M JUST... KIND OF AT A LOSS. I'VE NEVER BEEN IN THIS SORT OF SITUATION BEFORE.
...How're you feeling about it, Yashima-senpai?
HUH?

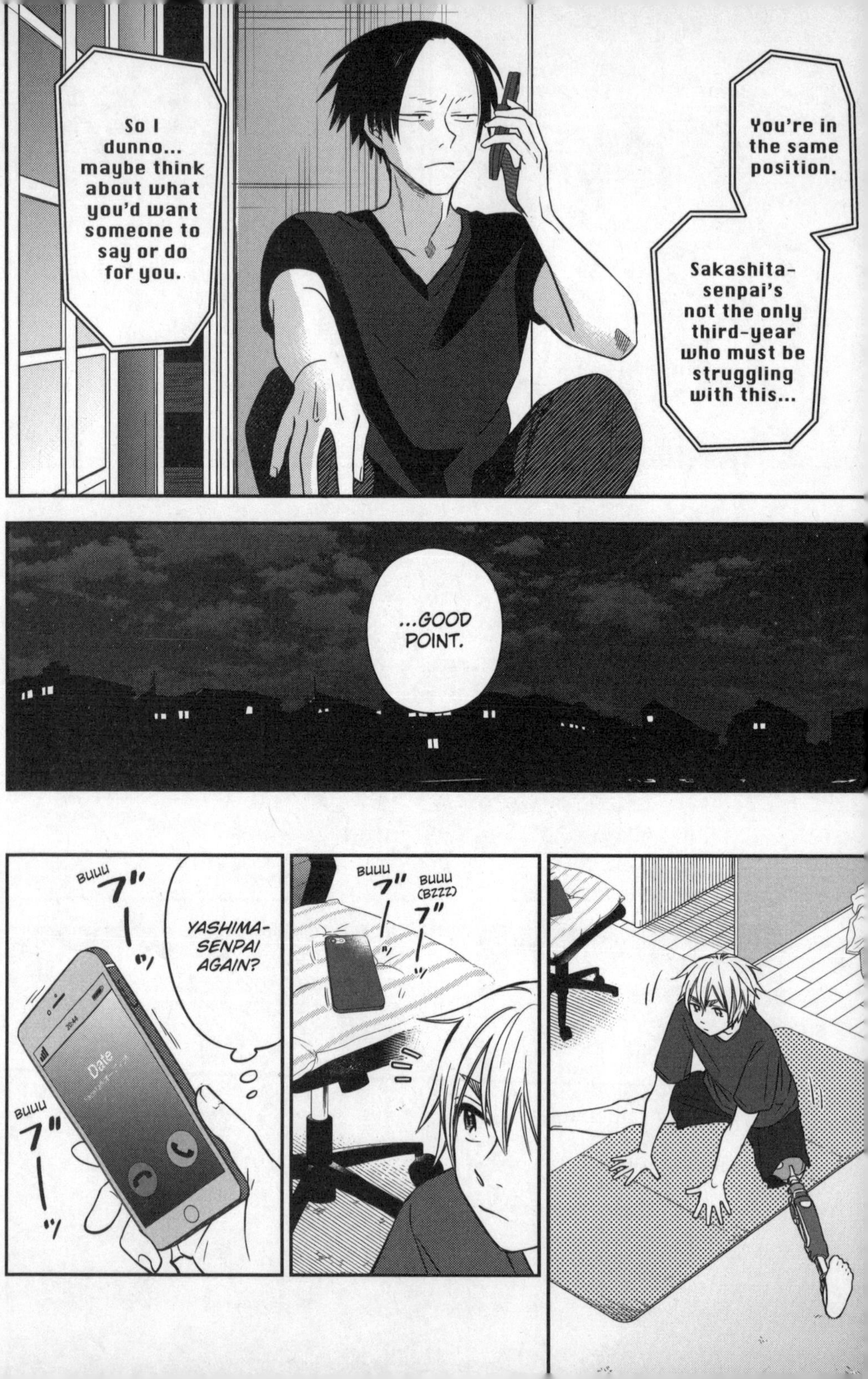
You're in the same position.
Sakashita-senpai's not the only third-year who must be struggling with this...
So I dunno... maybe think about what you'd want someone to say or do for you.
...GOOD POINT.
BUUU (BZZZ)
ブーッ
BUUU
ブーッ
YASHIMA-SENPAI AGAIN?
BUUU
ブーッ
Date
BUUU
ブーッ

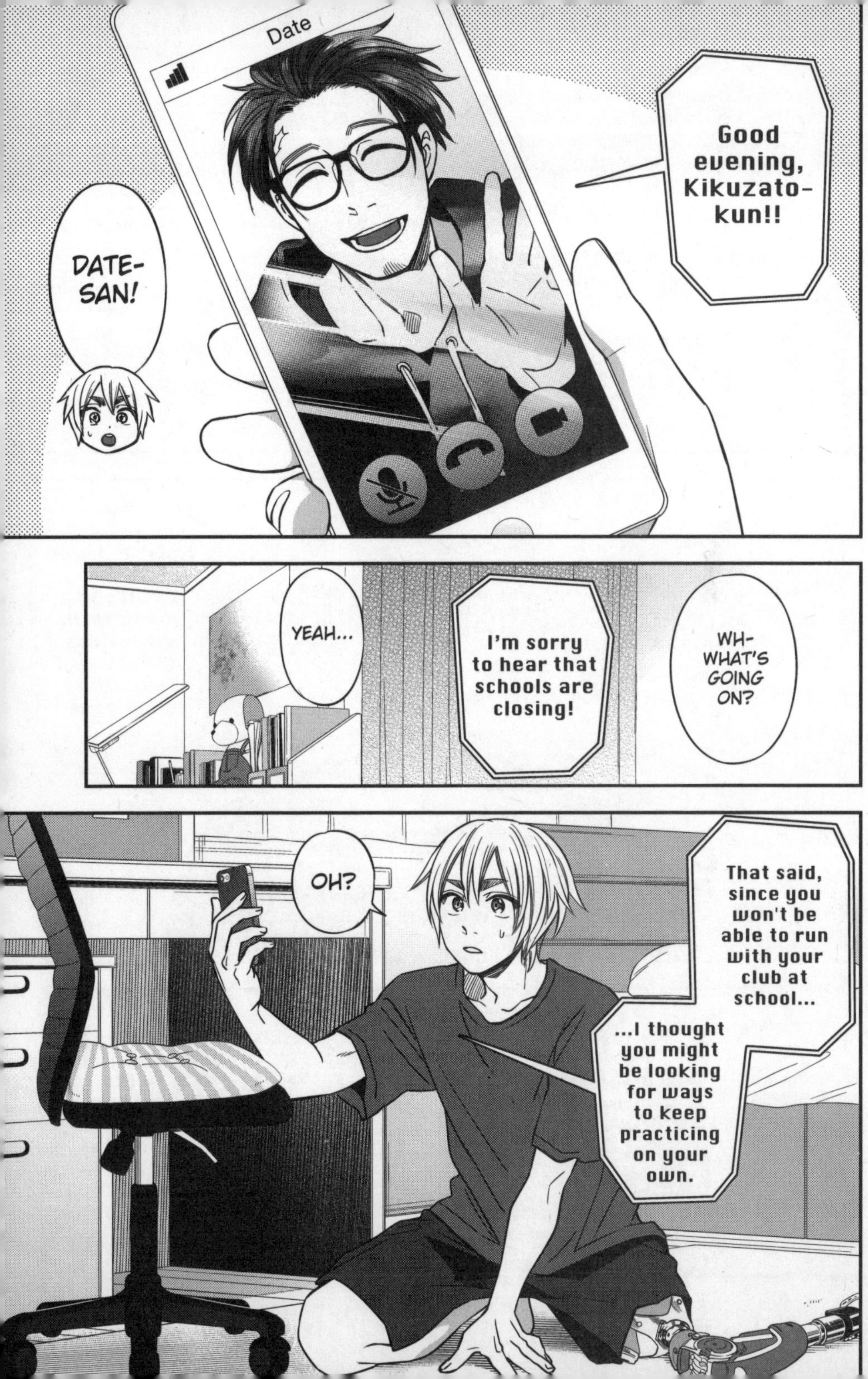
Date
Good evening, Kikuzato-kun!!
DATE-SAN!
WH-WHAT'S GOING ON?
I'm sorry to hear that schools are closing!
YEAH...
That said, since you won't be able to run with your club at school...
...I thought you might be looking for ways to keep practicing on your own.
OH?

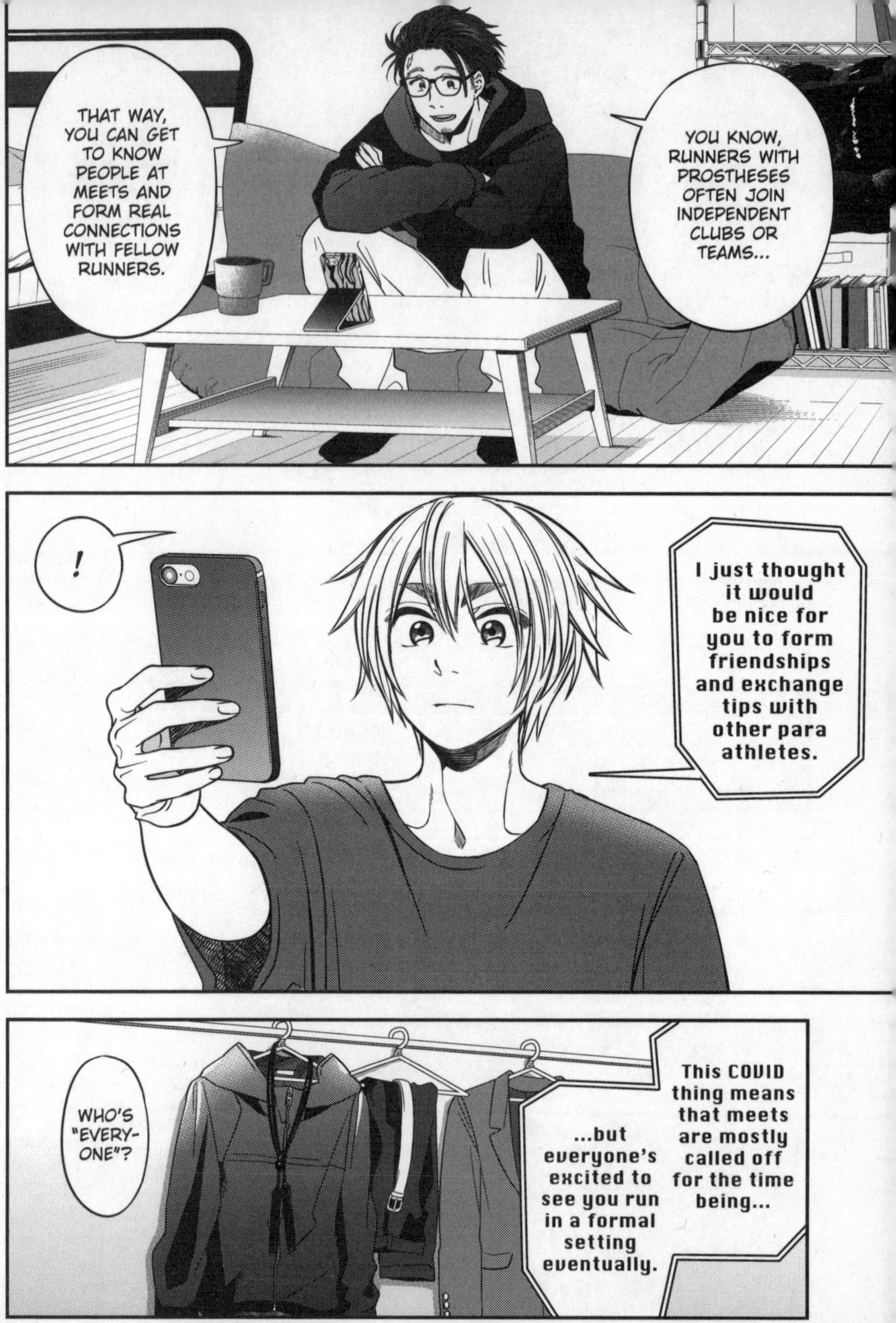
YOU KNOW, RUNNERS WITH PROSTHESES OFTEN JOIN INDEPENDENT CLUBS OR TEAMS...
THAT WAY, YOU CAN GET TO KNOW PEOPLE AT MEETS AND FORM REAL CONNECTIONS WITH FELLOW RUNNERS.
I just thought it would be nice for you to form friendships and exchange tips with other para athletes.
!
This COVID thing means that meets are mostly called off for the time being...
...but everyone's excited to see you run in a formal setting eventually.
WHO'S "EVERY-ONE"?

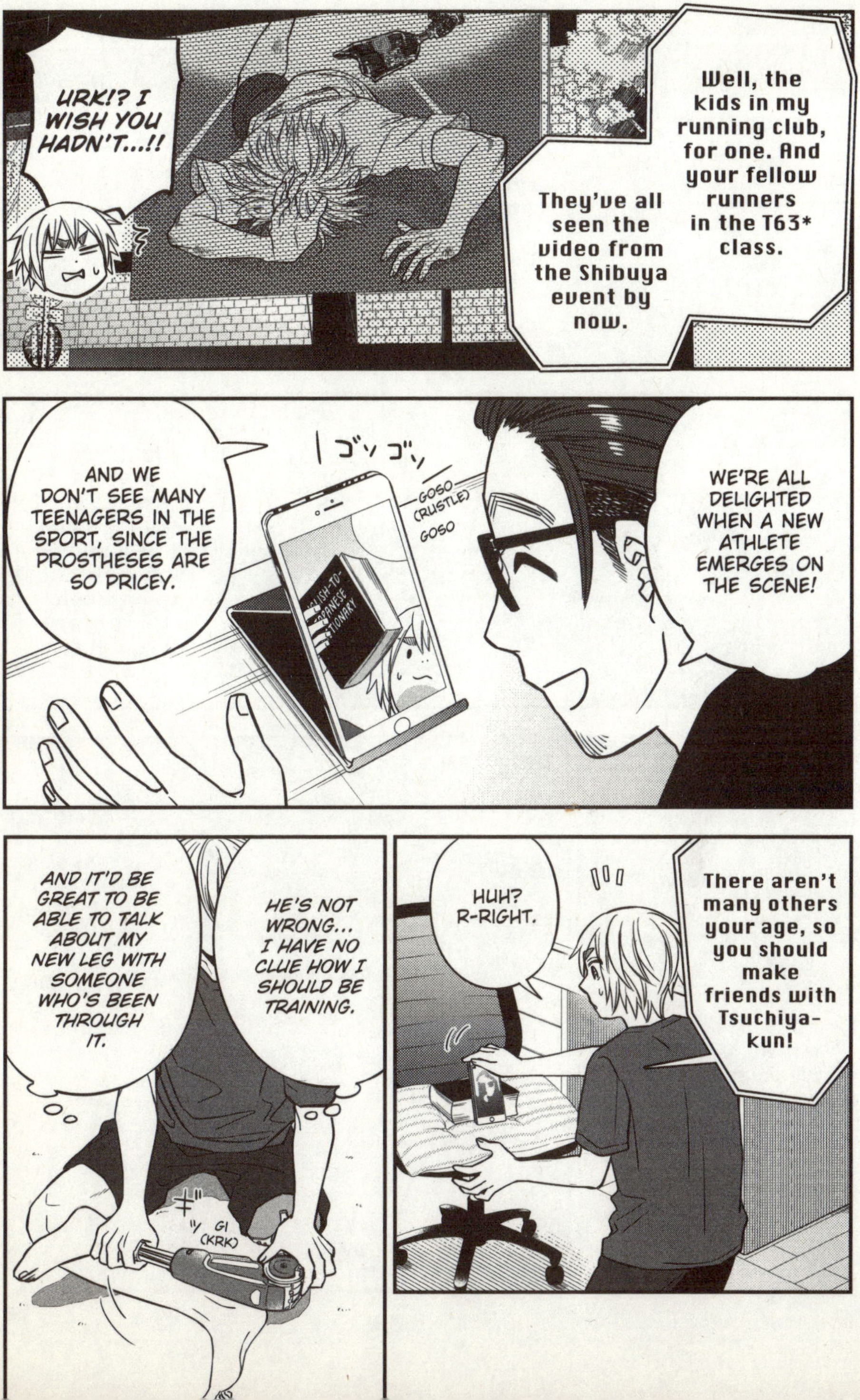
Well, the kids in my running club, for one. And your fellow runners in the T63* class.
They've all seen the video from the Shibuya event by now.
URK!? I WISH YOU HADN'T...!!
WE'RE ALL DELIGHTED WHEN A NEW ATHLETE EMERGES ON THE SCENE!
ゴソゴソ
GOSO (RUSTLE) GOSO
AND WE DON'T SEE MANY TEENAGERS IN THE SPORT, SINCE THE PROSTHESES ARE SO PRICEY.
There aren't many others your age, so you should make friends with Tsuchiya-kun!
HUH? R-RIGHT.
HE'S NOT WRONG... I HAVE NO CLUE HOW I SHOULD BE TRAINING.
AND IT'D BE GREAT TO BE ABLE TO TALK ABOUT MY NEW LEG WITH SOMEONE WHO'S BEEN THROUGH IT.
ギッ
GI (KRK)

*RUNNERS ARE DIVIDED INTO DIFFERENT CLASSES DEPENDING ON THE NATURE OF THEIR DISABILITY. T63 IS FOR THOSE WITH ABOVE-KNEE PROSTHESES, LIKE KIKUZATO. T64 IS FOR THOSE WITH BELOW-KNEE AMPUTATIONS.

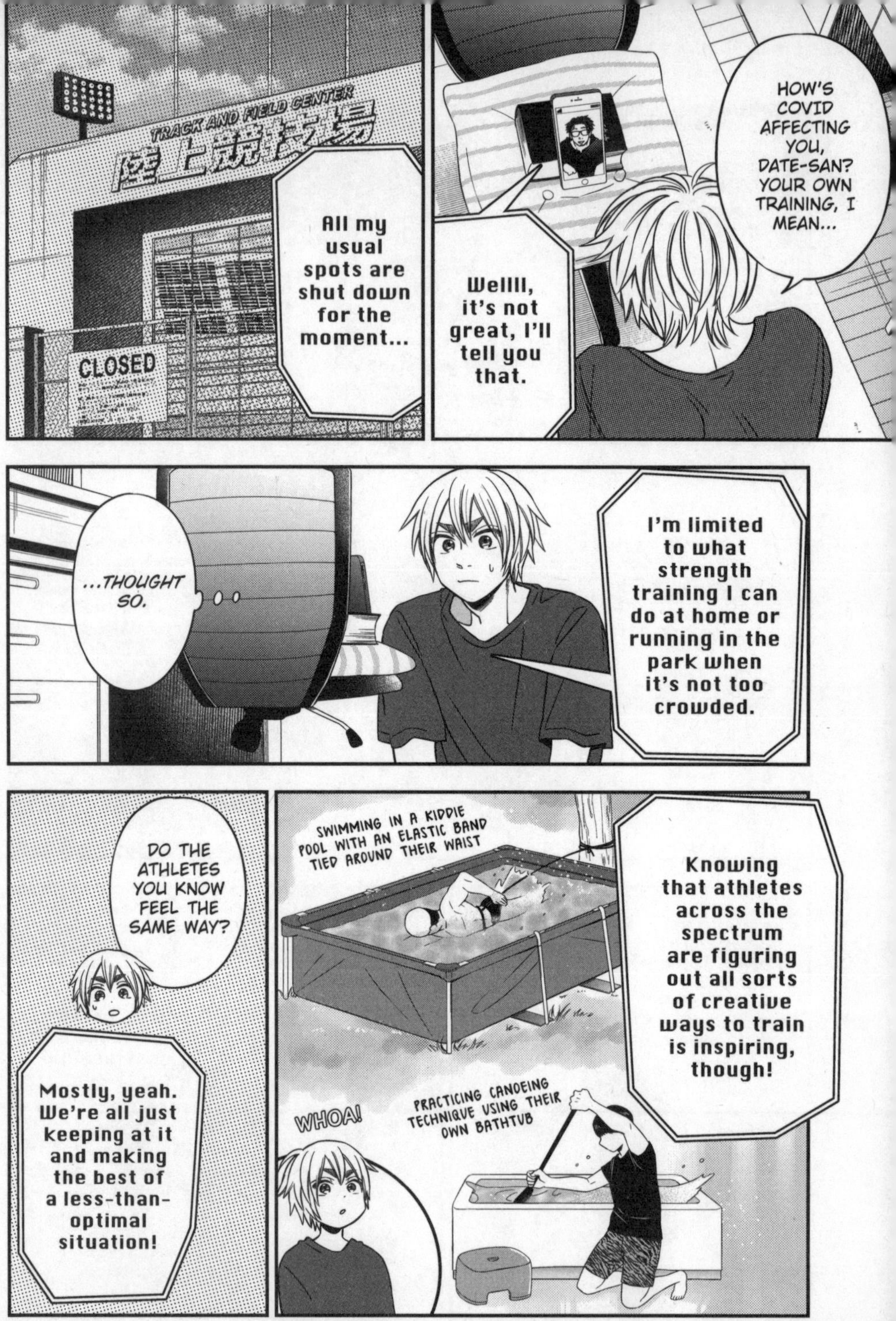

HOW'S COVID AFFECTING YOU, DATE-SAN? YOUR OWN TRAINING, I MEAN...
Wellll, it's not great, I'll tell you that.
TRACK AND FIELD CENTER
陸上競技場
CLOSED
All my usual spots are shut down for the moment...
I'm limited to what strength training I can do at home or running in the park when it's not too crowded.
...THOUGHT SO.
Knowing that athletes across the spectrum are figuring out all sorts of creative ways to train is inspiring, though!
SWIMMING IN A KIDDIE POOL WITH AN ELASTIC BAND TIED AROUND THEIR WAIST
PRACTICING CANOEING TECHNIQUE USING THEIR OWN BATHTUB
WHOA!
DO THE ATHLETES YOU KNOW FEEL THE SAME WAY?
Mostly, yeah. We're all just keeping at it and making the best of a less-than-optimal situation!

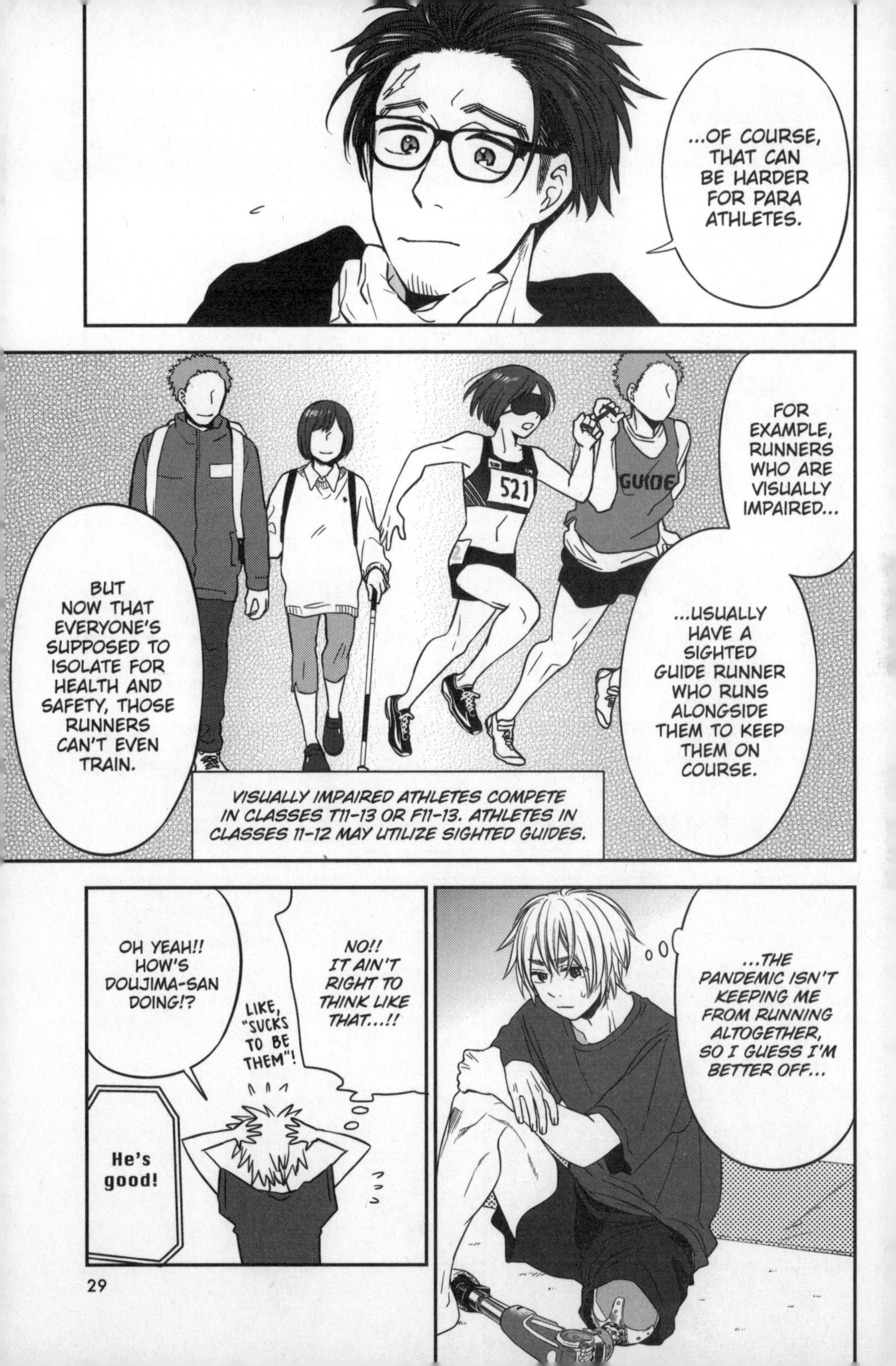
...OF COURSE, THAT CAN BE HARDER FOR PARA ATHLETES.
FOR EXAMPLE, RUNNERS WHO ARE VISUALLY IMPAIRED...
...USUALLY HAVE A SIGHTED GUIDE RUNNER WHO RUNS ALONGSIDE THEM TO KEEP THEM ON COURSE.
GUIDE
521
BUT NOW THAT EVERYONE'S SUPPOSED TO ISOLATE FOR HEALTH AND SAFETY, THOSE RUNNERS CAN'T EVEN TRAIN.
VISUALLY IMPAIRED ATHLETES COMPETE IN CLASSES T11-13 OR F11-13. ATHLETES IN CLASSES 11-12 MAY UTILIZE SIGHTED GUIDES.
...THE PANDEMIC ISN'T KEEPING ME FROM RUNNING ALTOGETHER, SO I GUESS I'M BETTER OFF...
NO!! IT AIN'T RIGHT TO THINK LIKE THAT...!!
LIKE, "SUCKS TO BE THEM"!
OH YEAH!! HOW'S DOUJIMA-SAN DOING!?
He's good!

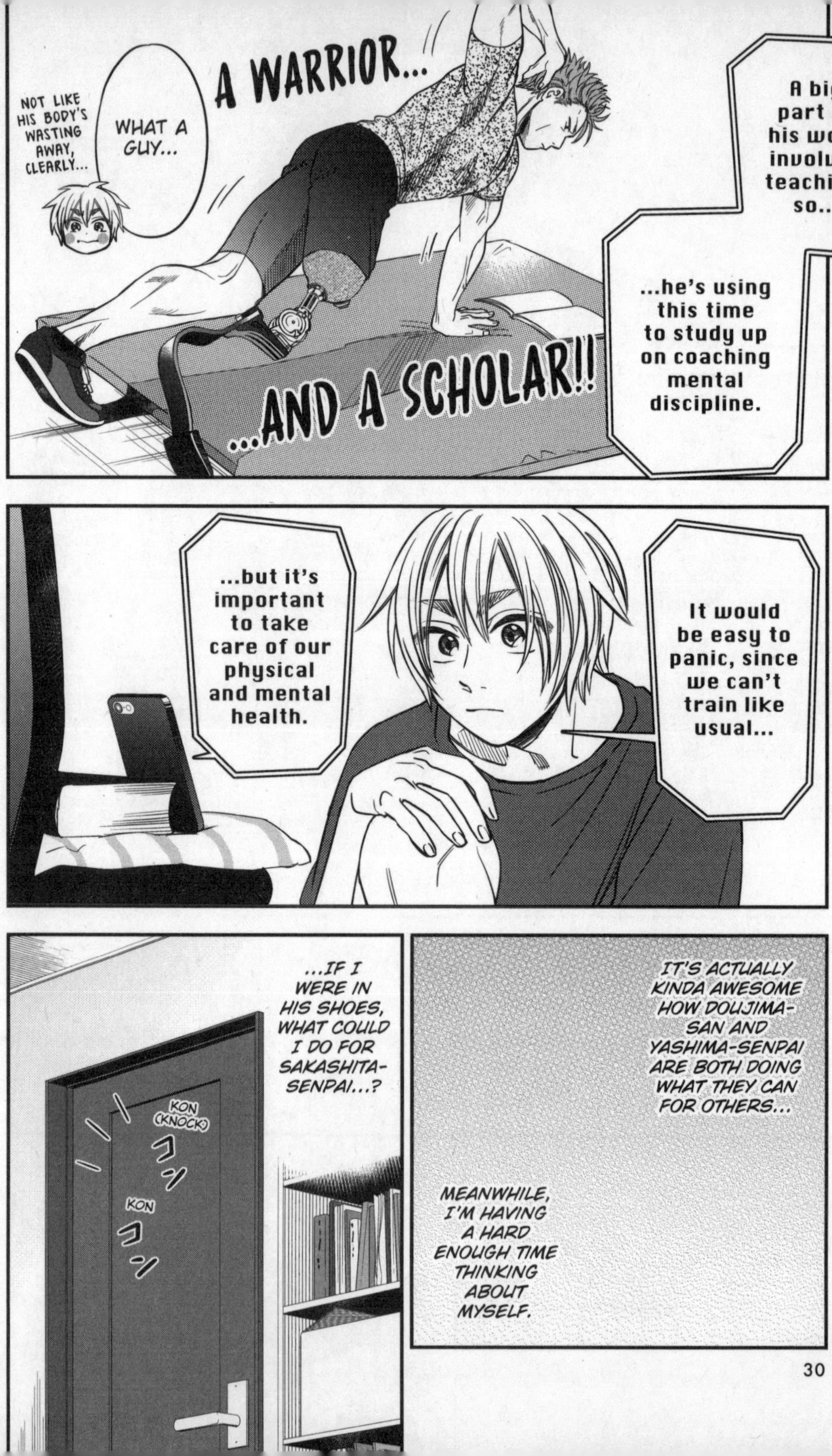
A big part of his work involves teaching, so...
...he's using this time to study up on coaching mental discipline.
A WARRIOR...
...AND A SCHOLAR!!
WHAT A GUY...
NOT LIKE HIS BODY'S WASTING AWAY, CLEARLY...
It would be easy to panic, since we can't train like usual...
...but it's important to take care of our physical and mental health.
IT'S ACTUALLY KINDA AWESOME HOW DOUJIMA-SAN AND YASHIMA-SENPAI ARE BOTH DOING WHAT THEY CAN FOR OTHERS...
MEANWHILE, I'M HAVING A HARD ENOUGH TIME THINKING ABOUT MYSELF.
...IF I WERE IN HIS SHOES, WHAT COULD I DO FOR SAKASHITA-SENPAI...?
KON (KNOCK)
KON

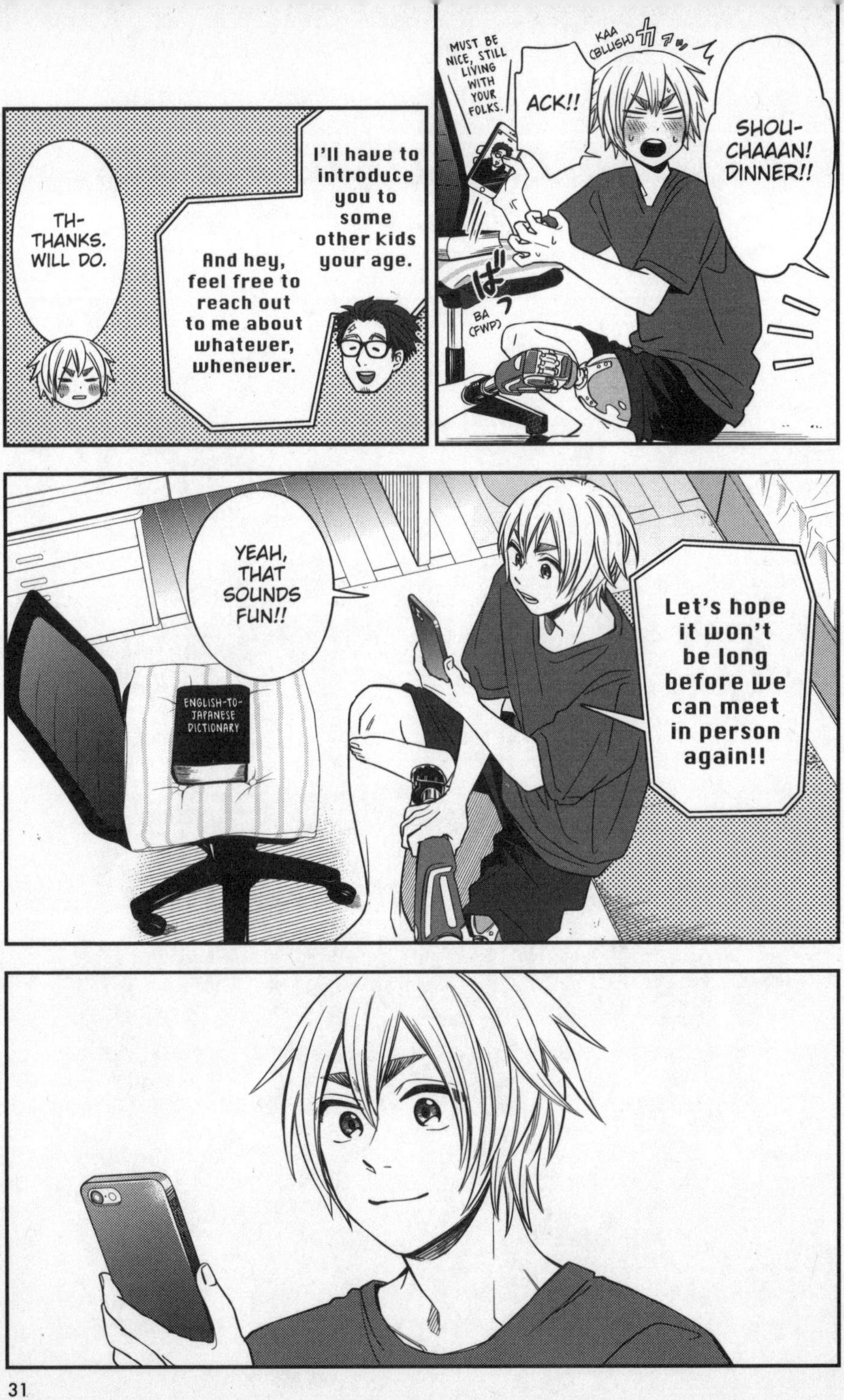
SHOU-CHAAAN! DINNER!!
KAA (BLUSH)
ACK!!
MUST BE NICE, STILL LIVING WITH YOUR FOLKS.
BA (FWP)
I'll have to introduce you to some other kids your age.
And hey, feel free to reach out to me about whatever, whenever.
TH-THANKS. WILL DO.
Let's hope it won't be long before we can meet in person again!!
YEAH, THAT SOUNDS FUN!!
ENGLISH-TO-JAPANESE DICTIONARY

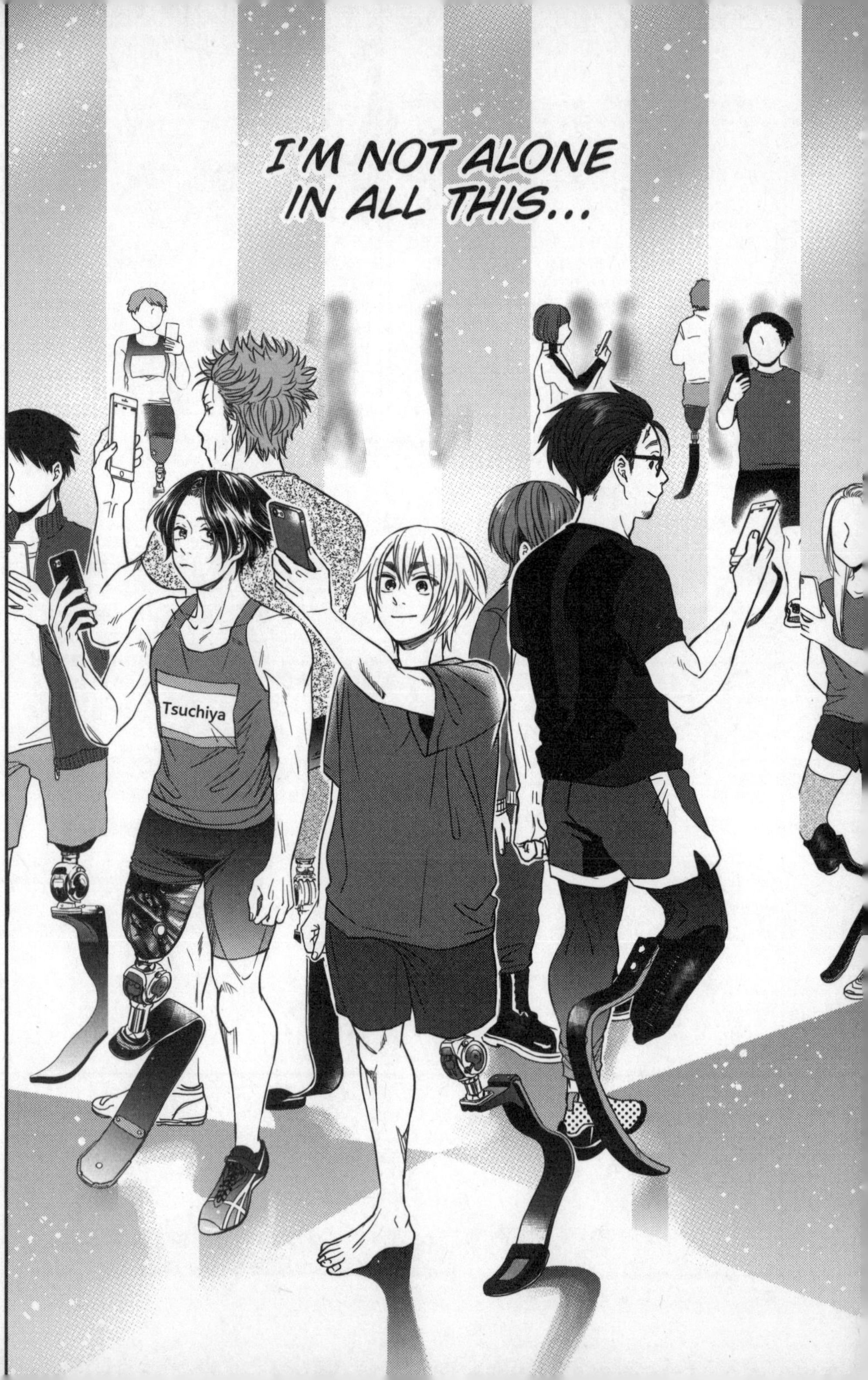
I'M NOT ALONE IN ALL THIS...
Tsuchiya

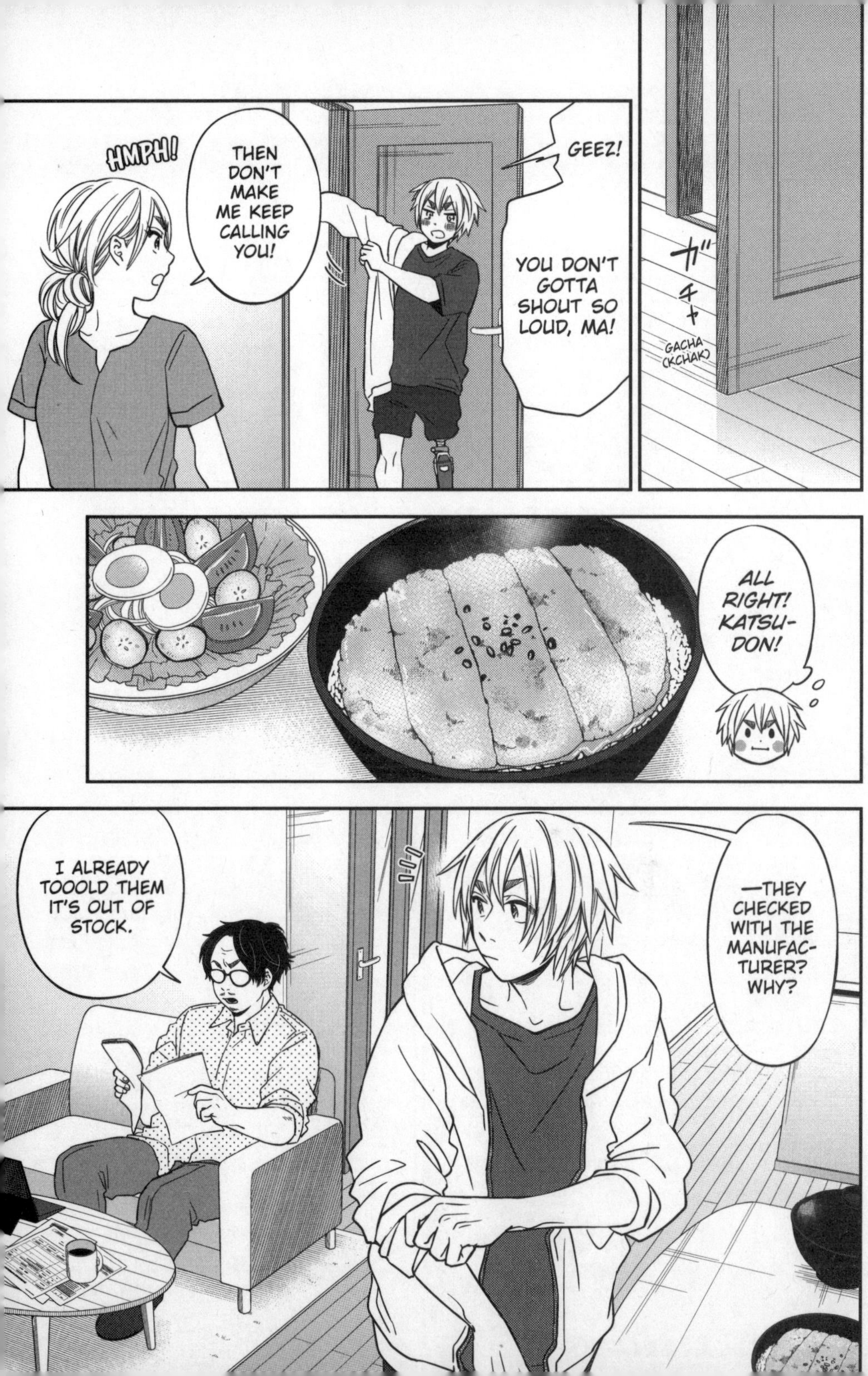
ガチャ
GACHA (KCHAK)
GEEZ!
YOU DON'T GOTTA SHOUT SO LOUD, MA!
THEN DON'T MAKE ME KEEP CALLING YOU!
HMPH!
ALL RIGHT! KATSU-DON!
—THEY CHECKED WITH THE MANUFAC-TURER? WHY?
I ALREADY TOOOLD THEM IT'S OUT OF STOCK.

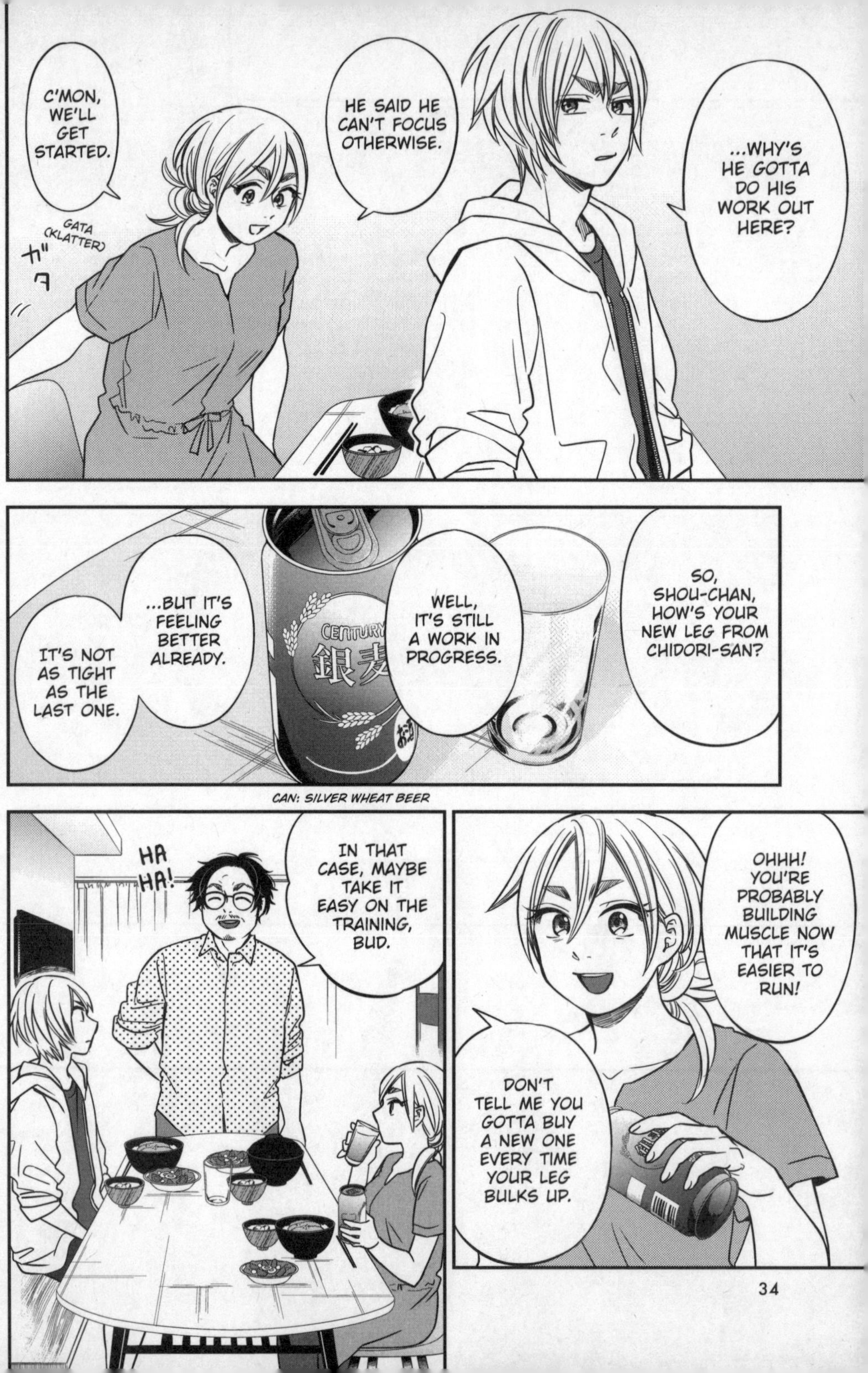
...WHY'S HE GOTTA DO HIS WORK OUT HERE?
HE SAID HE CAN'T FOCUS OTHERWISE.
C'MON, WE'LL GET STARTED.
ガタ
GATA (KLATTER)
SO, SHOU-CHAN, HOW'S YOUR NEW LEG FROM CHIDORI-SAN?
WELL, IT'S STILL A WORK IN PROGRESS.
CENTURY
銀麦
...BUT IT'S FEELING BETTER ALREADY.
IT'S NOT AS TIGHT AS THE LAST ONE.
CAN: SILVER WHEAT BEER
OHHH! YOU'RE PROBABLY BUILDING MUSCLE NOW THAT IT'S EASIER TO RUN!
DON'T TELL ME YOU GOTTA BUY A NEW ONE EVERY TIME YOUR LEG BULKS UP.
IN THAT CASE, MAYBE TAKE IT EASY ON THE TRAINING, BUD.
HA HA!

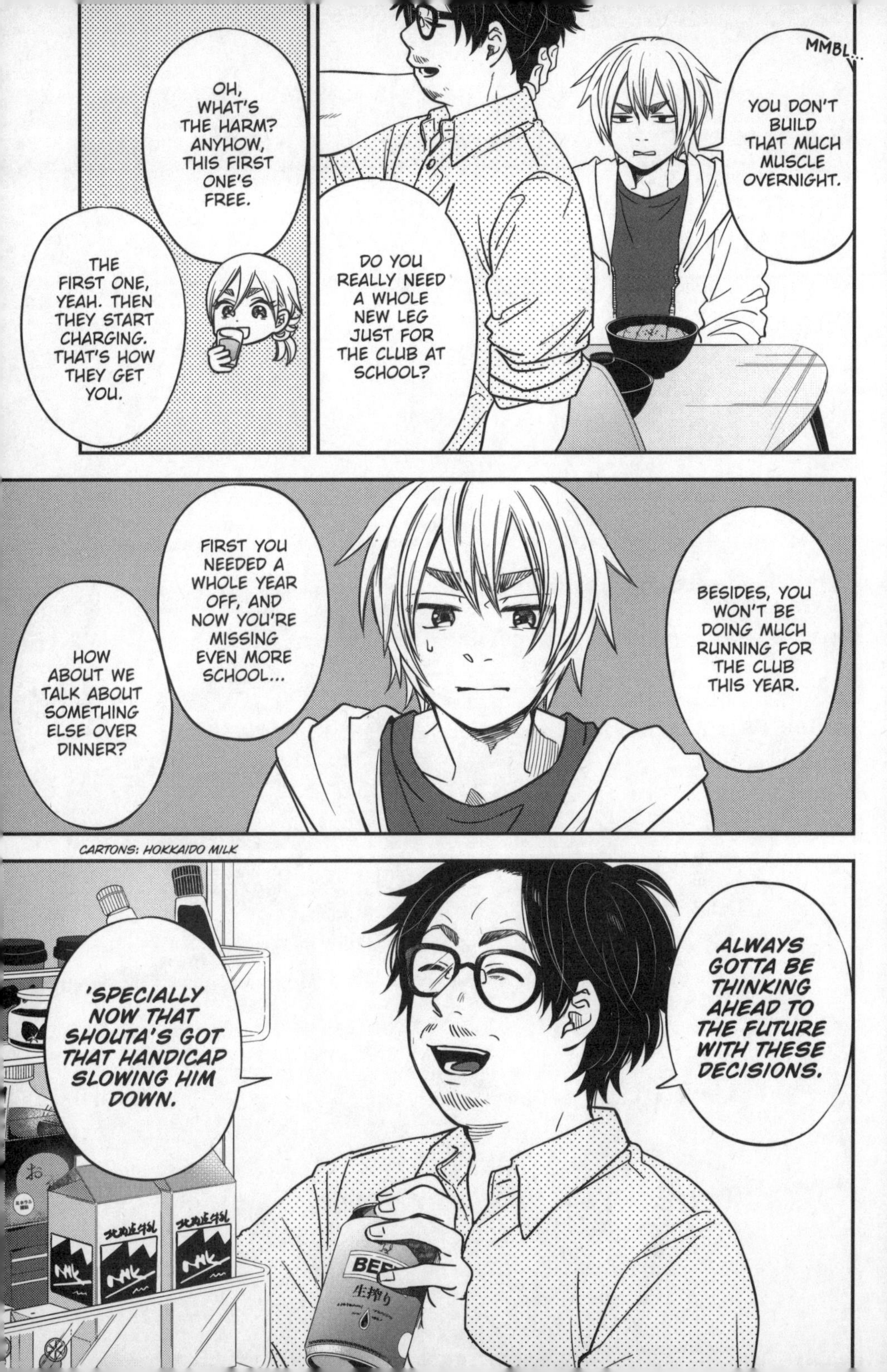
MMBL...
YOU DON'T BUILD THAT MUCH MUSCLE OVERNIGHT.
DO YOU REALLY NEED A WHOLE NEW LEG JUST FOR THE CLUB AT SCHOOL?
OH, WHAT'S THE HARM? ANYHOW, THIS FIRST ONE'S FREE.
THE FIRST ONE, YEAH. THEN THEY START CHARGING. THAT'S HOW THEY GET YOU.
BESIDES, YOU WON'T BE DOING MUCH RUNNING FOR THE CLUB THIS YEAR.
FIRST YOU NEEDED A WHOLE YEAR OFF, AND NOW YOU'RE MISSING EVEN MORE SCHOOL...
HOW ABOUT WE TALK ABOUT SOMETHING ELSE OVER DINNER?
CARTONS: HOKKAIDO MILK
ALWAYS GOTTA BE THINKING AHEAD TO THE FUTURE WITH THESE DECISIONS.
'SPECIALLY NOW THAT SHOUTA'S GOT THAT HANDICAP SLOWING HIM DOWN.

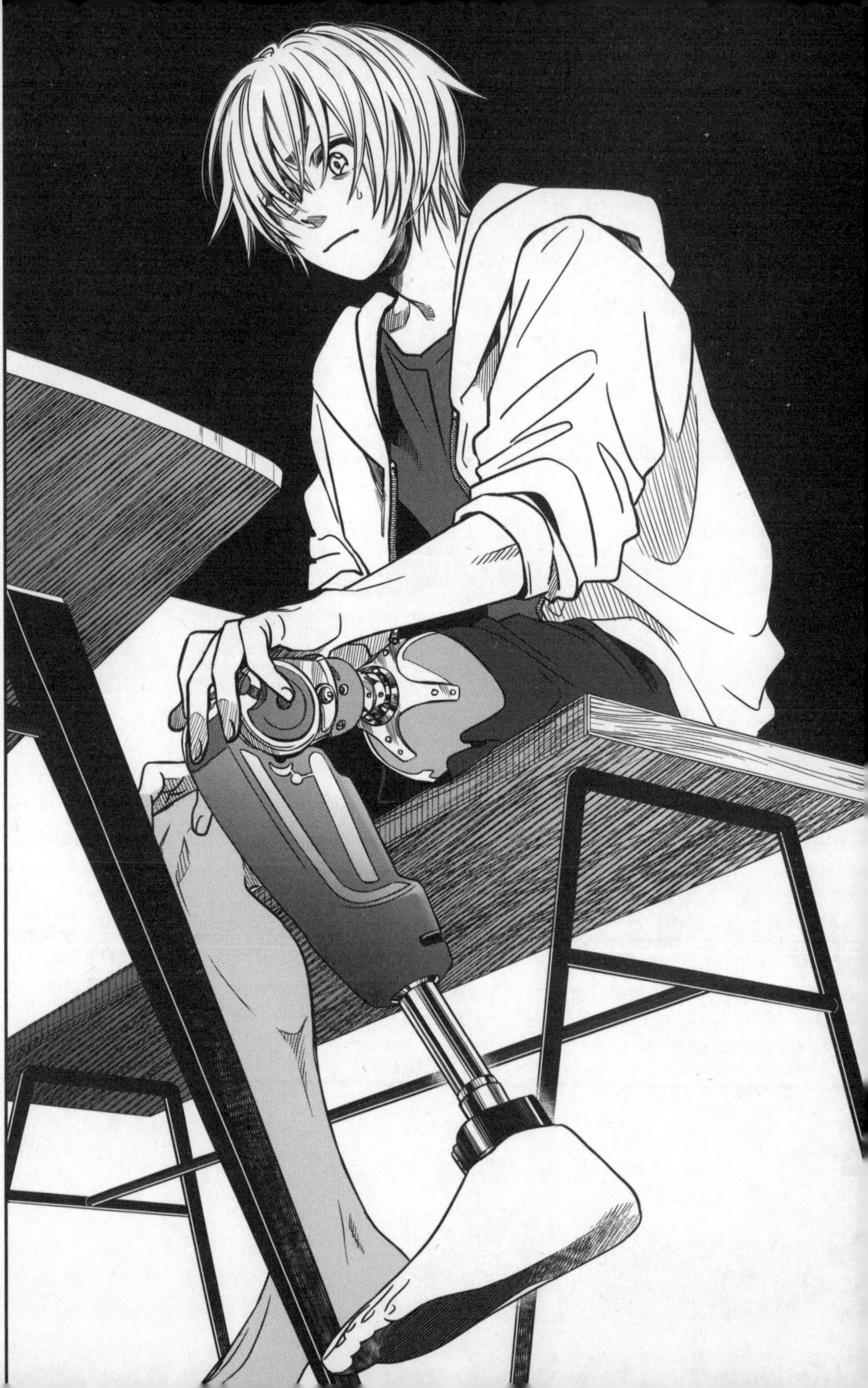

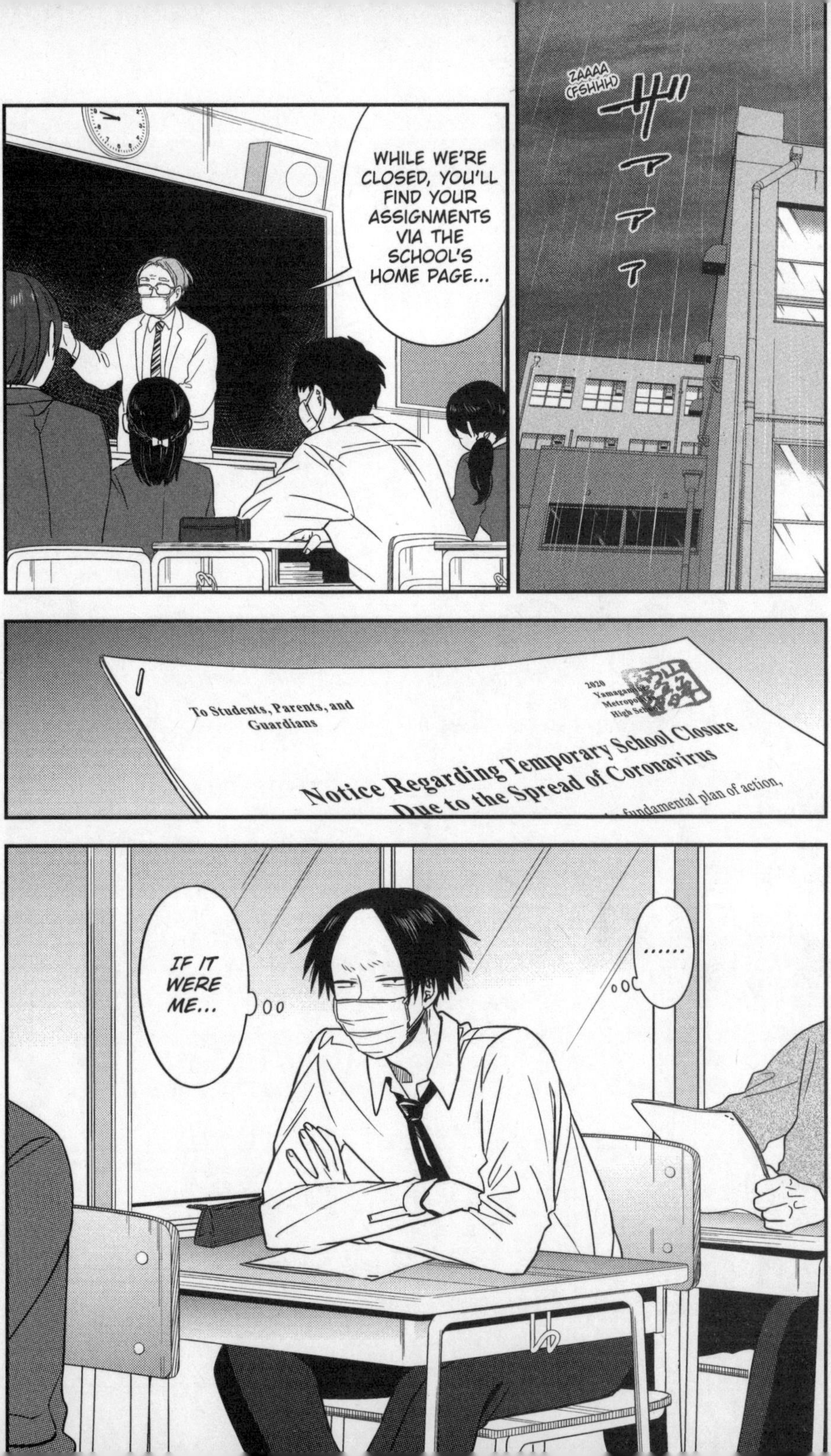
ザァァァ
ZAAAA (FSHHH)
WHILE WE'RE CLOSED, YOU'LL FIND YOUR ASSIGNMENTS VIA THE SCHOOL'S HOME PAGE...
To Students, Parents, and Guardians
2020
Notice Regarding Temporary School Closure Due to the Spread of Coronavirus
fundamental plan of action,
......
IF IT WERE ME...

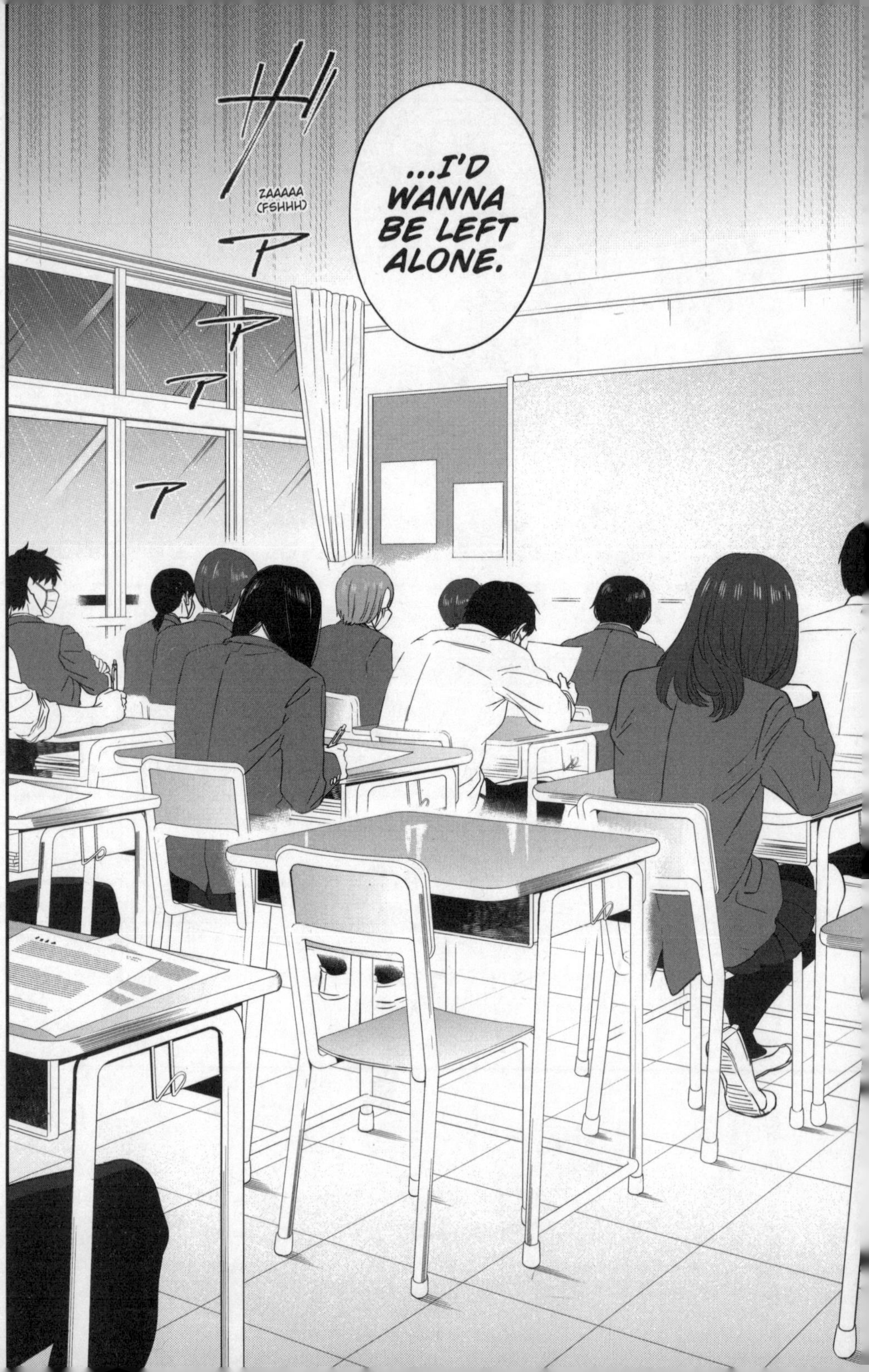
...I'D WANNA BE LEFT ALONE.
ZAAAAA (FSHHH)

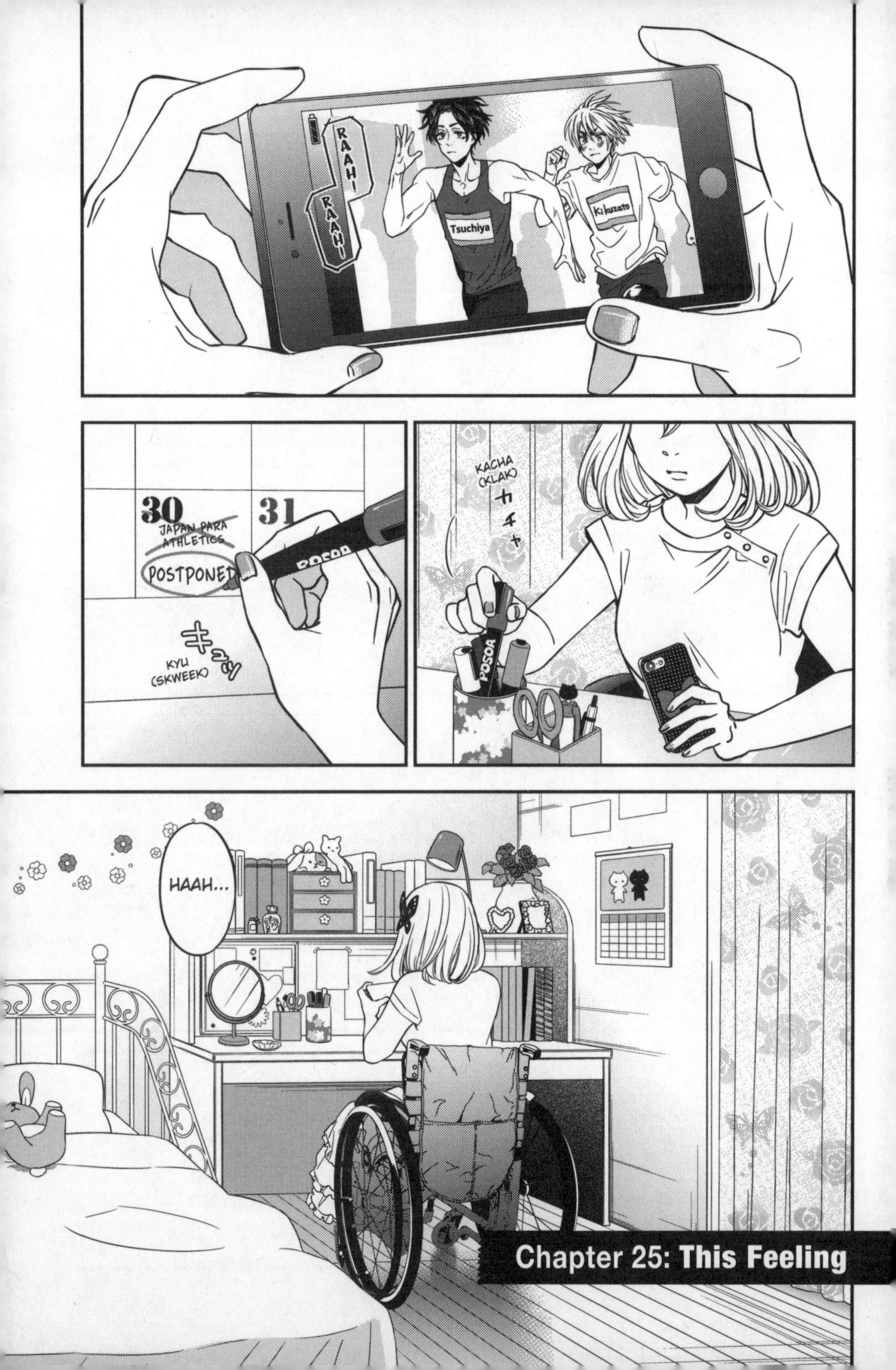
RAAH!
RAAH!
Tsuchiya
Kikuzato
KACHA (KLAK)
カチャ
30
31
JAPAN PARA ATHLETICS
POSTPONED
POSOA
キュッ
KYU (SKWEEK)
POSOA
HAAH...

Chapter 25: This Feeling

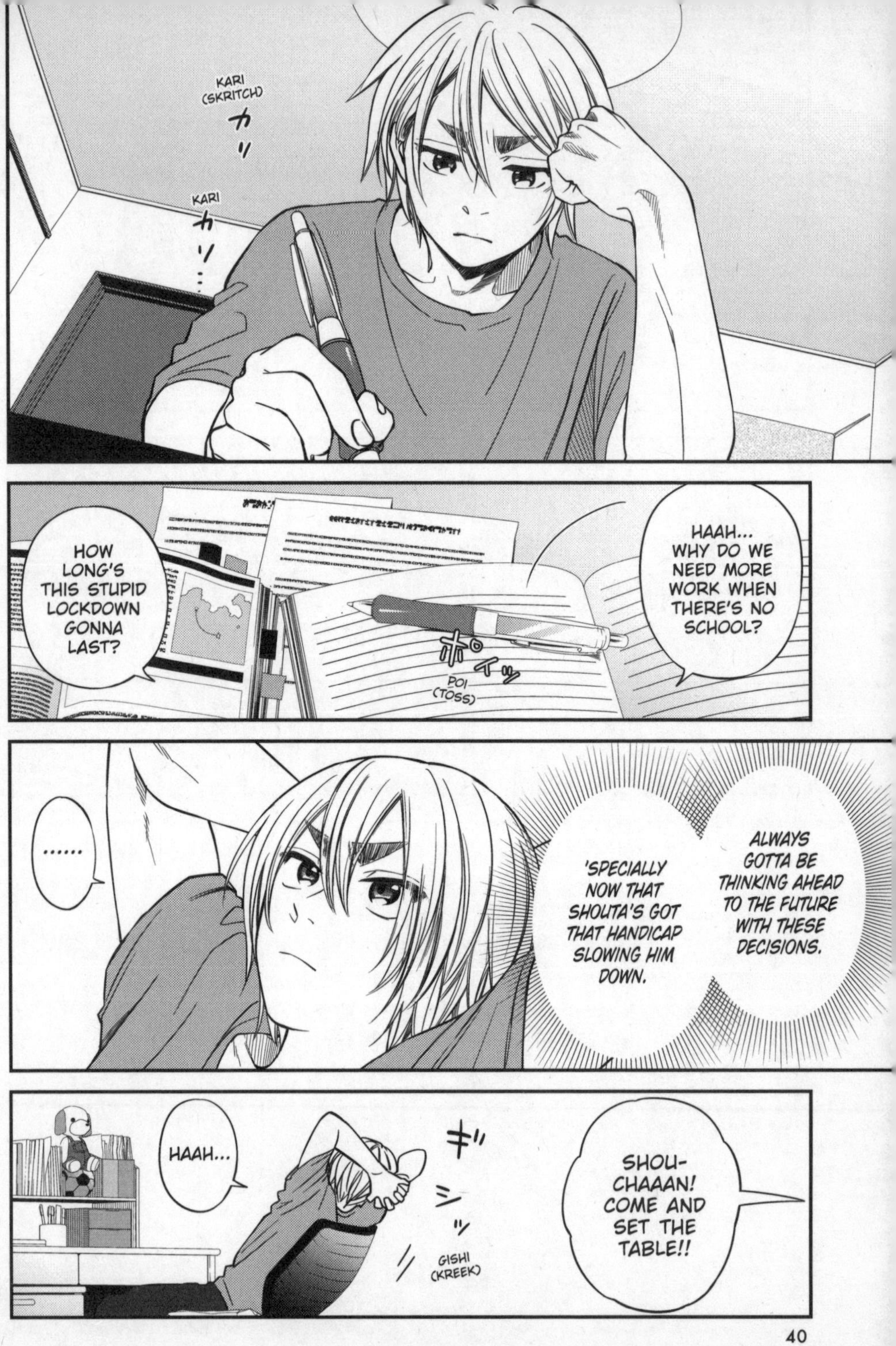
KARI (SKRITCH)
カッ
KARI
カッ…
HAAH... WHY DO WE NEED MORE WORK WHEN THERE'S NO SCHOOL?
ポイッ
POI (TOSS)
HOW LONG'S THIS STUPID LOCKDOWN GONNA LAST?
ALWAYS GOTTA BE THINKING AHEAD TO THE FUTURE WITH THESE DECISIONS.
'SPECIALLY NOW THAT SHOUTA'S GOT THAT HANDICAP SLOWING HIM DOWN.
......
SHOU-CHAAAN! COME AND SET THE TABLE!!
ギシッ
GISHI (KREEK)
HAAH...

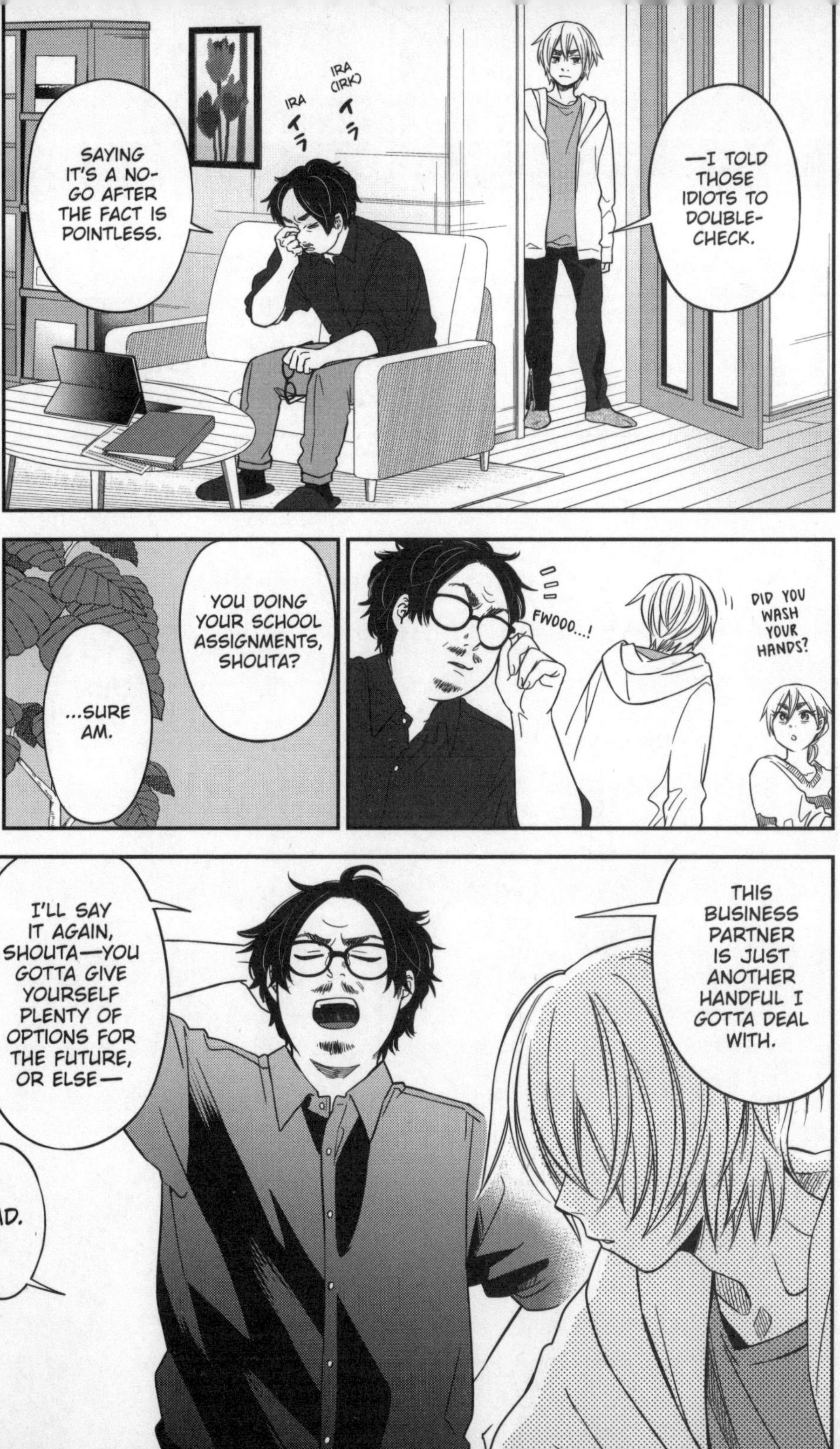
—I TOLD THOSE IDIOTS TO DOUBLE-CHECK.
IRA (IRK)
IRA
SAYING IT'S A NO-GO AFTER THE FACT IS POINTLESS.
DID YOU WASH YOUR HANDS?
FWOOO...!
YOU DOING YOUR SCHOOL ASSIGNMENTS, SHOUTA?
...SURE AM.
THIS BUSINESS PARTNER IS JUST ANOTHER HANDFUL I GOTTA DEAL WITH.
I'LL SAY IT AGAIN, SHOUTA—YOU GOTTA GIVE YOURSELF PLENTY OF OPTIONS FOR THE FUTURE, OR ELSE—
DAD.

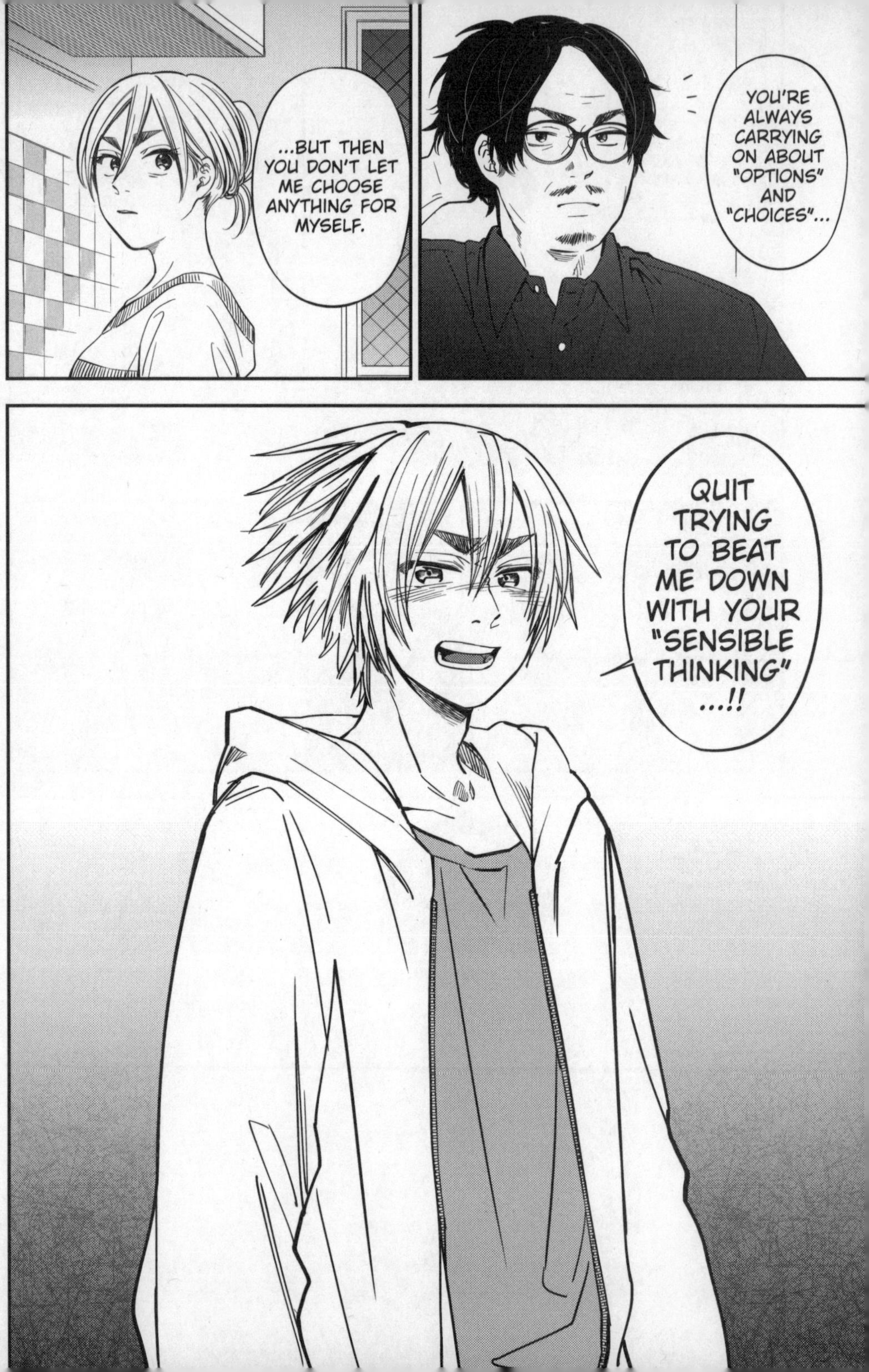
YOU'RE ALWAYS CARRYING ON ABOUT "OPTIONS" AND "CHOICES"...
...BUT THEN YOU DON'T LET ME CHOOSE ANYTHING FOR MYSELF.
QUIT TRYING TO BEAT ME DOWN WITH YOUR "SENSIBLE THINKING" ...!!

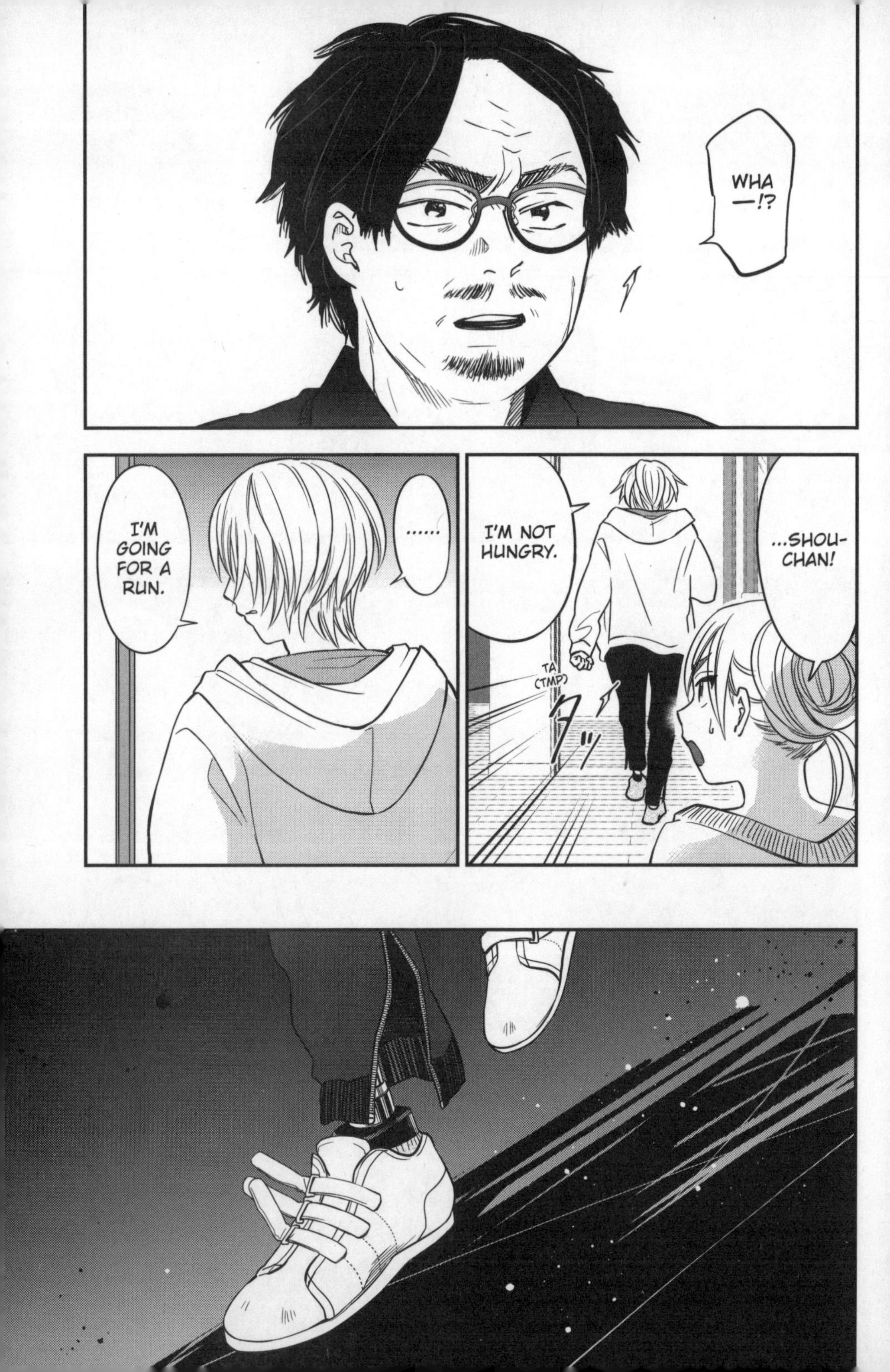
WHA—!?
...SHOU-CHAN!
I'M NOT HUNGRY.
TA (TMP)
......
I'M GOING FOR A RUN.

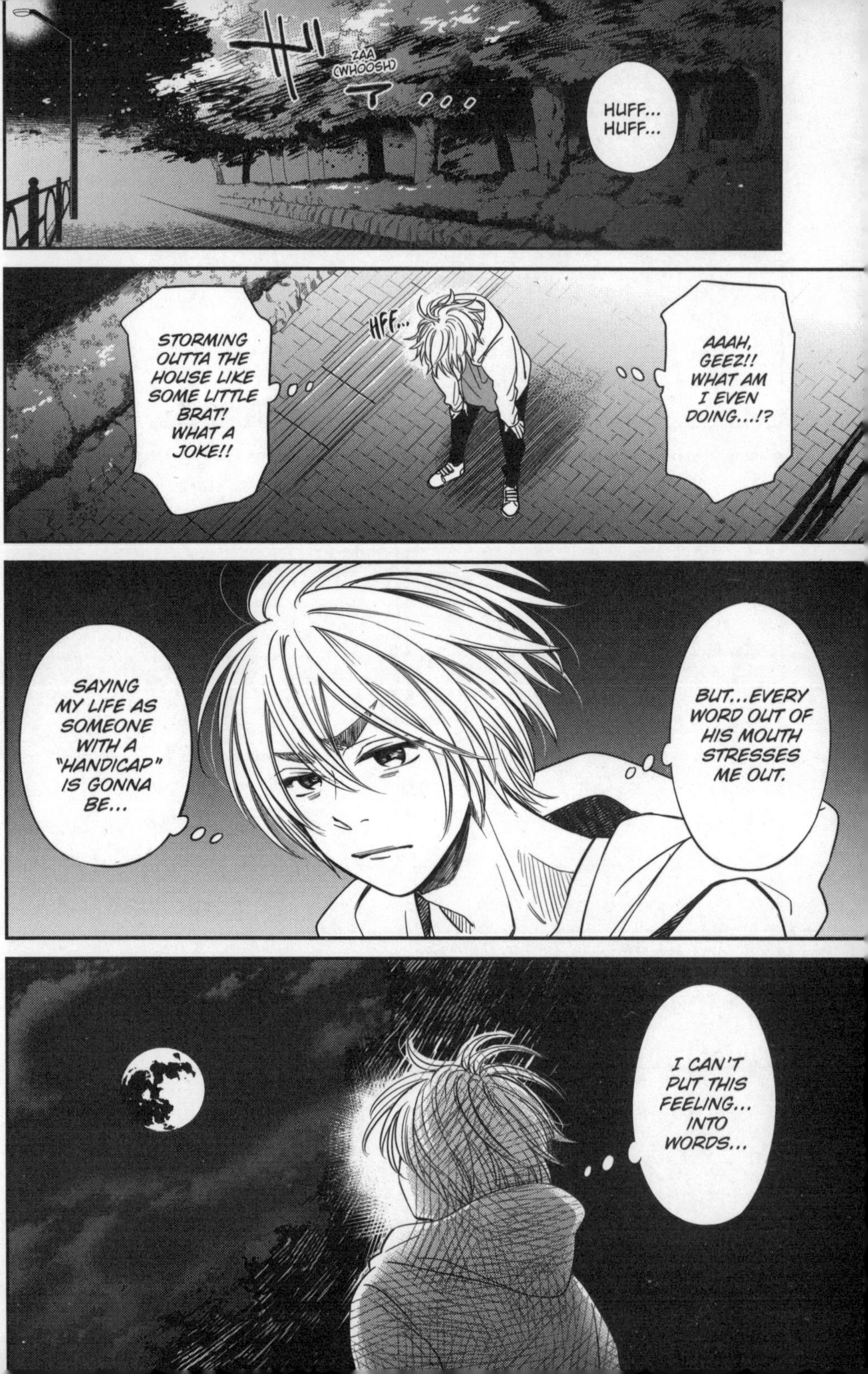

ZAA (WHOOSH)
HUFF... HUFF...
AAAH, GEEZ!! WHAT AM I EVEN DOING...!?
HFF...
STORMING OUTTA THE HOUSE LIKE SOME LITTLE BRAT! WHAT A JOKE!!
BUT...EVERY WORD OUT OF HIS MOUTH STRESSES ME OUT.
SAYING MY LIFE AS SOMEONE WITH A "HANDICAP" IS GONNA BE...
I CAN'T PUT THIS FEELING... INTO WORDS...

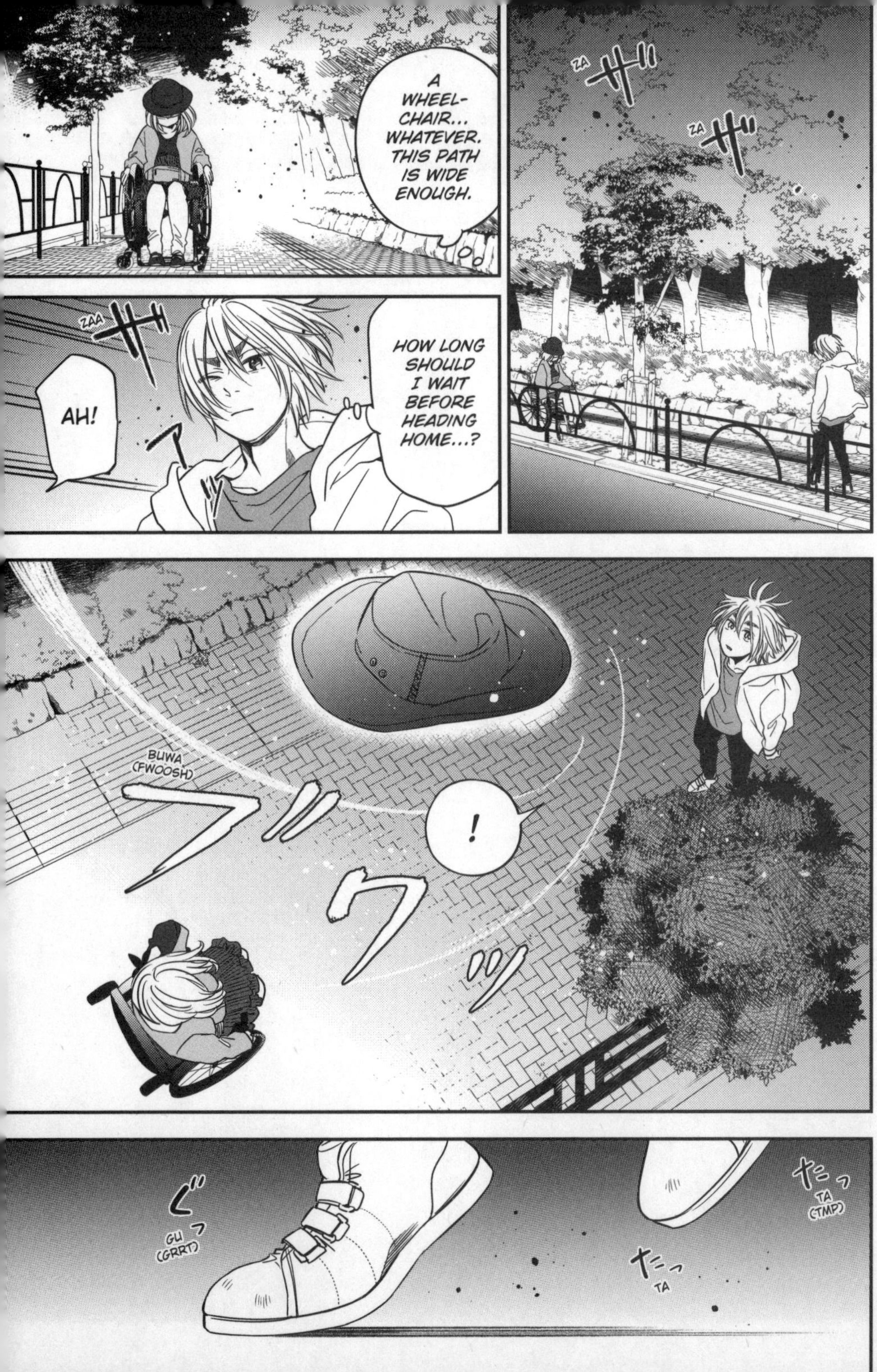
ZA
ZA
A WHEEL-CHAIR... WHATEVER. THIS PATH IS WIDE ENOUGH.
HOW LONG SHOULD I WAIT BEFORE HEADING HOME...?
ZAA
AH!
!
BUWA (FWOOSH)
TA (TMP)
TA
GU (GRRT)

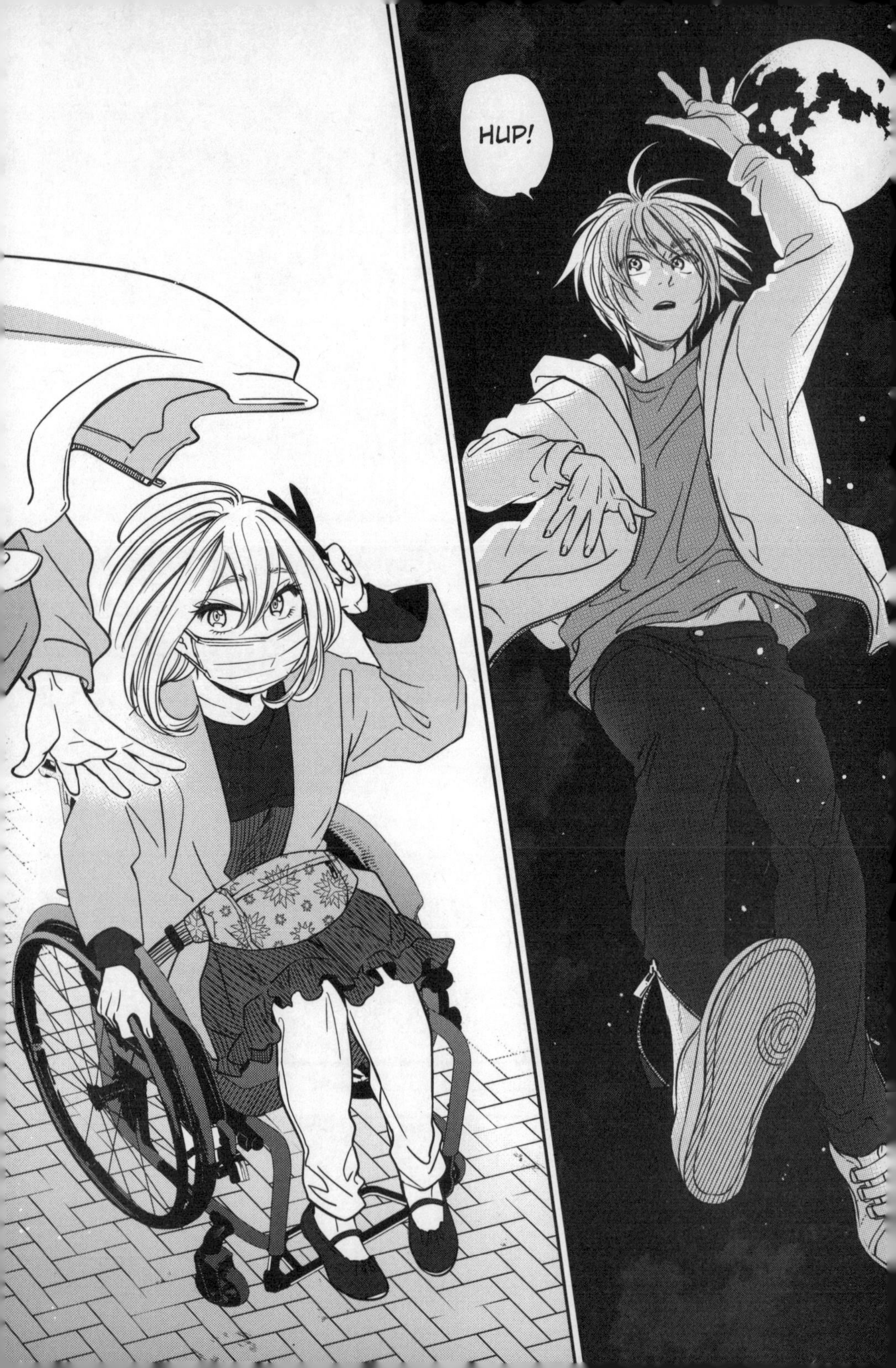
HUP!

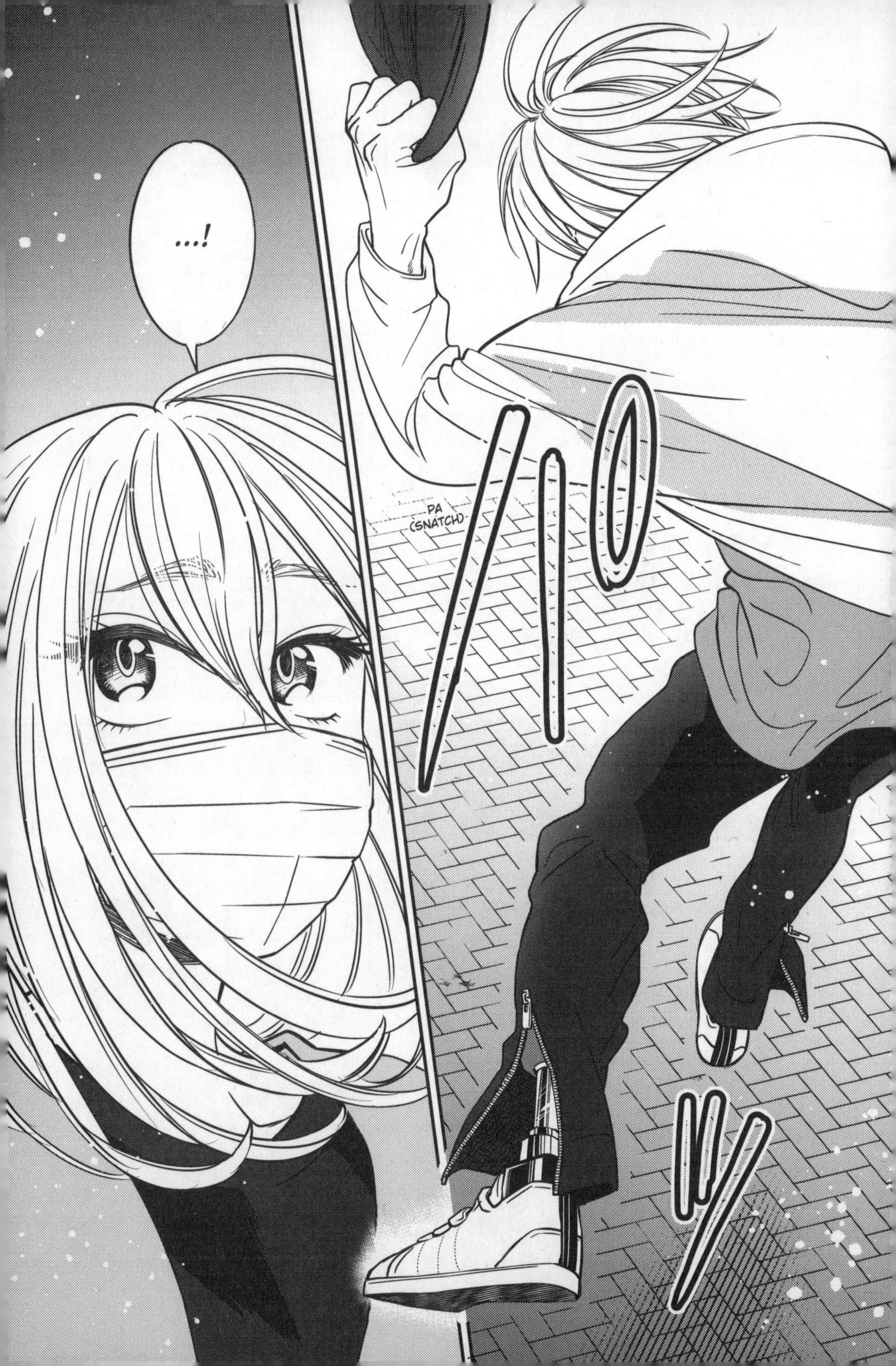
PA (SNATCH)
...!

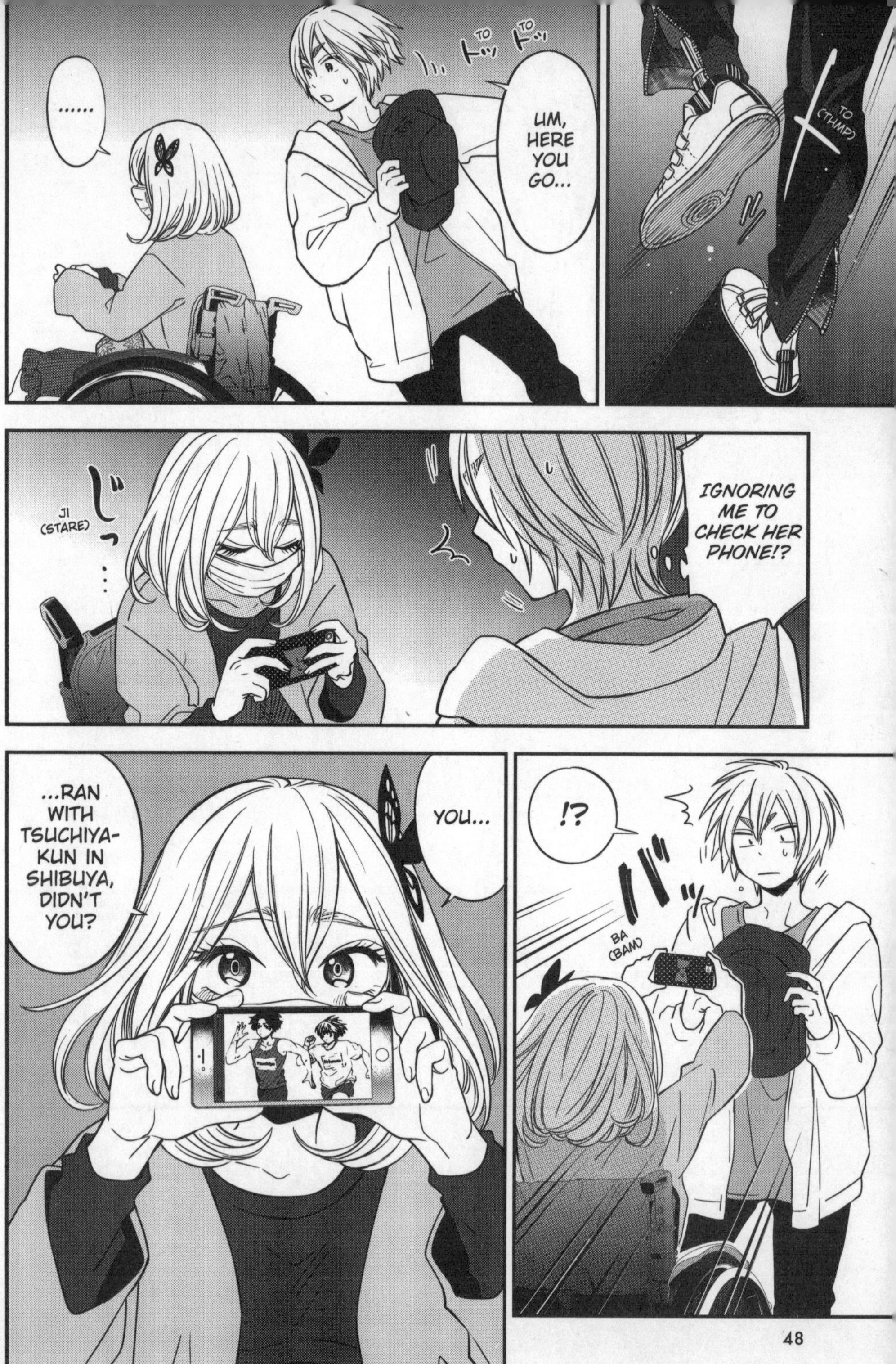

TO (THMP)
TO TO
UM, HERE YOU GO...
......
IGNORING ME TO CHECK HER PHONE!?
JI (STARE)
!?
BA (BAM)
YOU...
...RAN WITH TSUCHIYA-KUN IN SHIBUYA, DIDN'T YOU?

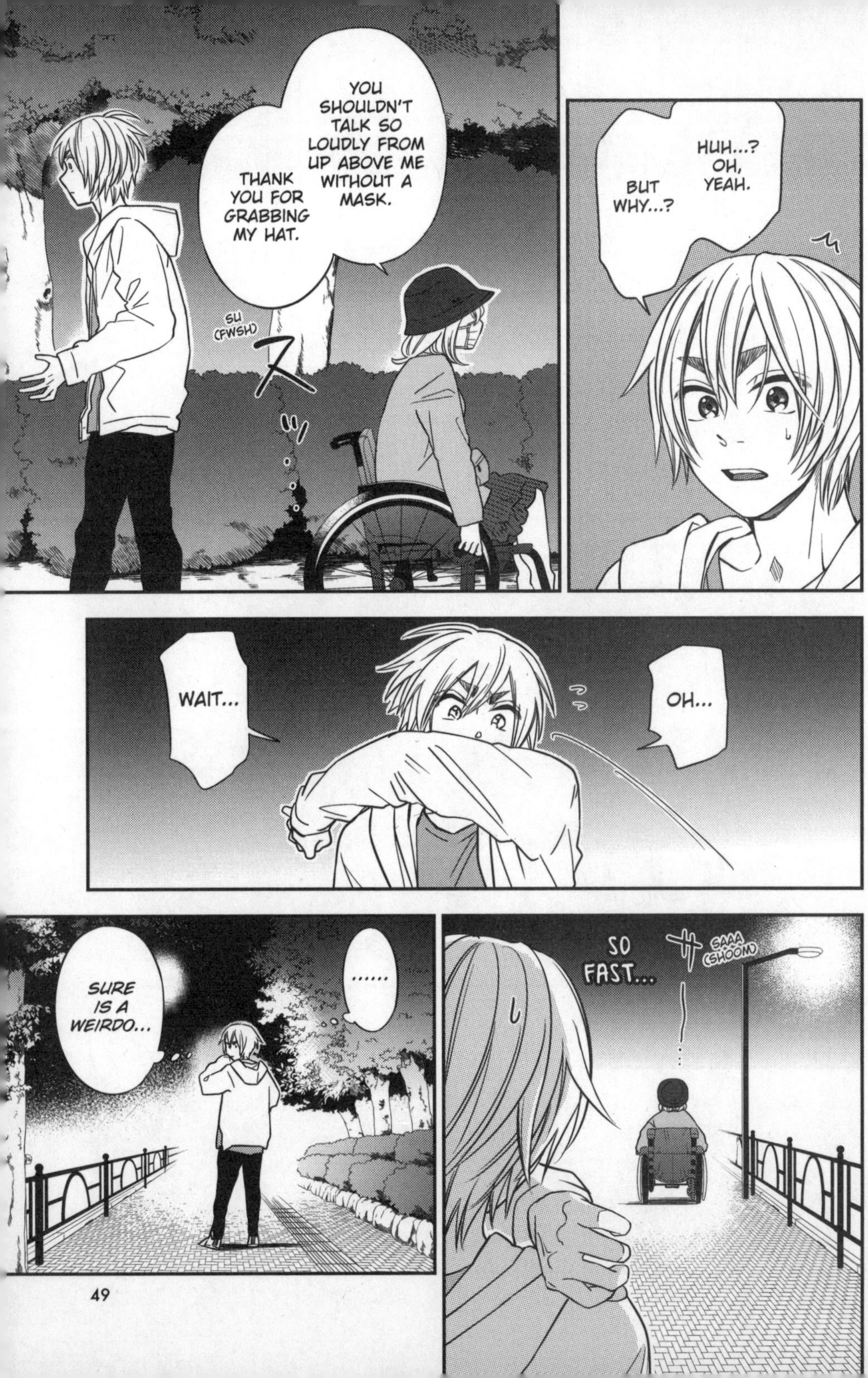
HUH...? OH, YEAH.
BUT WHY...?
YOU SHOULDN'T TALK SO LOUDLY FROM UP ABOVE ME WITHOUT A MASK.
THANK YOU FOR GRABBING MY HAT.
SU (FWSH)
OH...
WAIT...
SO FAST...
SAAA (SHOOM)
......
SURE IS A WEIRDO...

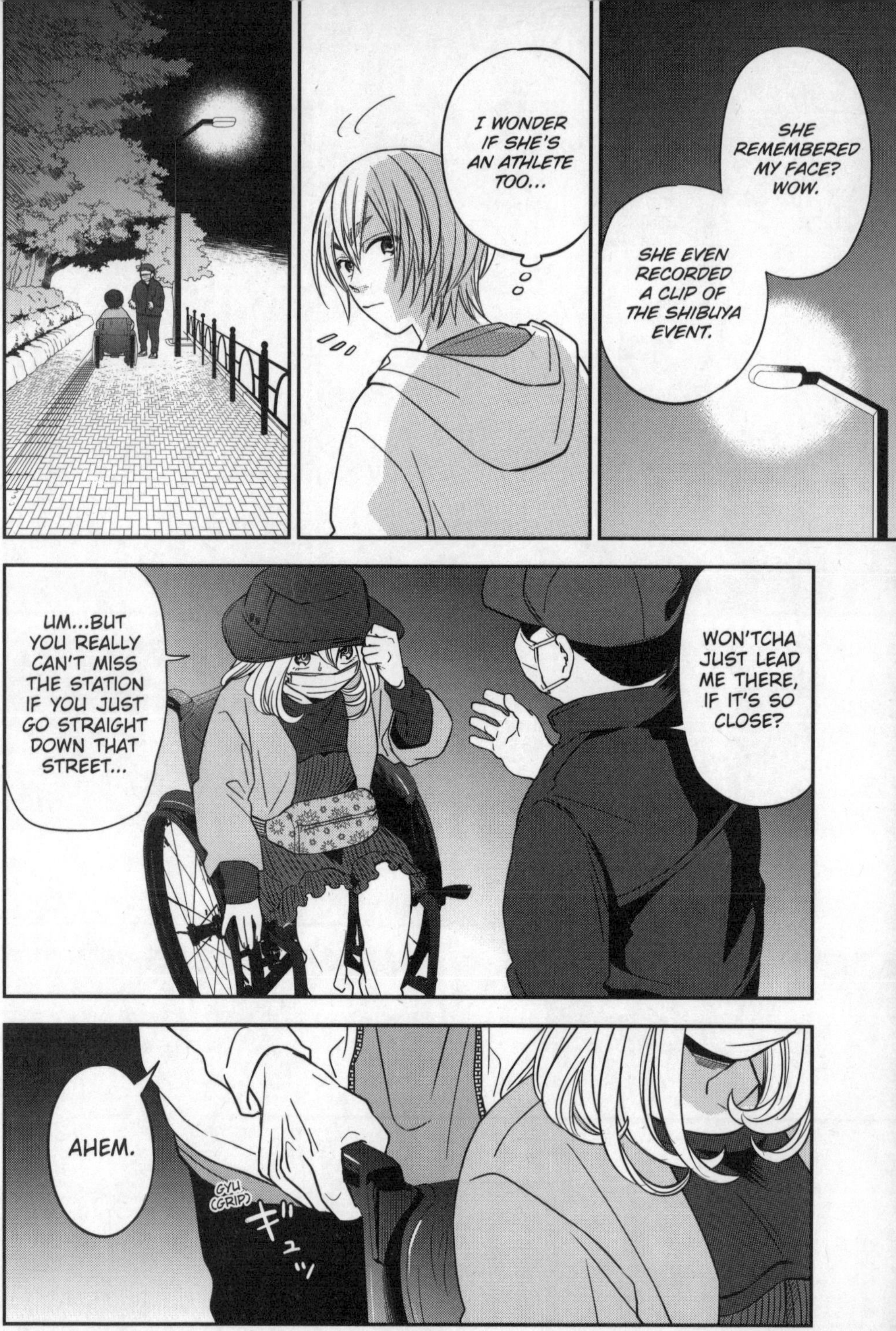
SHE REMEMBERED MY FACE? WOW.
SHE EVEN RECORDED A CLIP OF THE SHIBUYA EVENT.
I WONDER IF SHE'S AN ATHLETE TOO...
WON'TCHA JUST LEAD ME THERE, IF IT'S SO CLOSE?
UM...BUT YOU REALLY CAN'T MISS THE STATION IF YOU JUST GO STRAIGHT DOWN THAT STREET...
AHEM.
GYU (GRIP)
ギュッ

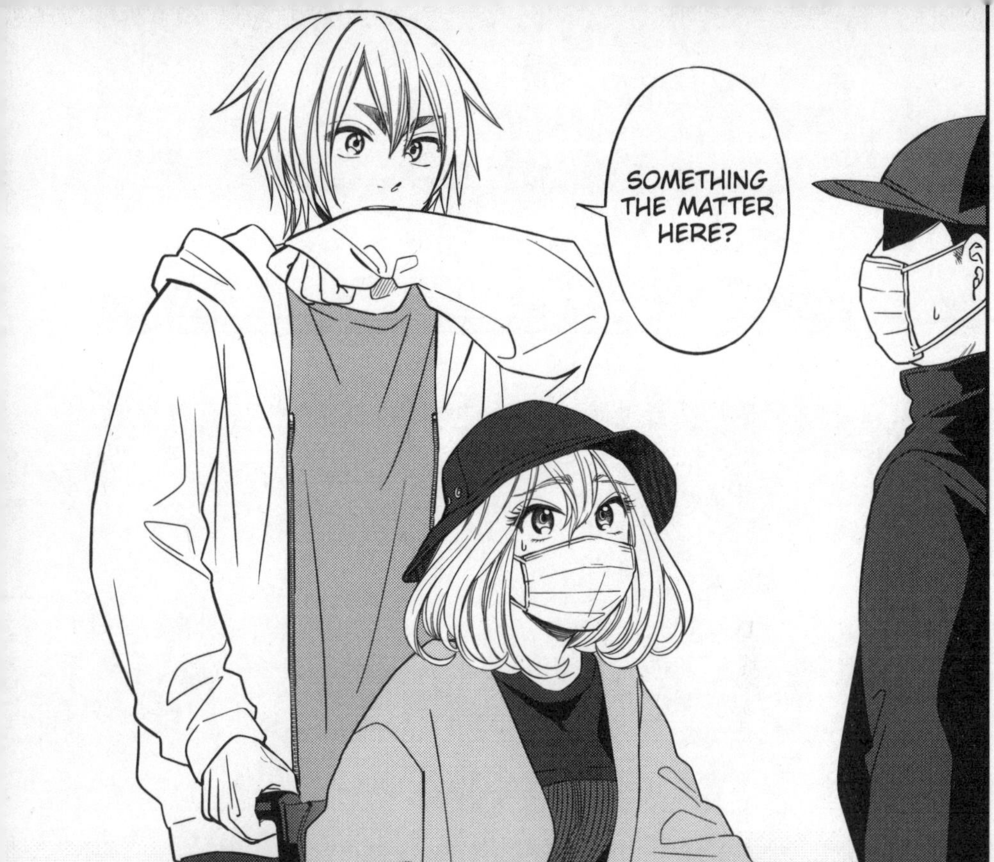
SOMETHING THE MATTER HERE?

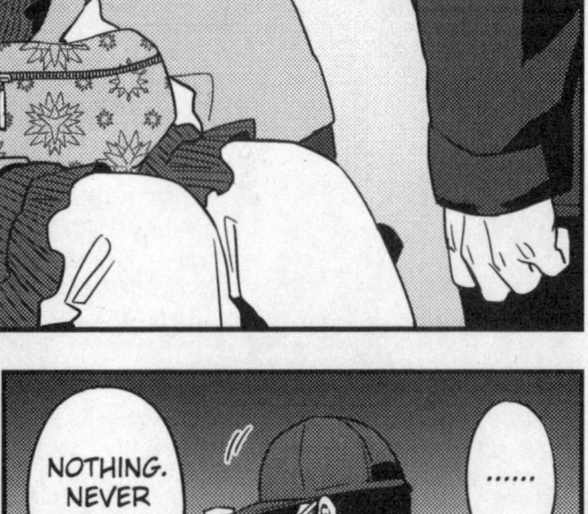
......
NOTHING. NEVER MIND...

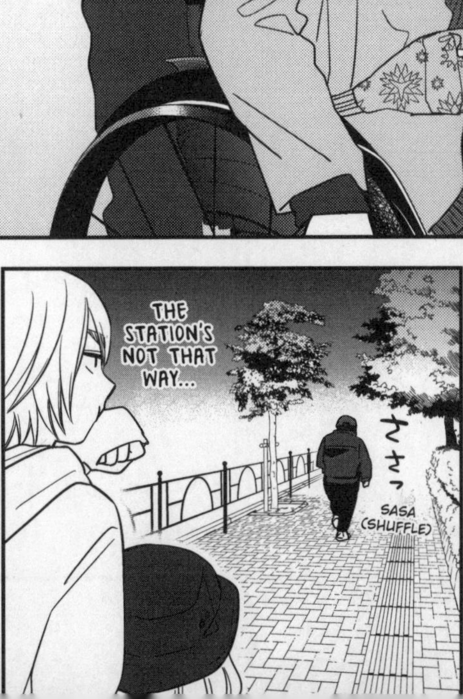
THE STATION'S NOT THAT WAY...
ささっ
SASA (SHUFFLE)

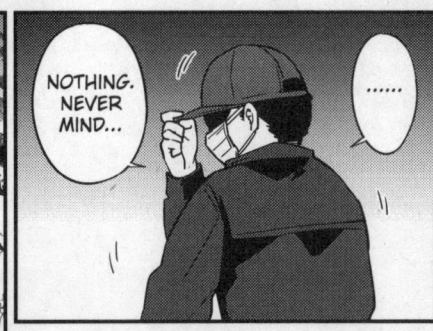

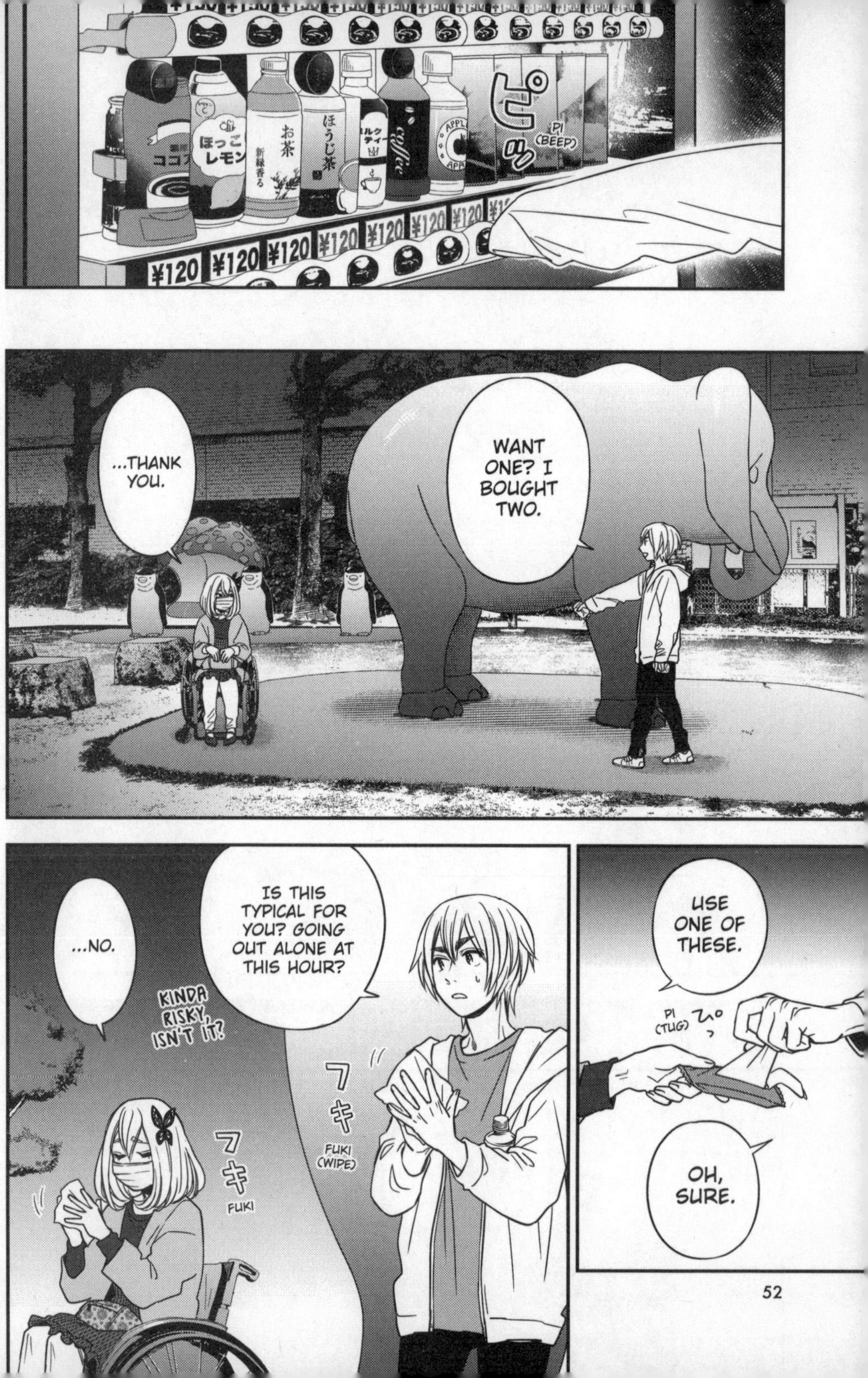
ピッ
PI (BEEP)
WANT ONE? I BOUGHT TWO.
...THANK YOU.
USE ONE OF THESE.
ぴっ
PI (TUG)
OH, SURE.
IS THIS TYPICAL FOR YOU? GOING OUT ALONE AT THIS HOUR?
KINDA RISKY, ISN'T IT?
...NO.
フキ
FUKI (WIPE)
フキ
FUKI

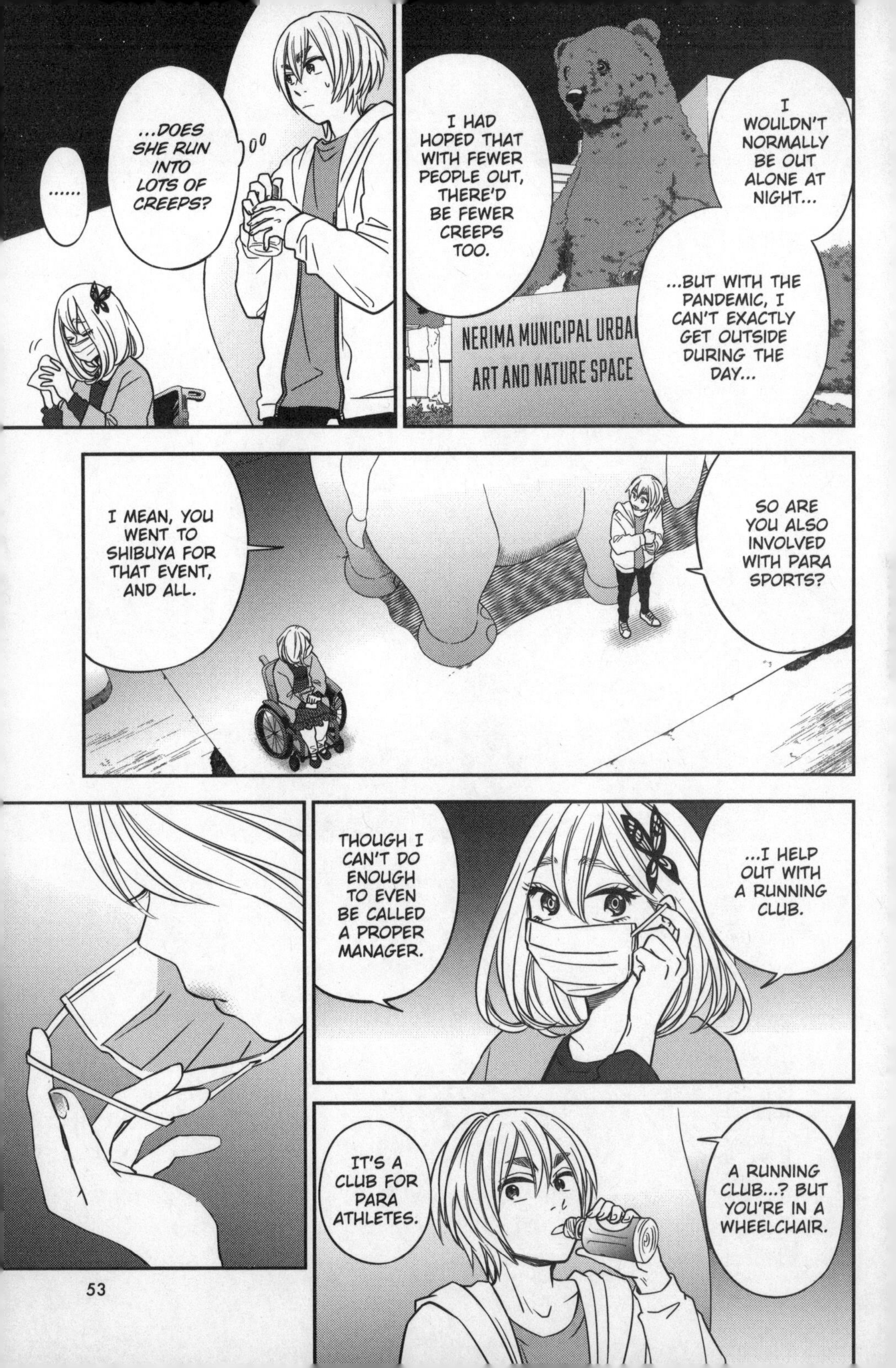
I WOULDN'T NORMALLY BE OUT ALONE AT NIGHT...
...BUT WITH THE PANDEMIC, I CAN'T EXACTLY GET OUTSIDE DURING THE DAY...
I HAD HOPED THAT WITH FEWER PEOPLE OUT, THERE'D BE FEWER CREEPS TOO.
NERIMA MUNICIPAL URBA
ART AND NATURE SPACE
...DOES SHE RUN INTO LOTS OF CREEPS?
......
SO ARE YOU ALSO INVOLVED WITH PARA SPORTS?
I MEAN, YOU WENT TO SHIBUYA FOR THAT EVENT, AND ALL.
...I HELP OUT WITH A RUNNING CLUB.
THOUGH I CAN'T DO ENOUGH TO EVEN BE CALLED A PROPER MANAGER.
A RUNNING CLUB...? BUT YOU'RE IN A WHEELCHAIR.
IT'S A CLUB FOR PARA ATHLETES.

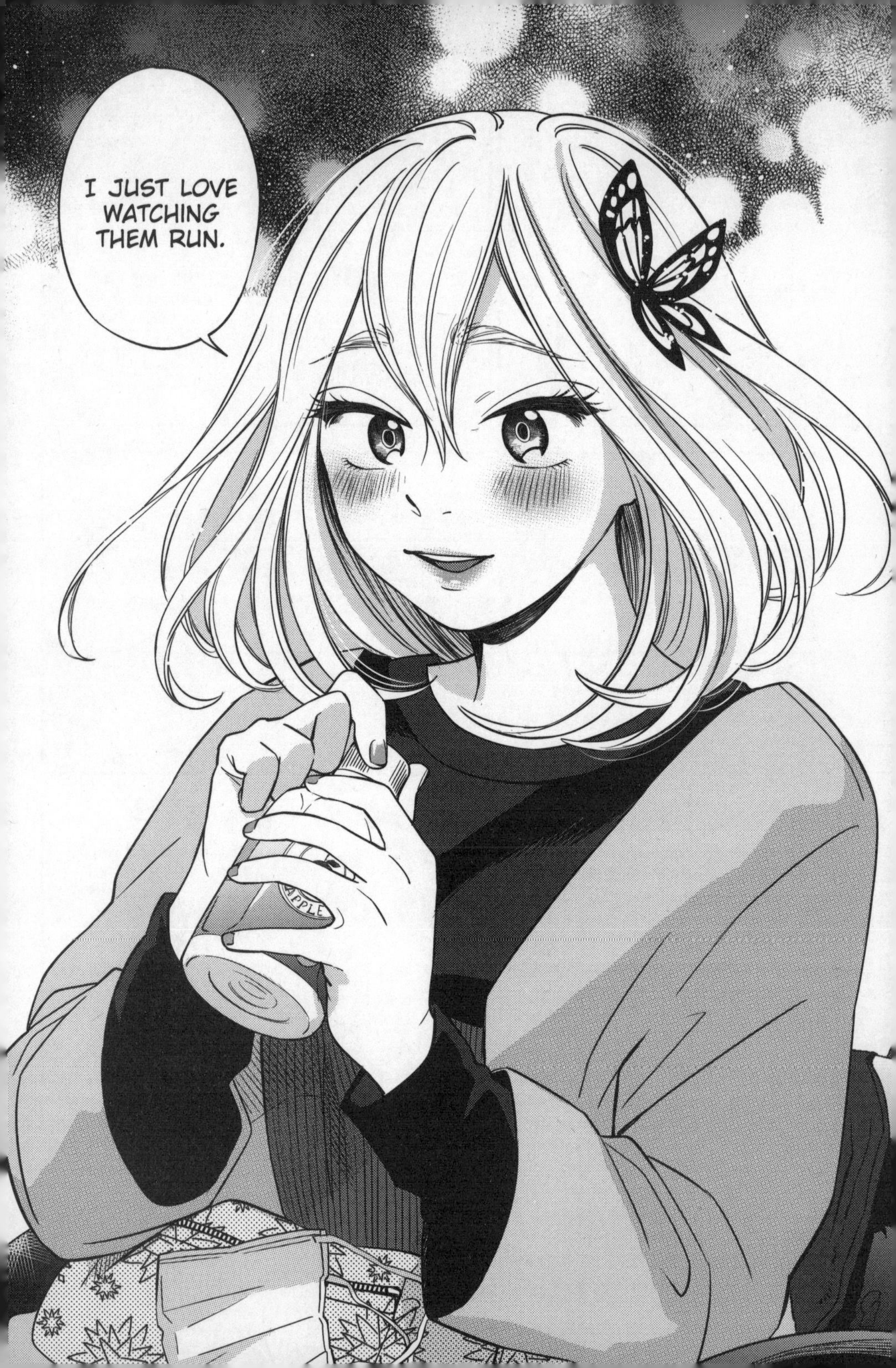
I JUST LOVE WATCHING THEM RUN.
APPLE

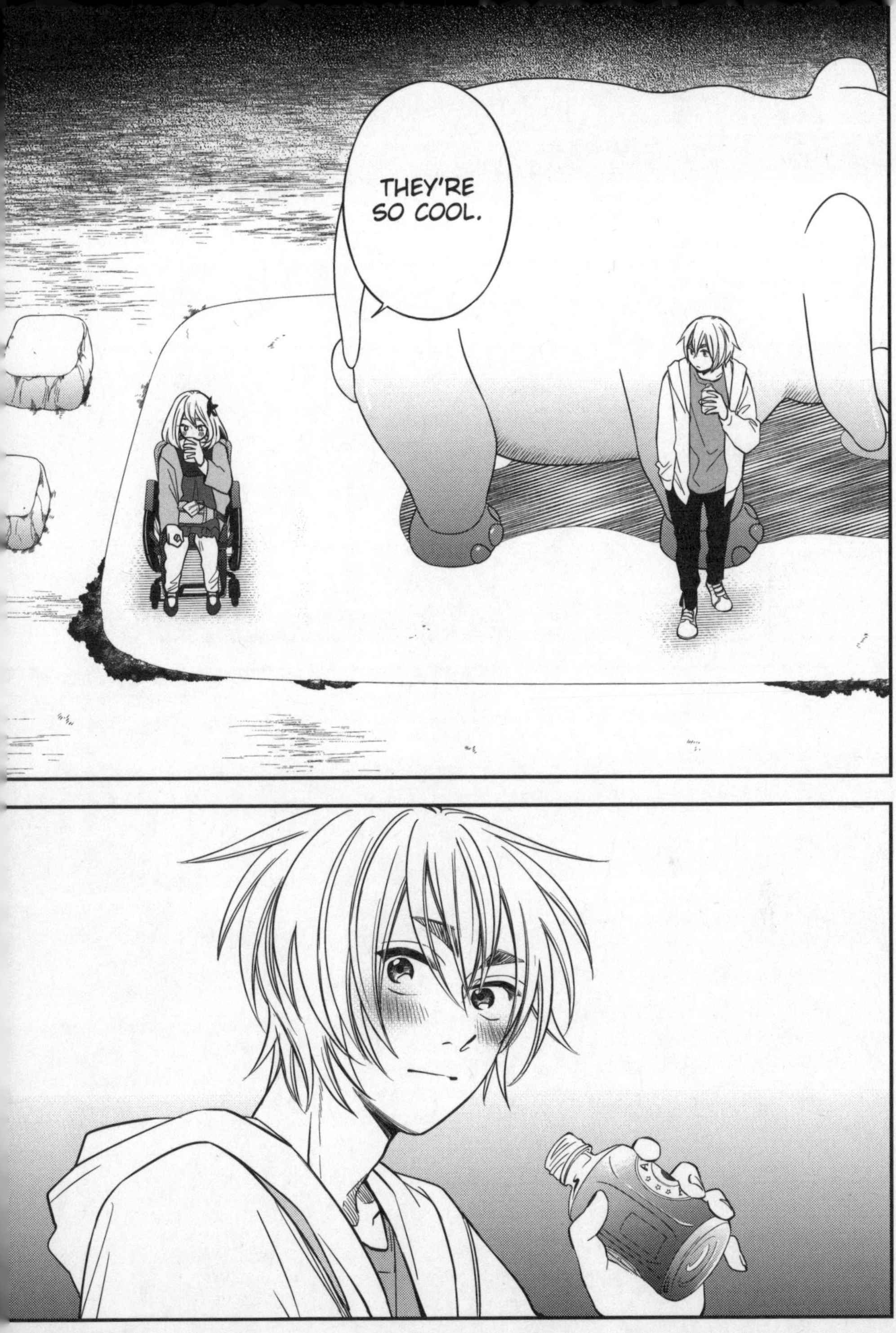
THEY'RE SO COOL.

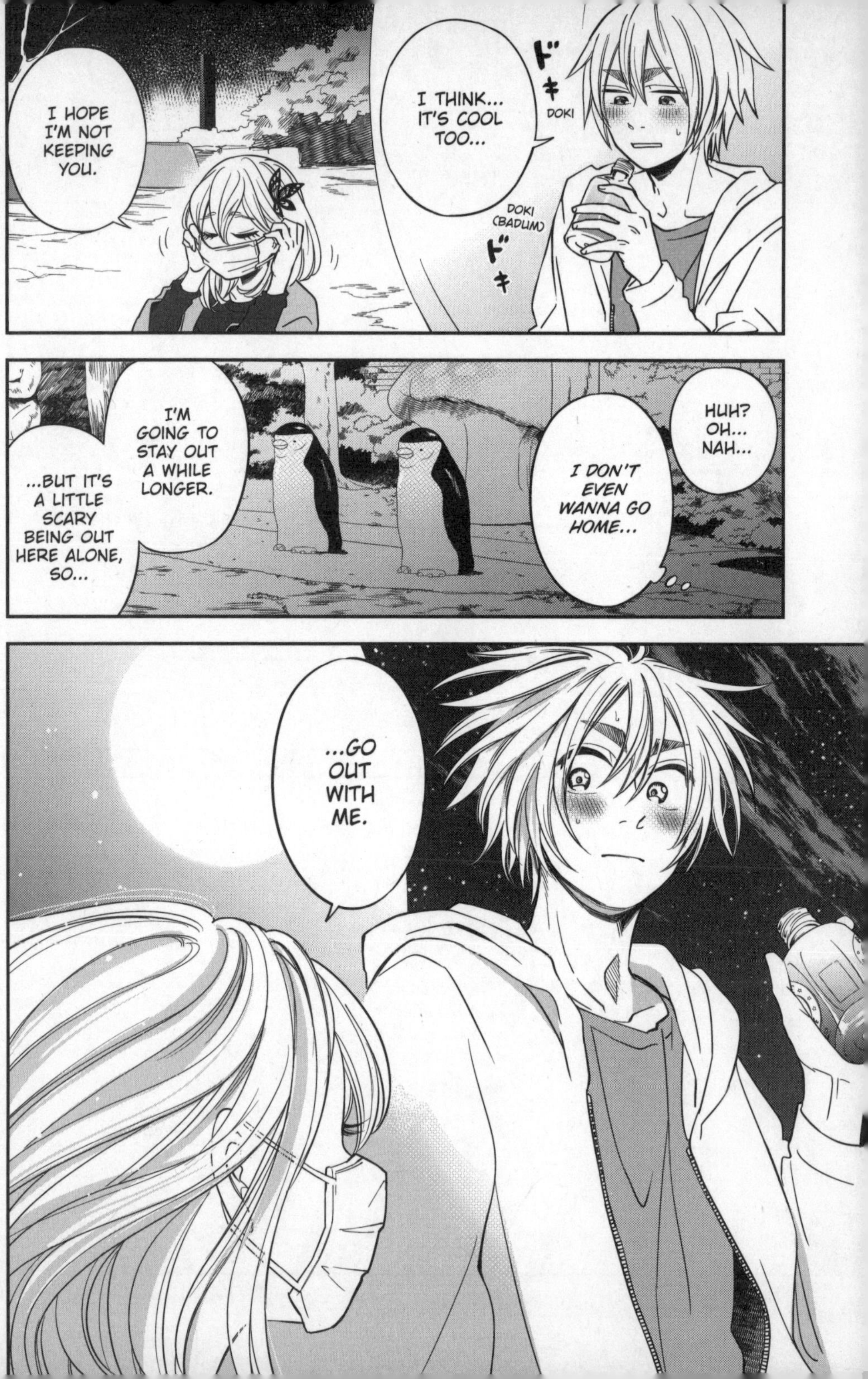
ドキ
DOKI
I THINK... IT'S COOL TOO...
DOKI (BADUM)
ドキ
I HOPE I'M NOT KEEPING YOU.
HUH? OH... NAH...
I DON'T EVEN WANNA GO HOME...
I'M GOING TO STAY OUT A WHILE LONGER.
...BUT IT'S A LITTLE SCARY BEING OUT HERE ALONE, SO...
...GO OUT WITH ME.

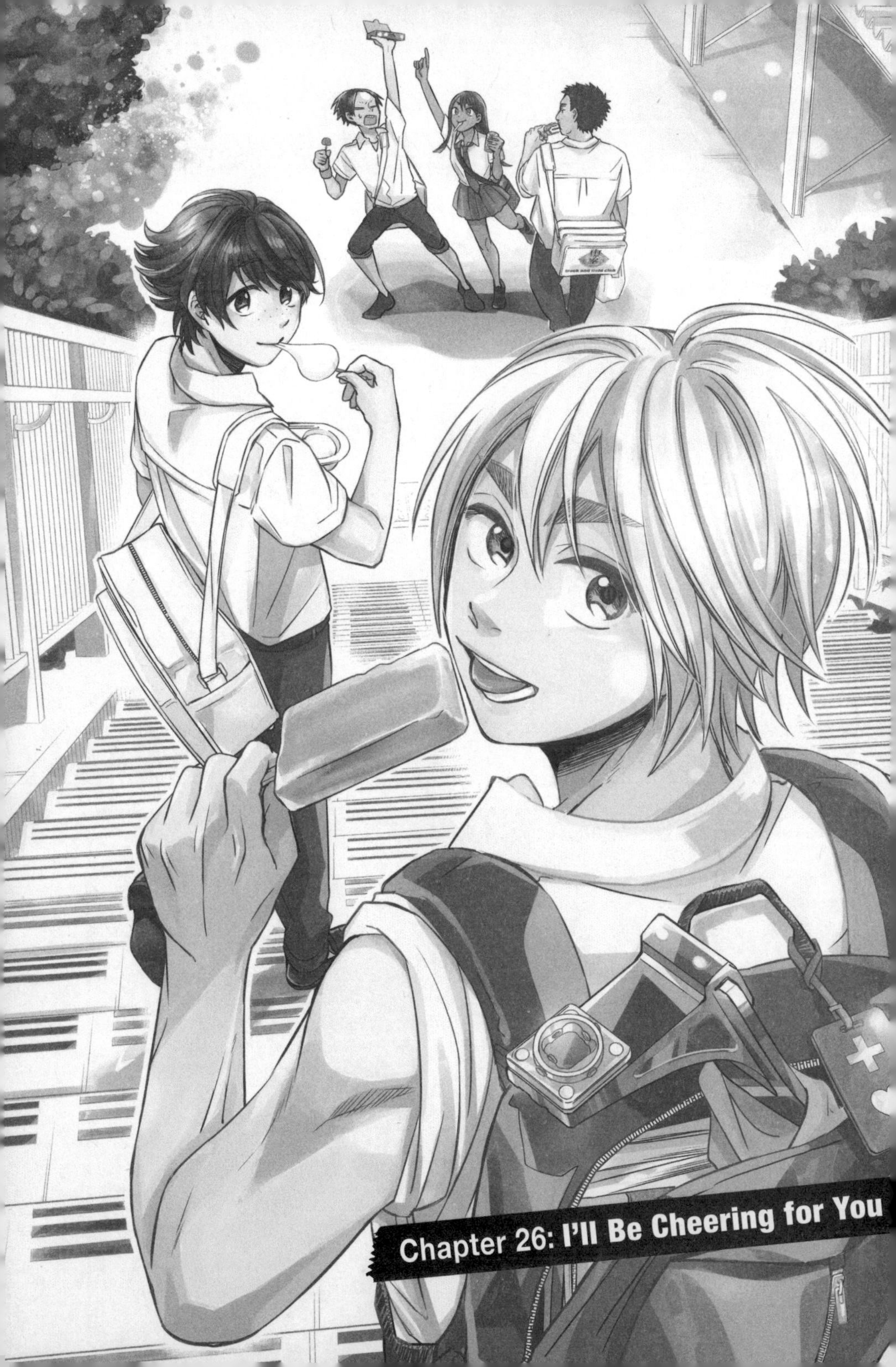
Chapter 26: I'll Be Cheering for You

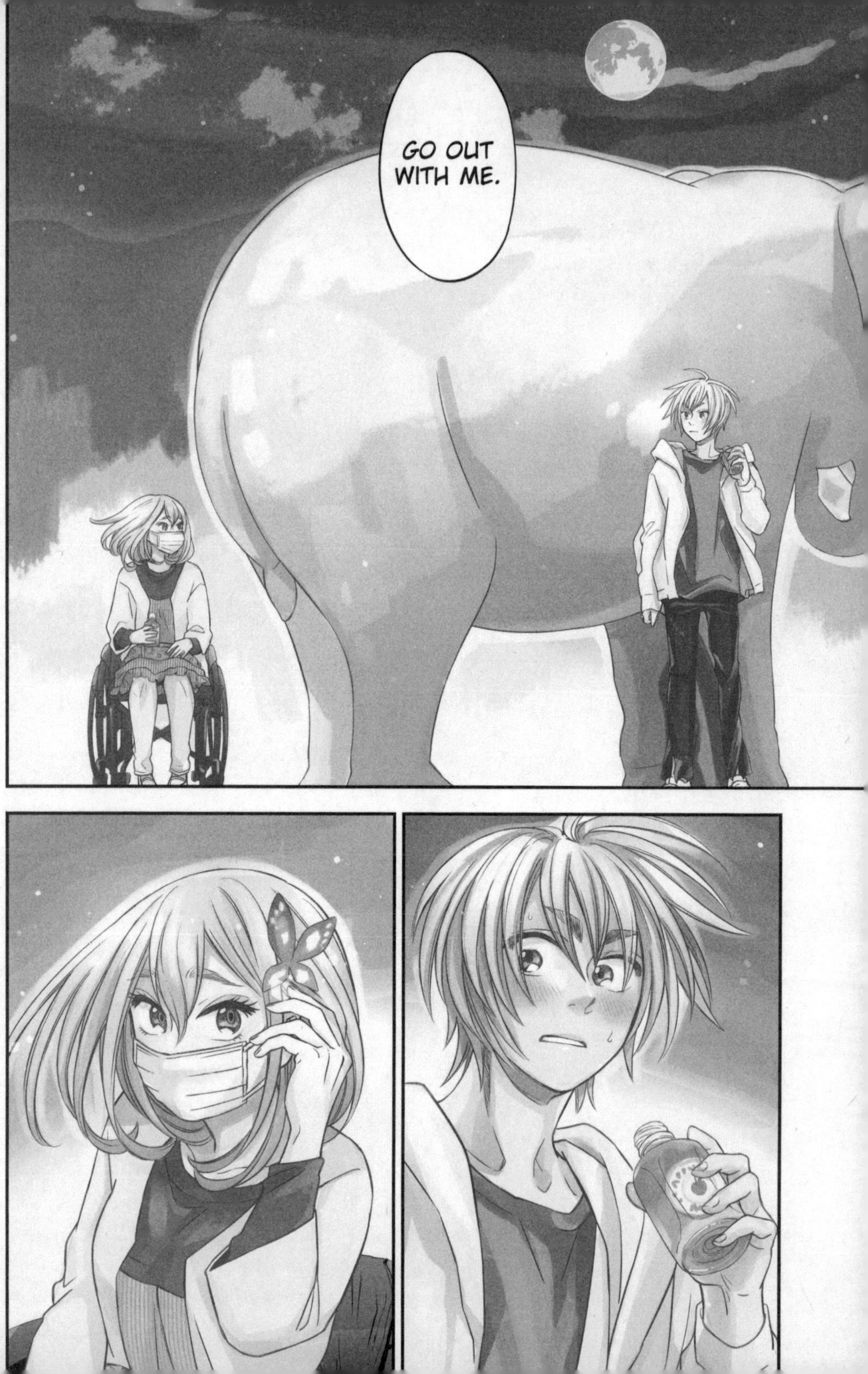
GO OUT
WITH ME.

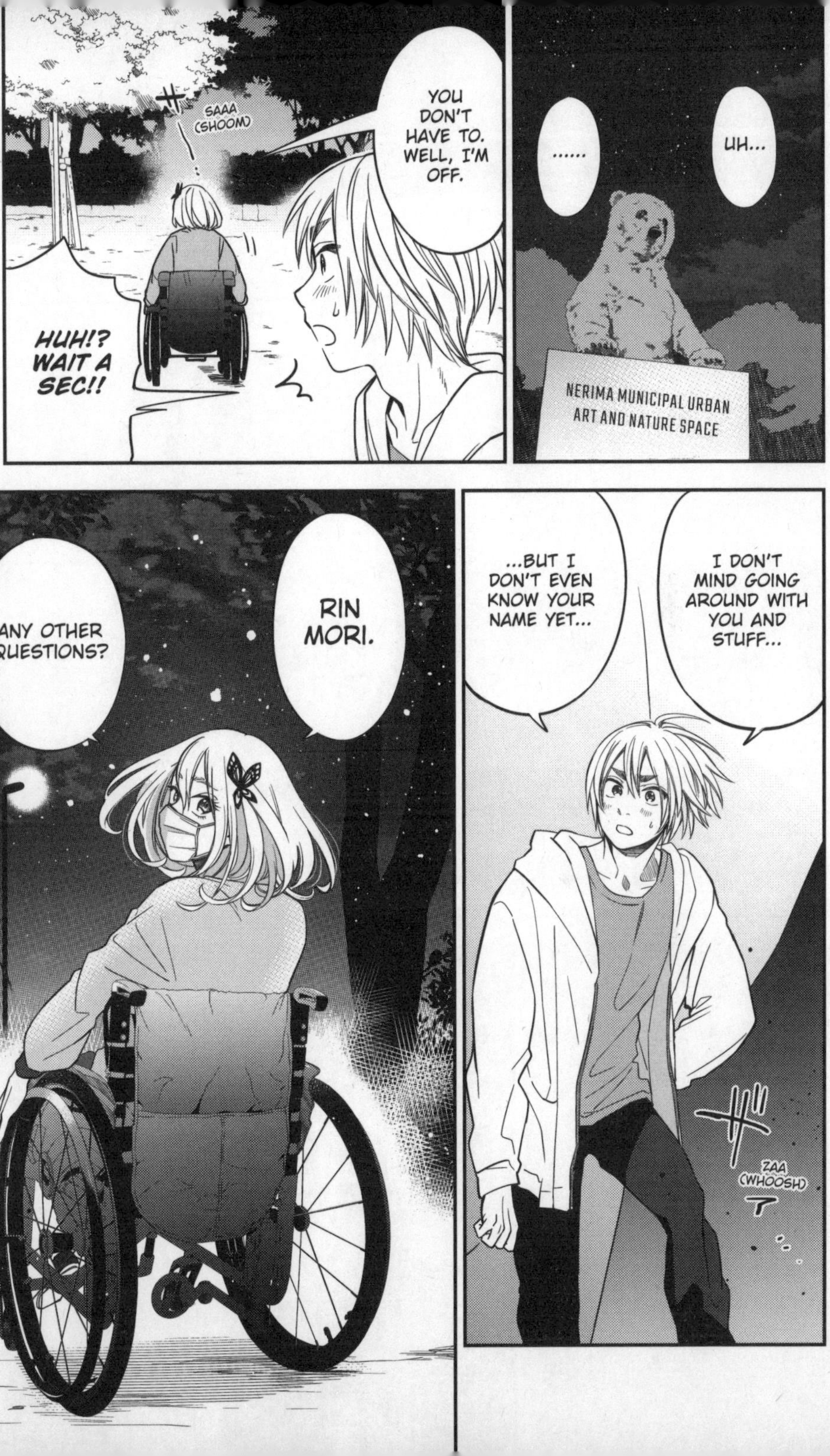
UH...
......
NERIMA MUNICIPAL URBAN ART AND NATURE SPACE
YOU DON'T HAVE TO. WELL, I'M OFF.
SAAA (SHOOM)
HUH!? WAIT A SEC!!
I DON'T MIND GOING AROUND WITH YOU AND STUFF...
...BUT I DON'T EVEN KNOW YOUR NAME YET...
ZAA (WHOOSH)
RIN MORI.
ANY OTHER QUESTIONS?

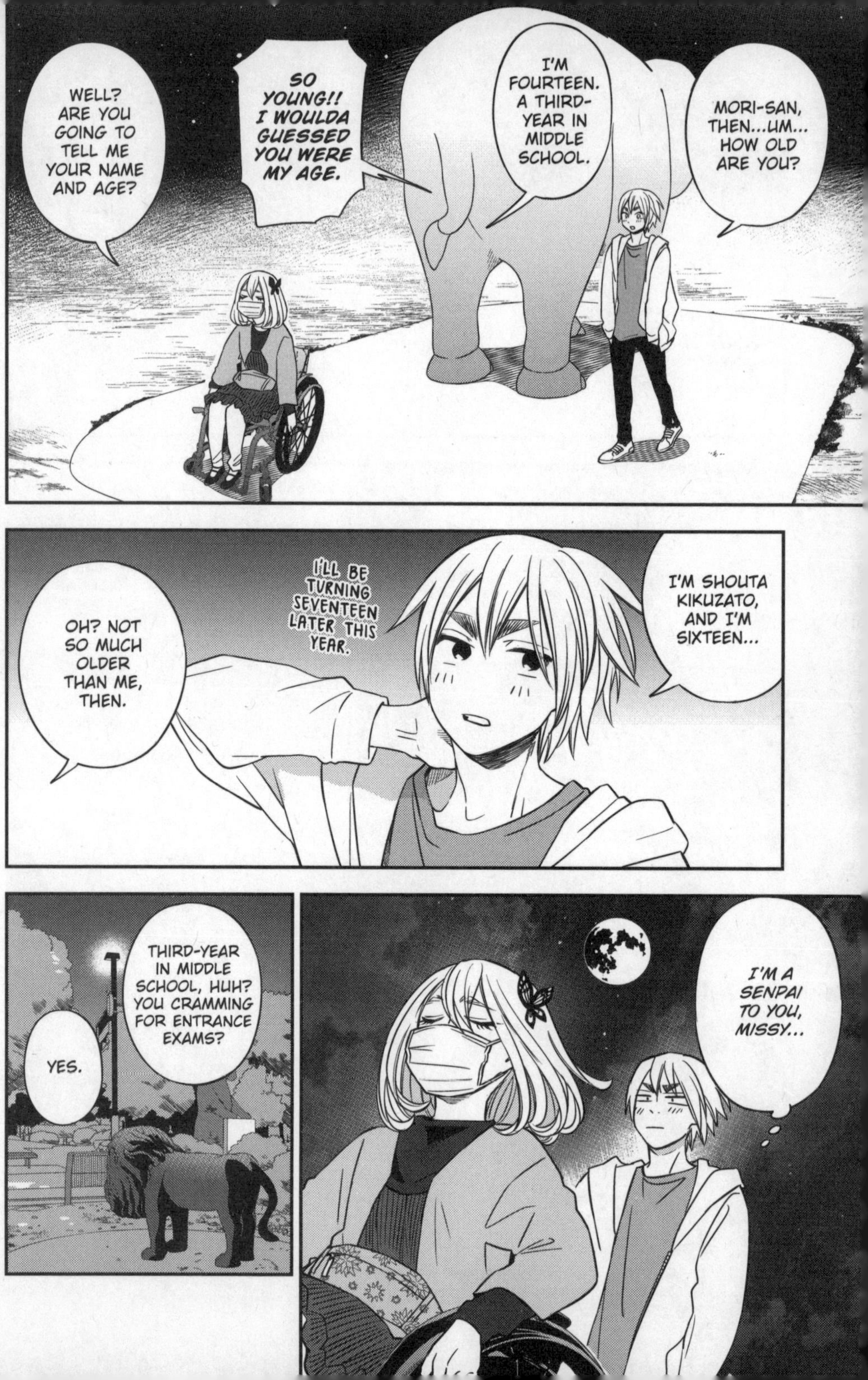
MORI-SAN, THEN...UM... HOW OLD ARE YOU?
I'M FOURTEEN. A THIRD-YEAR IN MIDDLE SCHOOL.
SO YOUNG!! I WOULDA GUESSED YOU WERE MY AGE.
WELL? ARE YOU GOING TO TELL ME YOUR NAME AND AGE?
I'M SHOUTA KIKUZATO, AND I'M SIXTEEN...
I'LL BE TURNING SEVENTEEN LATER THIS YEAR.
OH? NOT SO MUCH OLDER THAN ME, THEN.
I'M A SENPAI TO YOU, MISSY...
THIRD-YEAR IN MIDDLE SCHOOL, HUH? YOU CRAMMING FOR ENTRANCE EXAMS?
YES.

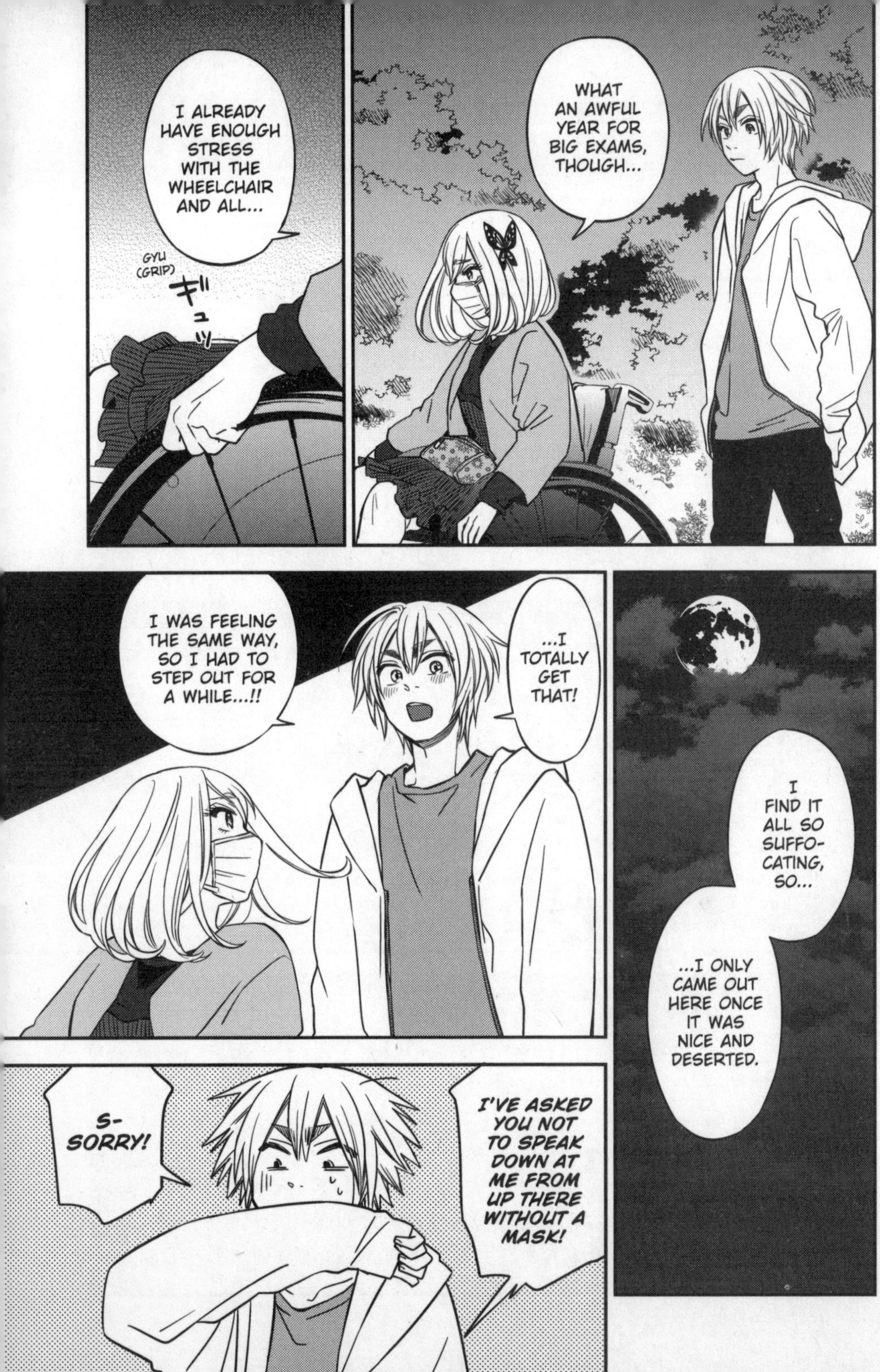
WHAT AN AWFUL YEAR FOR BIG EXAMS, THOUGH...
I ALREADY HAVE ENOUGH STRESS WITH THE WHEELCHAIR AND ALL...
GYU (GRIP)
ギュッ
I FIND IT ALL SO SUFFO-CATING, SO...
...I ONLY CAME OUT HERE ONCE IT WAS NICE AND DESERTED.
...I TOTALLY GET THAT!
I WAS FEELING THE SAME WAY, SO I HAD TO STEP OUT FOR A WHILE...!!
I'VE ASKED YOU NOT TO SPEAK DOWN AT ME FROM UP THERE WITHOUT A MASK!
S-SORRY!

I CAN'T BELIEVE YOU'RE OUT AND ABOUT WITHOUT ONE.
スッ
I KINDA LEFT IN A HURRY...
SORRY AGAIN...
GOSO (RUSTLE) ゴソ
SU (FWP) すっ
せっ SE (SHWP)
さ SA (SHP)
THAT HANDKERCHIEF IS BRAND NEW, SO YOU CAN HAVE IT.
WHOA, YOU MEAN IT? THANKS.
THE PRINT'S A LITTLE MUCH FOR ME, BUT...
ドキ DOKI
IT SMELLS REALLY GOOD...
WHAT'S THAT SCENT...?
スン SUN (SNIFF)
スン SUN
スン SUN
ドキ DOKI (BADUM)
LET'S HEAD THAT WAY.

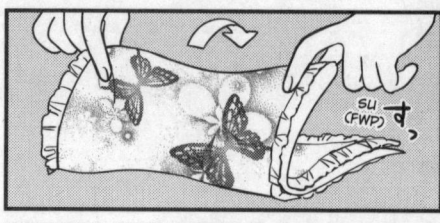

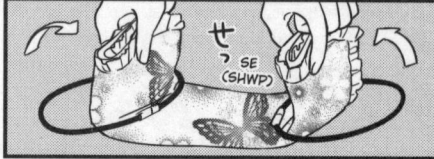

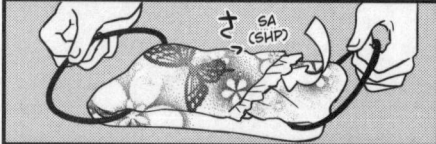

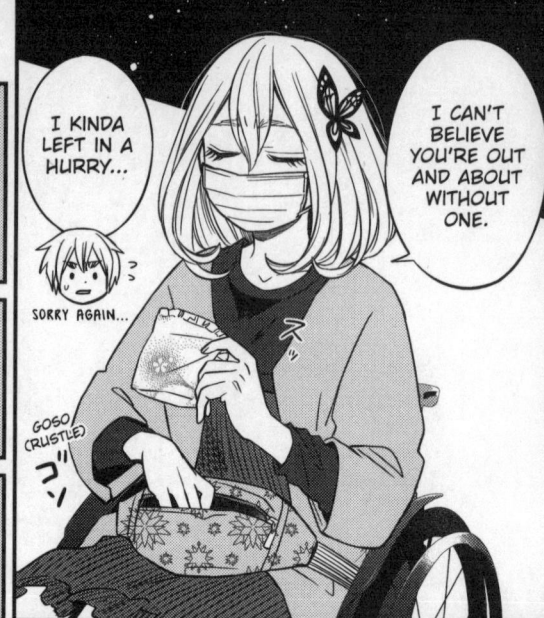

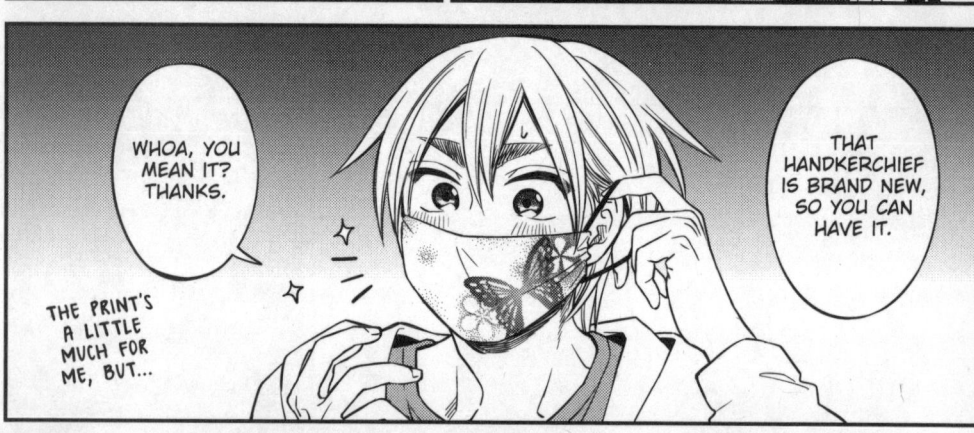

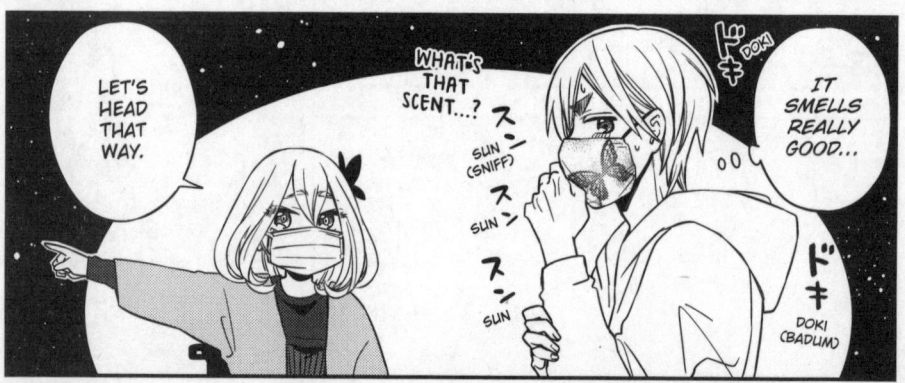

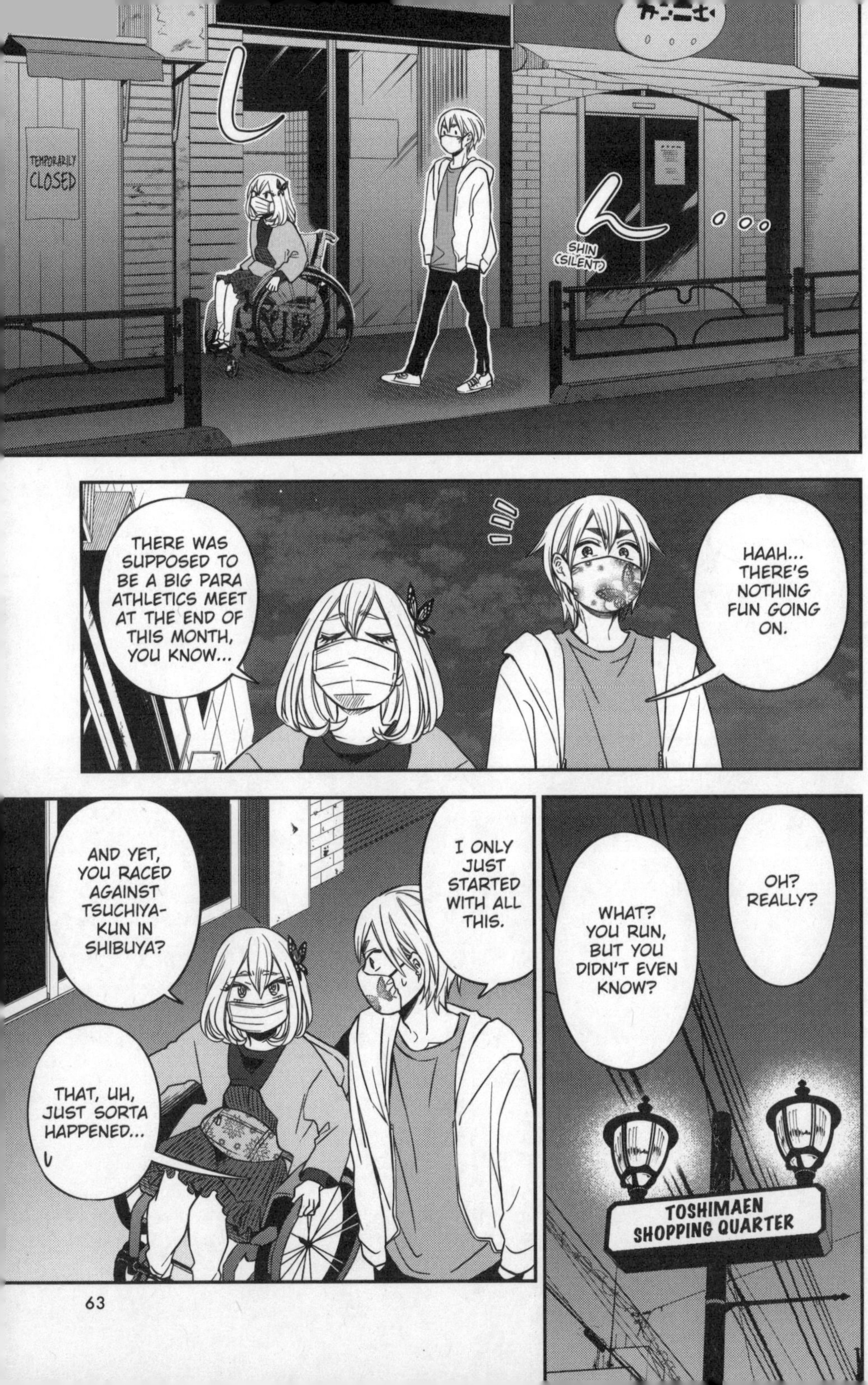
TEMPORARILY CLOSED
SHIN (SILENT)
HAAH... THERE'S NOTHING FUN GOING ON.
THERE WAS SUPPOSED TO BE A BIG PARA ATHLETICS MEET AT THE END OF THIS MONTH, YOU KNOW...
OH? REALLY?
WHAT? YOU RUN, BUT YOU DIDN'T EVEN KNOW?
TOSHIMAEN SHOPPING QUARTER
I ONLY JUST STARTED WITH ALL THIS.
AND YET, YOU RACED AGAINST TSUCHIYA-KUN IN SHIBUYA?
THAT, UH, JUST SORTA HAPPENED...

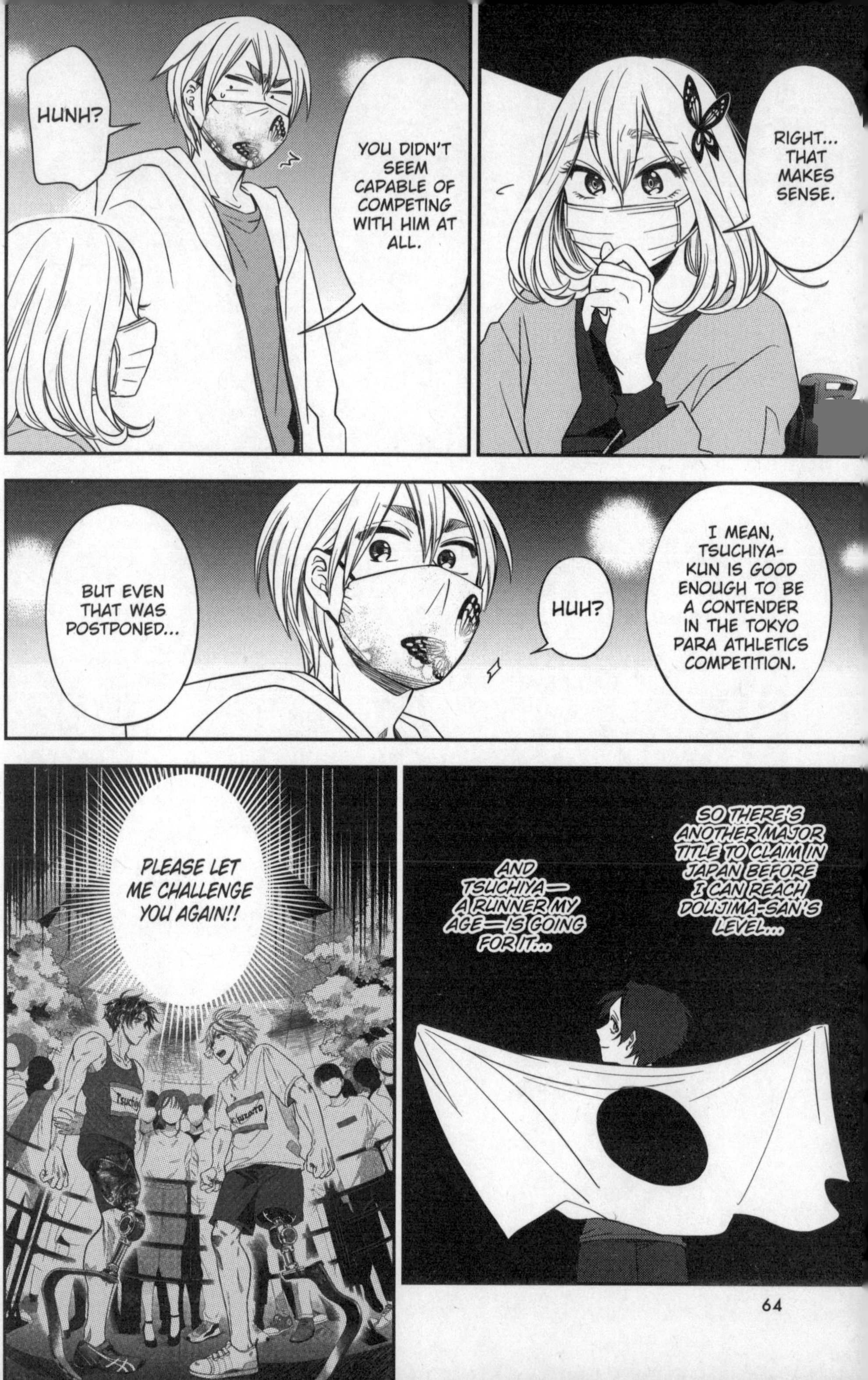
RIGHT... THAT MAKES SENSE.
YOU DIDN'T SEEM CAPABLE OF COMPETING WITH HIM AT ALL.
HUNH?
I MEAN, TSUCHIYA-KUN IS GOOD ENOUGH TO BE A CONTENDER IN THE TOKYO PARA ATHLETICS COMPETITION.
HUH?
BUT EVEN THAT WAS POSTPONED...
SO THERE'S ANOTHER MAJOR TITLE TO CLAIM IN JAPAN BEFORE I CAN REACH DOUJIMA-SAN'S LEVEL...
AND TSUCHIYA—A RUNNER MY AGE—IS GOING FOR IT...
PLEASE LET ME CHALLENGE YOU AGAIN!!

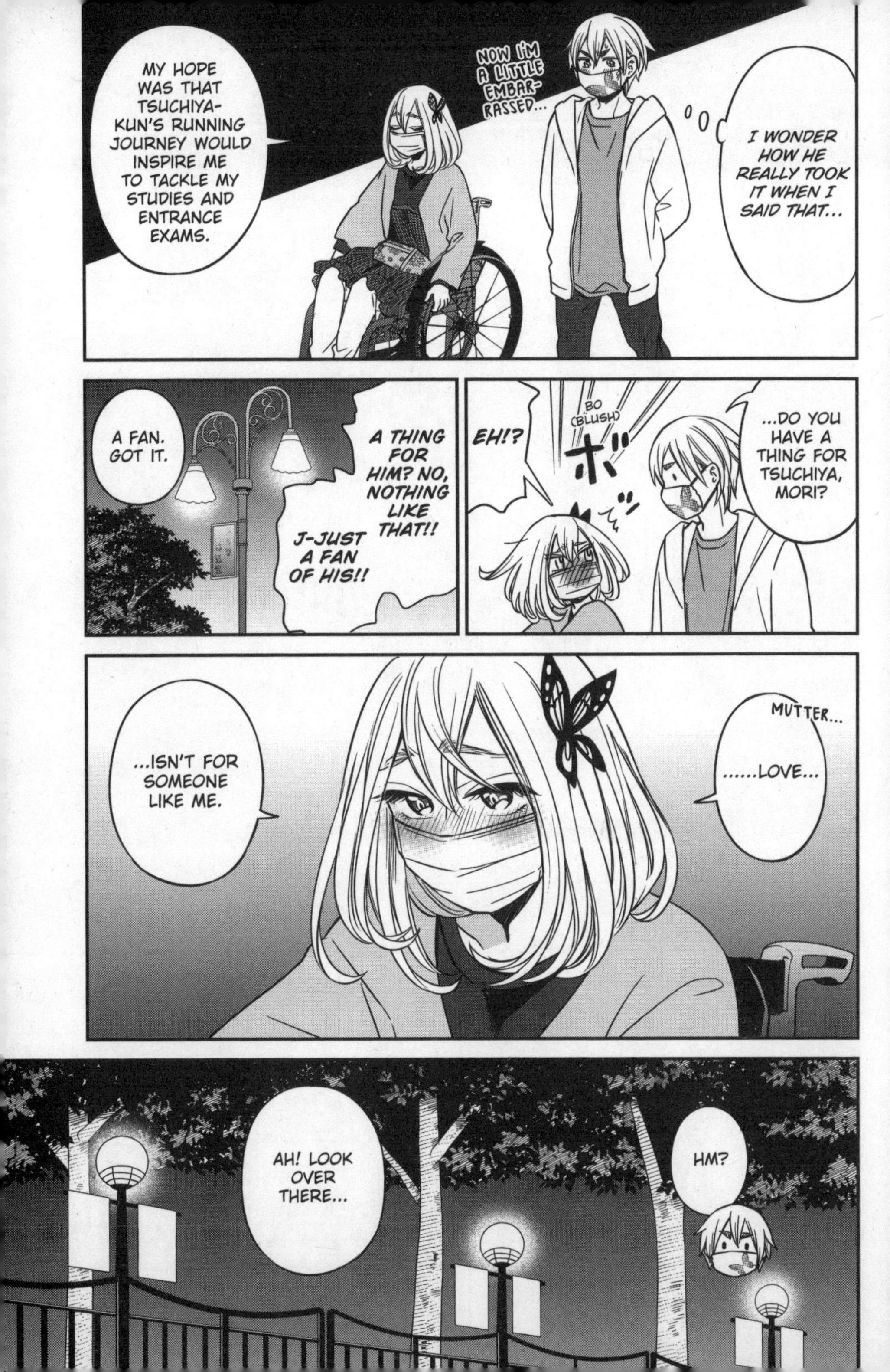
MY HOPE WAS THAT TSUCHIYA-KUN'S RUNNING JOURNEY WOULD INSPIRE ME TO TACKLE MY STUDIES AND ENTRANCE EXAMS.
NOW I'M A LITTLE EMBARRASSED...
I WONDER HOW HE REALLY TOOK IT WHEN I SAID THAT...
...DO YOU HAVE A THING FOR TSUCHIYA, MORI?
BO (BLUSH)
EH!?
A THING FOR HIM? NO, NOTHING LIKE THAT!!
J-JUST A FAN OF HIS!!
A FAN. GOT IT.
MUTTER...
......LOVE...
...ISN'T FOR SOMEONE LIKE ME.
AH! LOOK OVER THERE...
HM?

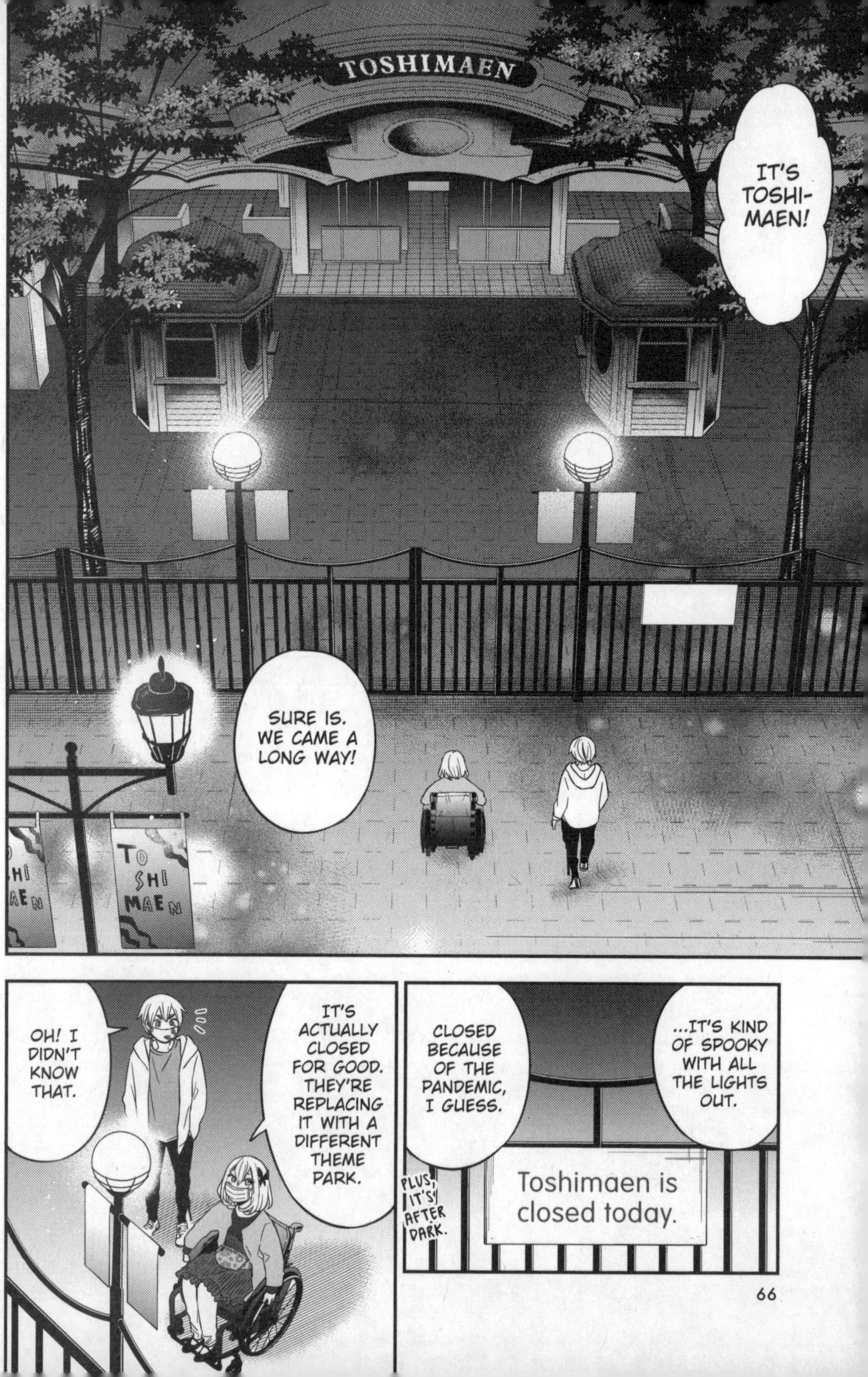
TOSHIMAEN
IT'S TOSHI-MAEN!
SURE IS. WE CAME A LONG WAY!
TO SHI MAEN
...IT'S KIND OF SPOOKY WITH ALL THE LIGHTS OUT.
CLOSED BECAUSE OF THE PANDEMIC, I GUESS.
PLUS, IT'S AFTER DARK.
Toshimaen is closed today.
IT'S ACTUALLY CLOSED FOR GOOD. THEY'RE REPLACING IT WITH A DIFFERENT THEME PARK.
OH! I DIDN'T KNOW THAT.

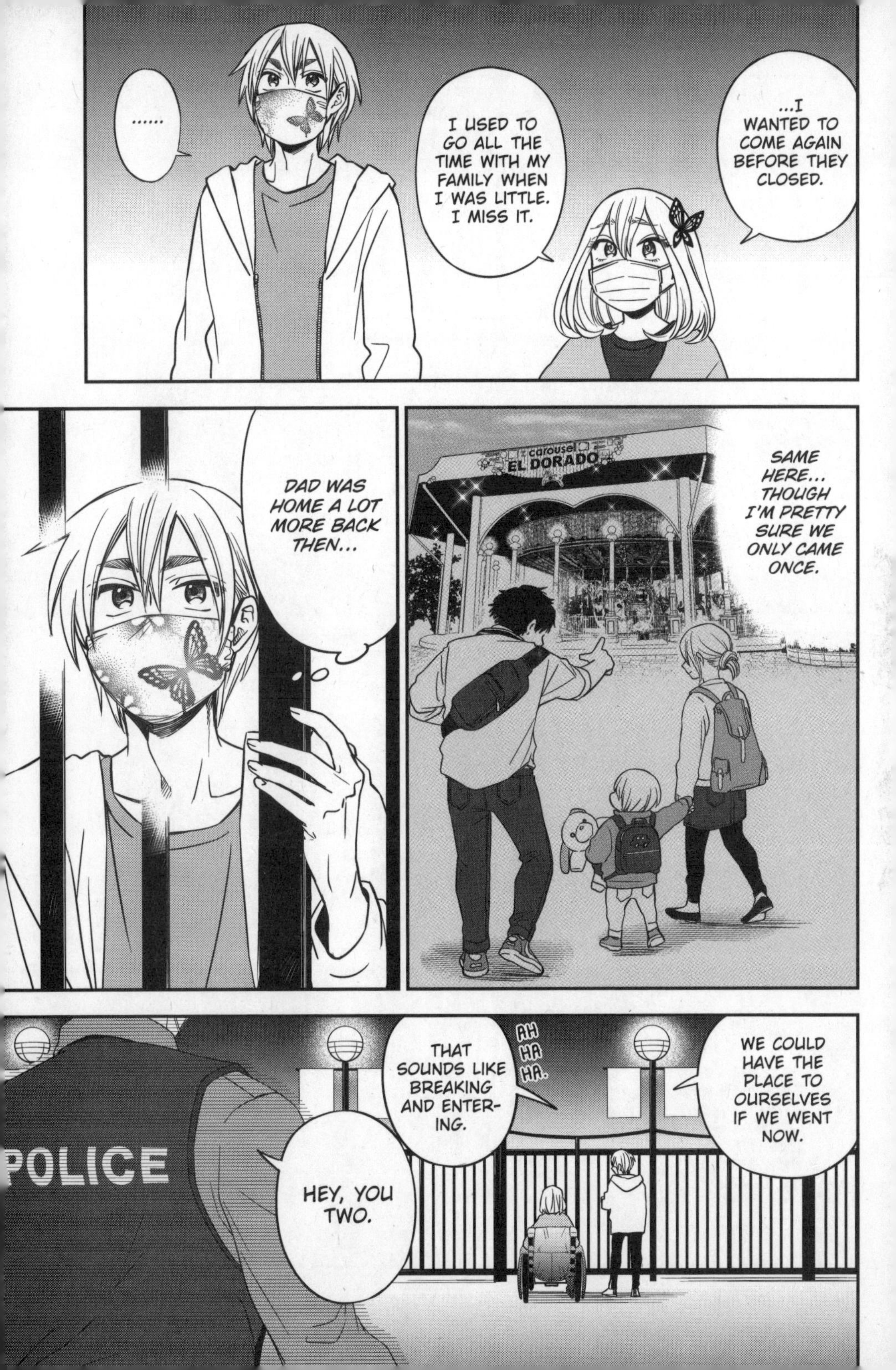
...I WANTED TO COME AGAIN BEFORE THEY CLOSED.
I USED TO GO ALL THE TIME WITH MY FAMILY WHEN I WAS LITTLE. I MISS IT.
......
carousel
EL DORADO
SAME HERE... THOUGH I'M PRETTY SURE WE ONLY CAME ONCE.
DAD WAS HOME A LOT MORE BACK THEN...
WE COULD HAVE THE PLACE TO OURSELVES IF WE WENT NOW.
AH HA HA.
THAT SOUNDS LIKE BREAKING AND ENTER-ING.
HEY, YOU TWO.
POLICE

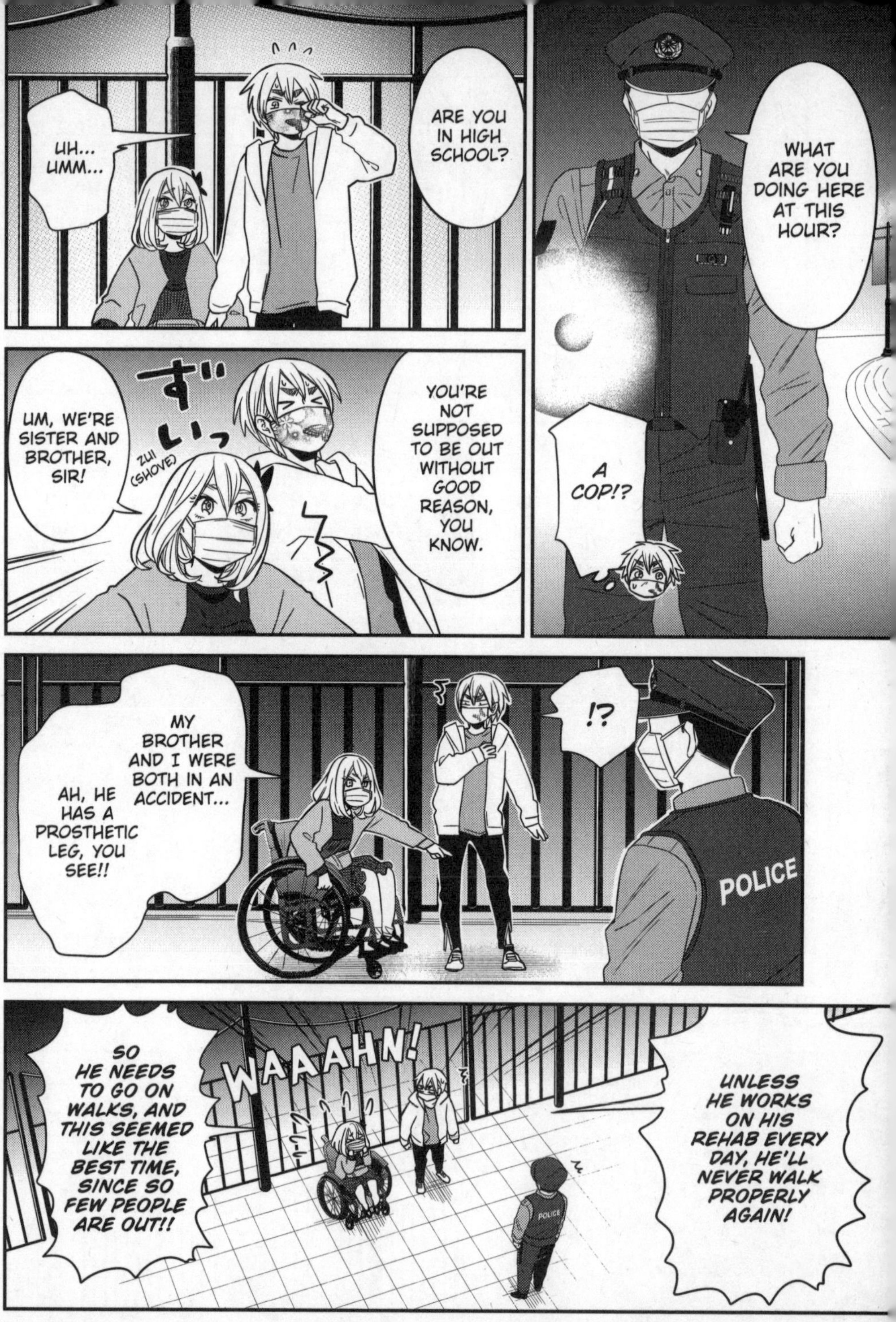
WHAT ARE YOU DOING HERE AT THIS HOUR?
A COP!?
ARE YOU IN HIGH SCHOOL?
UH... UMM...
YOU'RE NOT SUPPOSED TO BE OUT WITHOUT GOOD REASON, YOU KNOW.
ずいっ
ZUI (SHOVE)
UM, WE'RE SISTER AND BROTHER, SIR!
!?
MY BROTHER AND I WERE BOTH IN AN ACCIDENT...
AH, HE HAS A PROSTHETIC LEG, YOU SEE!!
POLICE
SO HE NEEDS TO GO ON WALKS, AND THIS SEEMED LIKE THE BEST TIME, SINCE SO FEW PEOPLE ARE OUT!!
WAAAHN!
UNLESS HE WORKS ON HIS REHAB EVERY DAY, HE'LL NEVER WALK PROPERLY AGAIN!
POLICE

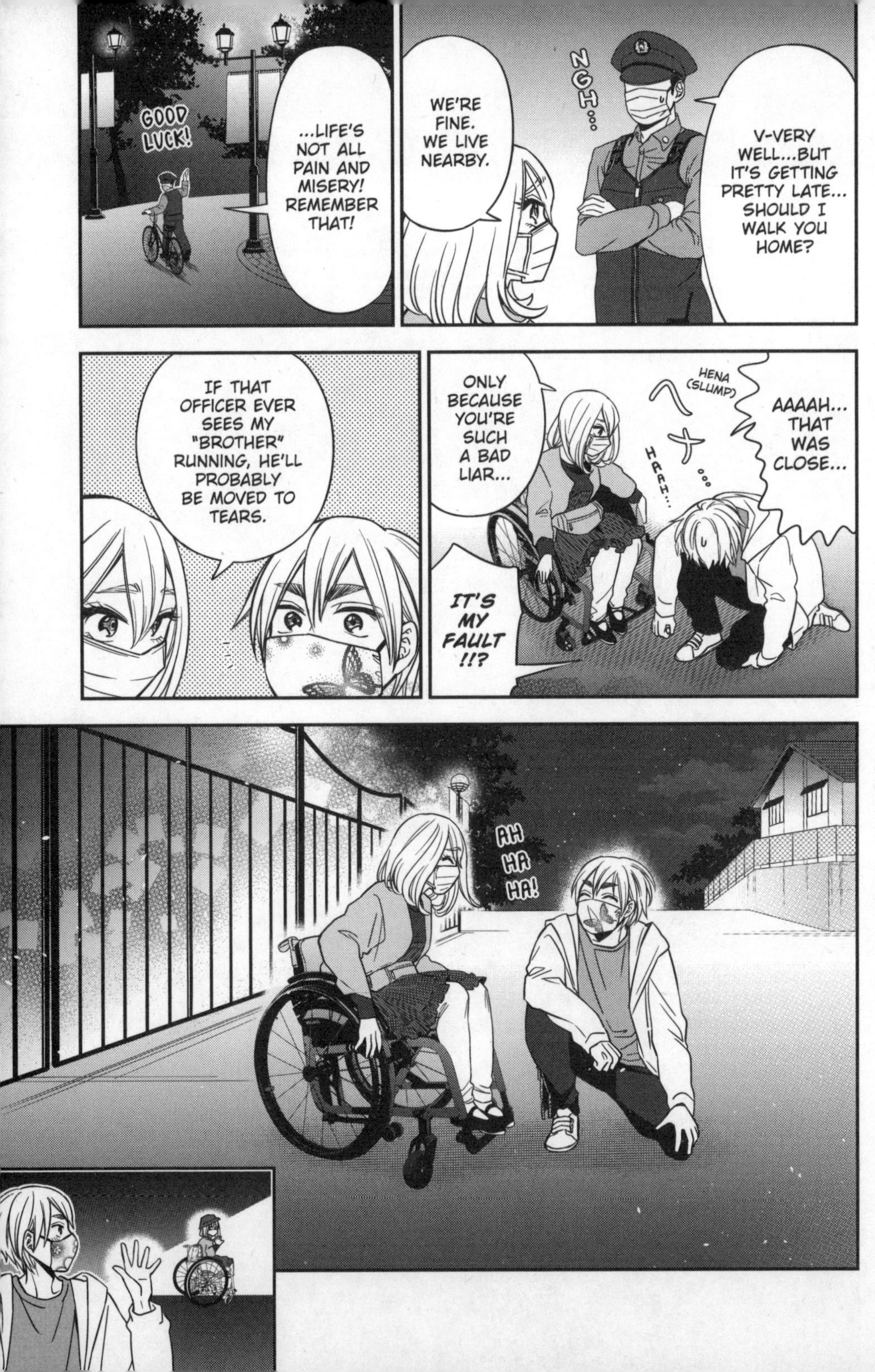
V-VERY WELL...BUT IT'S GETTING PRETTY LATE... SHOULD I WALK YOU HOME?
NGH...
WE'RE FINE. WE LIVE NEARBY.
...LIFE'S NOT ALL PAIN AND MISERY! REMEMBER THAT!
GOOD LUCK!
AAAAH... THAT WAS CLOSE...
HENA (SLUMP)
HAAH...
ONLY BECAUSE YOU'RE SUCH A BAD LIAR...
IT'S MY FAULT!!?
IF THAT OFFICER EVER SEES MY "BROTHER" RUNNING, HE'LL PROBABLY BE MOVED TO TEARS.
AH HA HA!

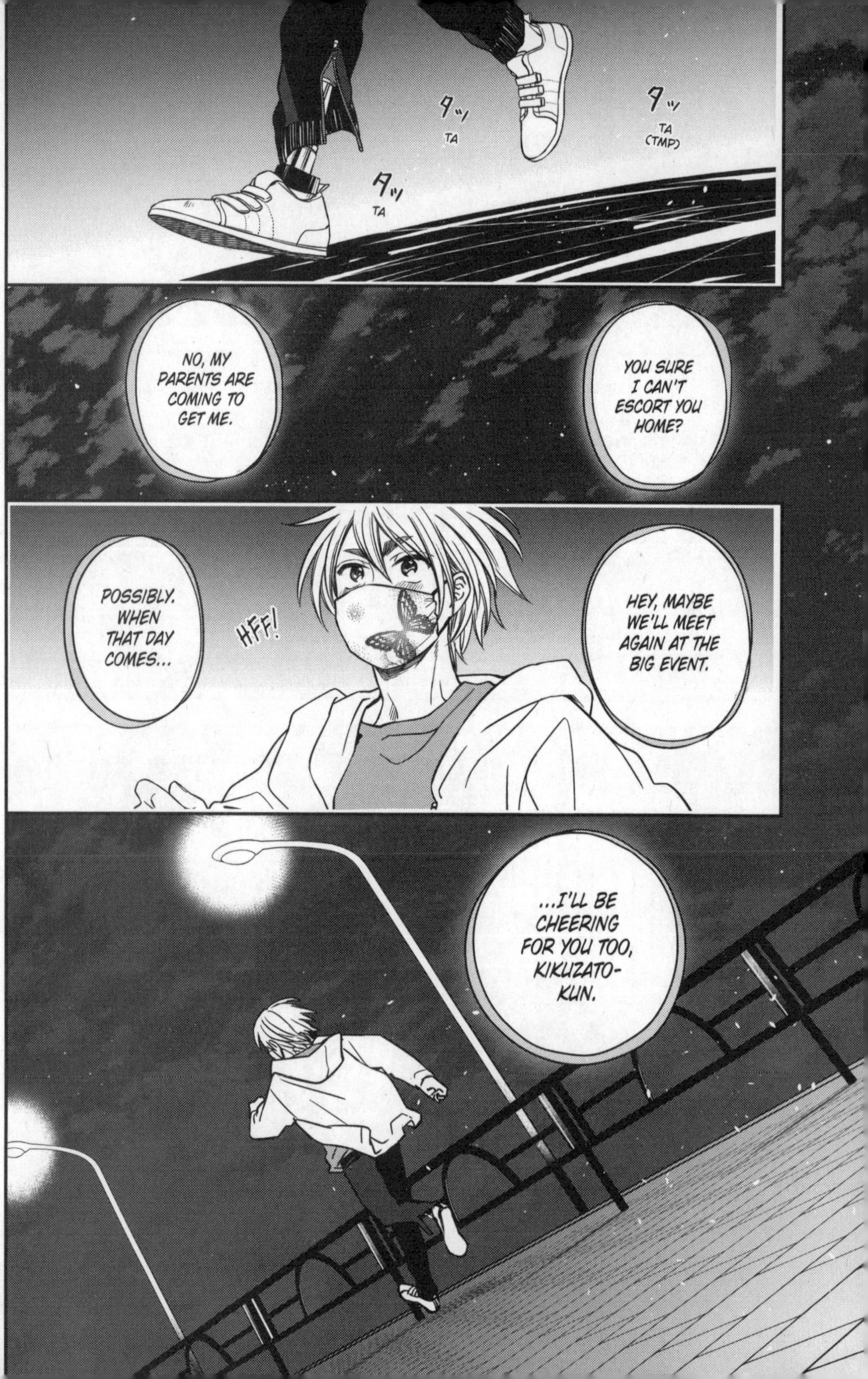

タッ
TA (TMP)
タッ
TA
タッ
TA
YOU SURE I CAN'T ESCORT YOU HOME?
NO, MY PARENTS ARE COMING TO GET ME.
HEY, MAYBE WE'LL MEET AGAIN AT THE BIG EVENT.
HFF!
POSSIBLY. WHEN THAT DAY COMES...
...I'LL BE CHEERING FOR YOU TOO, KIKUZATO-KUN.

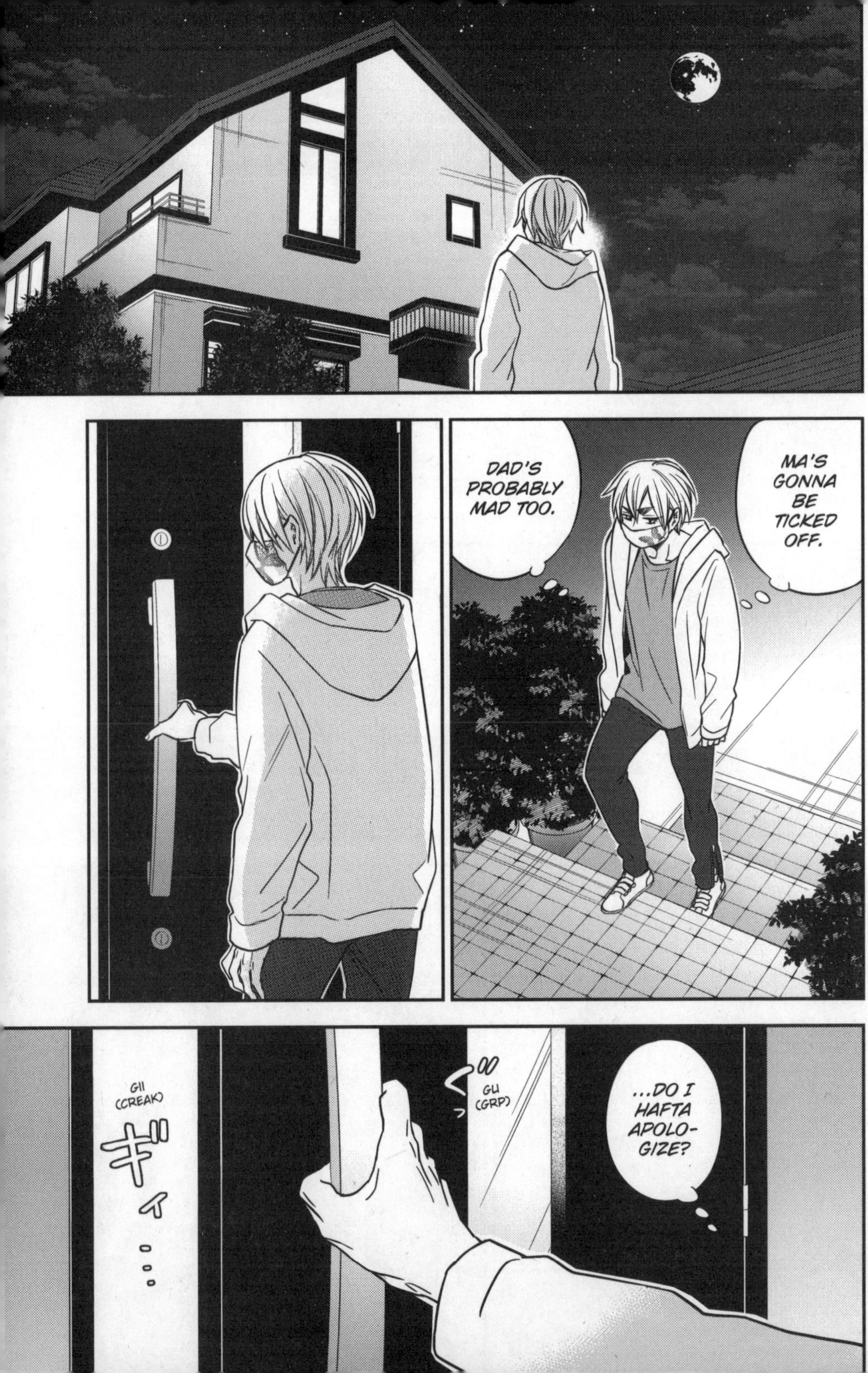
MA'S GONNA BE TICKED OFF.
DAD'S PROBABLY MAD TOO.
...DO I HAFTA APOLO-GIZE?
GU (GRP)
GII (CREAK)
ギィ…

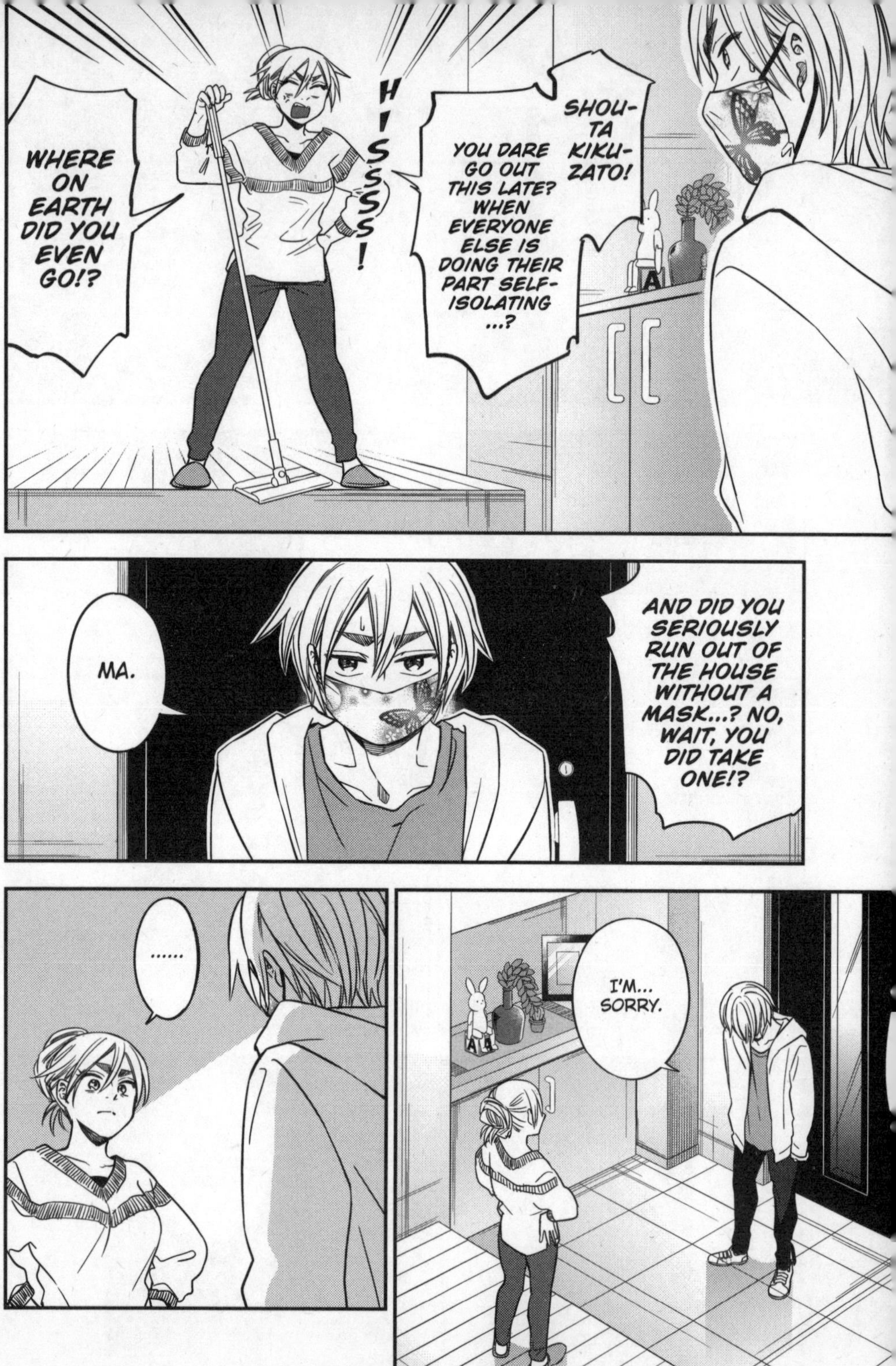
SHOUTA KIKUZATO!
YOU DARE GO OUT THIS LATE? WHEN EVERYONE ELSE IS DOING THEIR PART SELF-ISOLATING ...?
HISSSS!
WHERE ON EARTH DID YOU EVEN GO!?
AND DID YOU SERIOUSLY RUN OUT OF THE HOUSE WITHOUT A MASK...? NO, WAIT, YOU DID TAKE ONE!?
MA.
I'M... SORRY.
......

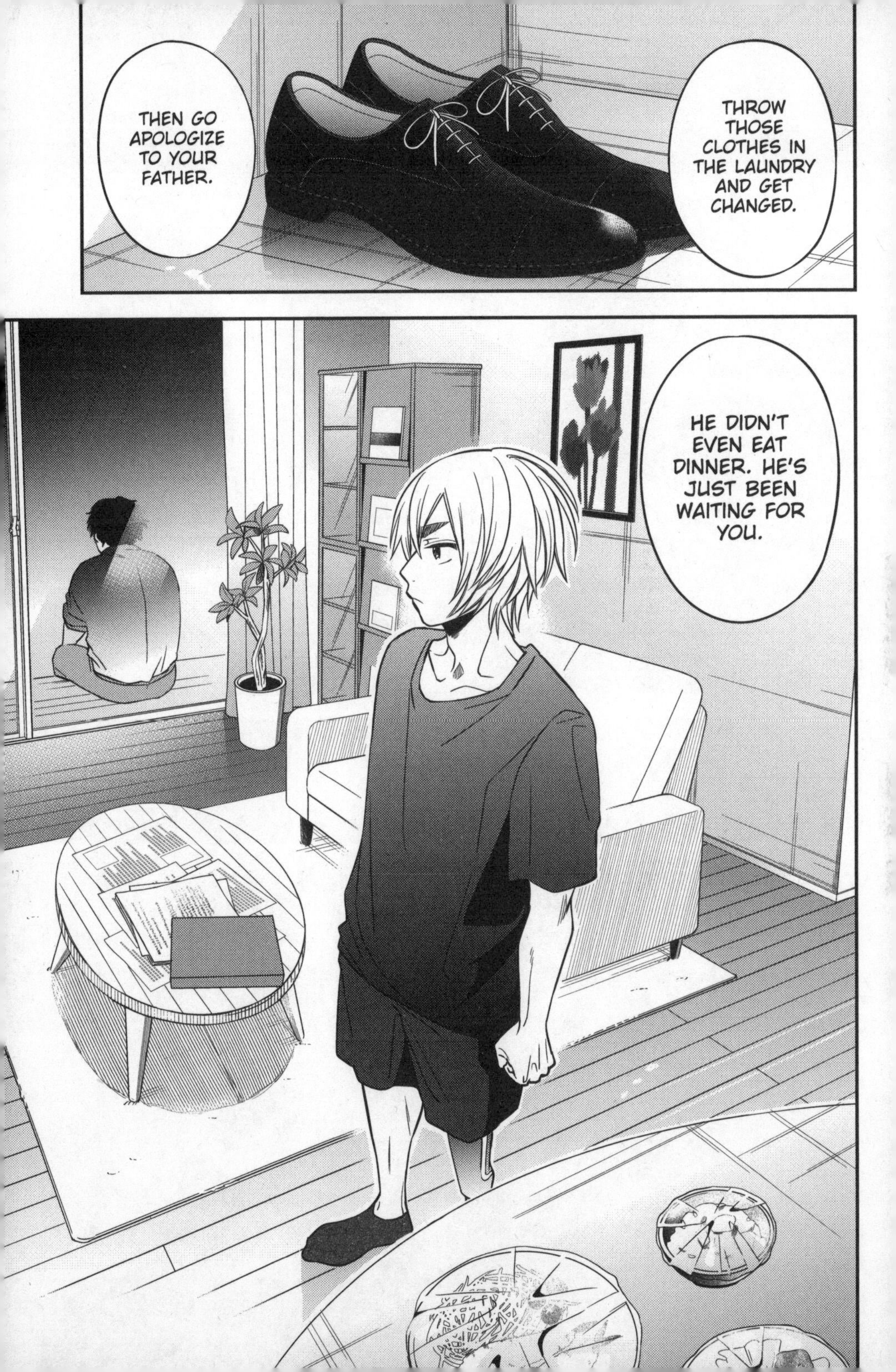
THROW THOSE CLOTHES IN THE LAUNDRY AND GET CHANGED.
THEN GO APOLOGIZE TO YOUR FATHER.
HE DIDN'T EVEN EAT DINNER. HE'S JUST BEEN WAITING FOR YOU.

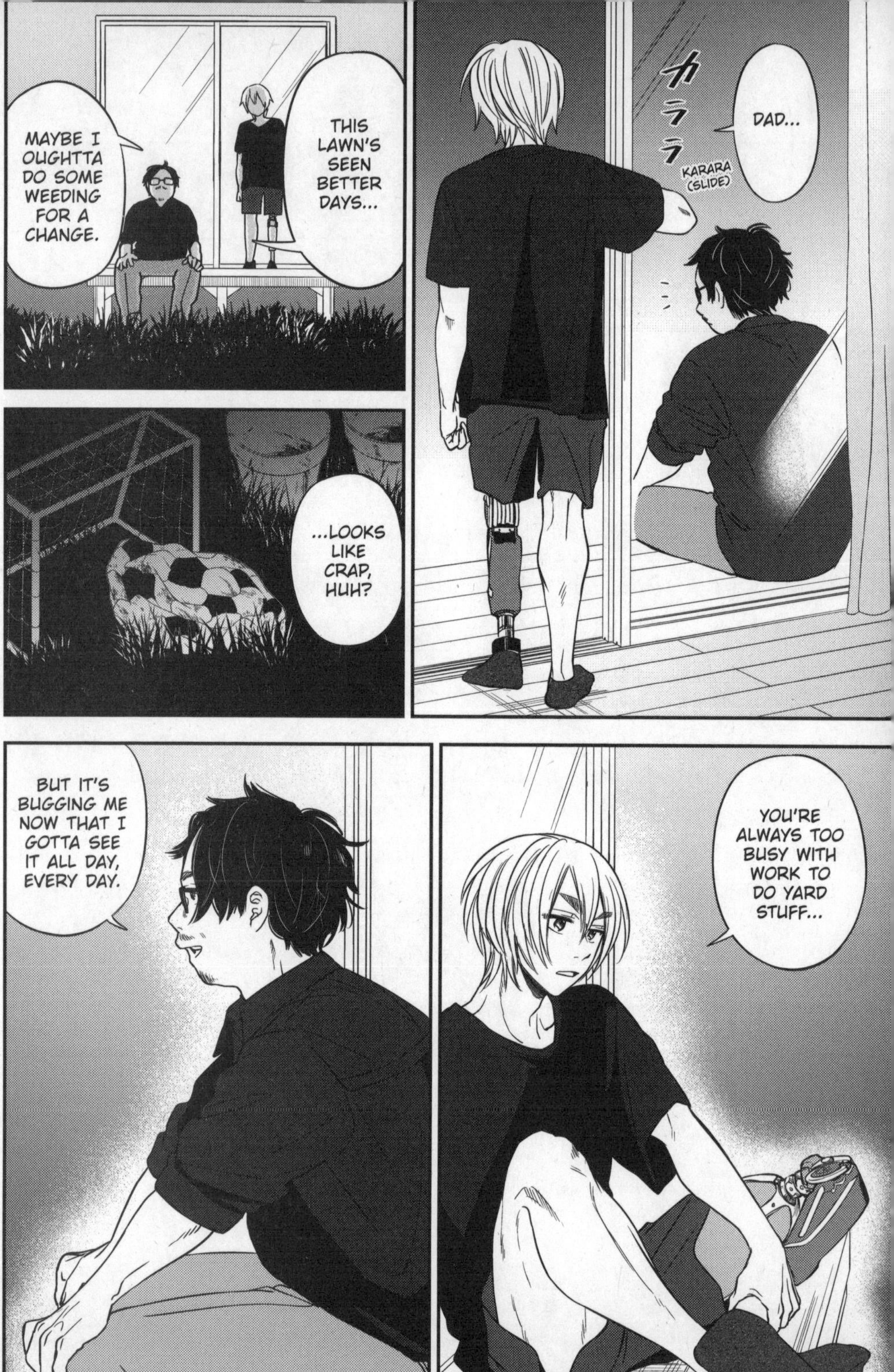
カララ
KARARA (SLIDE)
DAD...
THIS LAWN'S SEEN BETTER DAYS...
MAYBE I OUGHTTA DO SOME WEEDING FOR A CHANGE.
...LOOKS LIKE CRAP, HUH?
YOU'RE ALWAYS TOO BUSY WITH WORK TO DO YARD STUFF...
BUT IT'S BUGGING ME NOW THAT I GOTTA SEE IT ALL DAY, EVERY DAY.

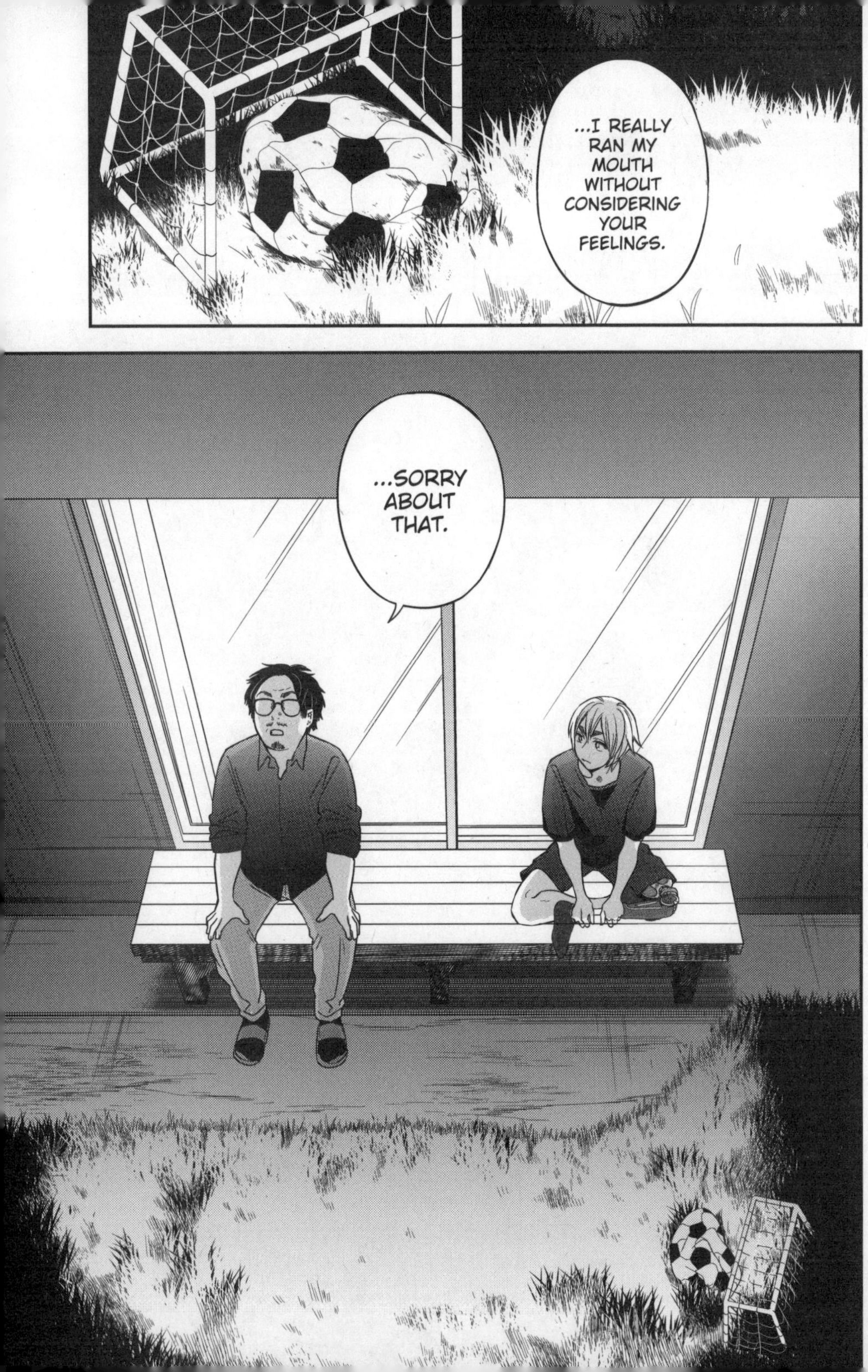
...I REALLY RAN MY MOUTH WITHOUT CONSIDERING YOUR FEELINGS.
...SORRY ABOUT THAT.

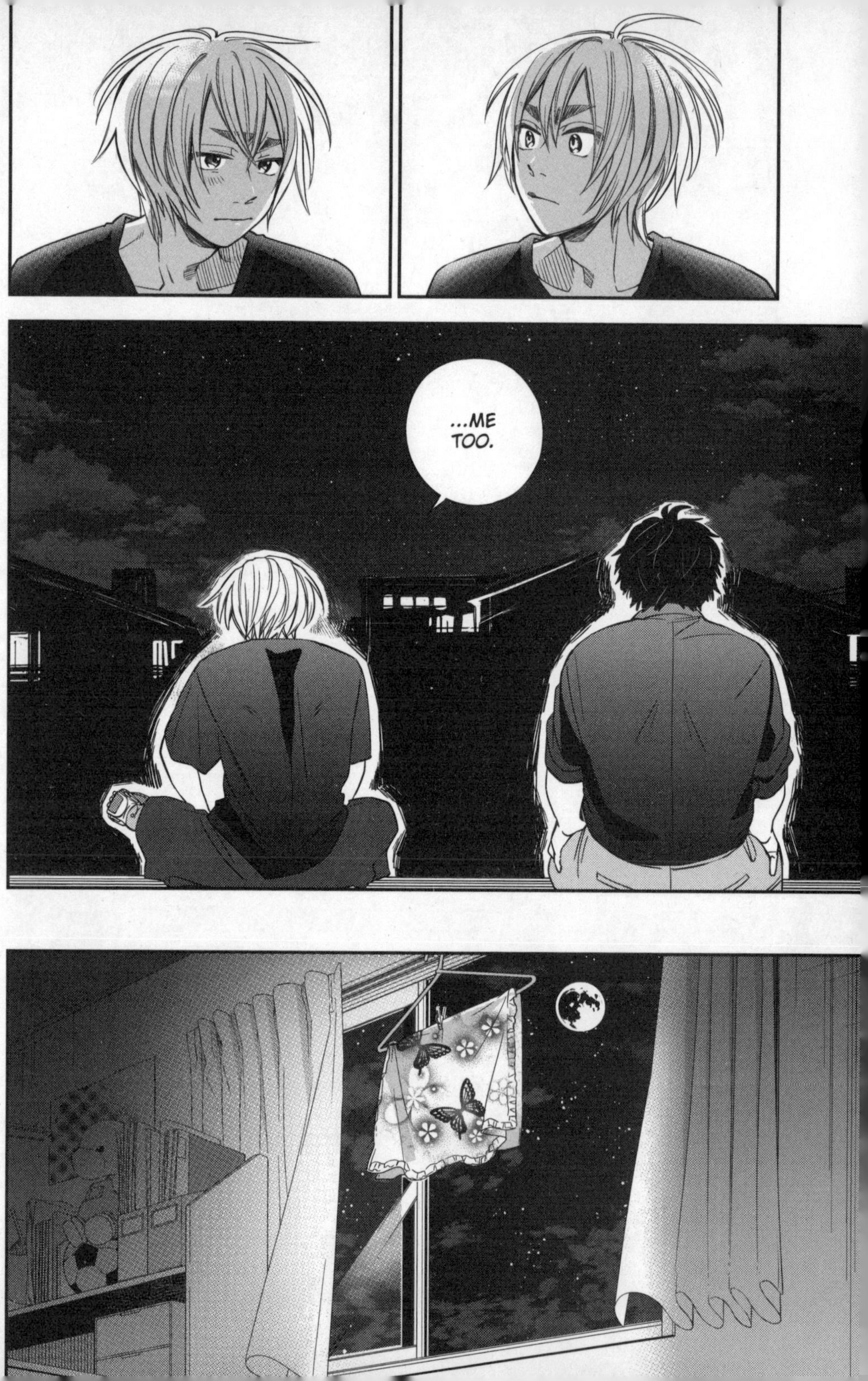
...ME TOO.

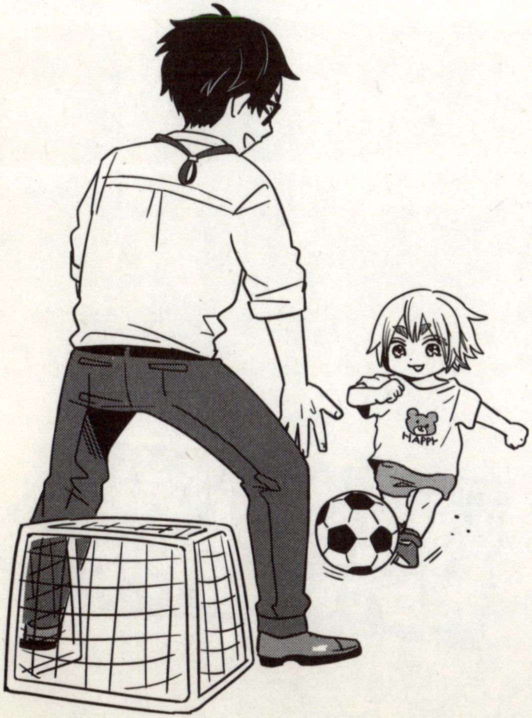
HAPPY

RUN ON YOUR NEW LEGS

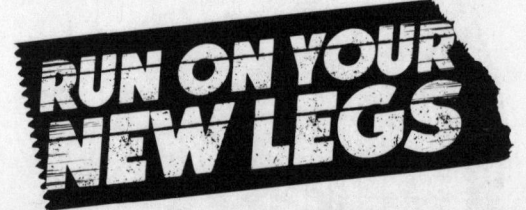

CHIRP
CHIRP
CHIRP...
バチッ
BACHI (SMAK)
JIRIRIRIRI (BEE-BEE-BEEP)
MNH...
CHIRP!
CHIRP!
Chapter 27: I Ain't Giving Up
KATSUN (THUD)
TON (TMP)

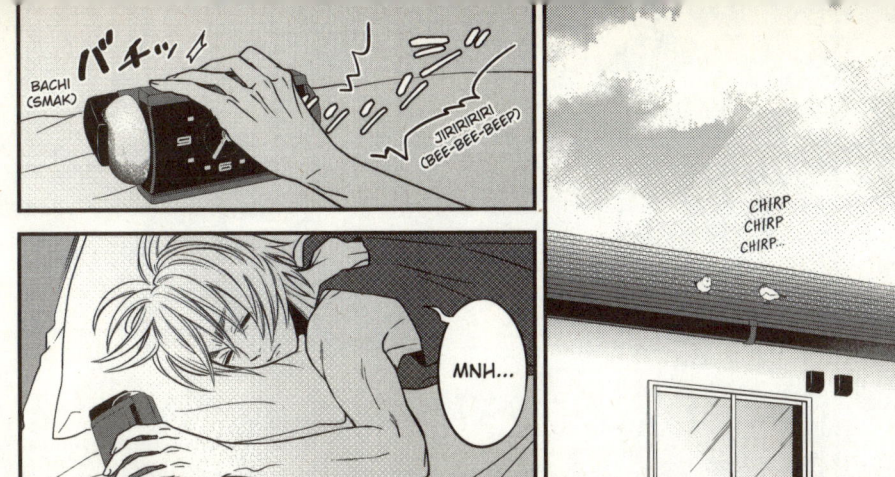

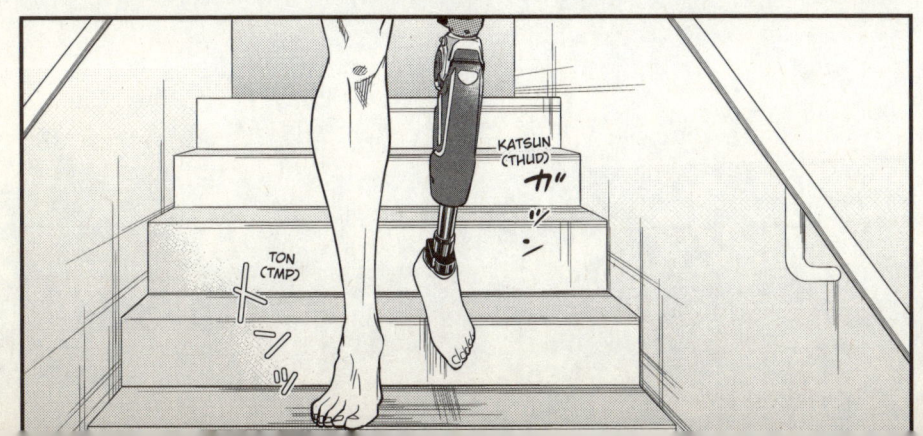

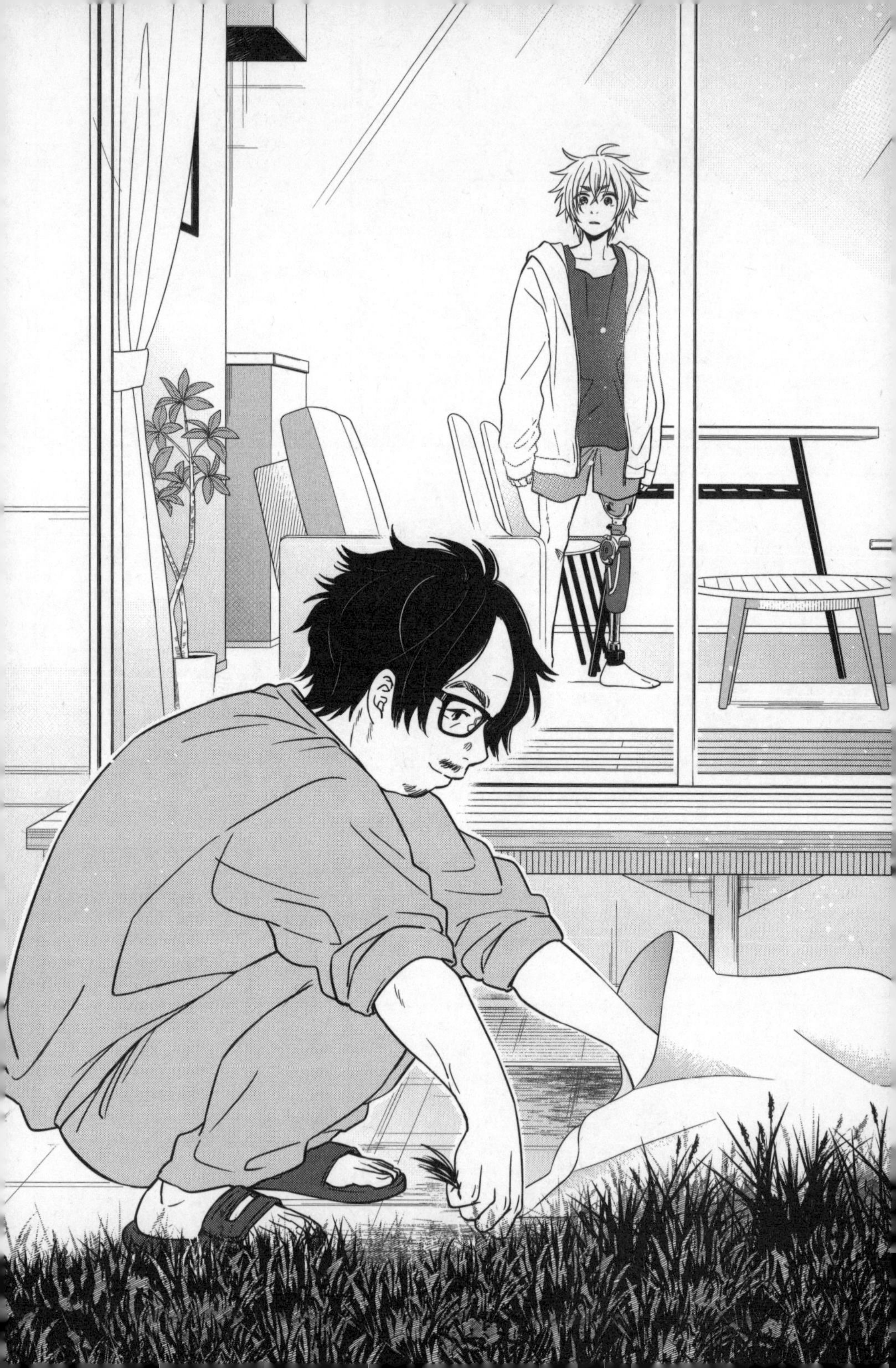

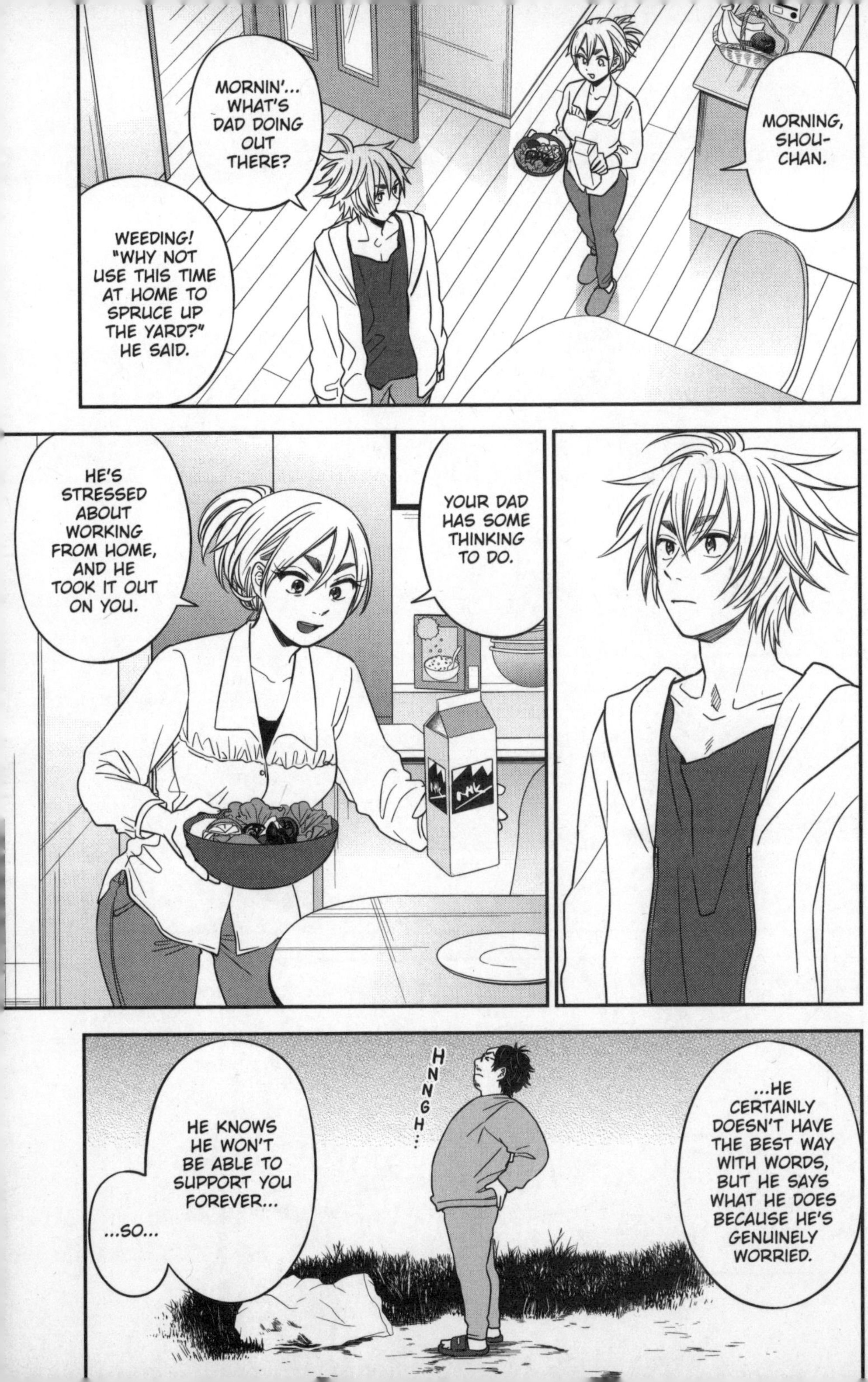
MORNING, SHOU-CHAN.
MORNIN'... WHAT'S DAD DOING OUT THERE?
WEEDING! "WHY NOT USE THIS TIME AT HOME TO SPRUCE UP THE YARD?" HE SAID.
YOUR DAD HAS SOME THINKING TO DO.
HE'S STRESSED ABOUT WORKING FROM HOME, AND HE TOOK IT OUT ON YOU.
...HE CERTAINLY DOESN'T HAVE THE BEST WAY WITH WORDS, BUT HE SAYS WHAT HE DOES BECAUSE HE'S GENUINELY WORRIED.
HNNGH...
HE KNOWS HE WON'T BE ABLE TO SUPPORT YOU FOREVER...
...SO...

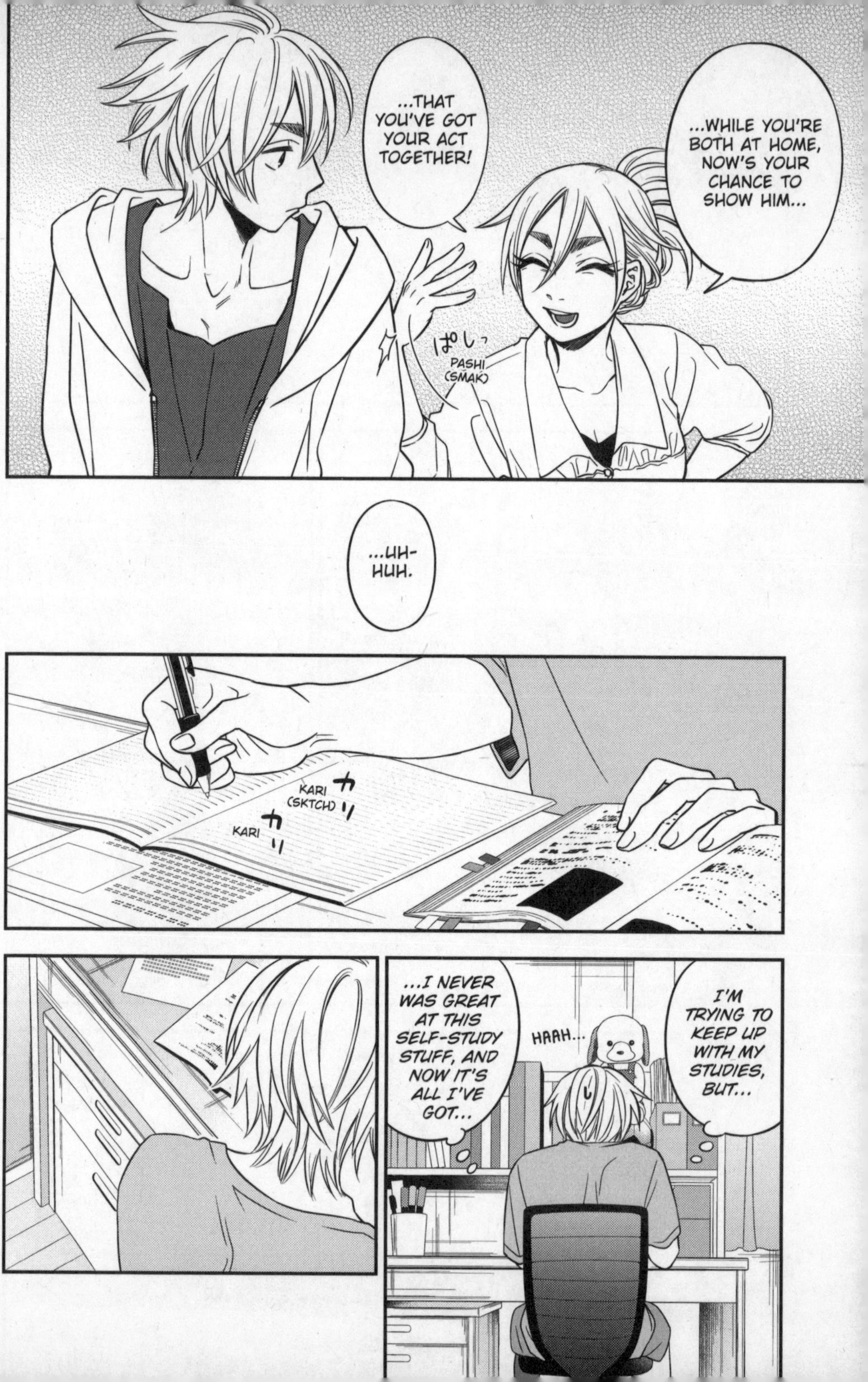
...WHILE YOU'RE BOTH AT HOME, NOW'S YOUR CHANCE TO SHOW HIM...
...THAT YOU'VE GOT YOUR ACT TOGETHER!
ぱしっ
PASHI (SMAK)
...UH-HUH.
カリ
KARI (SKTCH)
カリ
KARI
I'M TRYING TO KEEP UP WITH MY STUDIES, BUT...
HAAAH...
...I NEVER WAS GREAT AT THIS SELF-STUDY STUFF, AND NOW IT'S ALL I'VE GOT...

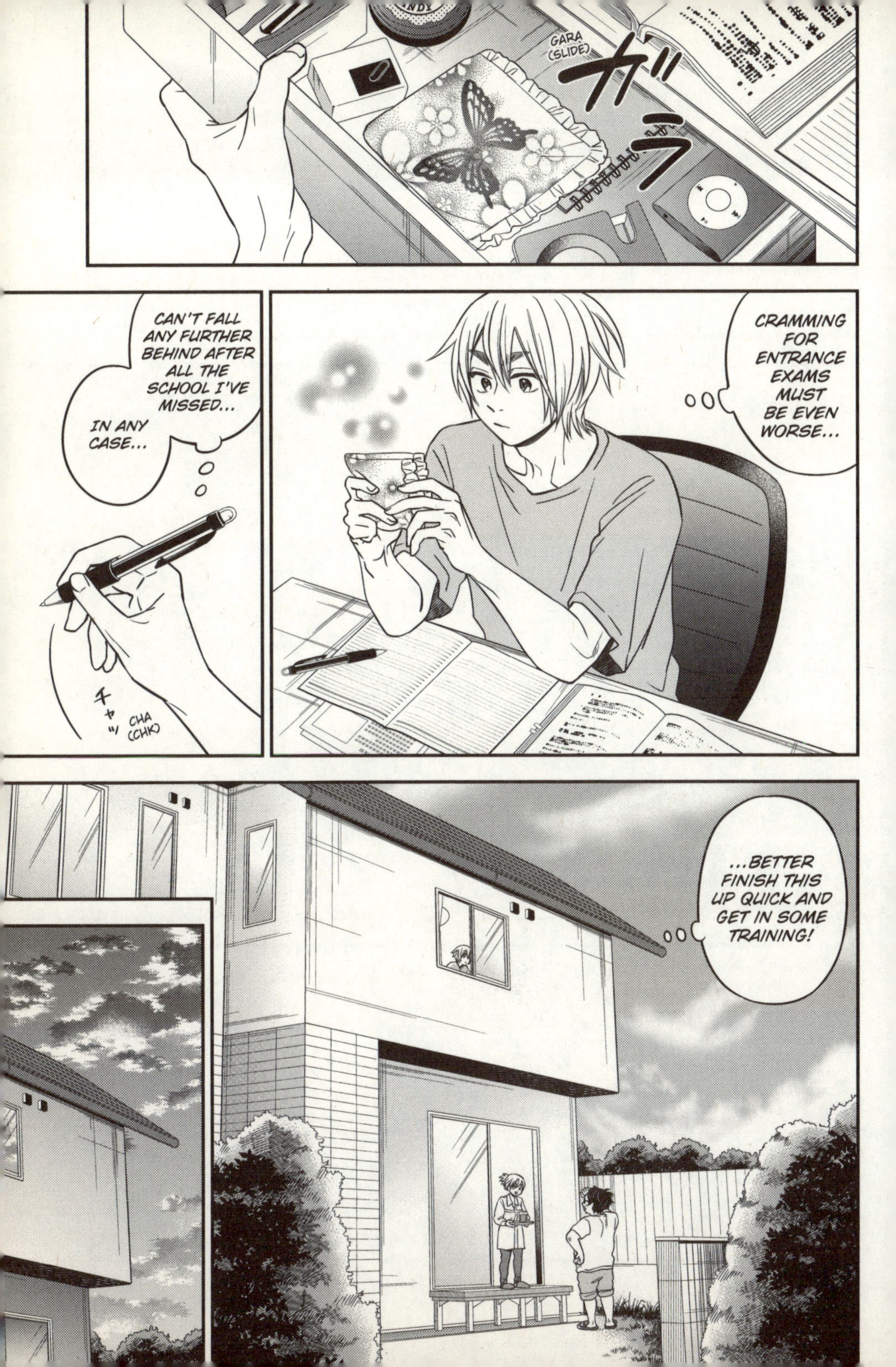
ガラ
GARA (SLIDE)
CRAMMING FOR ENTRANCE EXAMS MUST BE EVEN WORSE...
CAN'T FALL ANY FURTHER BEHIND AFTER ALL THE SCHOOL I'VE MISSED...
IN ANY CASE...
チャッ
CHA (CHK)
...BETTER FINISH THIS UP QUICK AND GET IN SOME TRAINING!

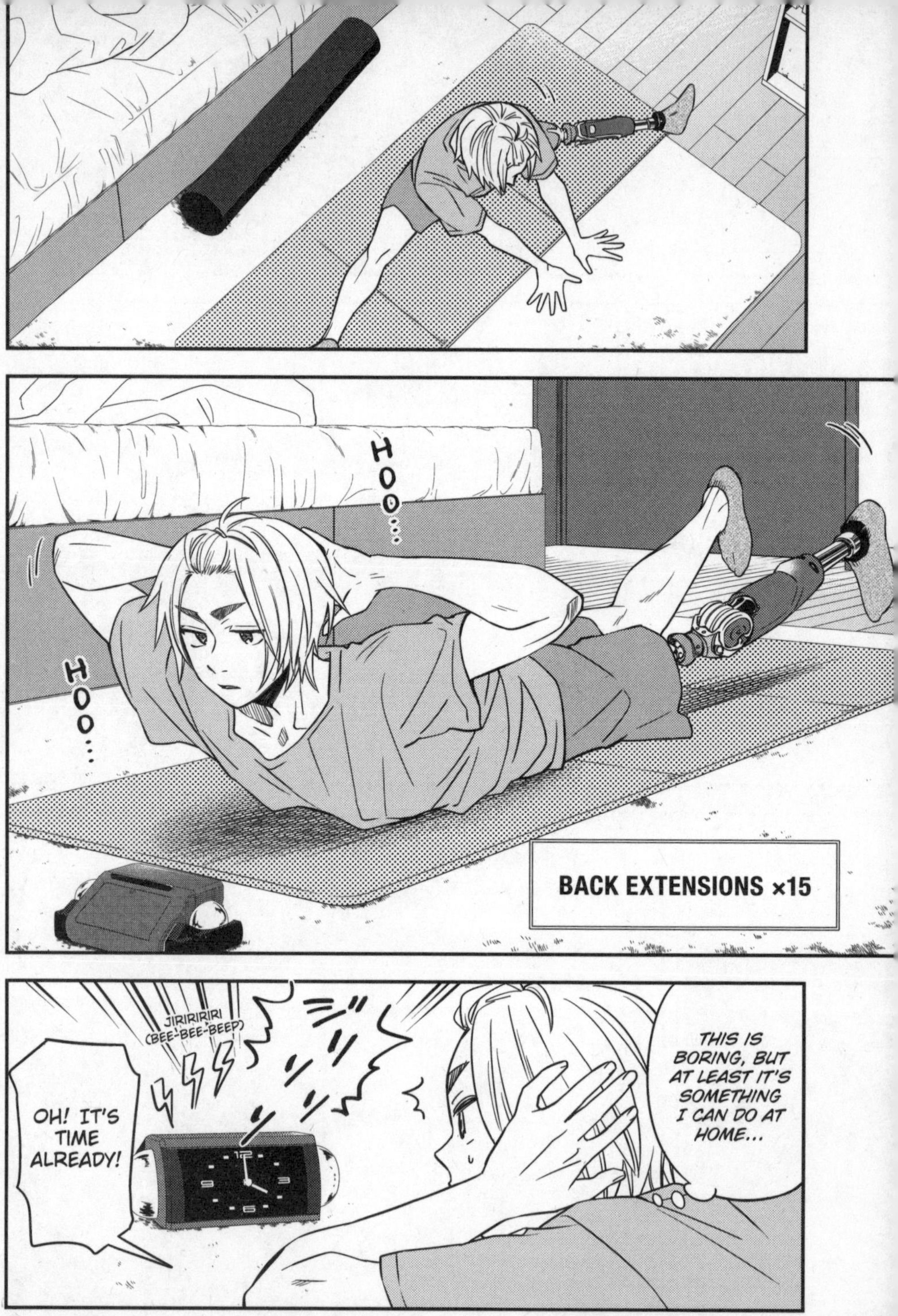

HOO...
HOO...
BACK EXTENSIONS ×15
THIS IS BORING, BUT AT LEAST IT'S SOMETHING I CAN DO AT HOME...
JIRIRIRIRI (BEE-BEE-BEEP)
OH! IT'S TIME ALREADY!

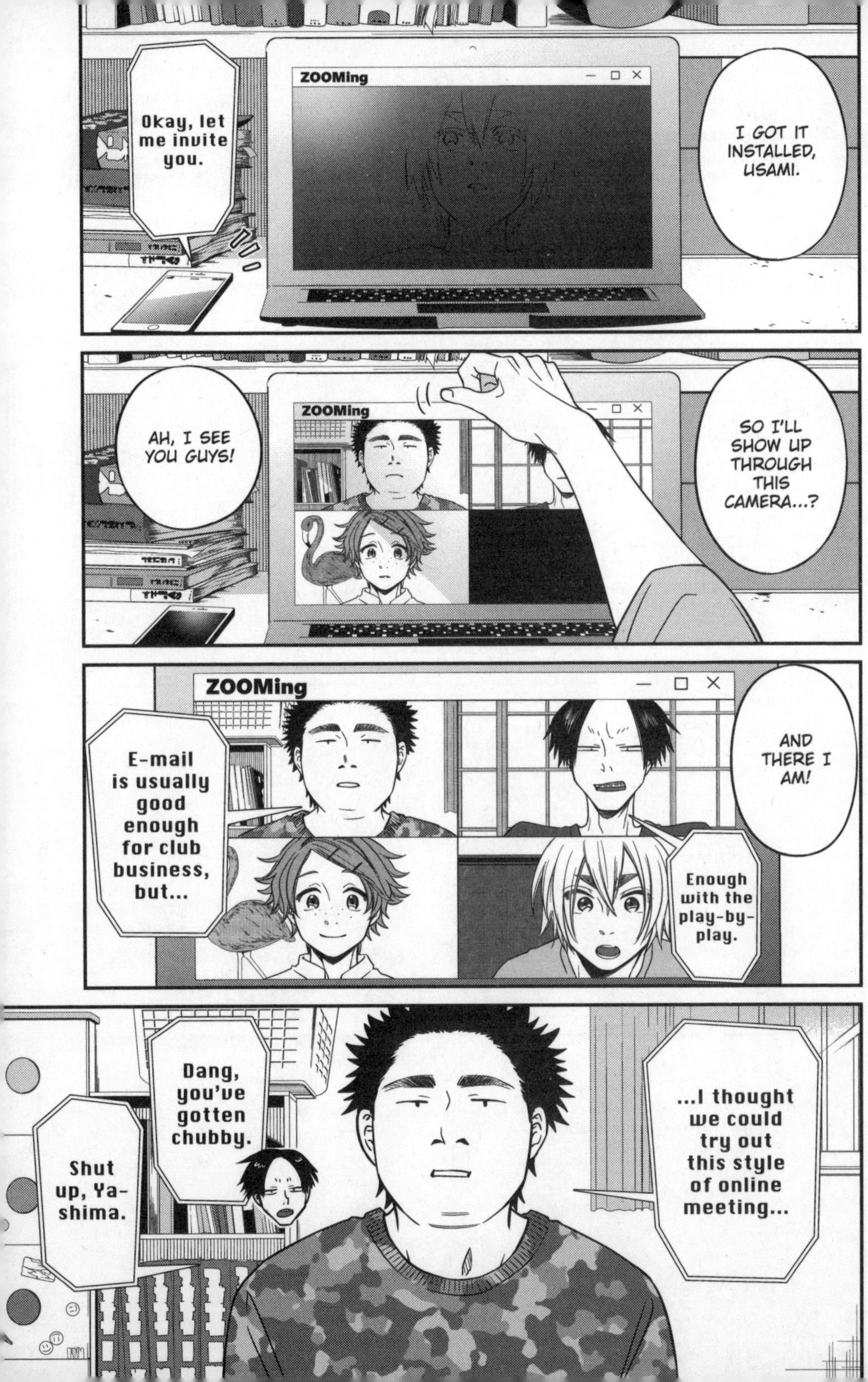
ZOOMing
I GOT IT INSTALLED, USAMI.
Okay, let me invite you.
ZOOMing
SO I'LL SHOW UP THROUGH THIS CAMERA...?
AH, I SEE YOU GUYS!
ZOOMing
AND THERE I AM!
Enough with the play-by-play.
E-mail is usually good enough for club business, but...
...I thought we could try out this style of online meeting...
Dang, you've gotten chubby.
Shut up, Ya-shima.

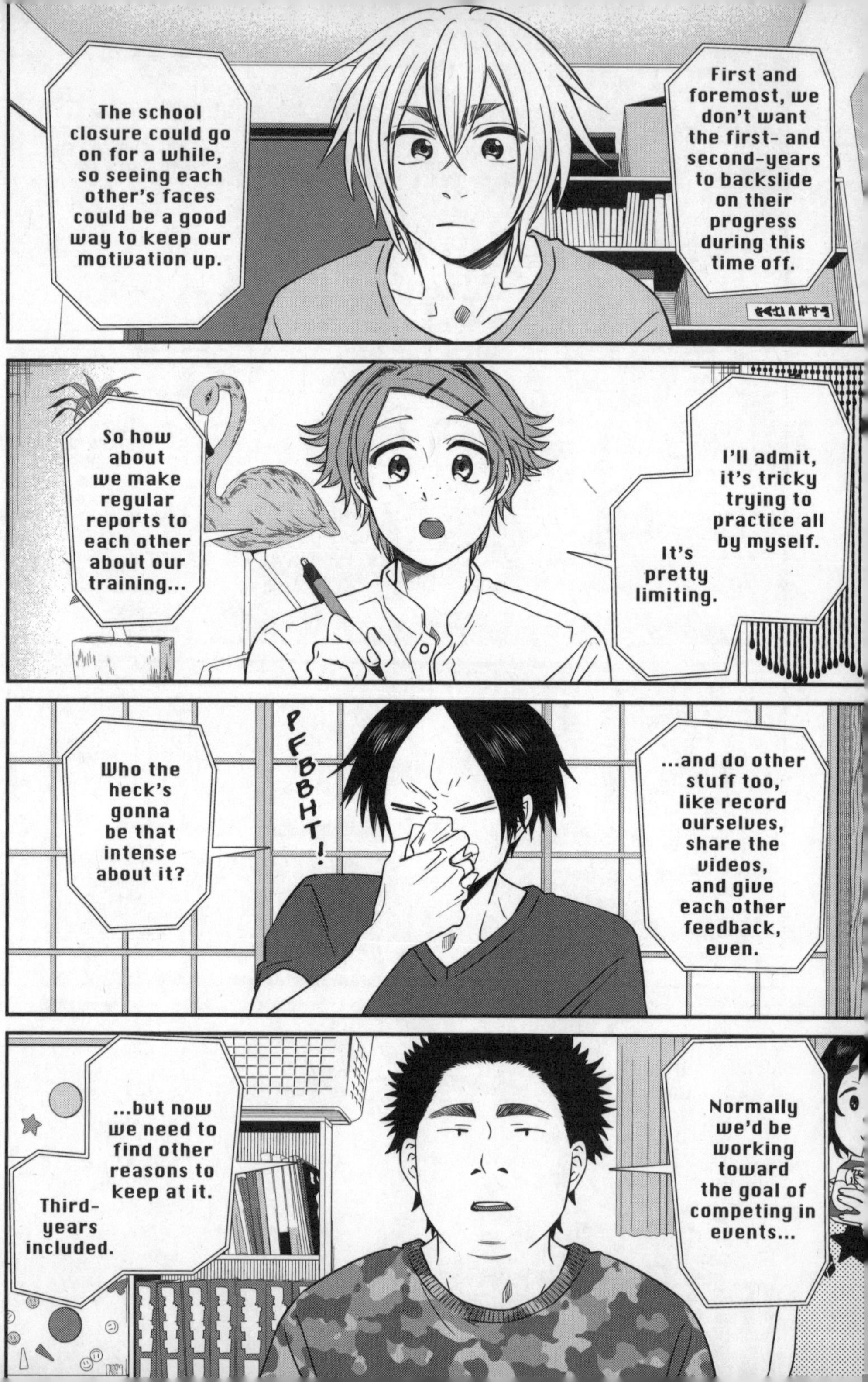
First and foremost, we don't want the first- and second-years to backslide on their progress during this time off.
The school closure could go on for a while, so seeing each other's faces could be a good way to keep our motivation up.
I'll admit, it's tricky trying to practice all by myself.
It's pretty limiting.
So how about we make regular reports to each other about our training...
...and do other stuff too, like record ourselves, share the videos, and give each other feedback, even.
PFBBHT!
Who the heck's gonna be that intense about it?
Normally we'd be working toward the goal of competing in events...
...but now we need to find other reasons to keep at it.
Third-years included.

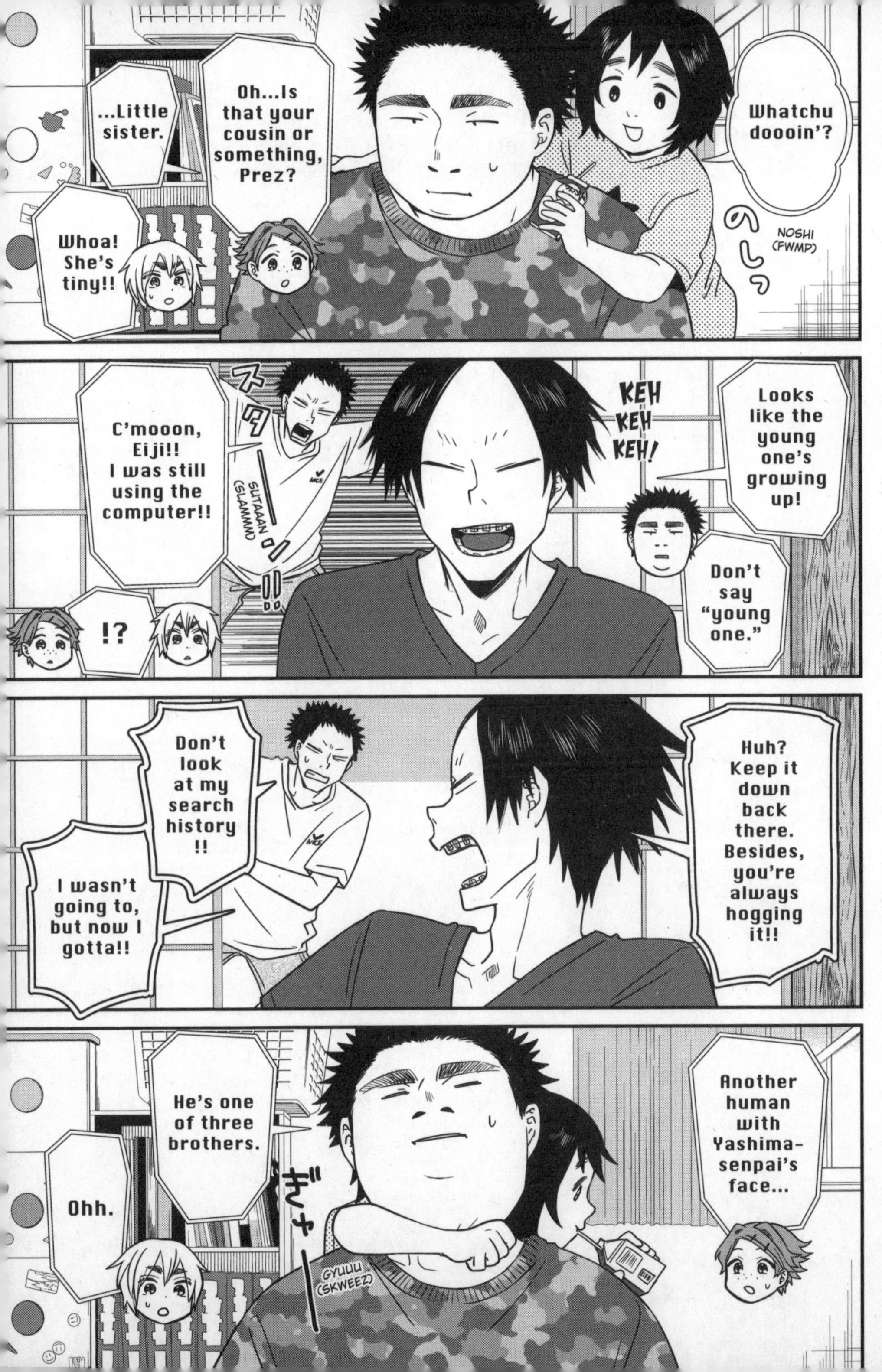

Whatchu doooin'?
のしっ
NOSHI (FWMP)
Oh...Is that your cousin or something, Prez?
...Little sister.
Whoa! She's tiny!!
Looks like the young one's growing up!
KEH KEH KEH!
Don't say "young one."
スターン!!
SUTAAAN (SLAMM)
C'mooon, Eiji!! I was still using the computer!!
!?
Huh? Keep it down back there. Besides, you're always hogging it!!
Don't look at my search history!!
I wasn't going to, but now I gotta!!
Another human with Yashima-senpai's face...
He's one of three brothers.
ぎゅー
GYUUU (SKWEEZ)
Ohh.

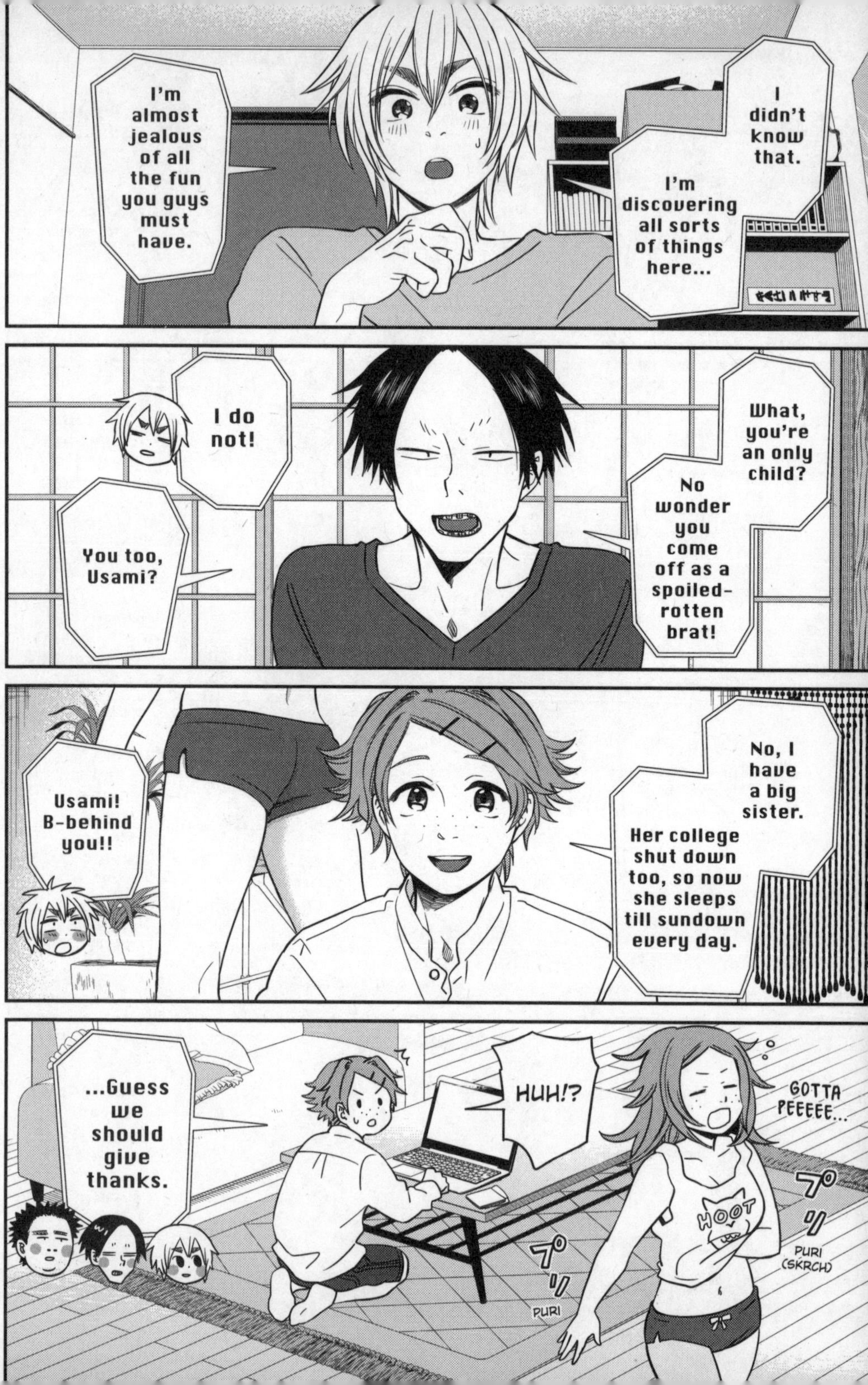
I didn't know that.
I'm discovering all sorts of things here...
I'm almost jealous of all the fun you guys must have.
What, you're an only child?
No wonder you come off as a spoiled-rotten brat!
I do not!
You too, Usami?
No, I have a big sister.
Her college shut down too, so now she sleeps till sundown every day.
Usami! B-behind you!!
GOTTA PEEEEE...
プリ
PURI (SKRCH)
HUH!?
プリ
PURI
...Guess we should give thanks.

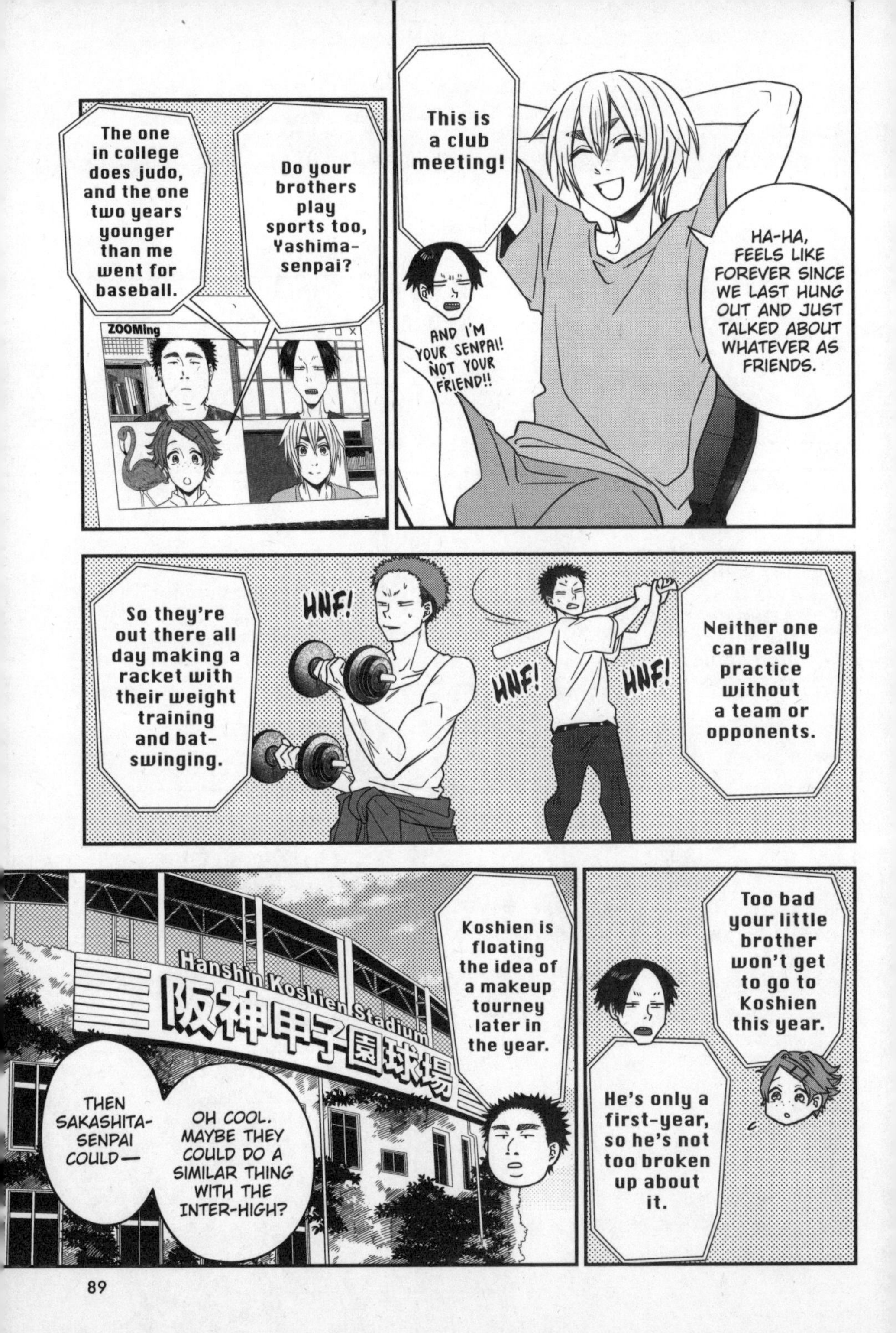
This is a club meeting!
HA-HA, FEELS LIKE FOREVER SINCE WE LAST HUNG OUT AND JUST TALKED ABOUT WHATEVER AS FRIENDS.
AND I'M YOUR SENPAI! NOT YOUR FRIEND!!
Do your brothers play sports too, Yashima-senpai?
The one in college does judo, and the one two years younger than me went for baseball.
ZOOMing
Neither one can really practice without a team or opponents.
HNF!
HNF!
HNF!
So they're out there all day making a racket with their weight training and bat-swinging.
Too bad your little brother won't get to go to Koshien this year.
He's only a first-year, so he's not too broken up about it.
Koshien is floating the idea of a makeup tourney later in the year.
Hanshin Koshien Stadium
阪神甲子園球場
OH COOL. MAYBE THEY COULD DO A SIMILAR THING WITH THE INTER-HIGH?
THEN SAKASHITA-SENPAI COULD—

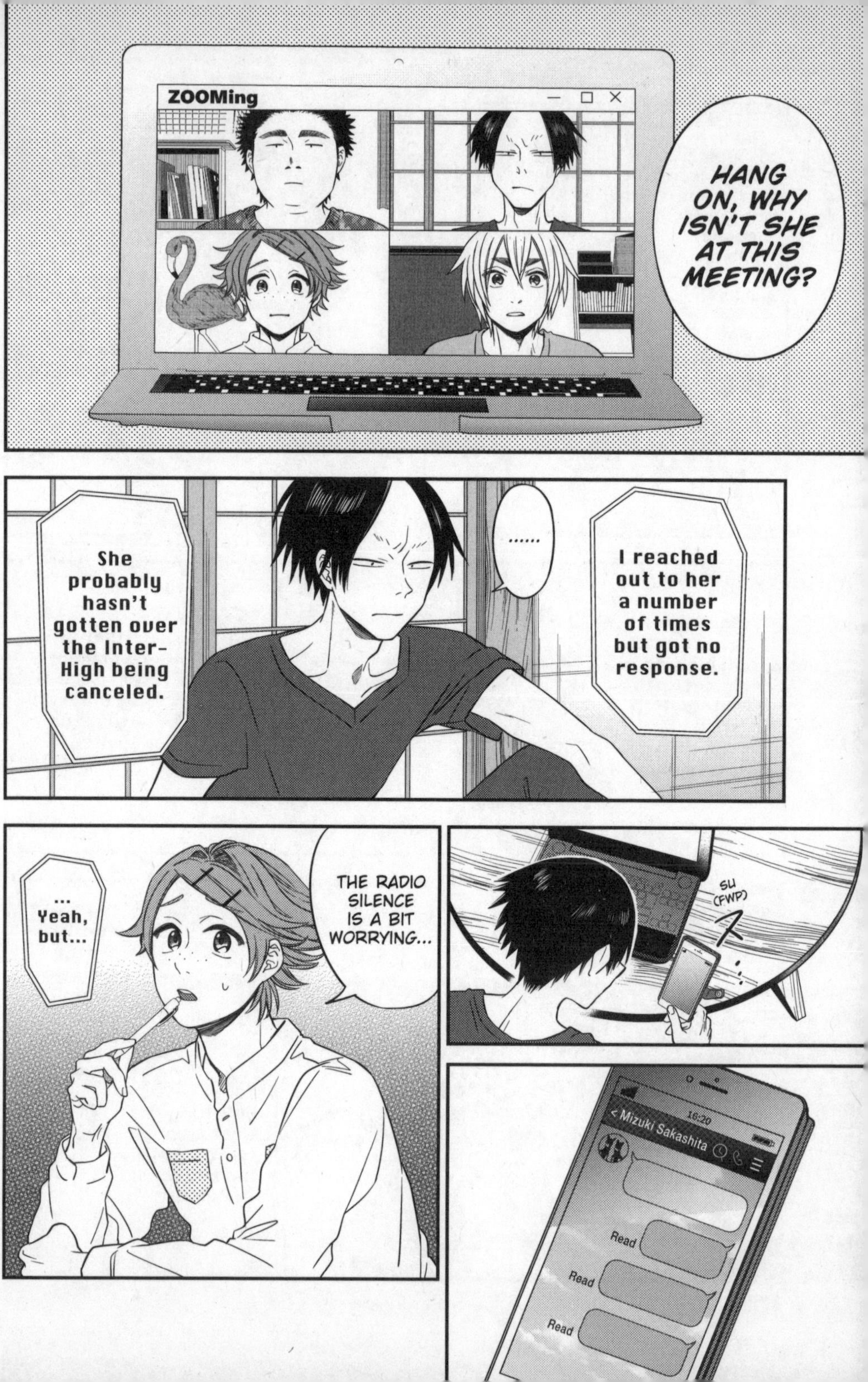
ZOOMing
HANG ON, WHY ISN'T SHE AT THIS MEETING?
......
I reached out to her a number of times but got no response.
She probably hasn't gotten over the Inter-High being canceled.
SU (FWP)
THE RADIO SILENCE IS A BIT WORRYING...
... Yeah, but...
16:20
< Mizuki Sakashita
Read
Read
Read

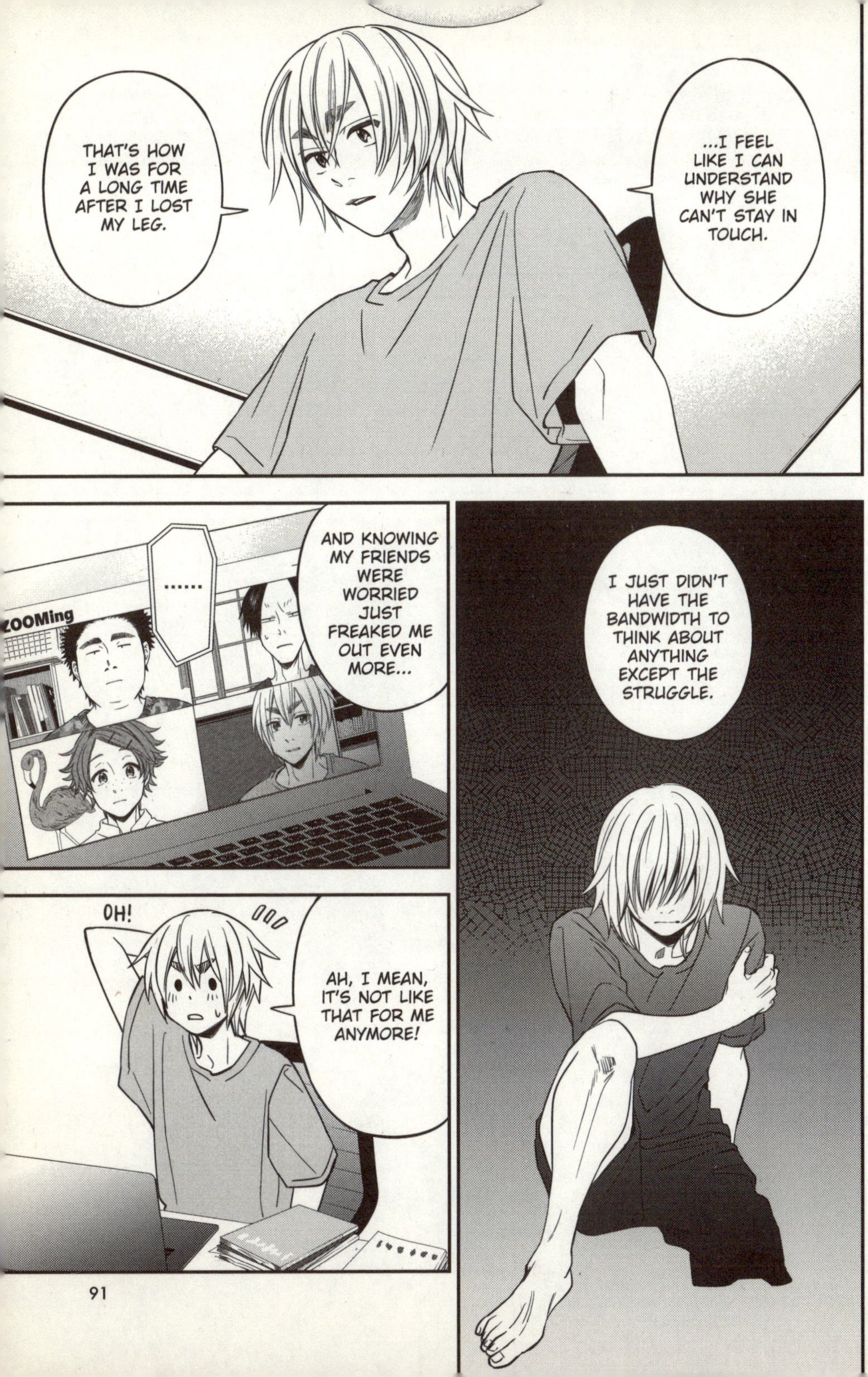
...I FEEL LIKE I CAN UNDERSTAND WHY SHE CAN'T STAY IN TOUCH.
THAT'S HOW I WAS FOR A LONG TIME AFTER I LOST MY LEG.
I JUST DIDN'T HAVE THE BANDWIDTH TO THINK ABOUT ANYTHING EXCEPT THE STRUGGLE.
AND KNOWING MY FRIENDS WERE WORRIED JUST FREAKED ME OUT EVEN MORE...
......
ZOOMing
OH!
AH, I MEAN, IT'S NOT LIKE THAT FOR ME ANYMORE!

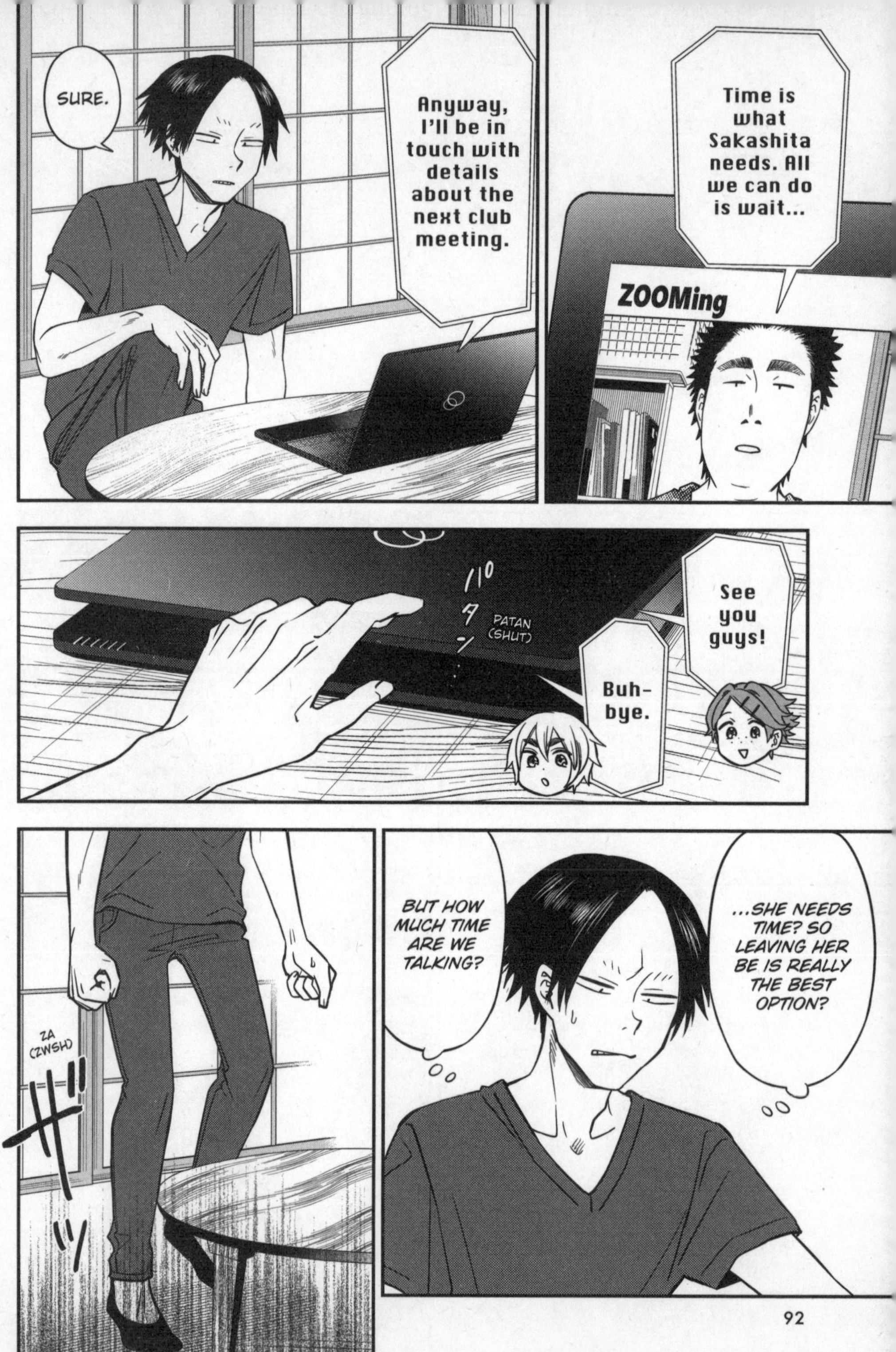
ZOOMing
Time is what Sakashita needs. All we can do is wait...
Anyway, I'll be in touch with details about the next club meeting.
SURE.
See you guys!
Buh-bye.
パタッ
PATAN (SHUT)
...SHE NEEDS TIME? SO LEAVING HER BE IS REALLY THE BEST OPTION?
BUT HOW MUCH TIME ARE WE TALKING?
ZA (ZWSH)
ザッ

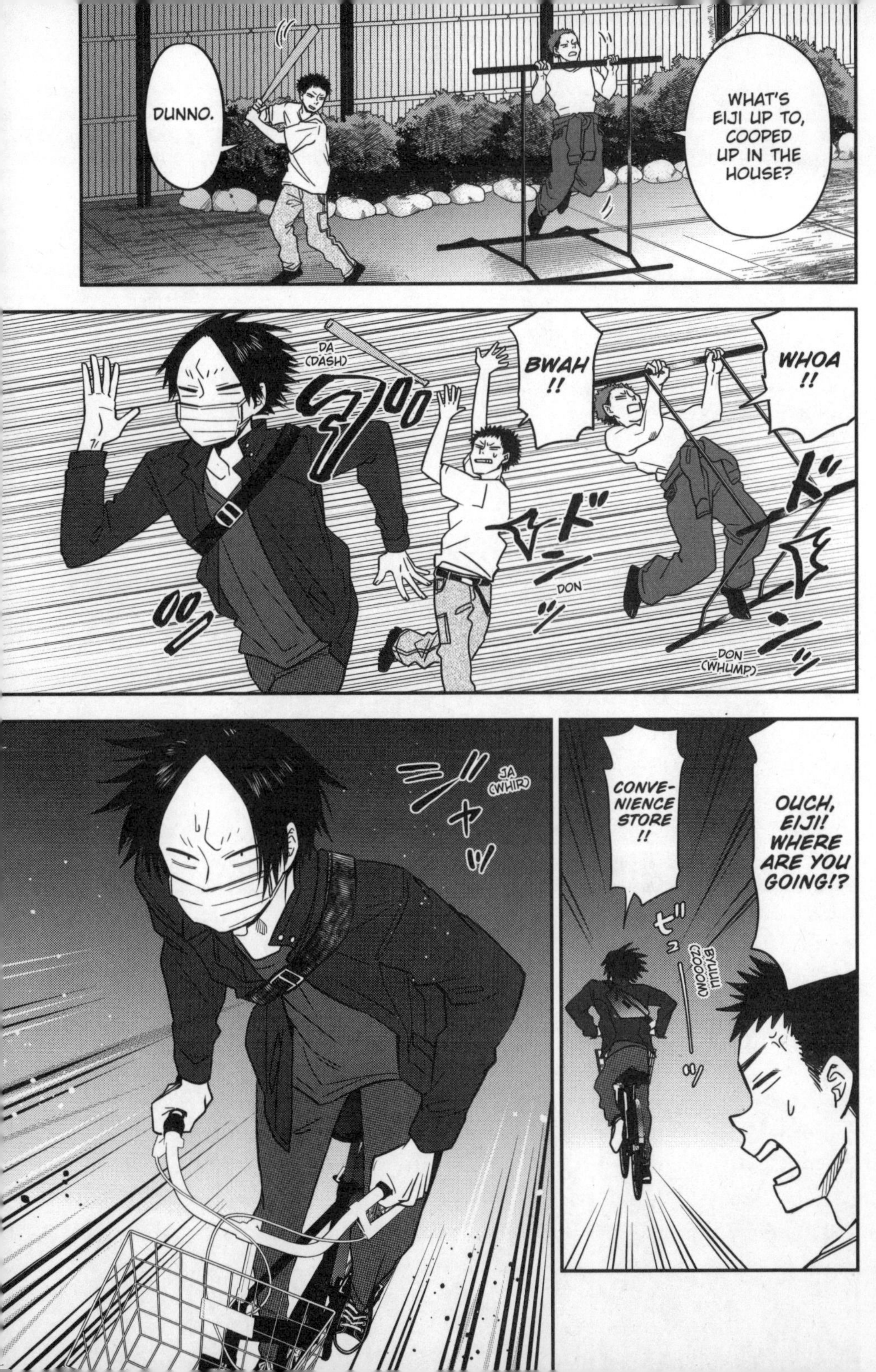
WHAT'S EIJI UP TO, COOPED UP IN THE HOUSE?
DUNNO.
WHOA !!
BWAH !!
DON (WHUMP)
DON
DA (DASH)
OUCH, EIJI! WHERE ARE YOU GOING!?
CONVENIENCE STORE !!
BYUUU (ZOOOOM)
JA (WHIR)

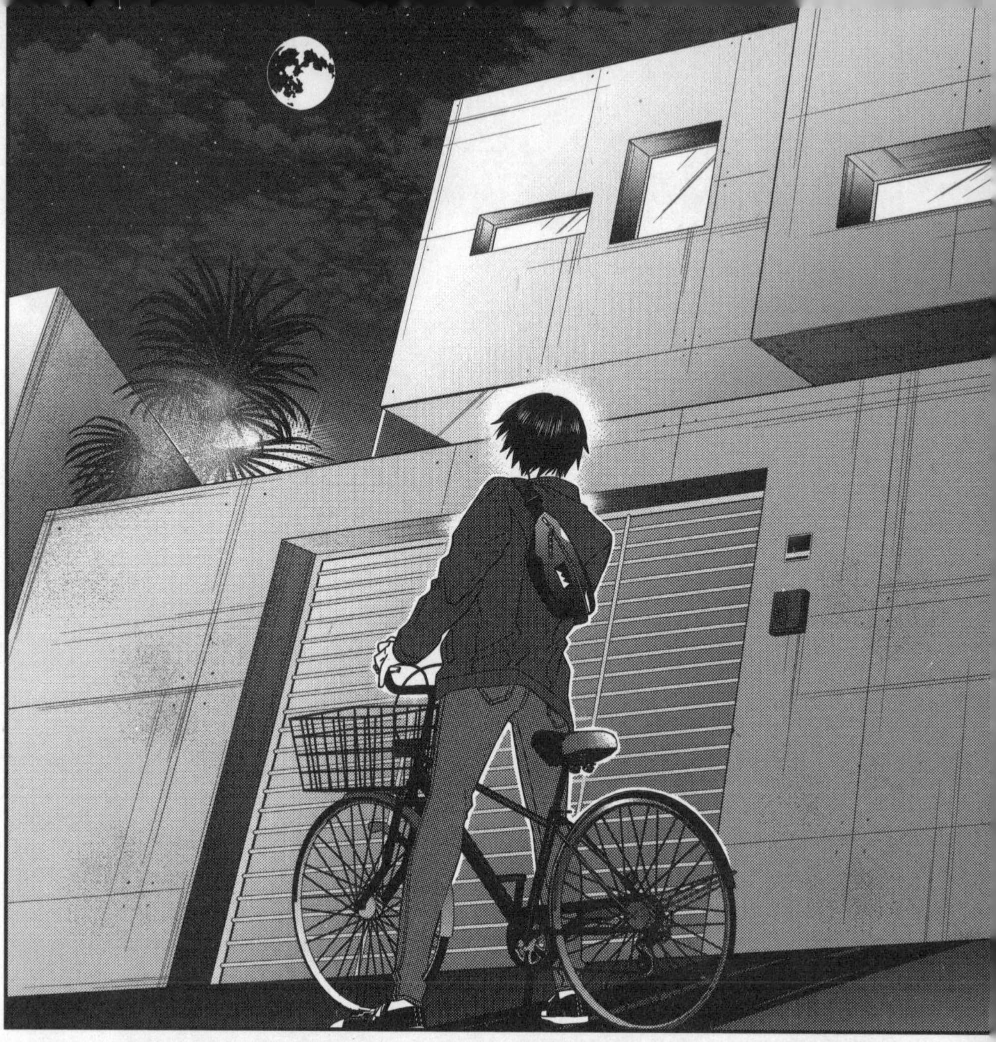

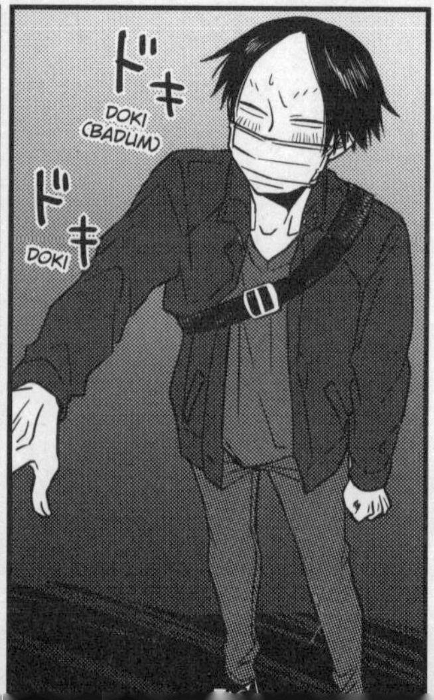
ドキ
DOKI (BADUM)
ドキ
DOKI

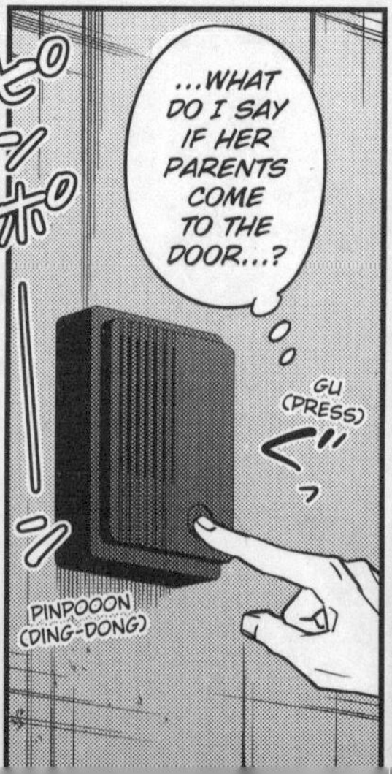
...WHAT DO I SAY IF HER PARENTS COME TO THE DOOR...?
ぐっ
GU (PRESS)
ピンポーン
PINPOOON (DING-DONG)

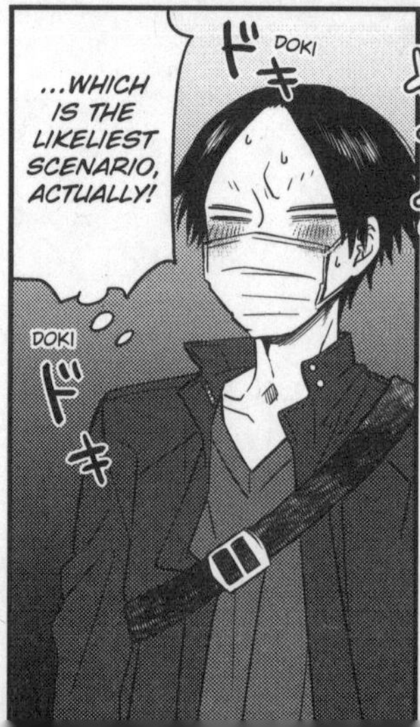
ドキ
DOKI
...WHICH IS THE LIKELIEST SCENARIO, ACTUALLY!
DOKI
ドキ

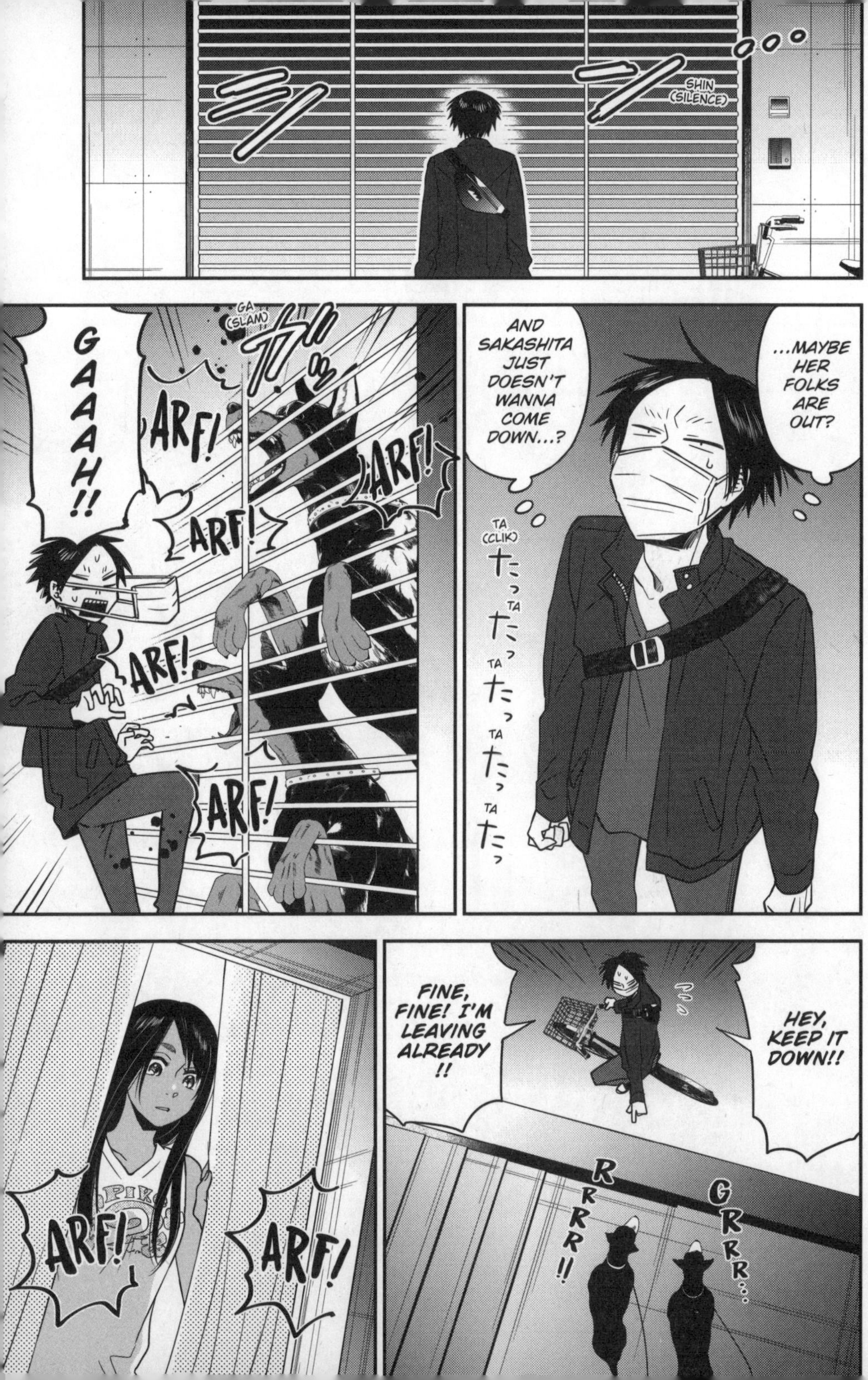
SHIN (SILENCE)
...MAYBE HER FOLKS ARE OUT?
AND SAKASHITA JUST DOESN'T WANNA COME DOWN...?
TA (CLIK)
たっ
TA
たっ
TA
たっ
TA
たっ
TA
たっ
GA (SLAM)
GAAAAH!!
ARF!
ARF!
ARF!
ARF!
ARF!
HEY, KEEP IT DOWN!!
FINE, FINE! I'M LEAVING ALREADY!!
GRRR...
RRRR!!
ARF!
ARF!

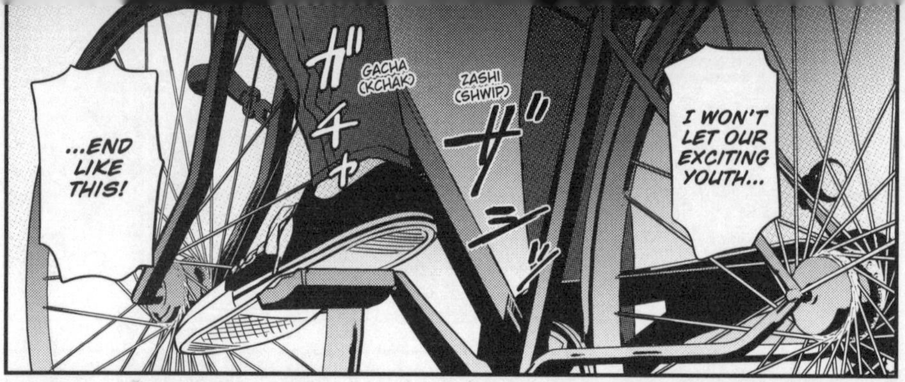
I WON'T LET OUR EXCITING YOUTH...
ZASHI (SHWIP)
GACHA (KCHAK)
...END LIKE THIS!
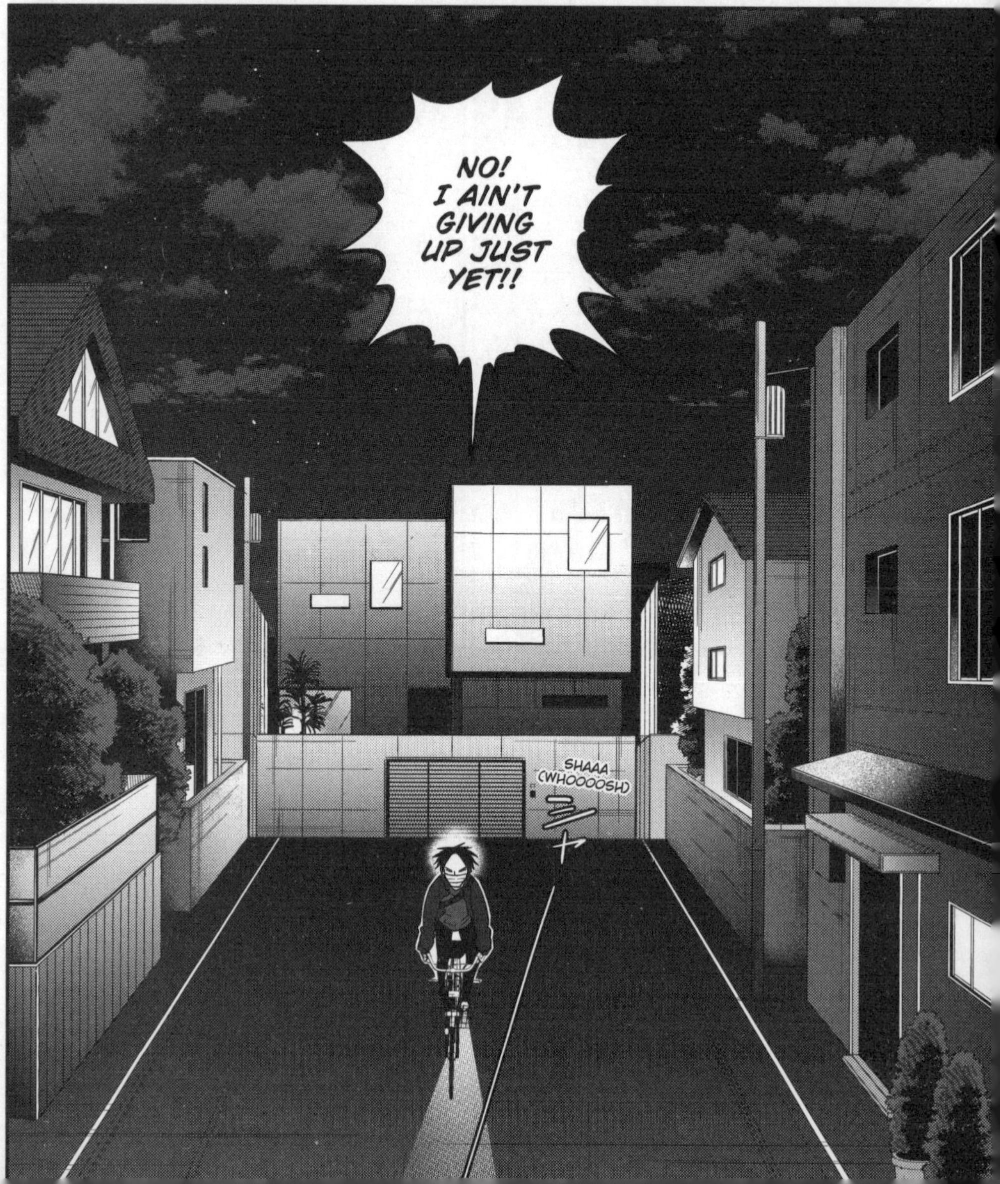
NO! I AIN'T GIVING UP JUST YET!!
SHAAA (WHOOOOSH)

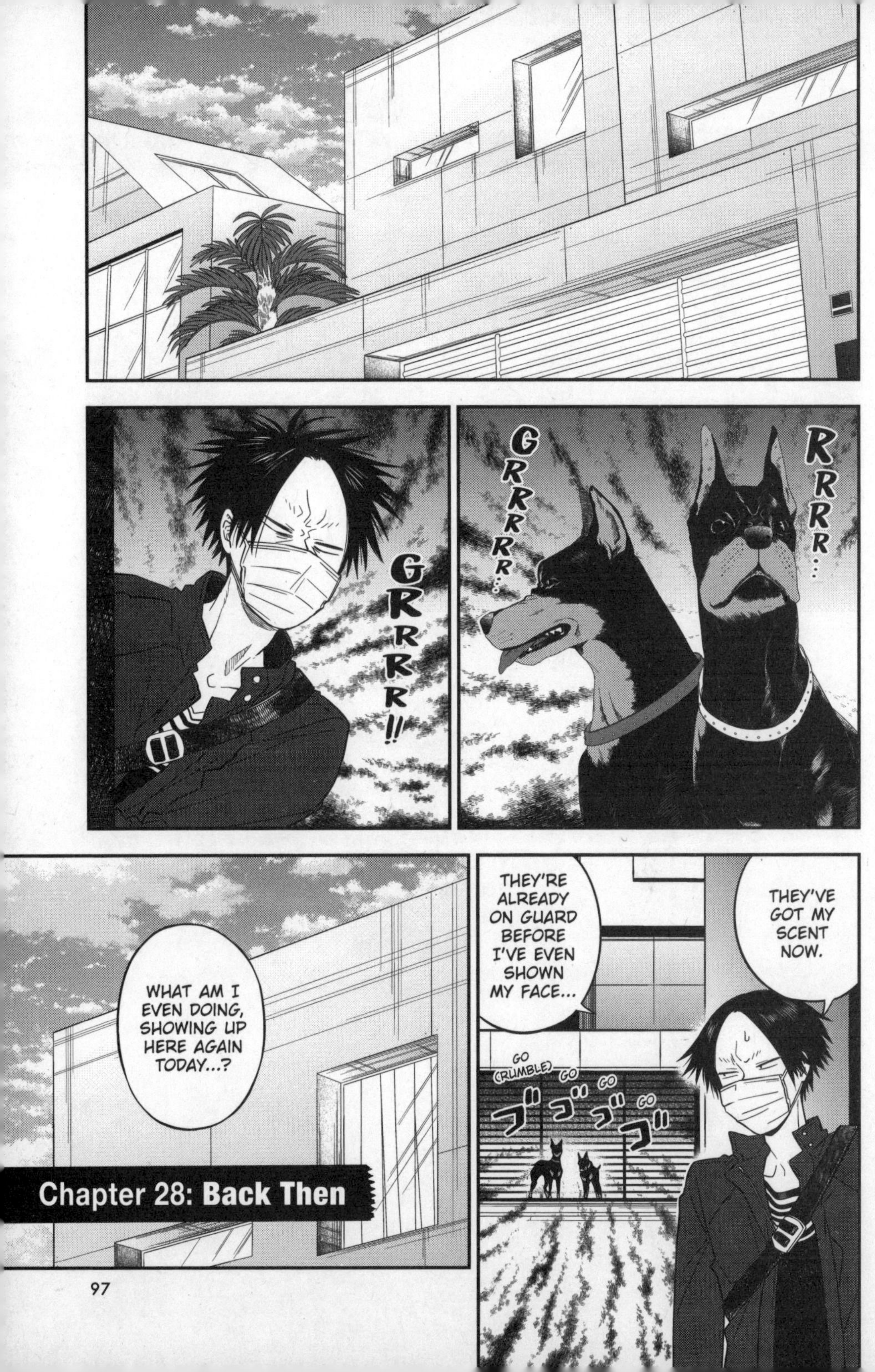
RRRR...
GRRRRR...
GRRRR!!
THEY'VE GOT MY SCENT NOW.
THEY'RE ALREADY ON GUARD BEFORE I'VE EVEN SHOWN MY FACE...
GO (RUMBLE) GO GO GO
ゴゴゴゴ
WHAT AM I EVEN DOING, SHOWING UP HERE AGAIN TODAY...?
Chapter 28: Back Then

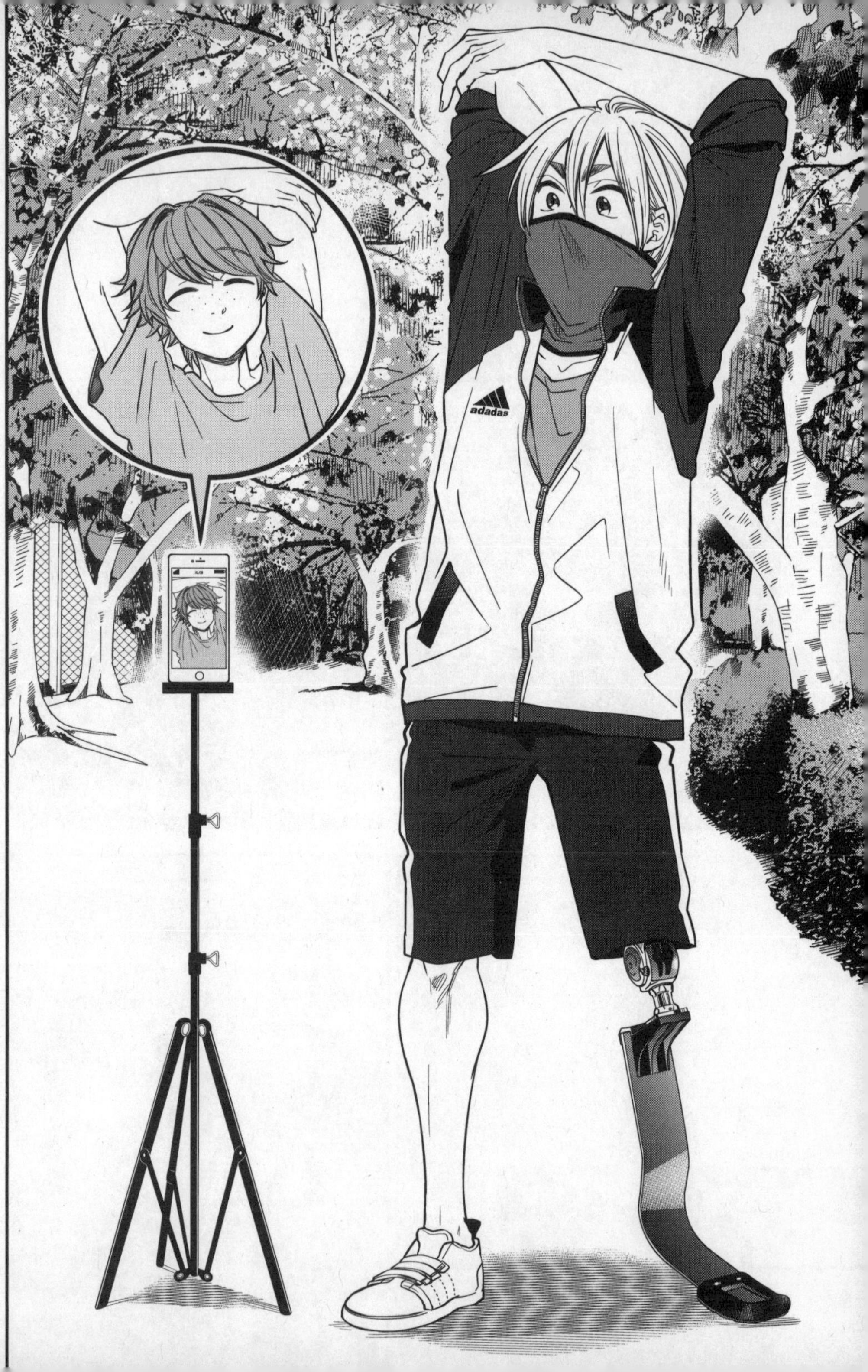
adadas

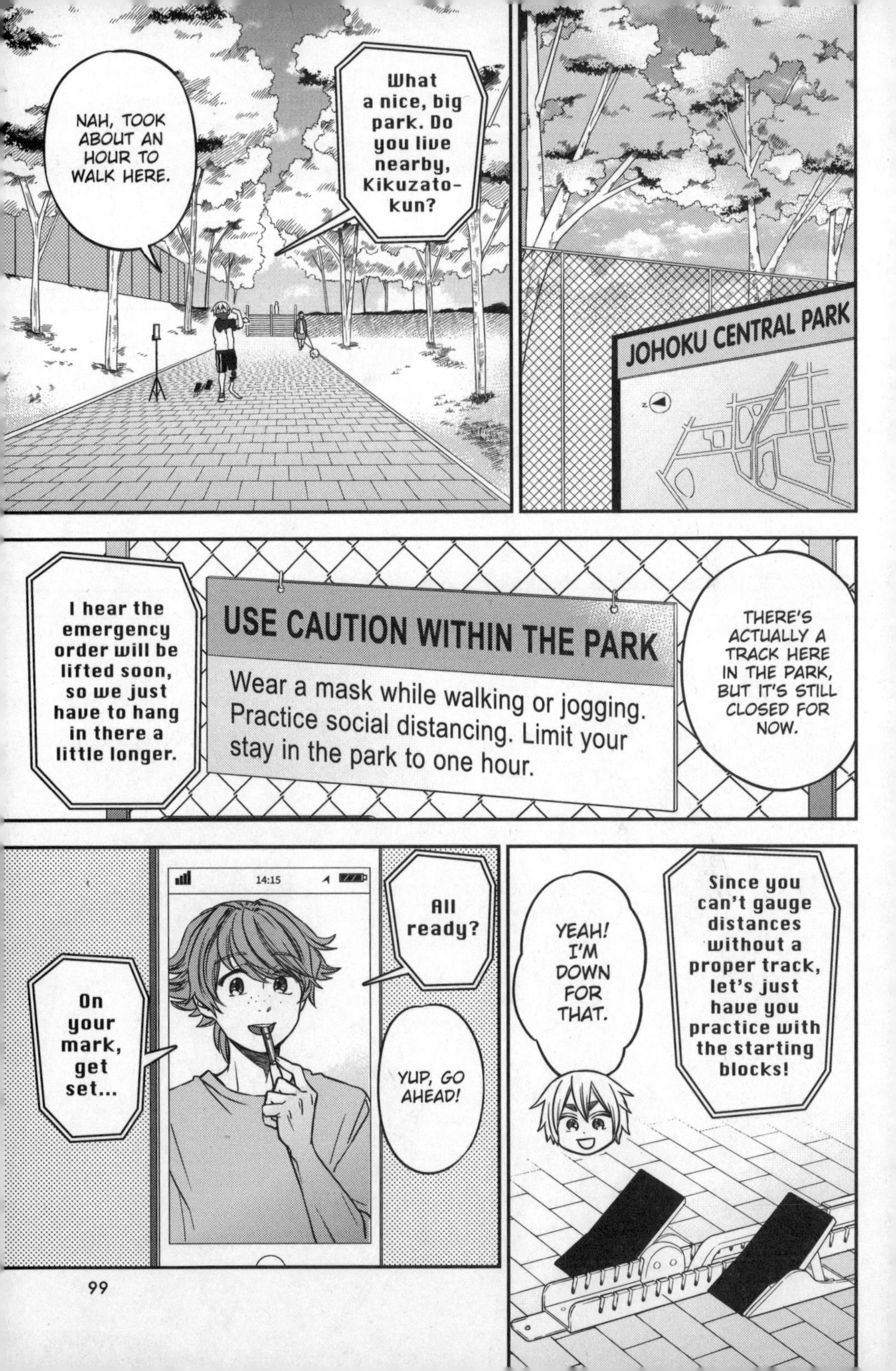

JOHOKU CENTRAL PARK
What a nice, big park. Do you live nearby, Kikuzato-kun?
NAH, TOOK ABOUT AN HOUR TO WALK HERE.
THERE'S ACTUALLY A TRACK HERE IN THE PARK, BUT IT'S STILL CLOSED FOR NOW.
USE CAUTION WITHIN THE PARK
Wear a mask while walking or jogging. Practice social distancing. Limit your stay in the park to one hour.
I hear the emergency order will be lifted soon, so we just have to hang in there a little longer.
Since you can't gauge distances without a proper track, let's just have you practice with the starting blocks!
YEAH! I'M DOWN FOR THAT.
14:15
All ready?
YUP, GO AHEAD!
On your mark, get set...

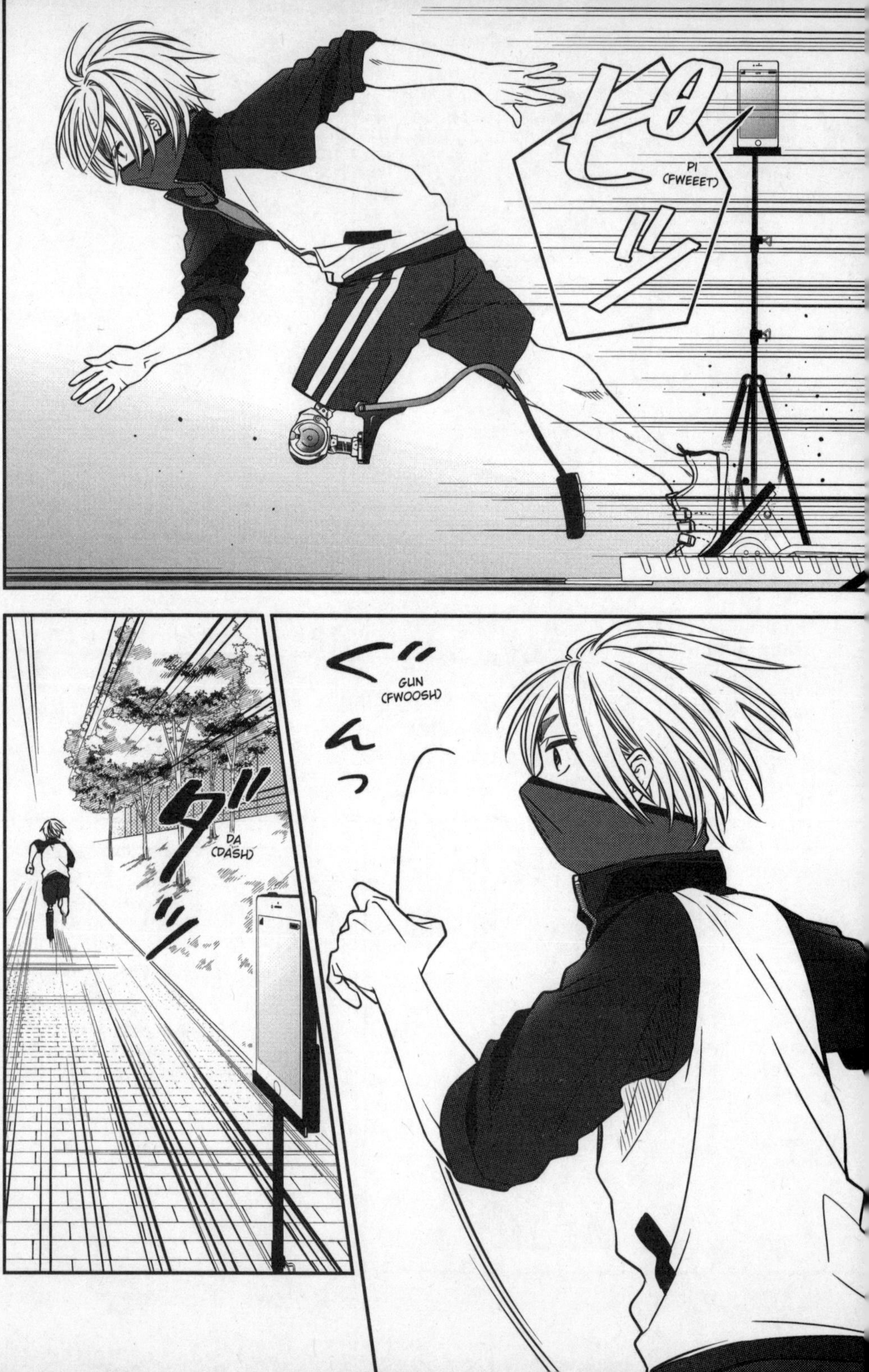
ピッ
PI (FWEEET)
ぐんっ
GUN (FWOOSH)
ダッ
DA (DASH)

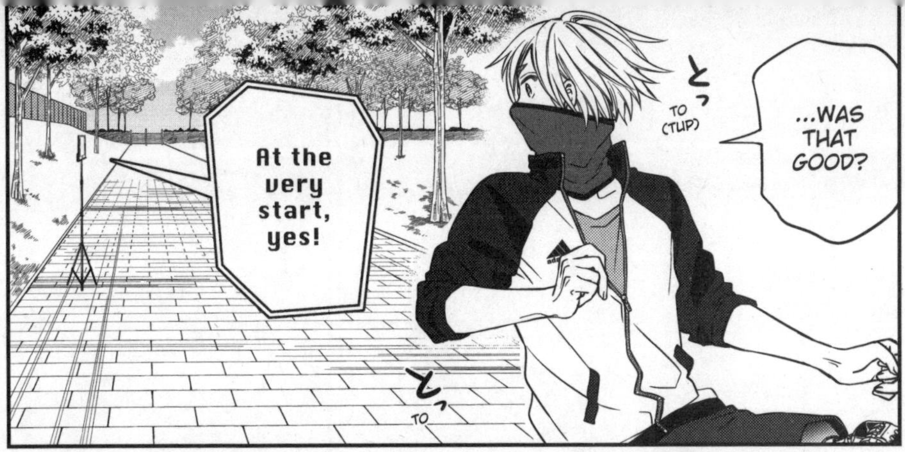
...WAS THAT GOOD?
TO (TUP)
At the very start, yes!
TO

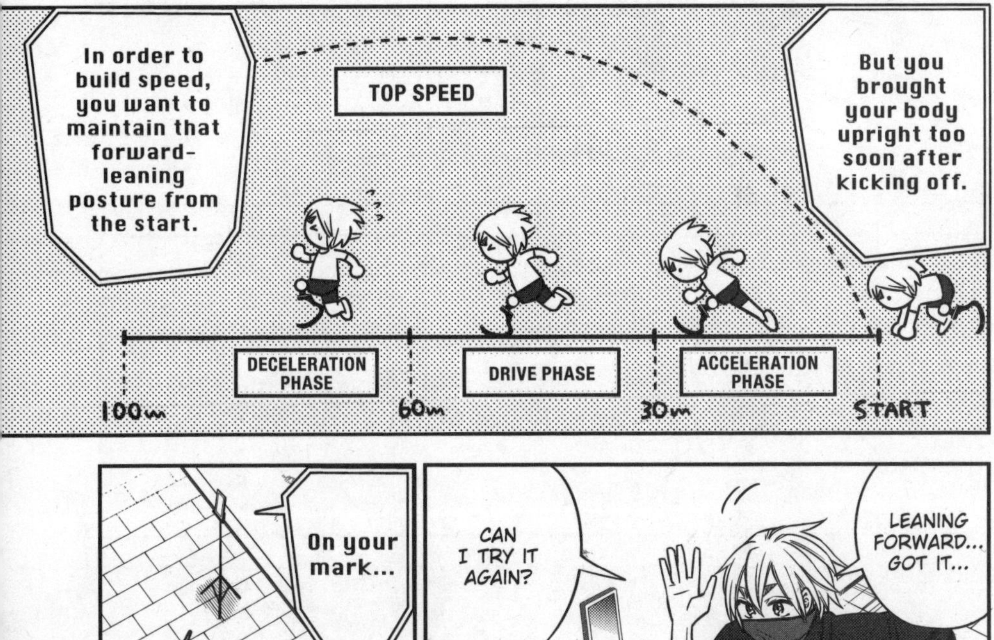
But you brought your body upright too soon after kicking off.
In order to build speed, you want to maintain that forward-leaning posture from the start.
TOP SPEED
START
ACCELERATION PHASE
30m
DRIVE PHASE
60m
DECELERATION PHASE
100m

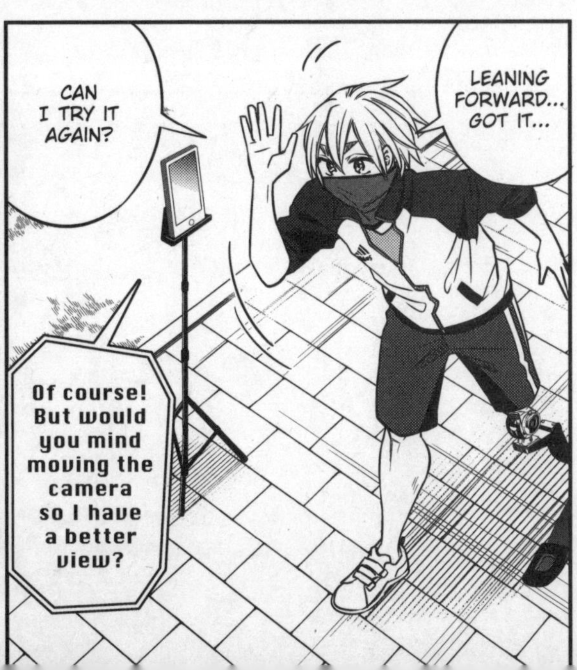
LEANING FORWARD... GOT IT...
CAN I TRY IT AGAIN?
Of course! But would you mind moving the camera so I have a better view?

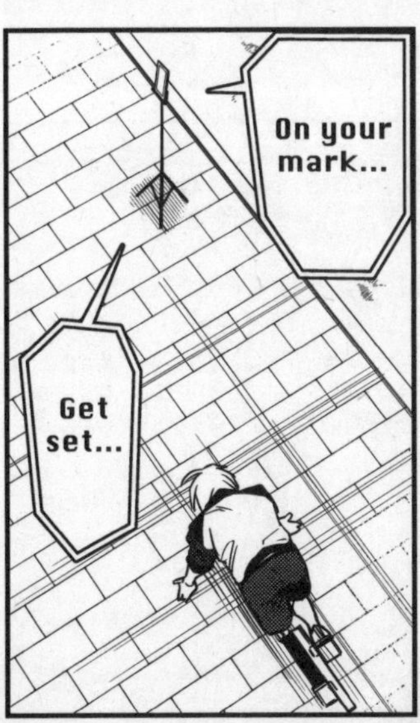
On your mark...
Get set...

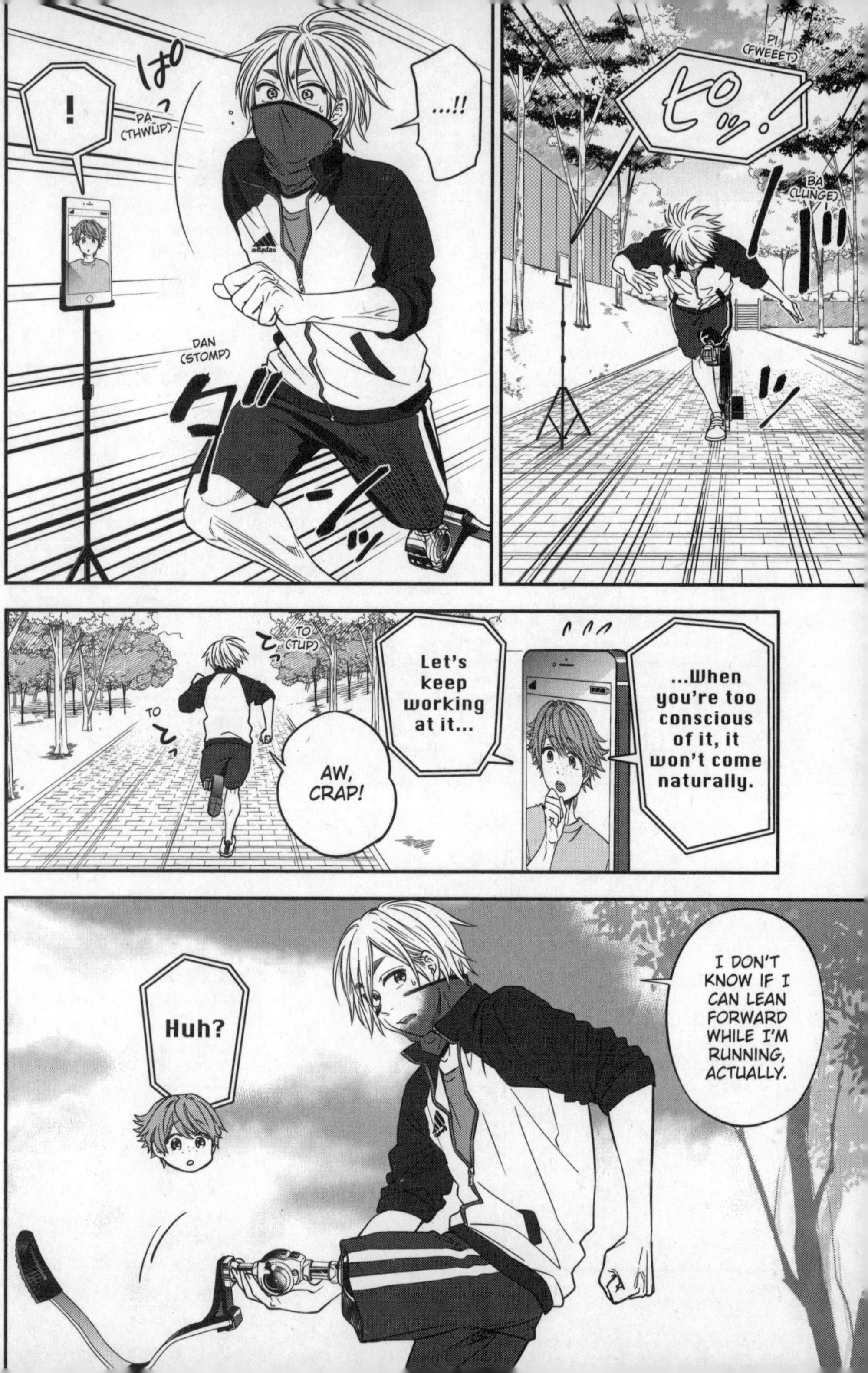
PI (FWEEET)
BA (LUNGE)
...!!
PA (THWUP)
!
DAN (STOMP)
...When you're too conscious of it, it won't come naturally.
Let's keep working at it...
TO (TUP)
AW, CRAP!
TO
I DON'T KNOW IF I CAN LEAN FORWARD WHILE I'M RUNNING, ACTUALLY.
Huh?

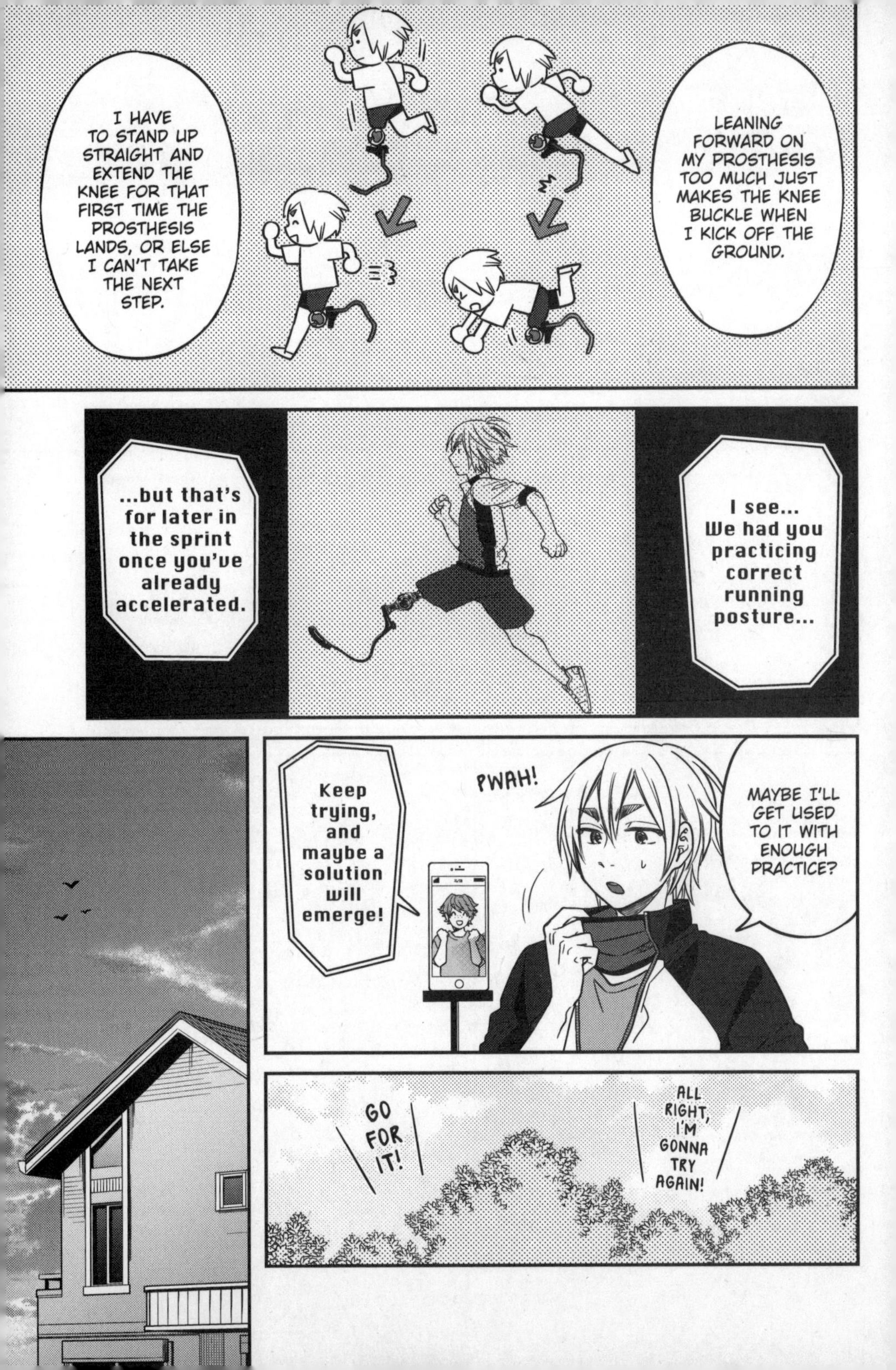
LEANING FORWARD ON MY PROSTHESIS TOO MUCH JUST MAKES THE KNEE BUCKLE WHEN I KICK OFF THE GROUND.
I HAVE TO STAND UP STRAIGHT AND EXTEND THE KNEE FOR THAT FIRST TIME THE PROSTHESIS LANDS, OR ELSE I CAN'T TAKE THE NEXT STEP.
I see... We had you practicing correct running posture...
...but that's for later in the sprint once you've already accelerated.
MAYBE I'LL GET USED TO IT WITH ENOUGH PRACTICE?
PWAH!
Keep trying, and maybe a solution will emerge!
ALL RIGHT, I'M GONNA TRY AGAIN!
GO FOR IT!

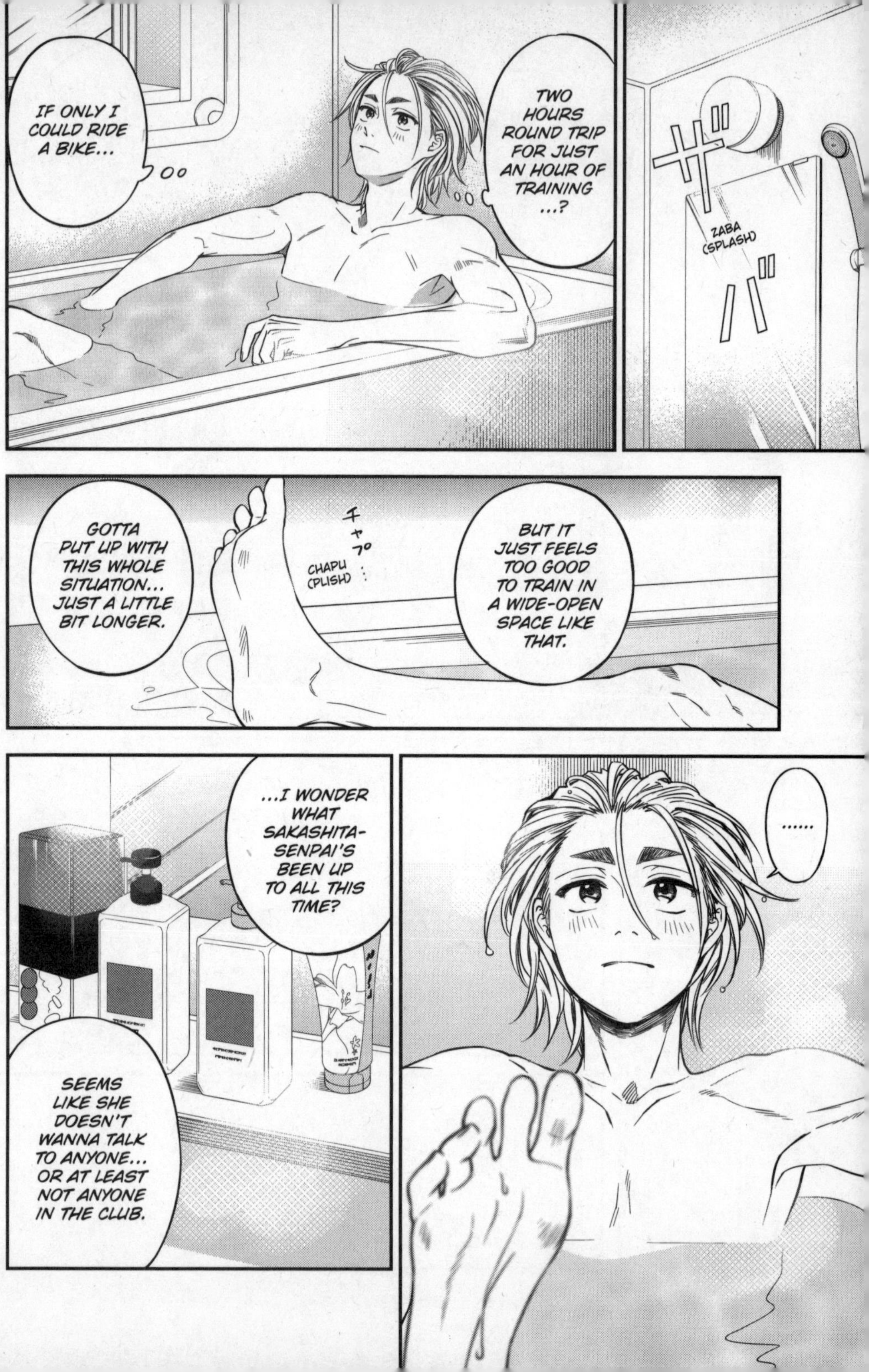
ザバ
ZABA (SPLASH)
TWO HOURS ROUND TRIP FOR JUST AN HOUR OF TRAINING ...?
IF ONLY I COULD RIDE A BIKE...
BUT IT JUST FEELS TOO GOOD TO TRAIN IN A WIDE-OPEN SPACE LIKE THAT.
チャプ
CHAPU (PLISH)
GOTTA PUT UP WITH THIS WHOLE SITUATION... JUST A LITTLE BIT LONGER.
......
...I WONDER WHAT SAKASHITA-SENPAI'S BEEN UP TO ALL THIS TIME?
SEEMS LIKE SHE DOESN'T WANNA TALK TO ANYONE... OR AT LEAST NOT ANYONE IN THE CLUB.

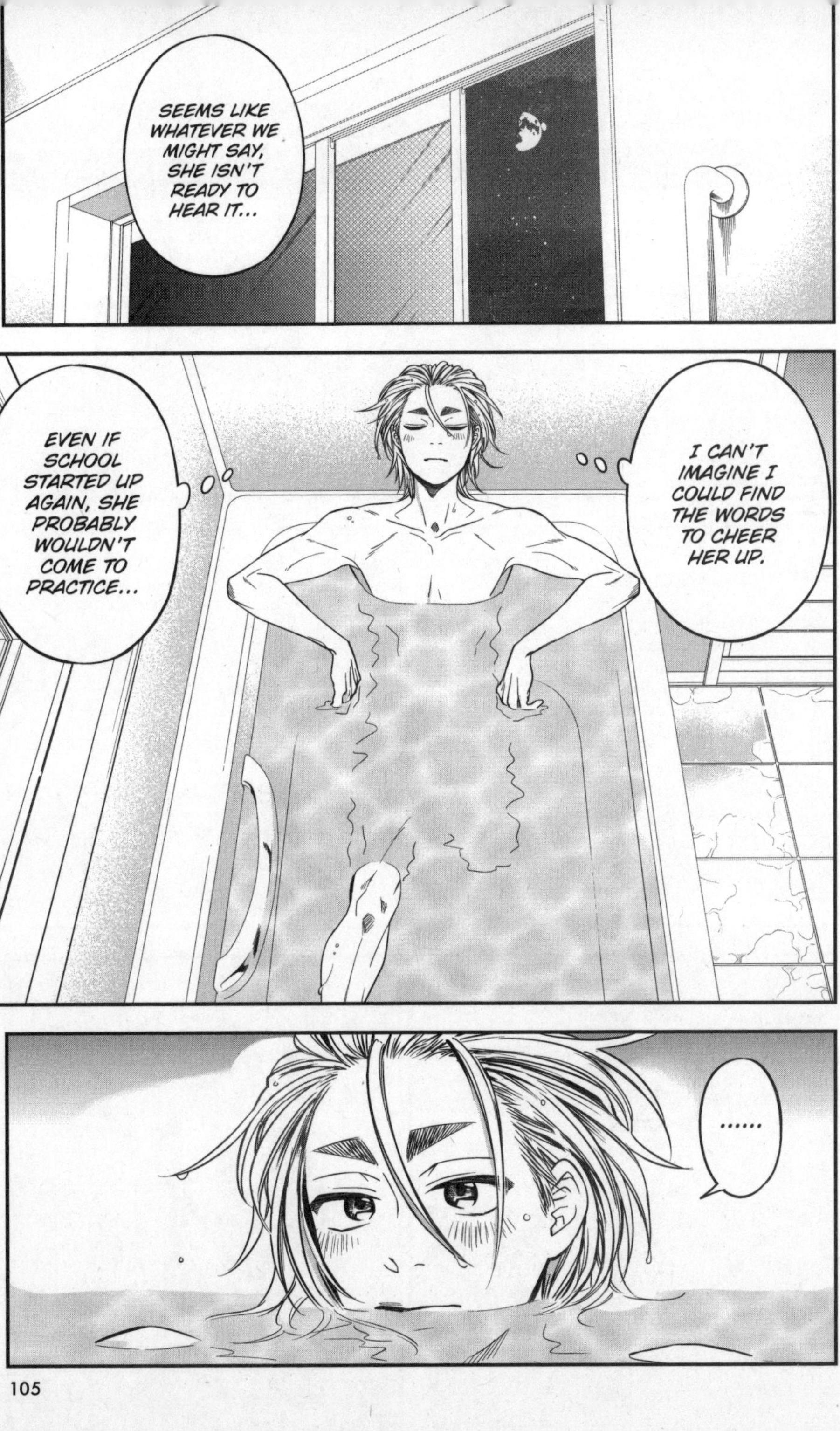
SEEMS LIKE WHATEVER WE MIGHT SAY, SHE ISN'T READY TO HEAR IT...
I CAN'T IMAGINE I COULD FIND THE WORDS TO CHEER HER UP.
EVEN IF SCHOOL STARTED UP AGAIN, SHE PROBABLY WOULDN'T COME TO PRACTICE...
......

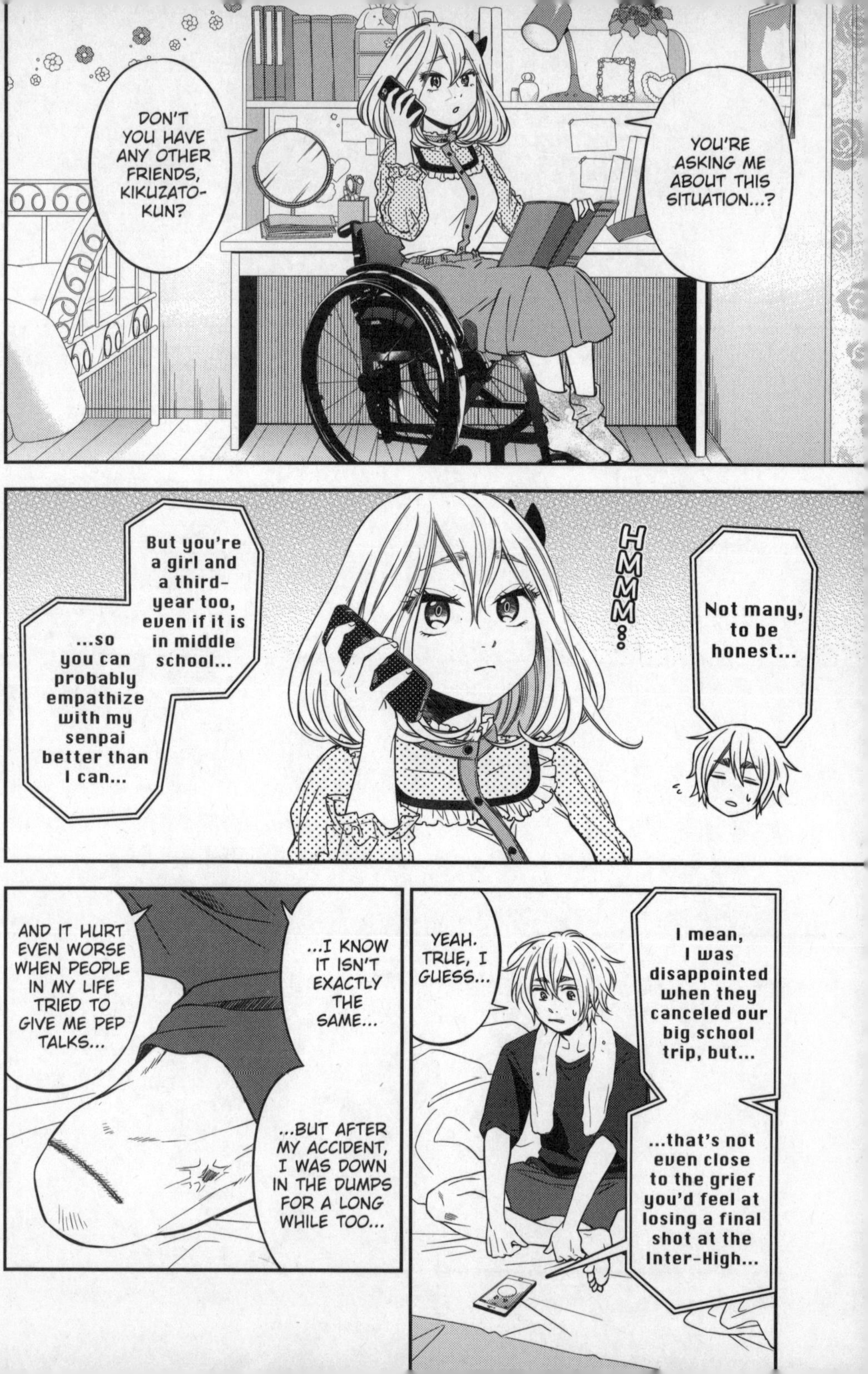

YOU'RE ASKING ME ABOUT THIS SITUATION...?
DON'T YOU HAVE ANY OTHER FRIENDS, KIKUZATO-KUN?
Not many, to be honest...
HMMM...
But you're a girl and a third-year too, even if it is in middle school...
...so you can probably empathize with my senpai better than I can...
I mean, I was disappointed when they canceled our big school trip, but...
...that's not even close to the grief you'd feel at losing a final shot at the Inter-High...
YEAH. TRUE, I GUESS...
...I KNOW IT ISN'T EXACTLY THE SAME...
...BUT AFTER MY ACCIDENT, I WAS DOWN IN THE DUMPS FOR A LONG WHILE TOO...
AND IT HURT EVEN WORSE WHEN PEOPLE IN MY LIFE TRIED TO GIVE ME PEP TALKS...

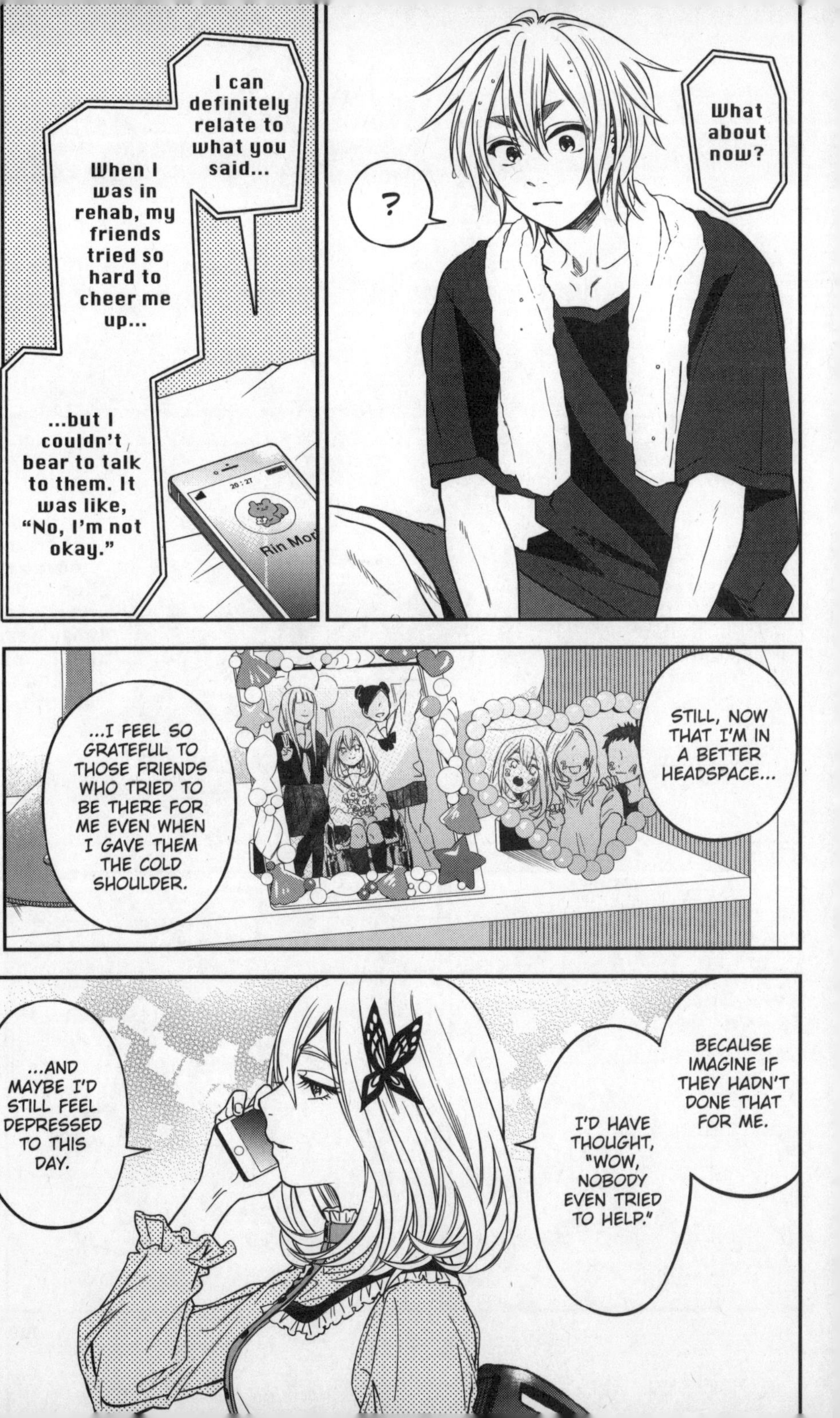
What about now?
?
I can definitely relate to what you said...
When I was in rehab, my friends tried so hard to cheer me up...
...but I couldn't bear to talk to them. It was like, "No, I'm not okay."
20:27
STILL, NOW THAT I'M IN A BETTER HEADSPACE...
...I FEEL SO GRATEFUL TO THOSE FRIENDS WHO TRIED TO BE THERE FOR ME EVEN WHEN I GAVE THEM THE COLD SHOULDER.
BECAUSE IMAGINE IF THEY HADN'T DONE THAT FOR ME.
I'D HAVE THOUGHT, "WOW, NOBODY EVEN TRIED TO HELP."
...AND MAYBE I'D STILL FEEL DEPRESSED TO THIS DAY.

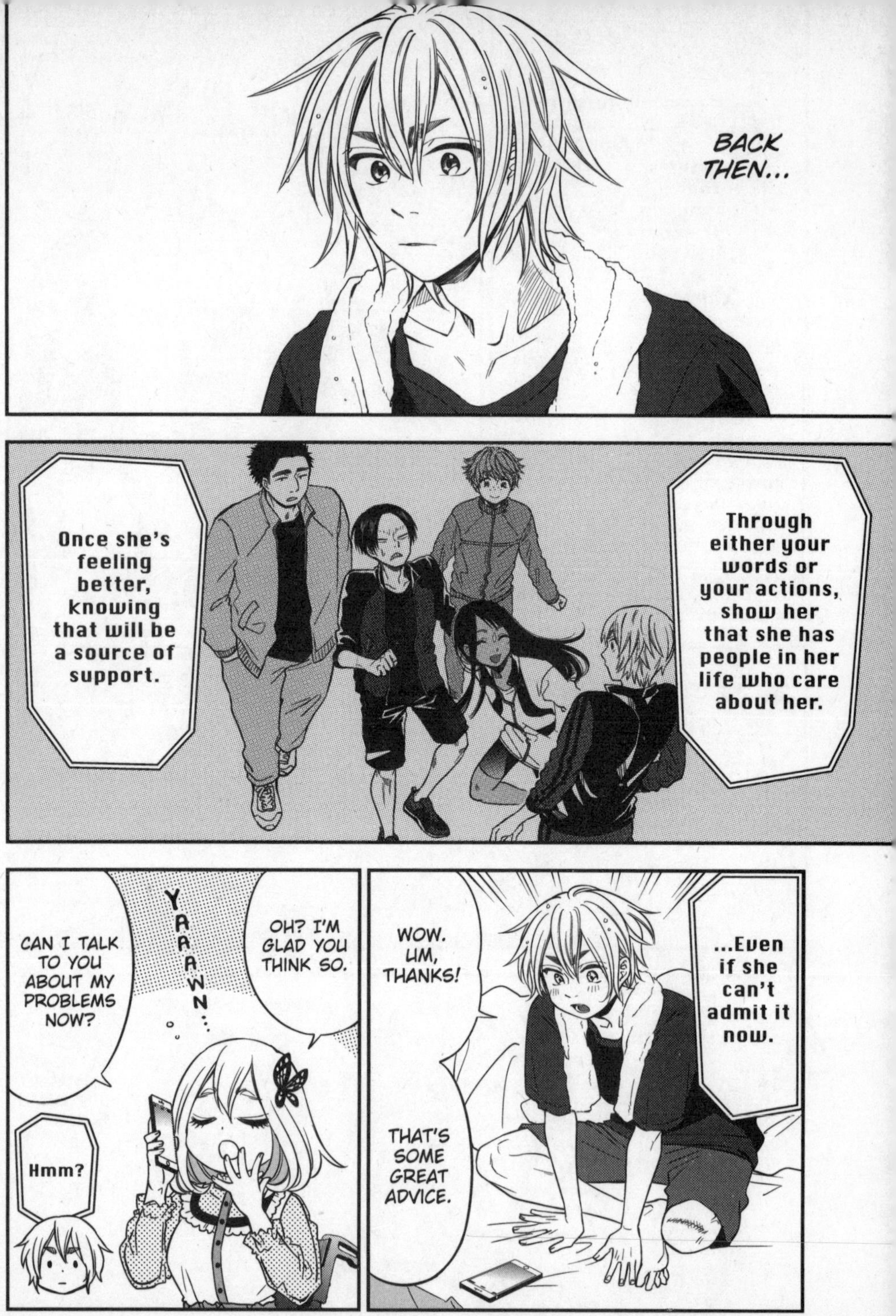
BACK THEN...
Through either your words or your actions, show her that she has people in her life who care about her.
Once she's feeling better, knowing that will be a source of support.
...Even if she can't admit it now.
WOW. UM, THANKS!
THAT'S SOME GREAT ADVICE.
OH? I'M GLAD YOU THINK SO.
YAAAWN...
CAN I TALK TO YOU ABOUT MY PROBLEMS NOW?
Hmm?

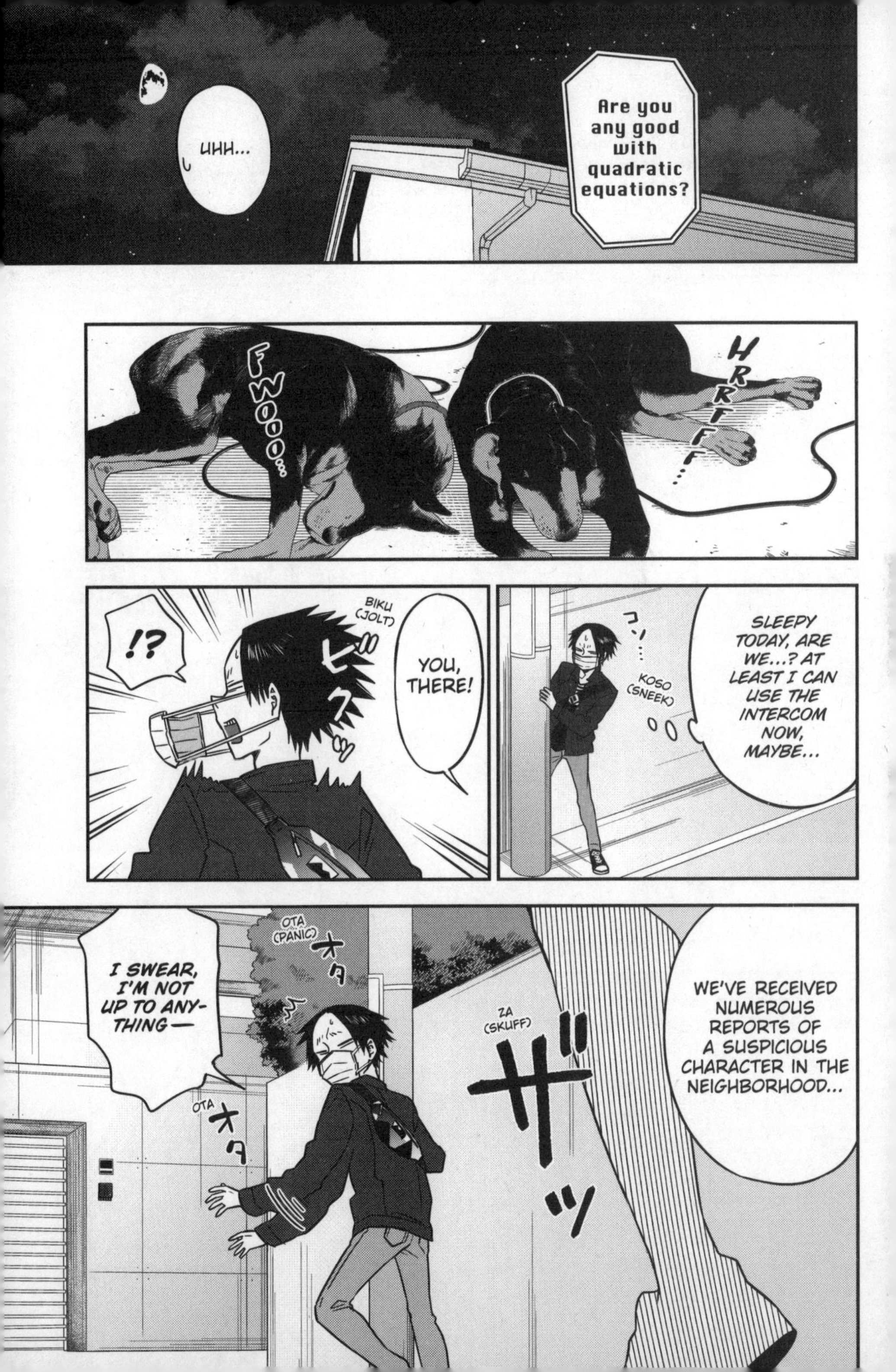

Are you any good with quadratic equations?
UHH...
HRRFFF...
FWOOO...
SLEEPY TODAY, ARE WE...? AT LEAST I CAN USE THE INTERCOM NOW, MAYBE...
KOSO (SNEEK)
YOU, THERE!
BIKU (JOLT)
!?
WE'VE RECEIVED NUMEROUS REPORTS OF A SUSPICIOUS CHARACTER IN THE NEIGHBORHOOD...
ZA (SKUFF)
OTA (PANIC)
I SWEAR, I'M NOT UP TO ANY-THING—
OTA

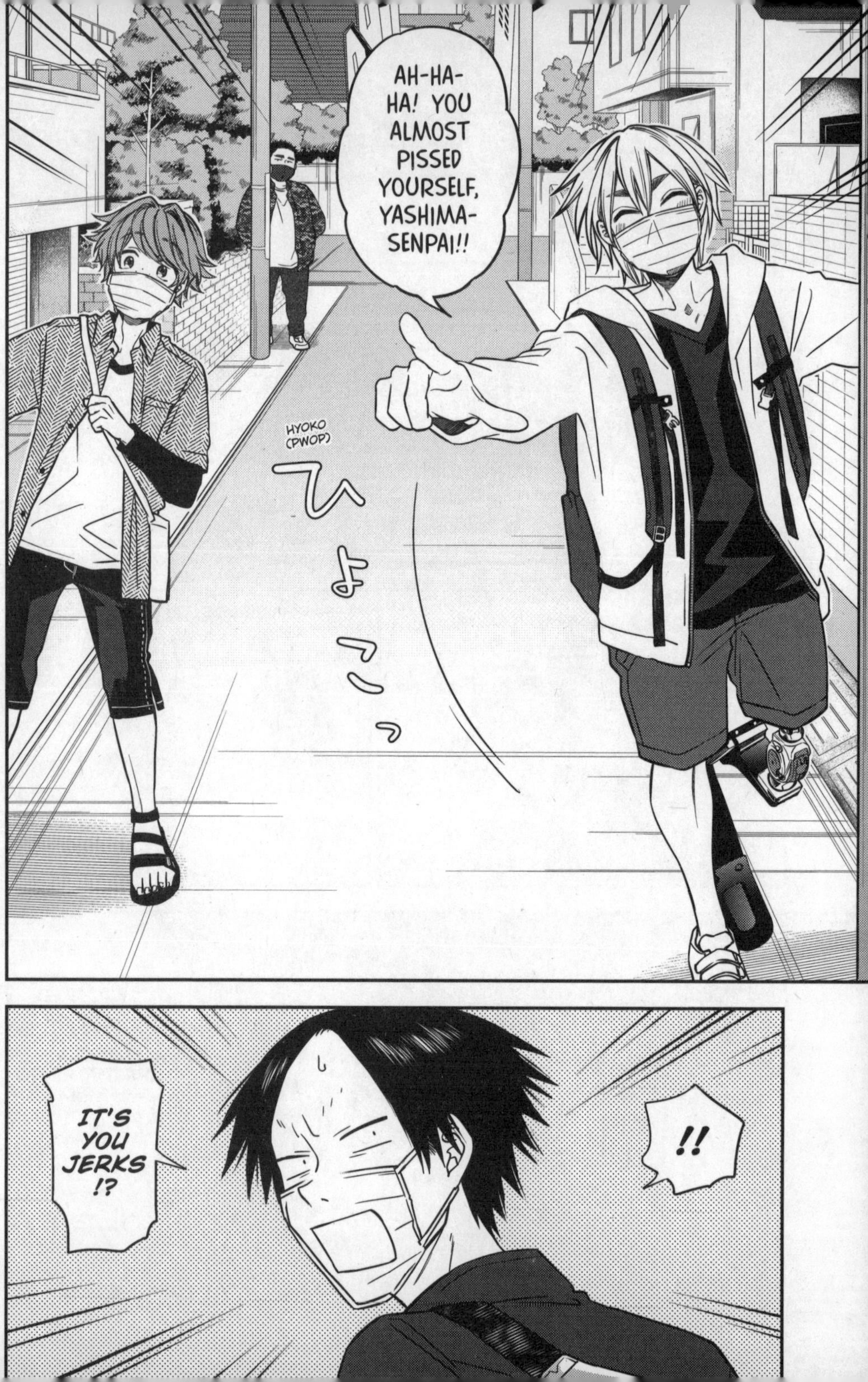
AH-HA-HA! YOU ALMOST PISSED YOURSELF, YASHIMA-SENPAI!!
ひょこっ
HYOKO (PWOP)
!!
IT'S YOU JERKS !?

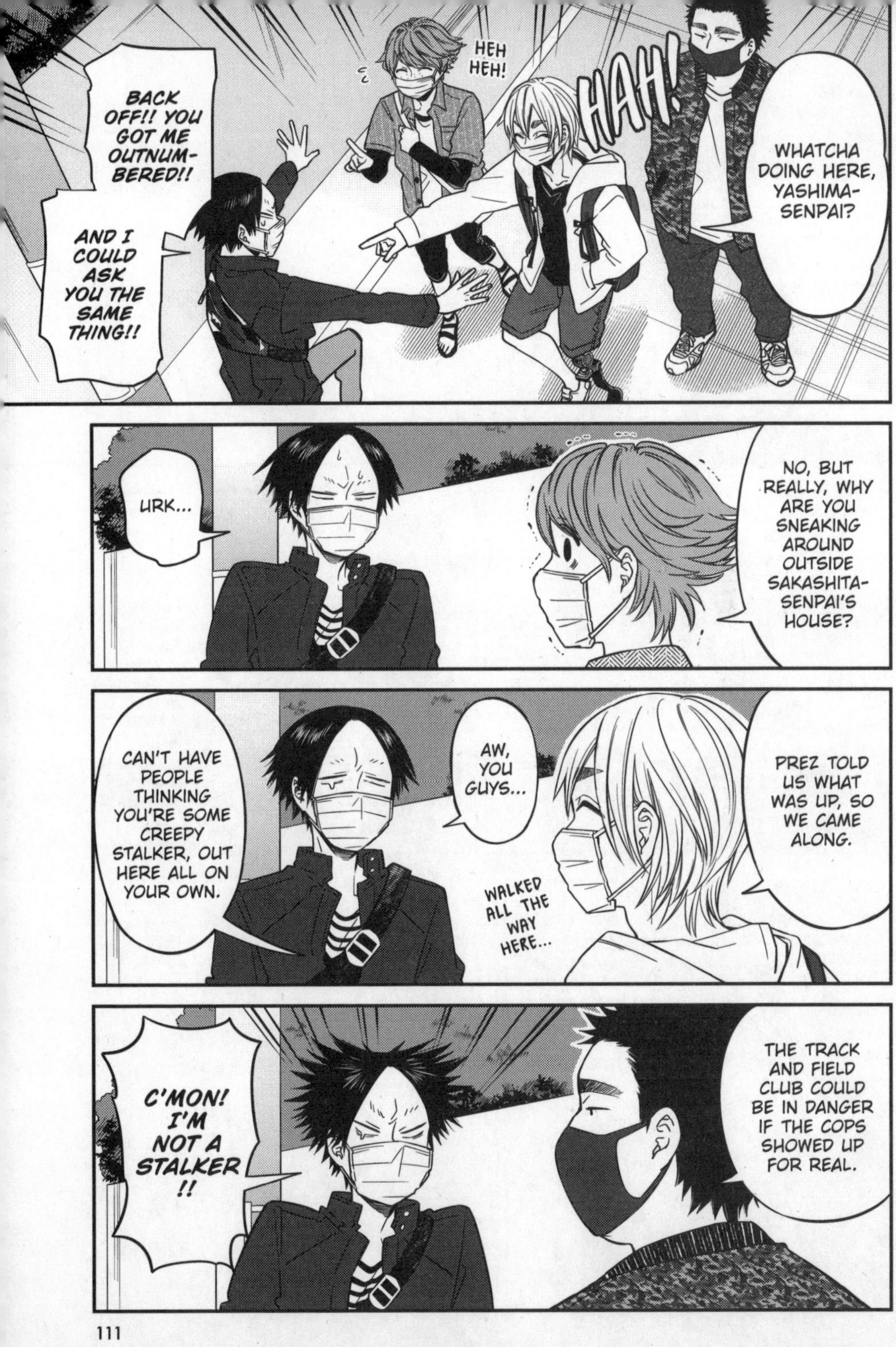
WHATCHA DOING HERE, YASHIMA-SENPAI?
HAH!
HEH HEH!
BACK OFF!! YOU GOT ME OUTNUM-BERED!!
AND I COULD ASK YOU THE SAME THING!!
NO, BUT REALLY, WHY ARE YOU SNEAKING AROUND OUTSIDE SAKASHITA-SENPAI'S HOUSE?
URK...
PREZ TOLD US WHAT WAS UP, SO WE CAME ALONG.
WALKED ALL THE WAY HERE...
AW, YOU GUYS...
CAN'T HAVE PEOPLE THINKING YOU'RE SOME CREEPY STALKER, OUT HERE ALL ON YOUR OWN.
THE TRACK AND FIELD CLUB COULD BE IN DANGER IF THE COPS SHOWED UP FOR REAL.
C'MON! I'M NOT A STALKER!!

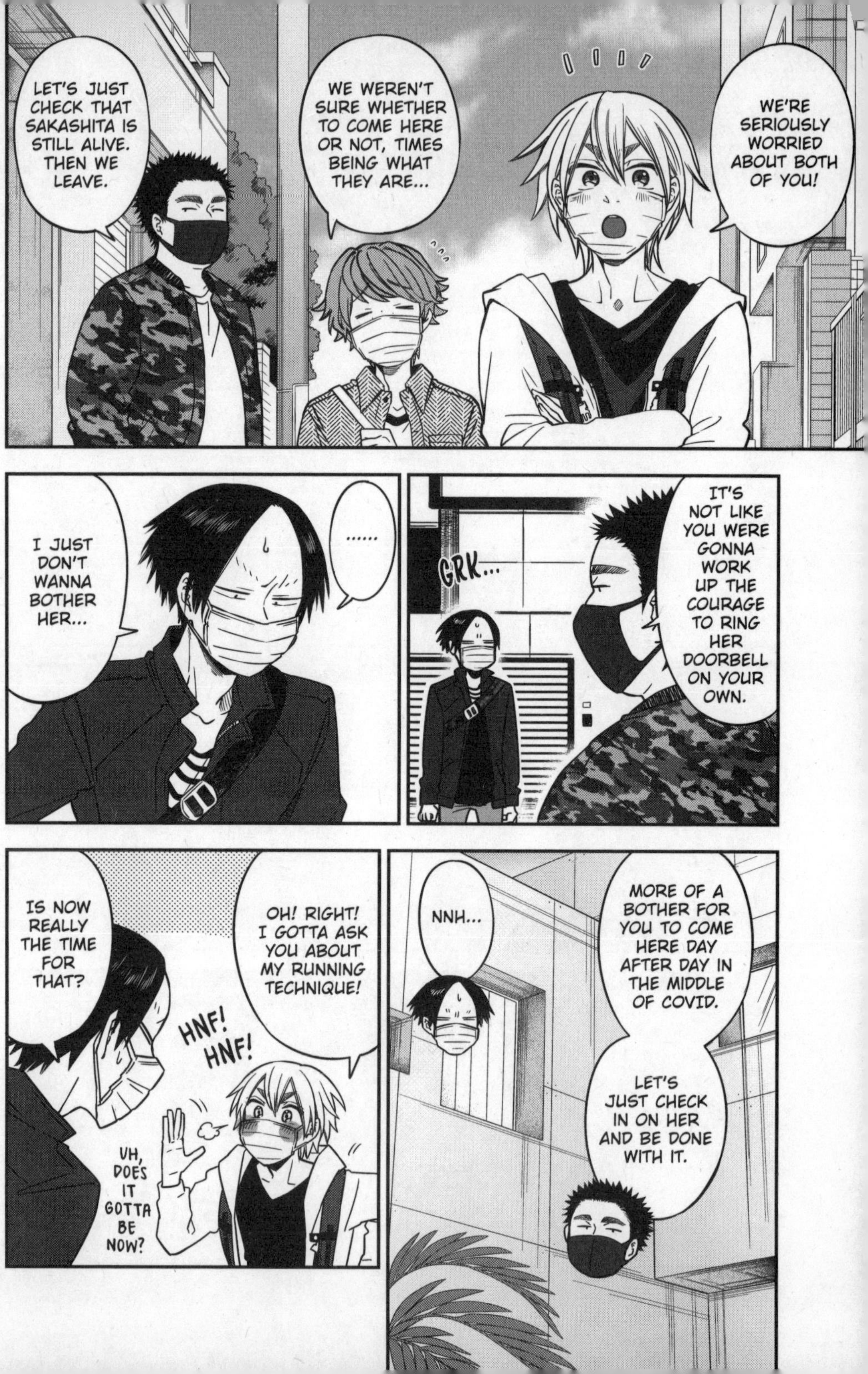
WE'RE SERIOUSLY WORRIED ABOUT BOTH OF YOU!
WE WEREN'T SURE WHETHER TO COME HERE OR NOT, TIMES BEING WHAT THEY ARE...
LET'S JUST CHECK THAT SAKASHITA IS STILL ALIVE. THEN WE LEAVE.
IT'S NOT LIKE YOU WERE GONNA WORK UP THE COURAGE TO RING HER DOORBELL ON YOUR OWN.
GRK...
......
I JUST DON'T WANNA BOTHER HER...
MORE OF A BOTHER FOR YOU TO COME HERE DAY AFTER DAY IN THE MIDDLE OF COVID.
NNH...
LET'S JUST CHECK IN ON HER AND BE DONE WITH IT.
OH! RIGHT! I GOTTA ASK YOU ABOUT MY RUNNING TECHNIQUE!
IS NOW REALLY THE TIME FOR THAT?
HNF! HNF!
UH, DOES IT GOTTA BE NOW?

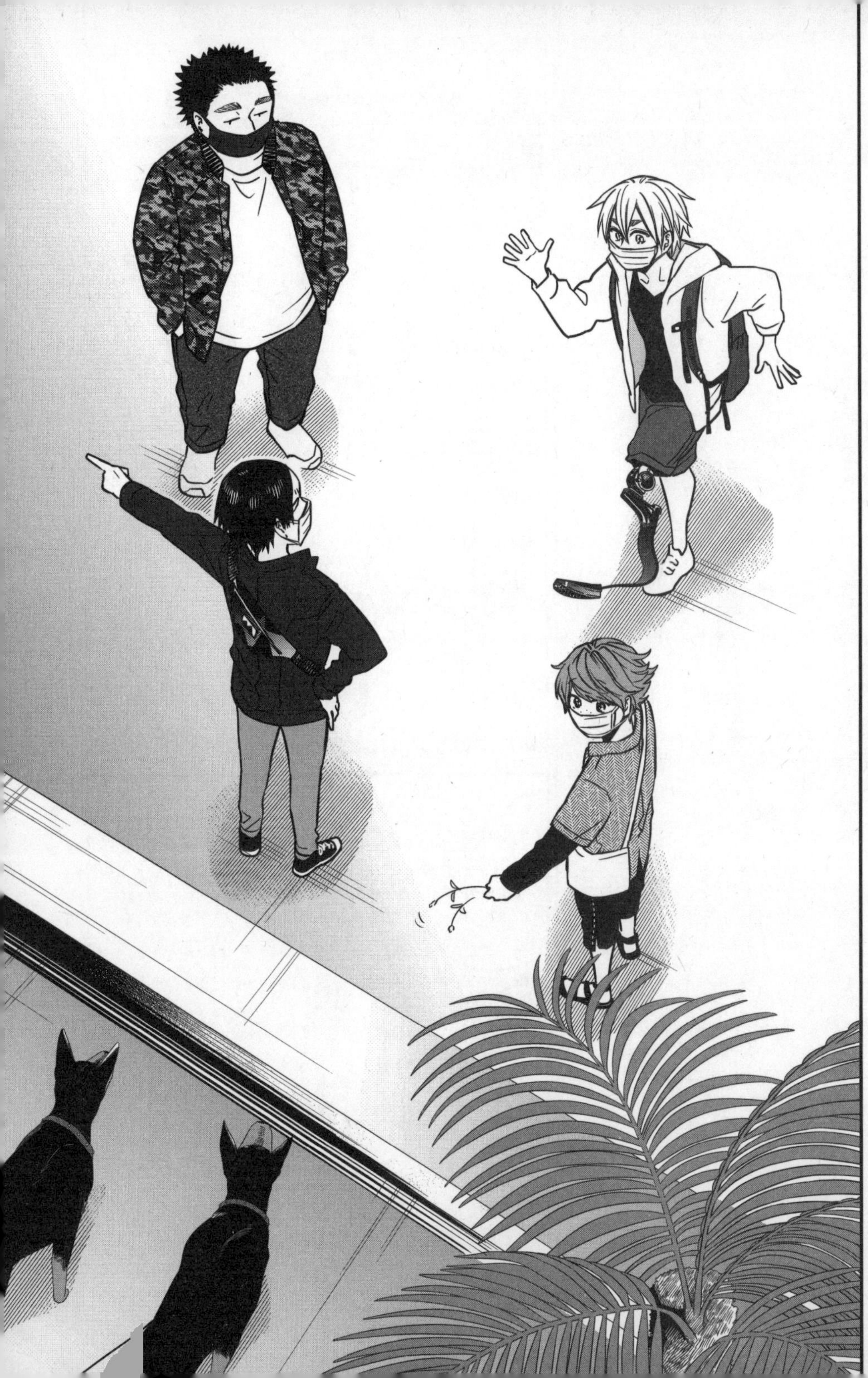

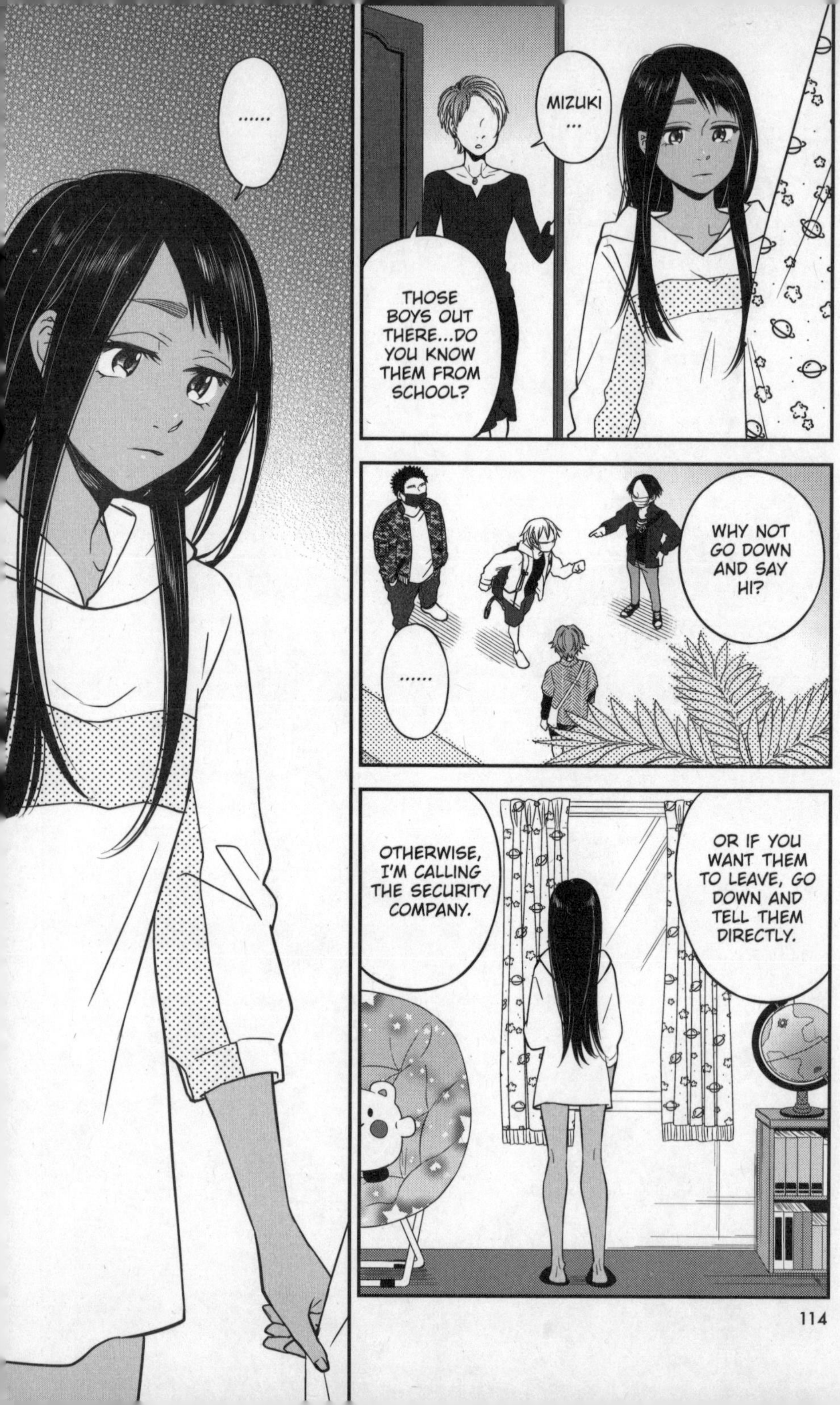
MIZUKI ...
THOSE BOYS OUT THERE...DO YOU KNOW THEM FROM SCHOOL?
WHY NOT GO DOWN AND SAY HI?
......
OR IF YOU WANT THEM TO LEAVE, GO DOWN AND TELL THEM DIRECTLY.
OTHERWISE, I'M CALLING THE SECURITY COMPANY.
......

Chapter 29: That Same Sky

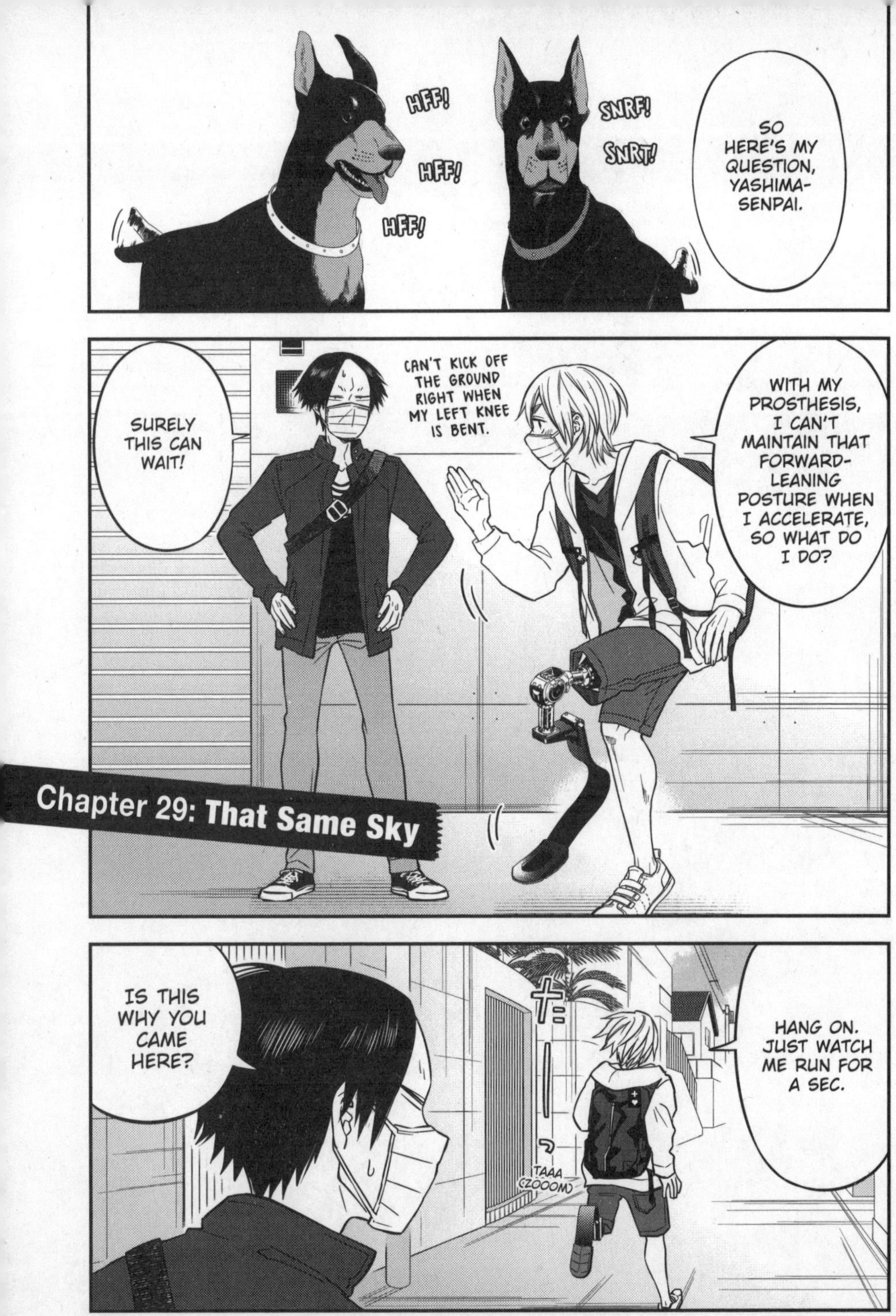
SO HERE'S MY QUESTION, YASHIMA-SENPAI.
SNRF!
SNRT!
HFF!
HFF!
HFF!
WITH MY PROSTHESIS, I CAN'T MAINTAIN THAT FORWARD-LEANING POSTURE WHEN I ACCELERATE, SO WHAT DO I DO?
CAN'T KICK OFF THE GROUND RIGHT WHEN MY LEFT KNEE IS BENT.
SURELY THIS CAN WAIT!
HANG ON. JUST WATCH ME RUN FOR A SEC.
TAAA (ZOOOM)
IS THIS WHY YOU CAME HERE?

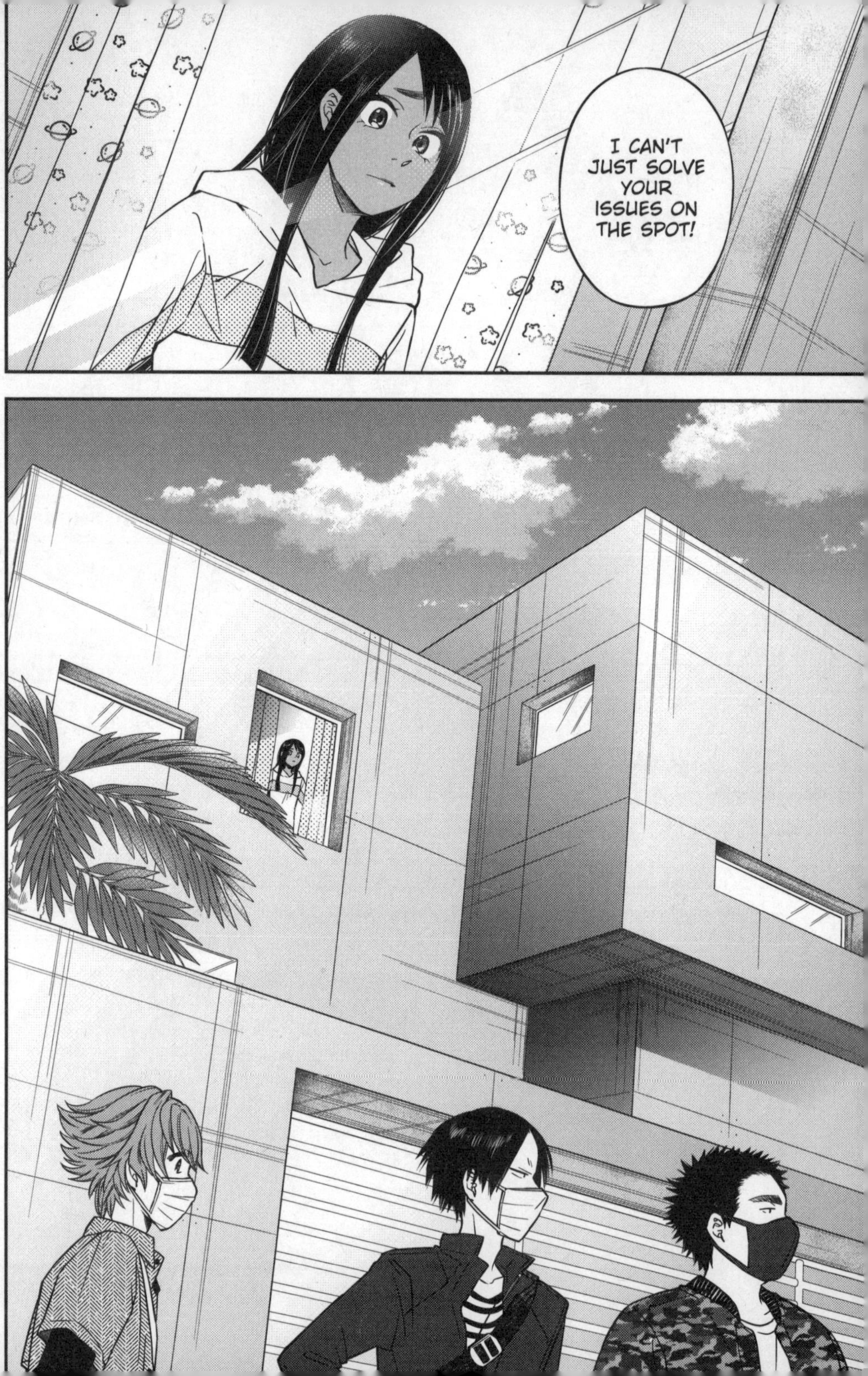
I CAN'T JUST SOLVE YOUR ISSUES ON THE SPOT!

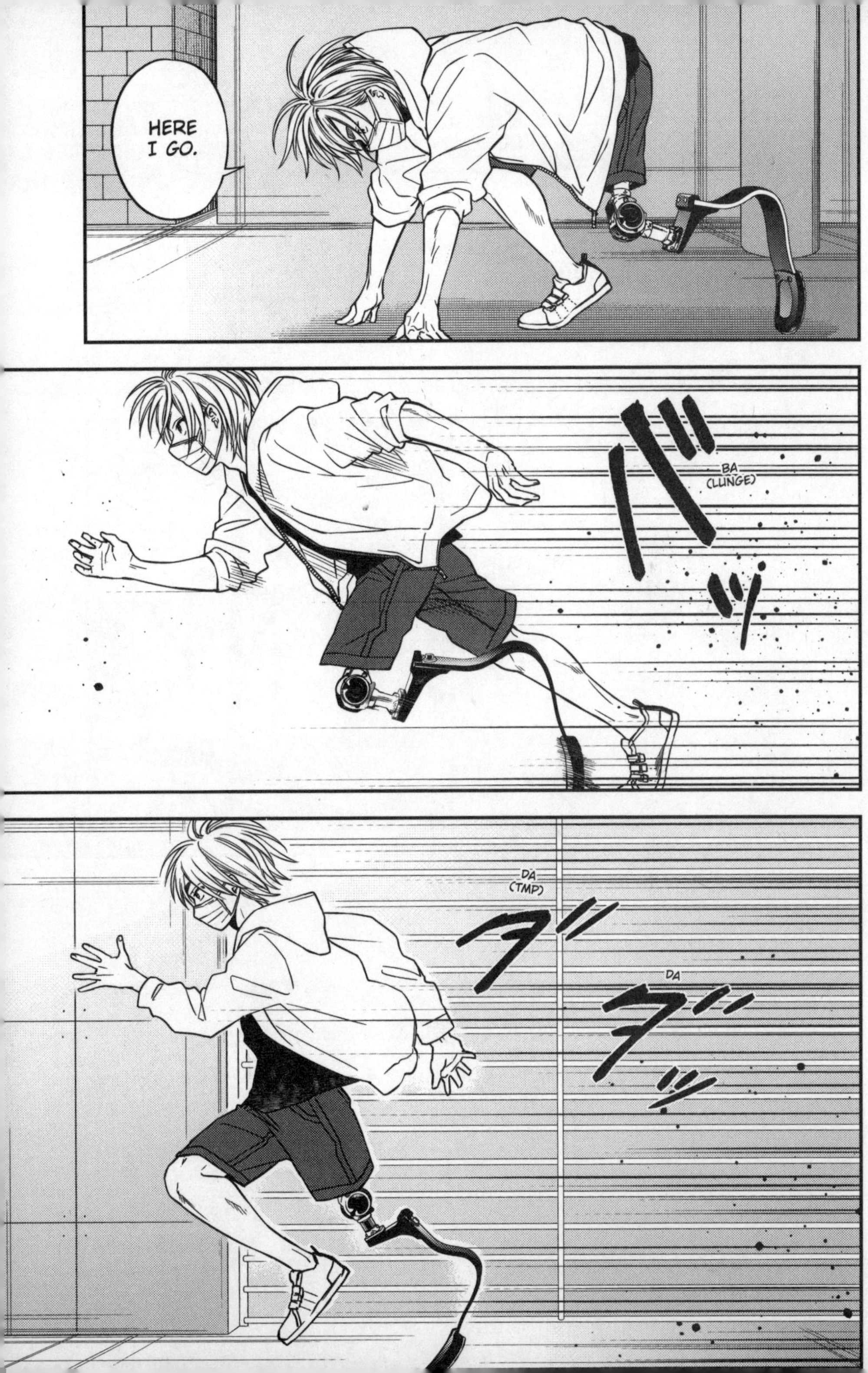
HERE I GO.
バッ
BA (LUNGE)
ダッ
DA (TMP)
ダッ
DA

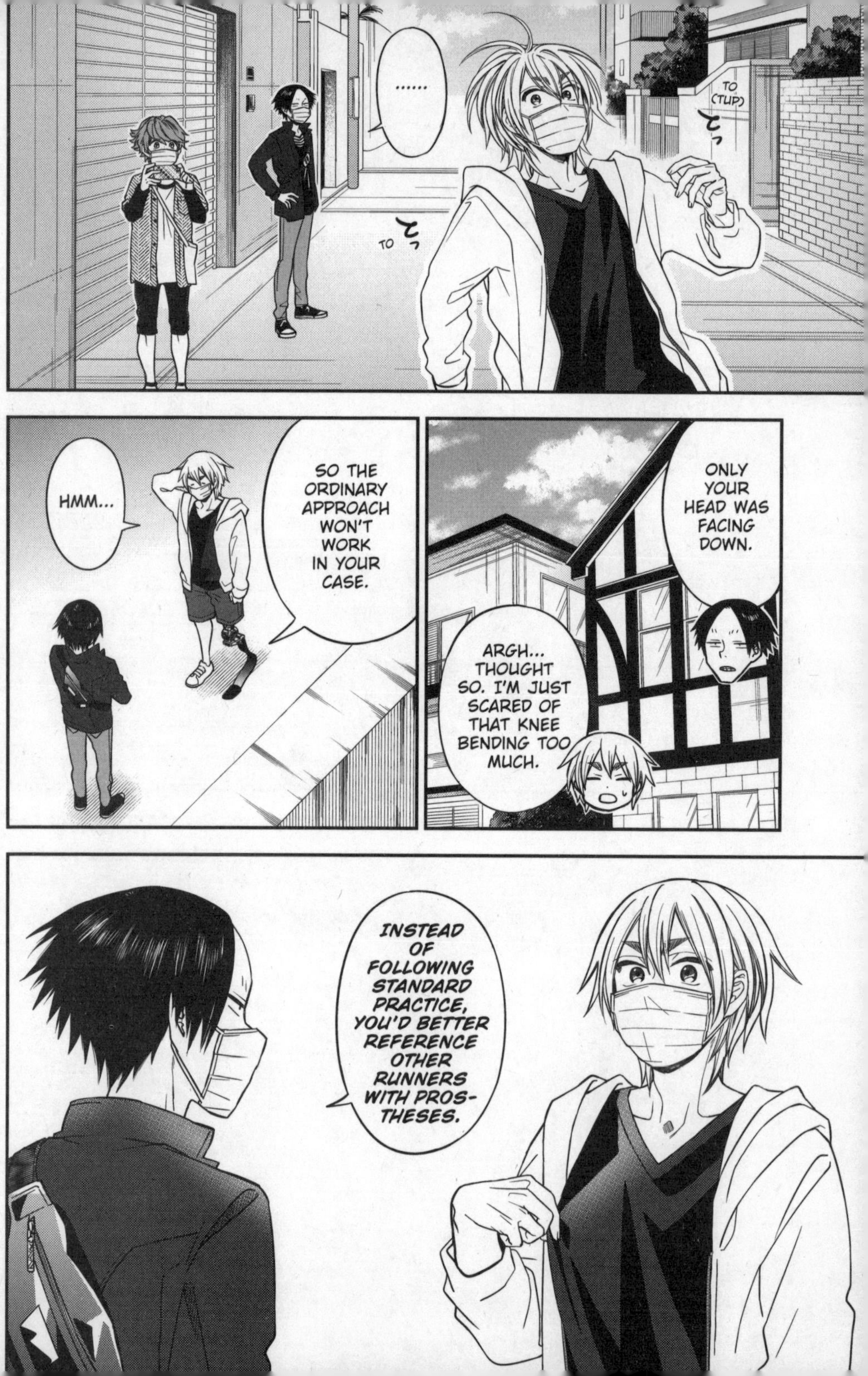
TO (TUP)
てっ
......
てっ
TO
ONLY YOUR HEAD WAS FACING DOWN.
ARGH... THOUGHT SO. I'M JUST SCARED OF THAT KNEE BENDING TOO MUCH.
SO THE ORDINARY APPROACH WON'T WORK IN YOUR CASE.
HMM...
INSTEAD OF FOLLOWING STANDARD PRACTICE, YOU'D BETTER REFERENCE OTHER RUNNERS WITH PROS-THESES.

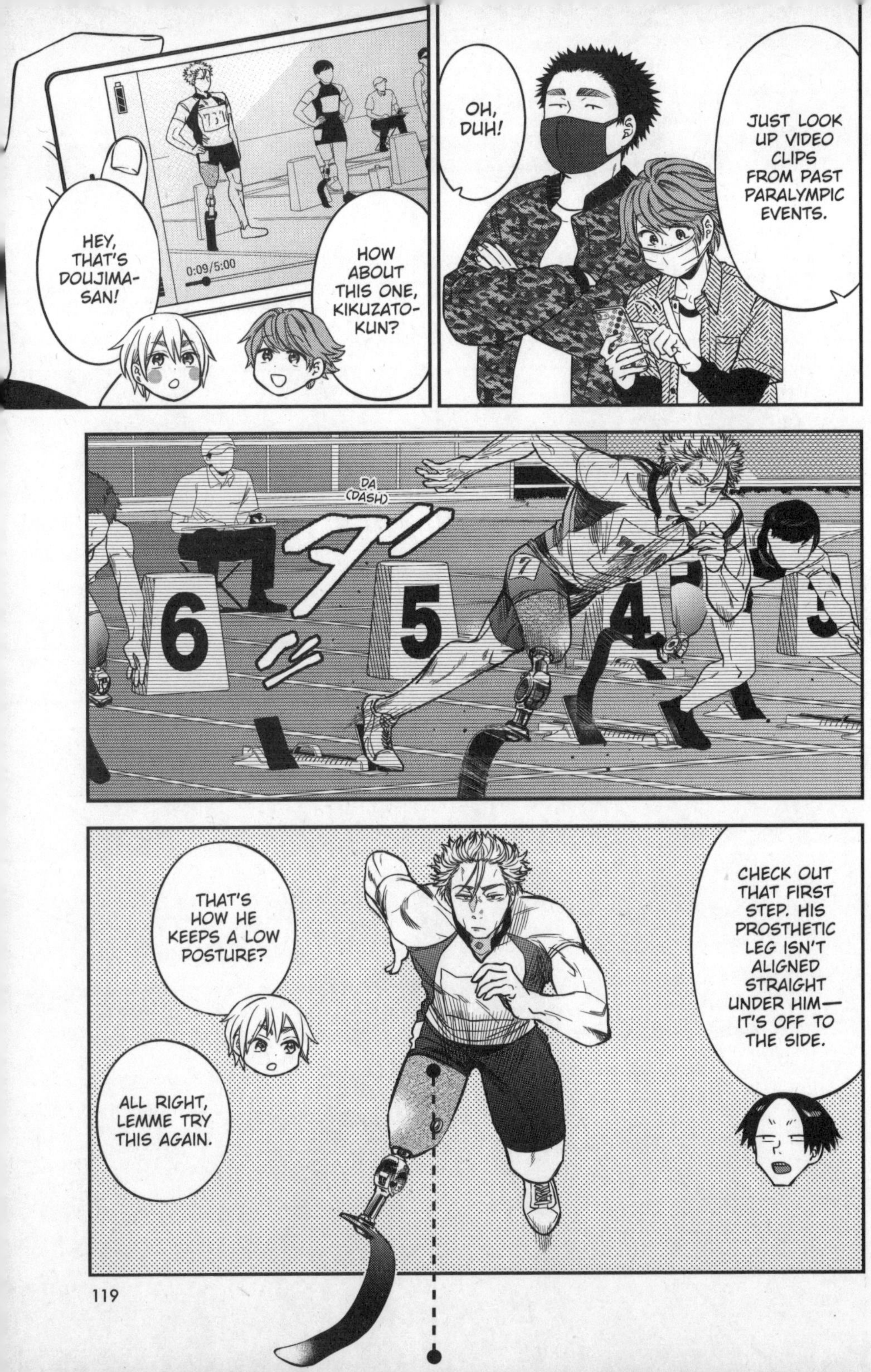
JUST LOOK UP VIDEO CLIPS FROM PAST PARALYMPIC EVENTS.
OH, DUH!
HOW ABOUT THIS ONE, KIKUZATO-KUN?
HEY, THAT'S DOUJIMA-SAN!
0:09/5:00
DA (DASH)
CHECK OUT THAT FIRST STEP. HIS PROSTHETIC LEG ISN'T ALIGNED STRAIGHT UNDER HIM—IT'S OFF TO THE SIDE.
THAT'S HOW HE KEEPS A LOW POSTURE?
ALL RIGHT, LEMME TRY THIS AGAIN.

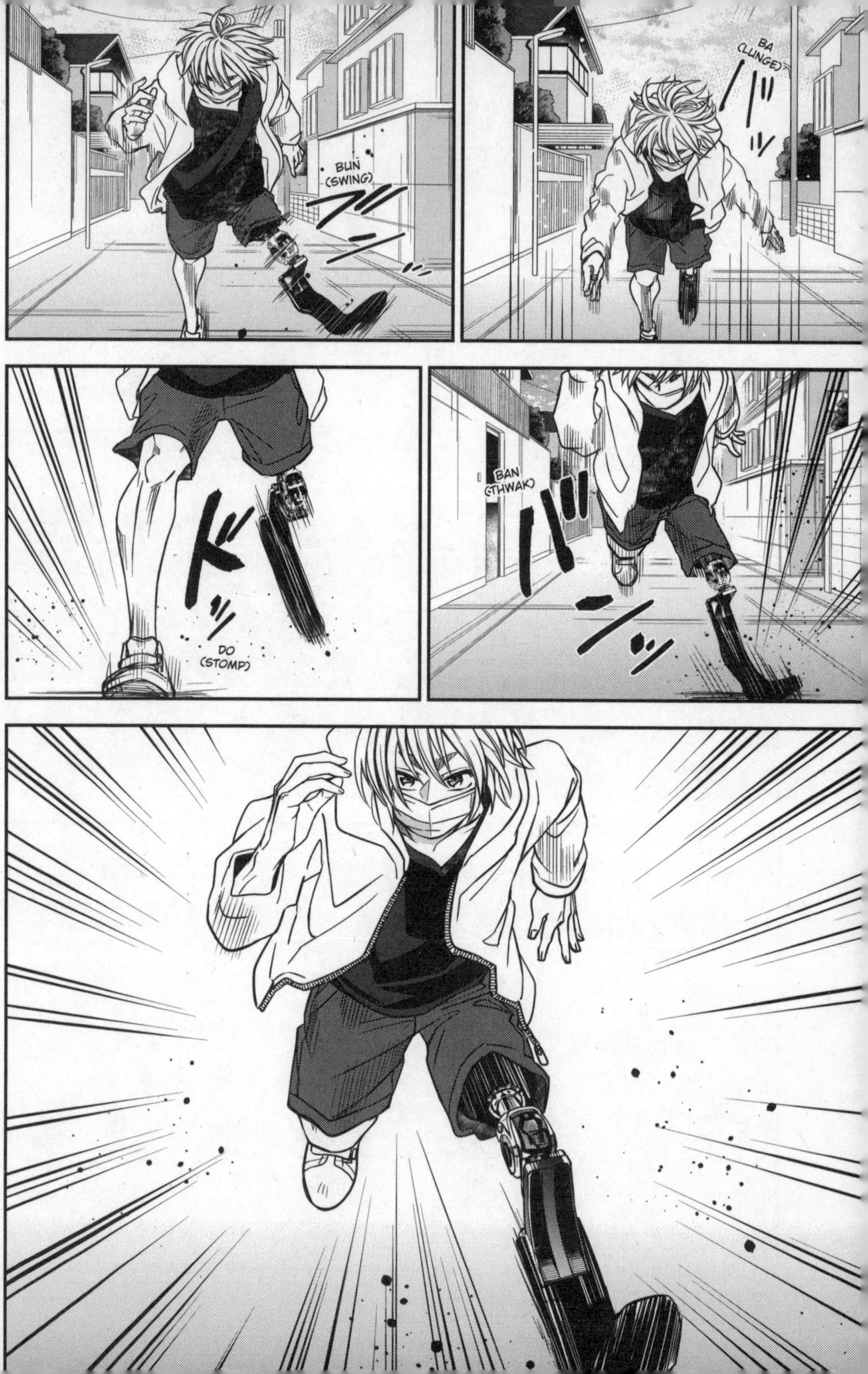
BA (LUNGE)
BUN (SWING)
BAN (THWAK)
DO (STOMP)

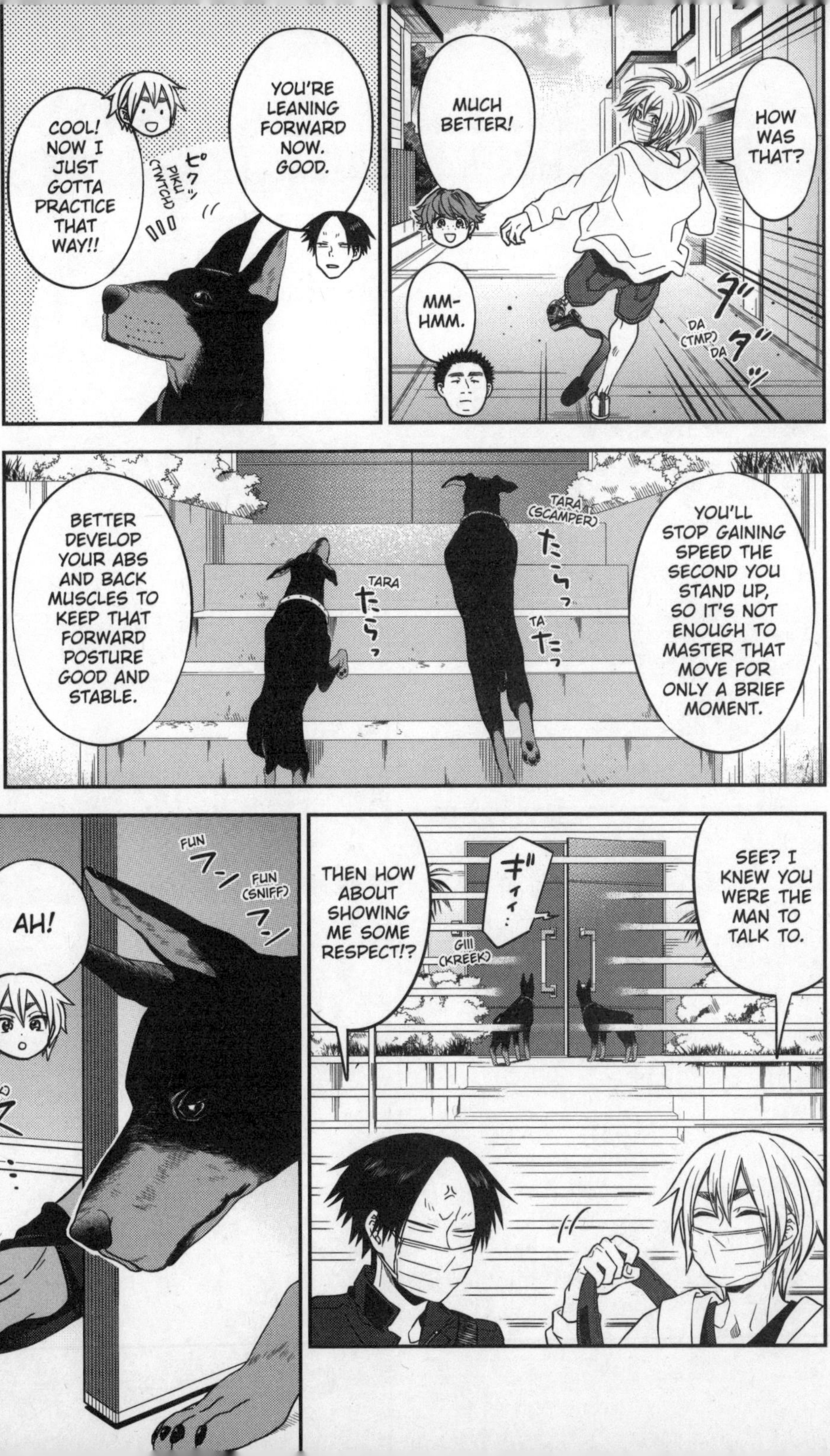

HOW WAS THAT?
MUCH BETTER!
MM-HMM.
DA (TMP) DA
YOU'RE LEANING FORWARD NOW. GOOD.
PIKU (TWTCH)
COOL! NOW I JUST GOTTA PRACTICE THAT WAY!!
YOU'LL STOP GAINING SPEED THE SECOND YOU STAND UP, SO IT'S NOT ENOUGH TO MASTER THAT MOVE FOR ONLY A BRIEF MOMENT.
TARA (SCAMPER)
TA
TARA
BETTER DEVELOP YOUR ABS AND BACK MUSCLES TO KEEP THAT FORWARD POSTURE GOOD AND STABLE.
SEE? I KNEW YOU WERE THE MAN TO TALK TO.
GIII (KREEK)
THEN HOW ABOUT SHOWING ME SOME RESPECT!?
FUN
FUN (SNIFF)
AH!
SU (SSK)

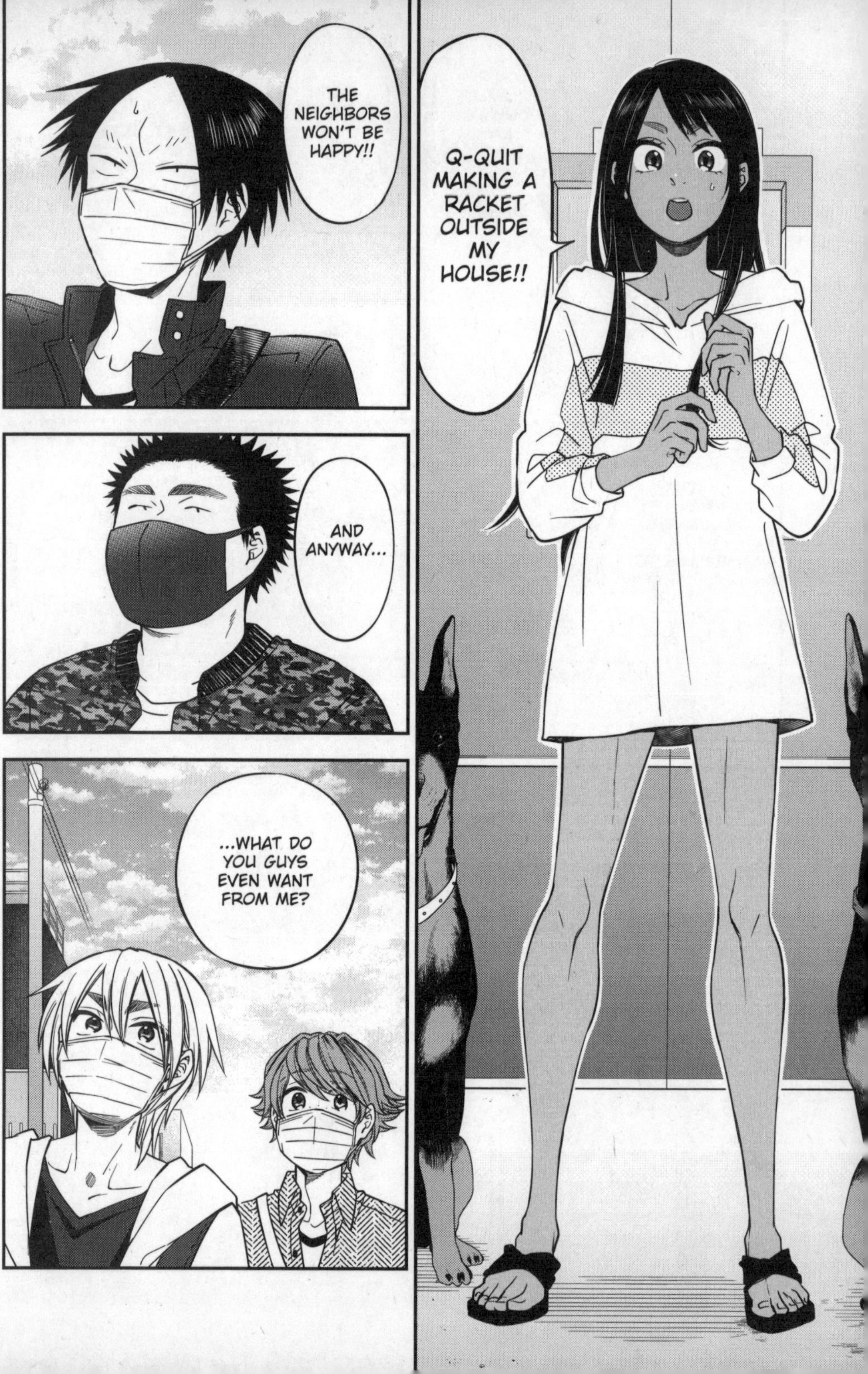
Q-QUIT MAKING A RACKET OUTSIDE MY HOUSE!!
THE NEIGHBORS WON'T BE HAPPY!!
AND ANYWAY...
...WHAT DO YOU GUYS EVEN WANT FROM ME?

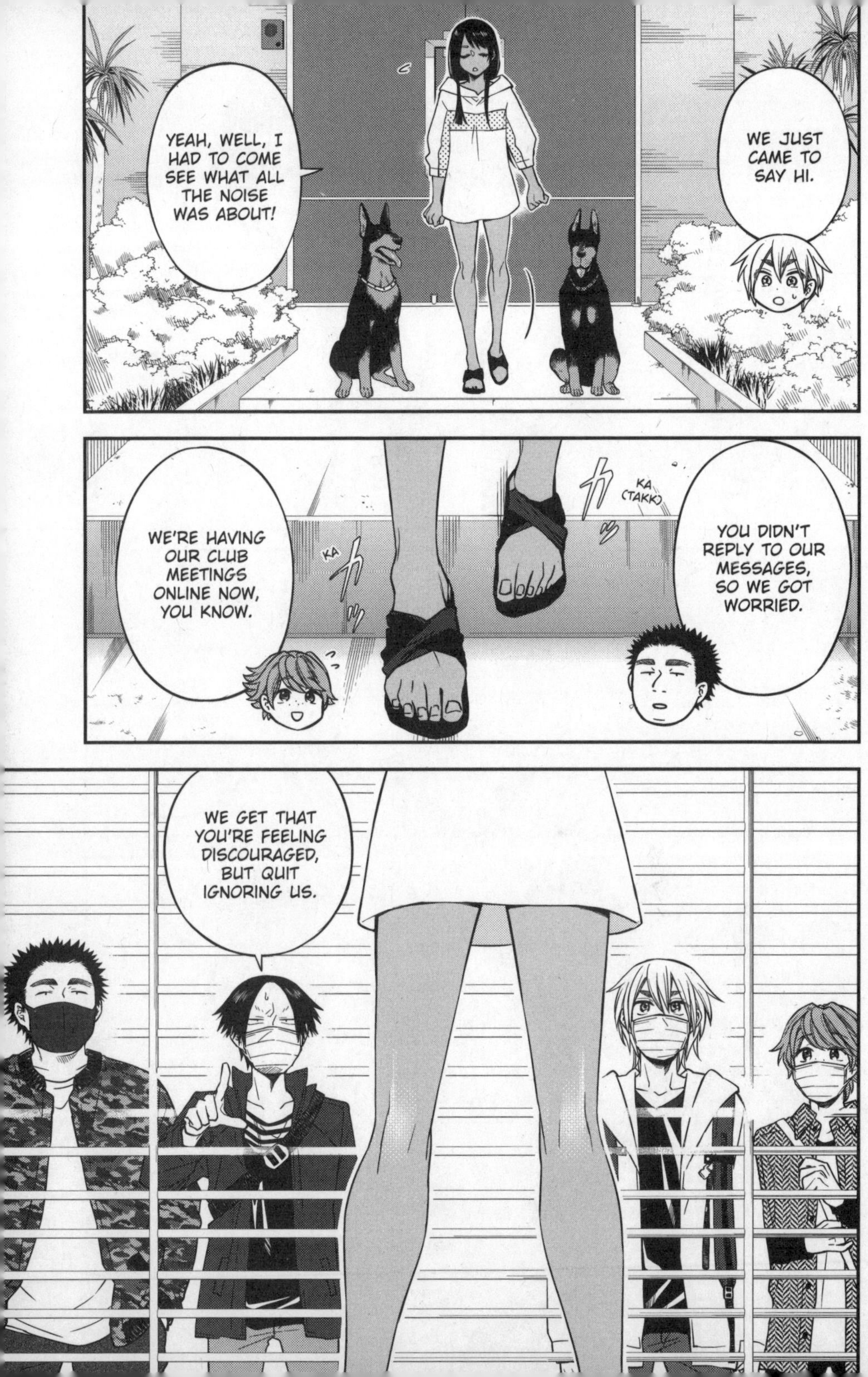
WE JUST CAME TO SAY HI.
YEAH, WELL, I HAD TO COME SEE WHAT ALL THE NOISE WAS ABOUT!
YOU DIDN'T REPLY TO OUR MESSAGES, SO WE GOT WORRIED.
KA (TAKK)
KA
WE'RE HAVING OUR CLUB MEETINGS ONLINE NOW, YOU KNOW.
WE GET THAT YOU'RE FEELING DISCOURAGED, BUT QUIT IGNORING US.

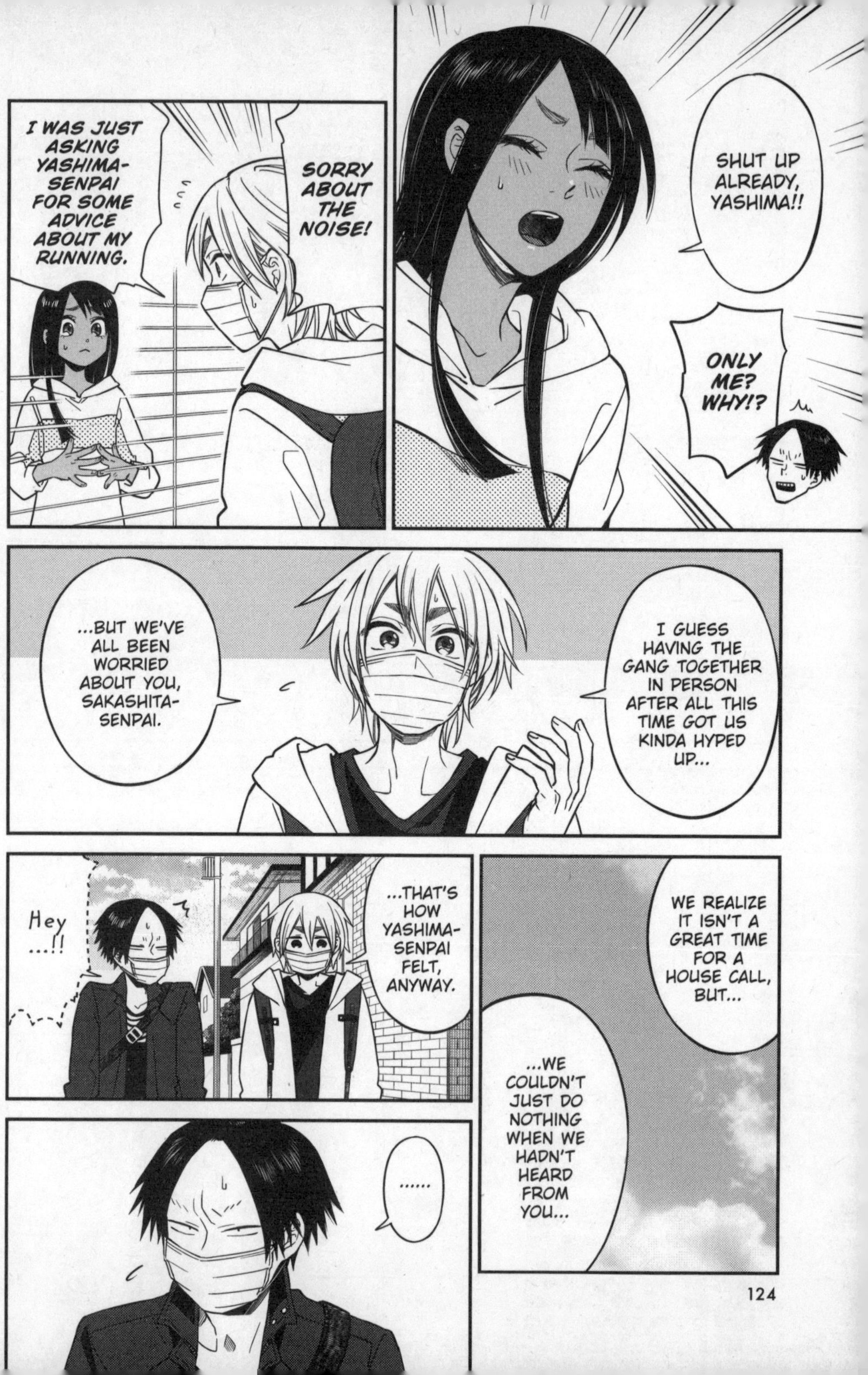
SHUT UP ALREADY, YASHIMA!!
ONLY ME? WHY!?
SORRY ABOUT THE NOISE!
I WAS JUST ASKING YASHIMA-SENPAI FOR SOME ADVICE ABOUT MY RUNNING.
I GUESS HAVING THE GANG TOGETHER IN PERSON AFTER ALL THIS TIME GOT US KINDA HYPED UP...
...BUT WE'VE ALL BEEN WORRIED ABOUT YOU, SAKASHITA-SENPAI.
WE REALIZE IT ISN'T A GREAT TIME FOR A HOUSE CALL, BUT...
...WE COULDN'T JUST DO NOTHING WHEN WE HADN'T HEARD FROM YOU...
...THAT'S HOW YASHIMA-SENPAI FELT, ANYWAY.
Hey ...!!
......

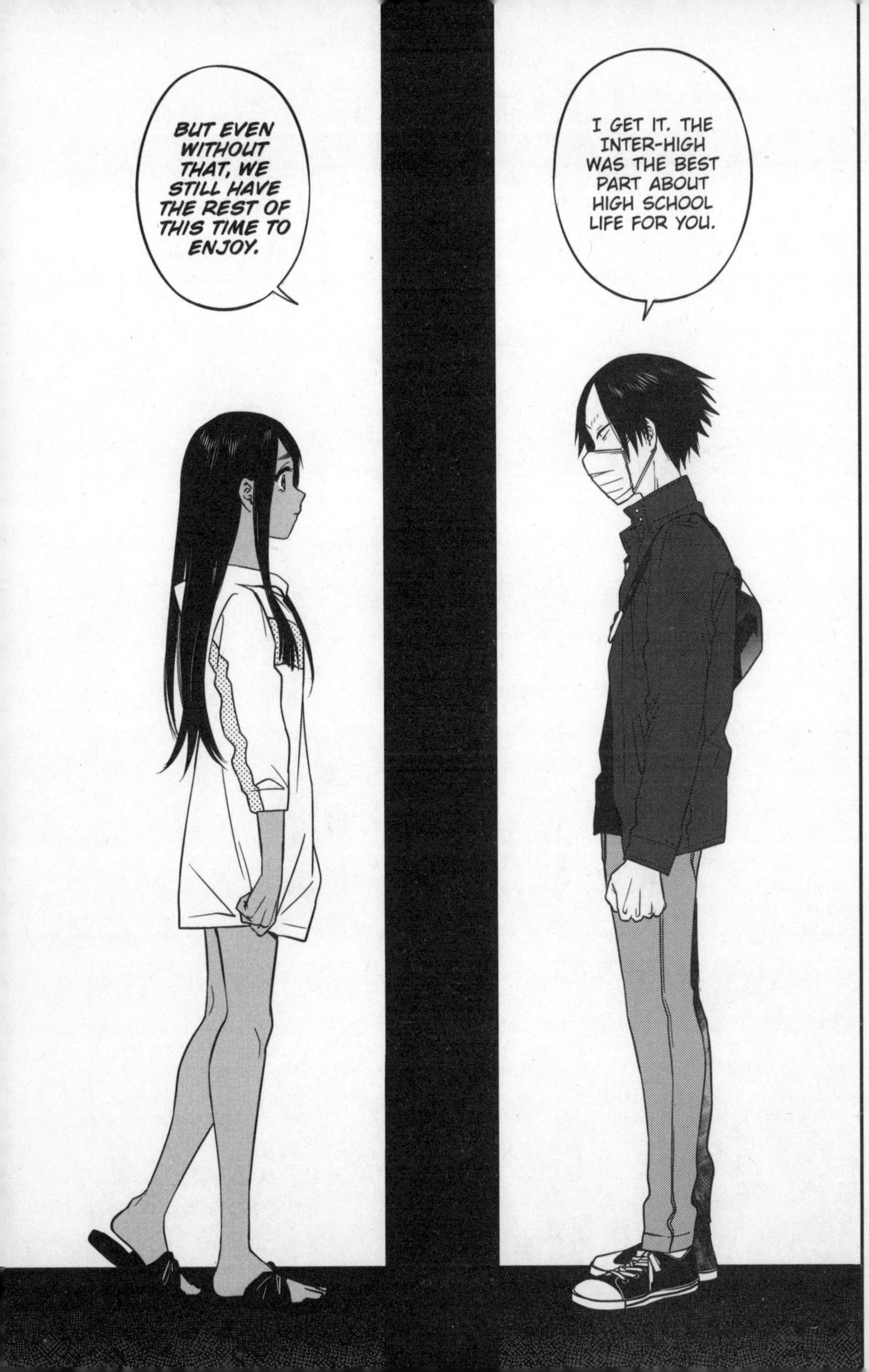
I GET IT. THE INTER-HIGH WAS THE BEST PART ABOUT HIGH SCHOOL LIFE FOR YOU.
BUT EVEN WITHOUT THAT, WE STILL HAVE THE REST OF THIS TIME TO ENJOY.

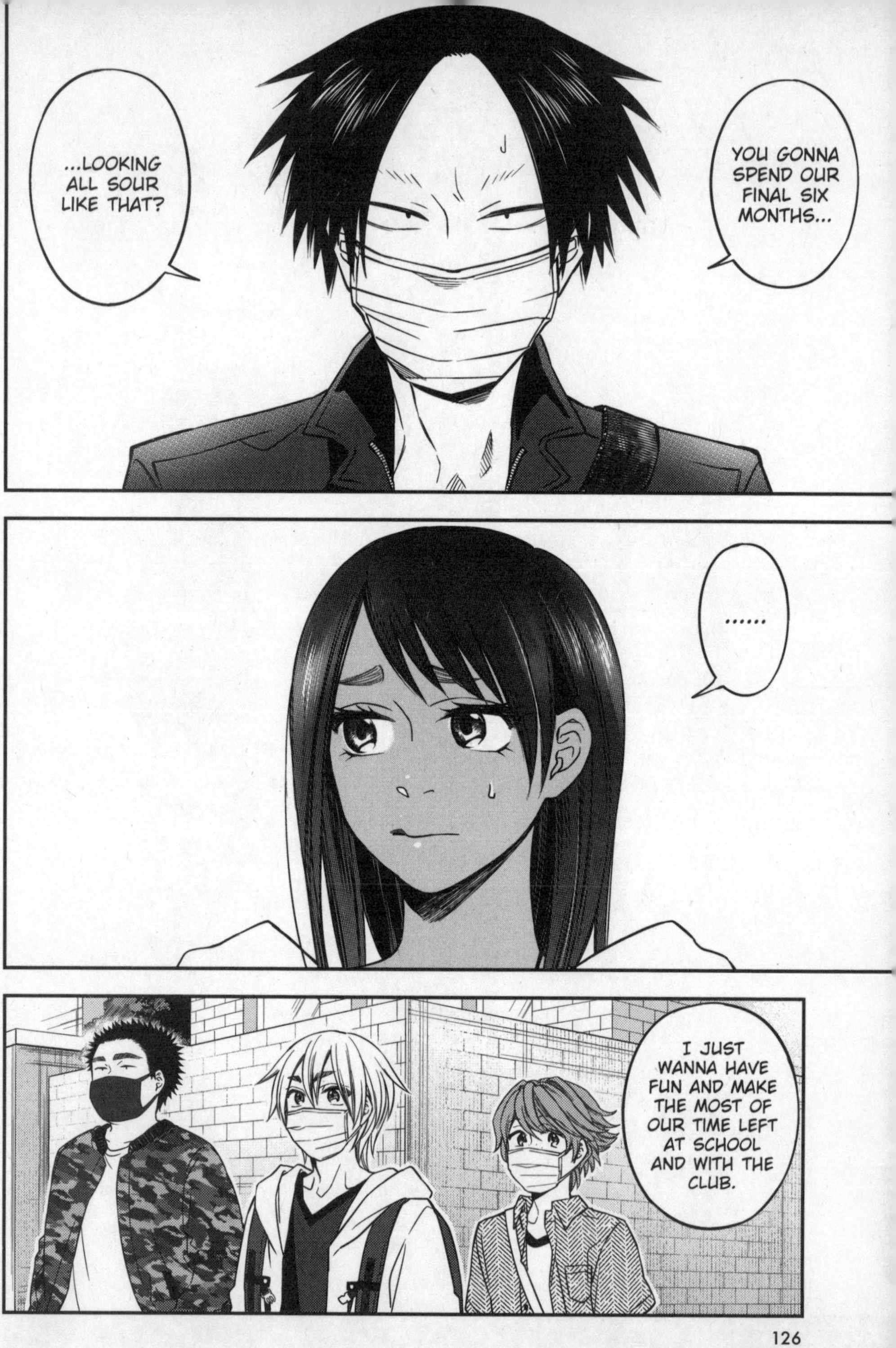
YOU GONNA SPEND OUR FINAL SIX MONTHS...
...LOOKING ALL SOUR LIKE THAT?
......
I JUST WANNA HAVE FUN AND MAKE THE MOST OF OUR TIME LEFT AT SCHOOL AND WITH THE CLUB.

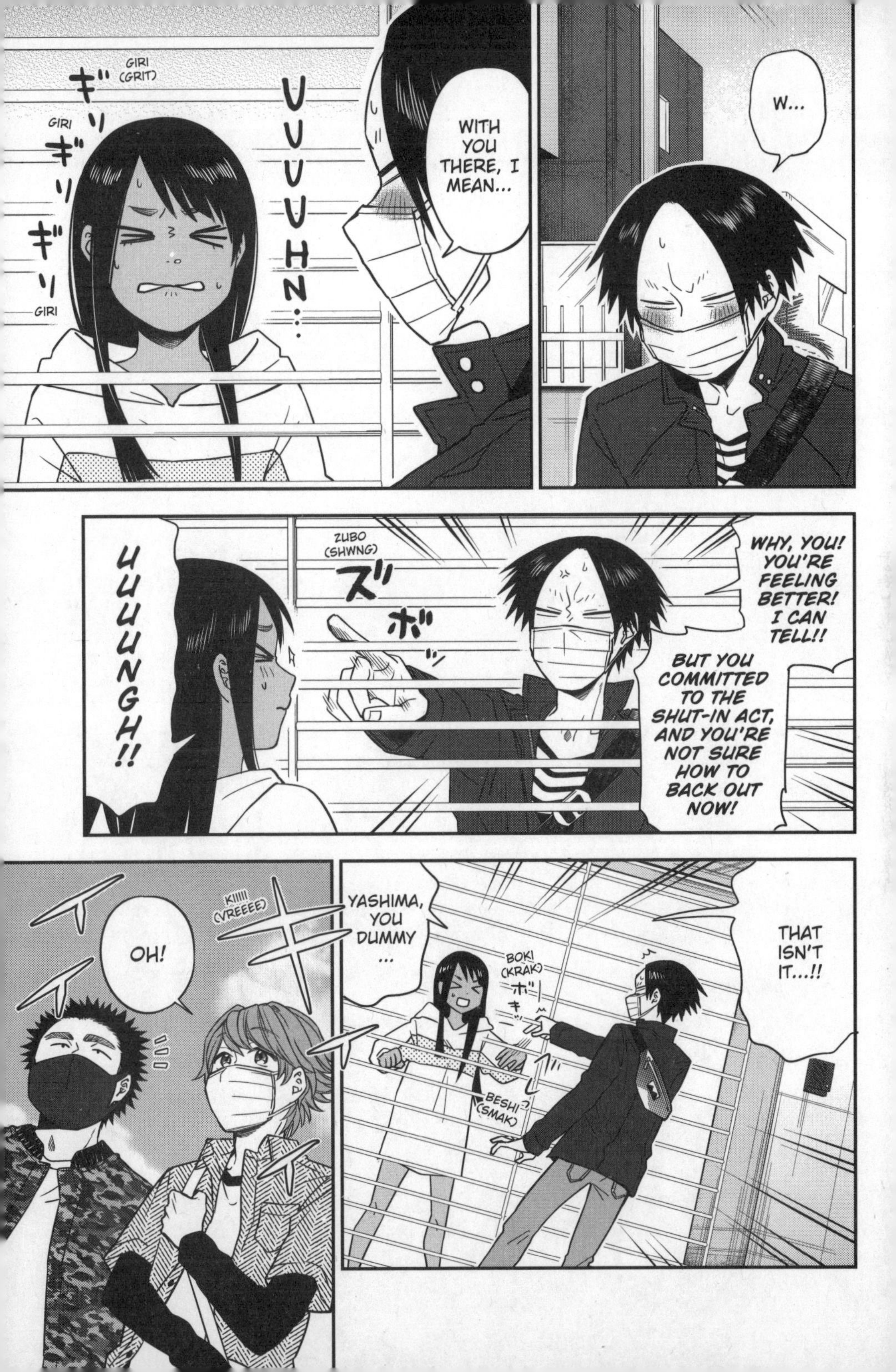
W...
WITH YOU THERE, I MEAN...
GIRI (GRIT)
GIRI
GIRI
UUUUHN...
WHY, YOU! YOU'RE FEELING BETTER! I CAN TELL!!
BUT YOU COMMITTED TO THE SHUT-IN ACT, AND YOU'RE NOT SURE HOW TO BACK OUT NOW!
ZUBO (SHWNG)
UUUUNGH!!
THAT ISN'T IT...!!
YASHIMA, YOU DUMMY ...
BOKI (KRAK)
BESHI (SMAK)
KIIIII (VREEEE)
OH!

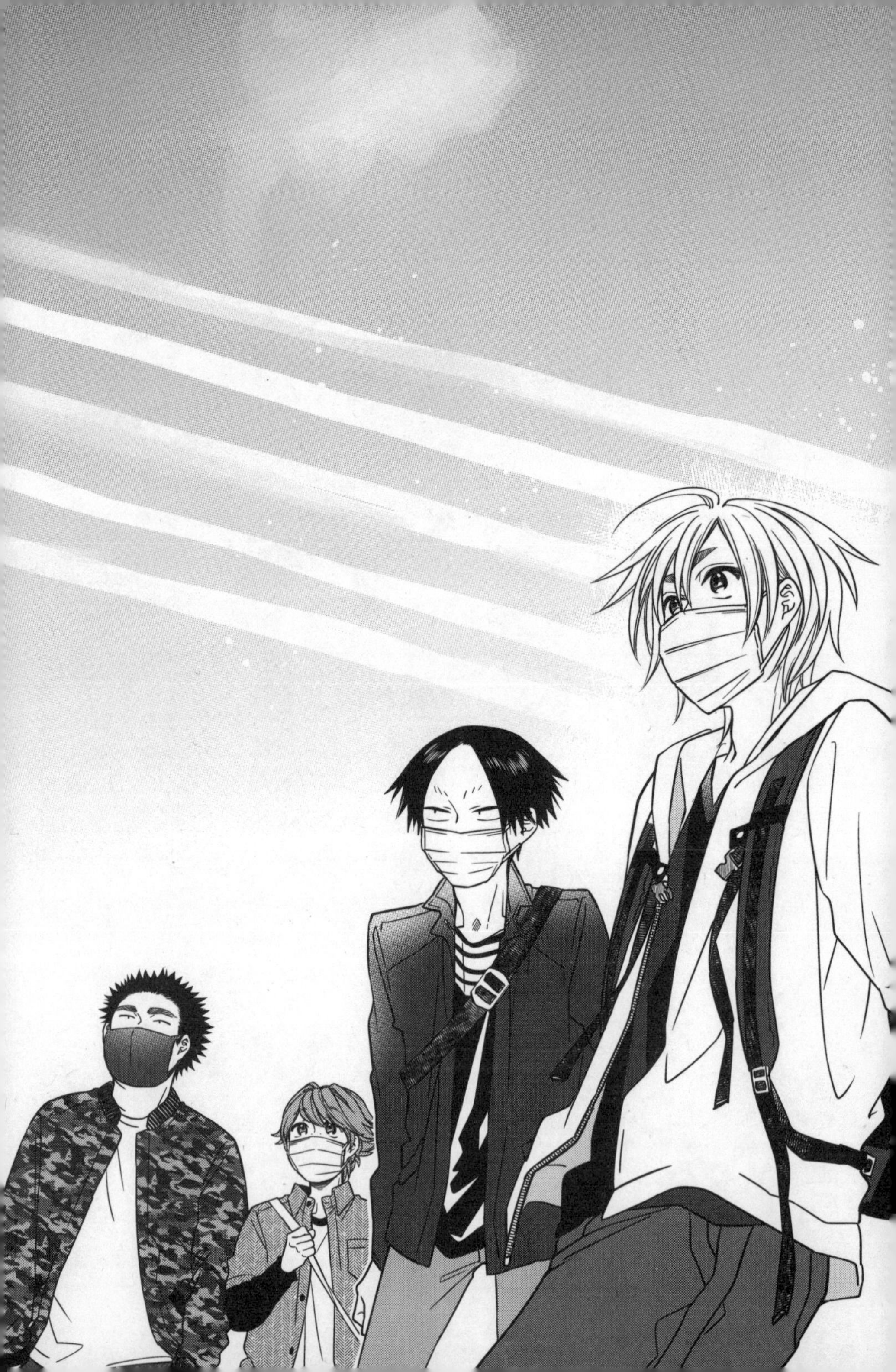

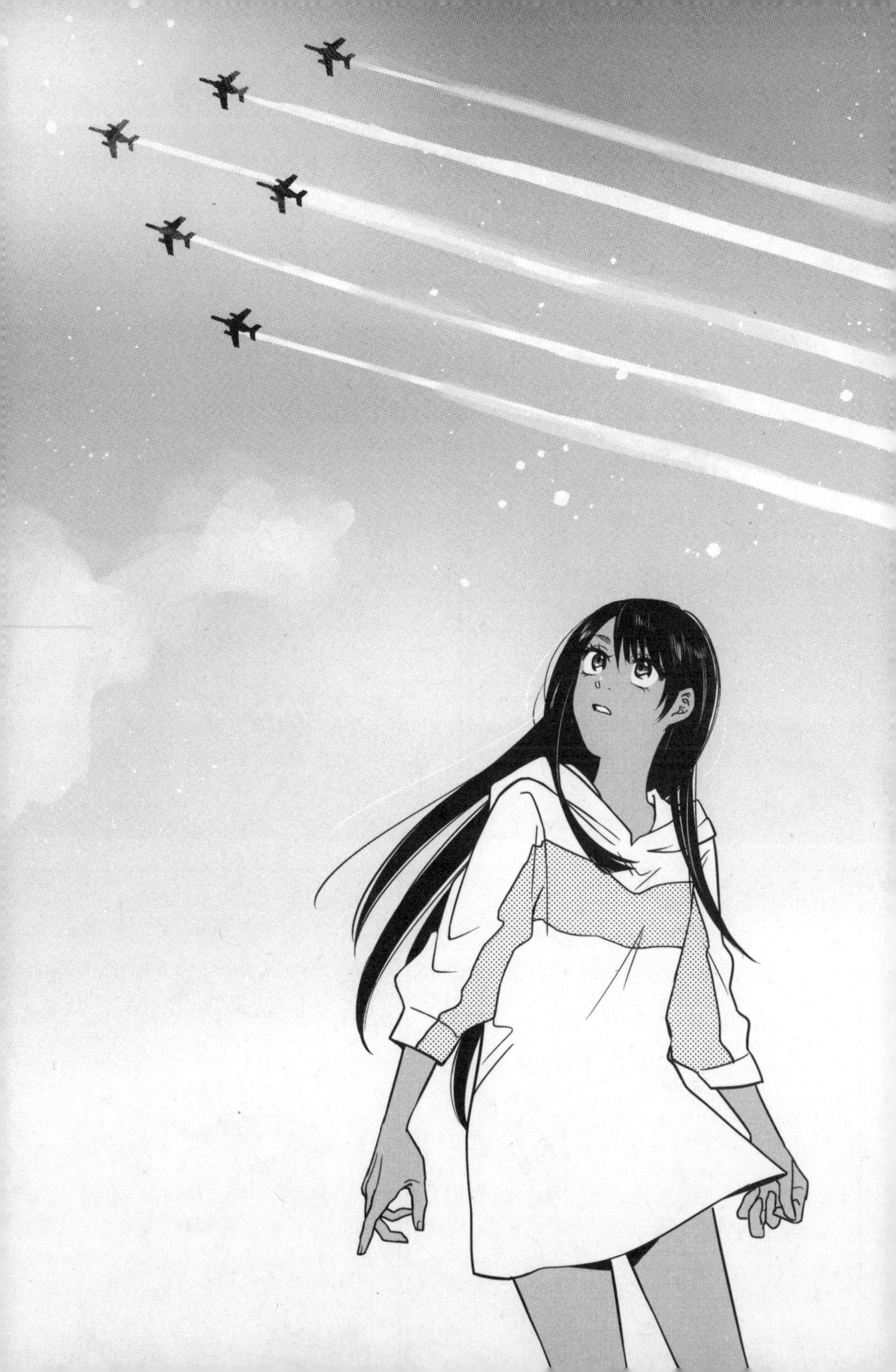

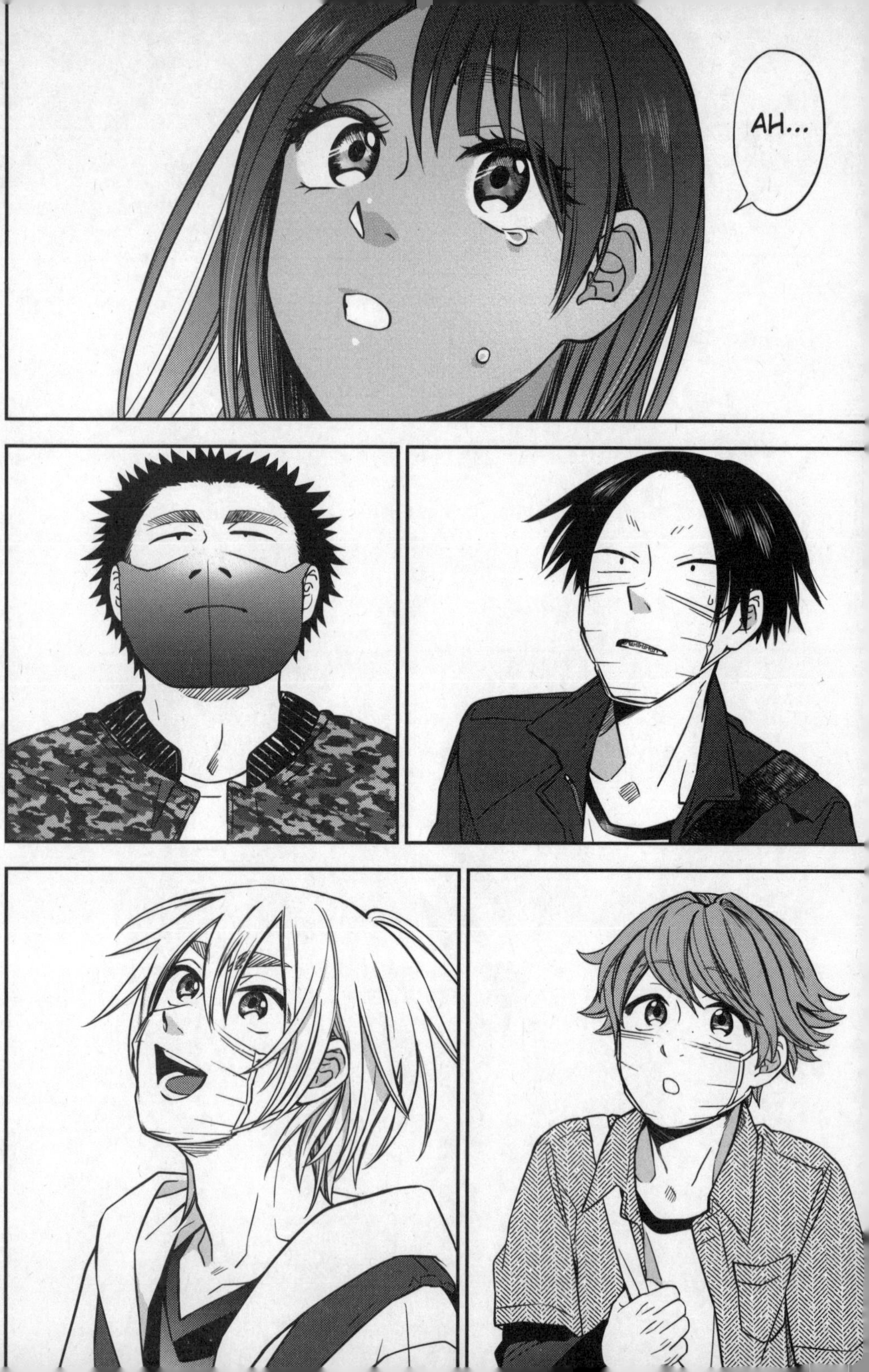
AH...

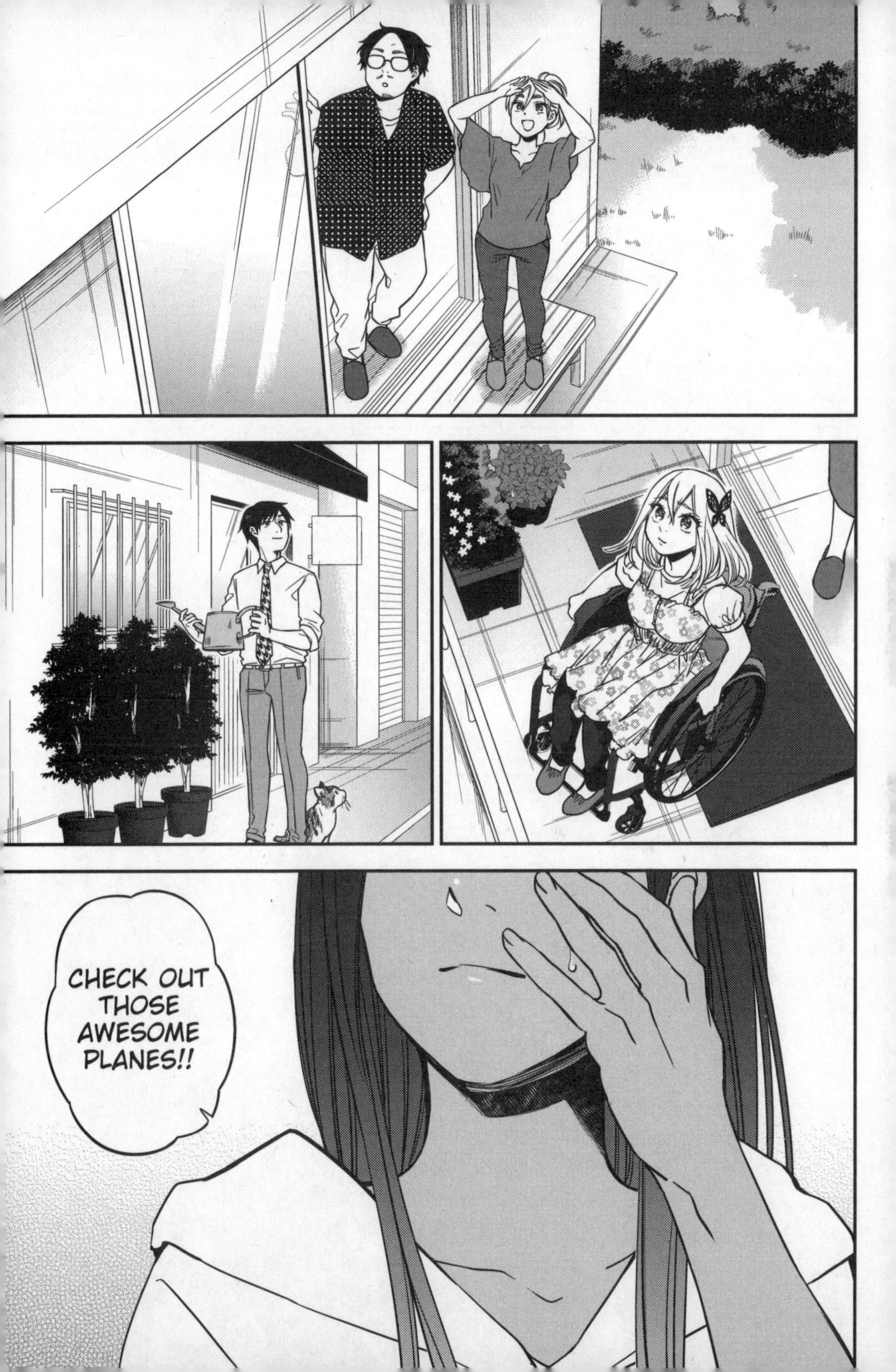
CHECK OUT THOSE AWESOME PLANES!!

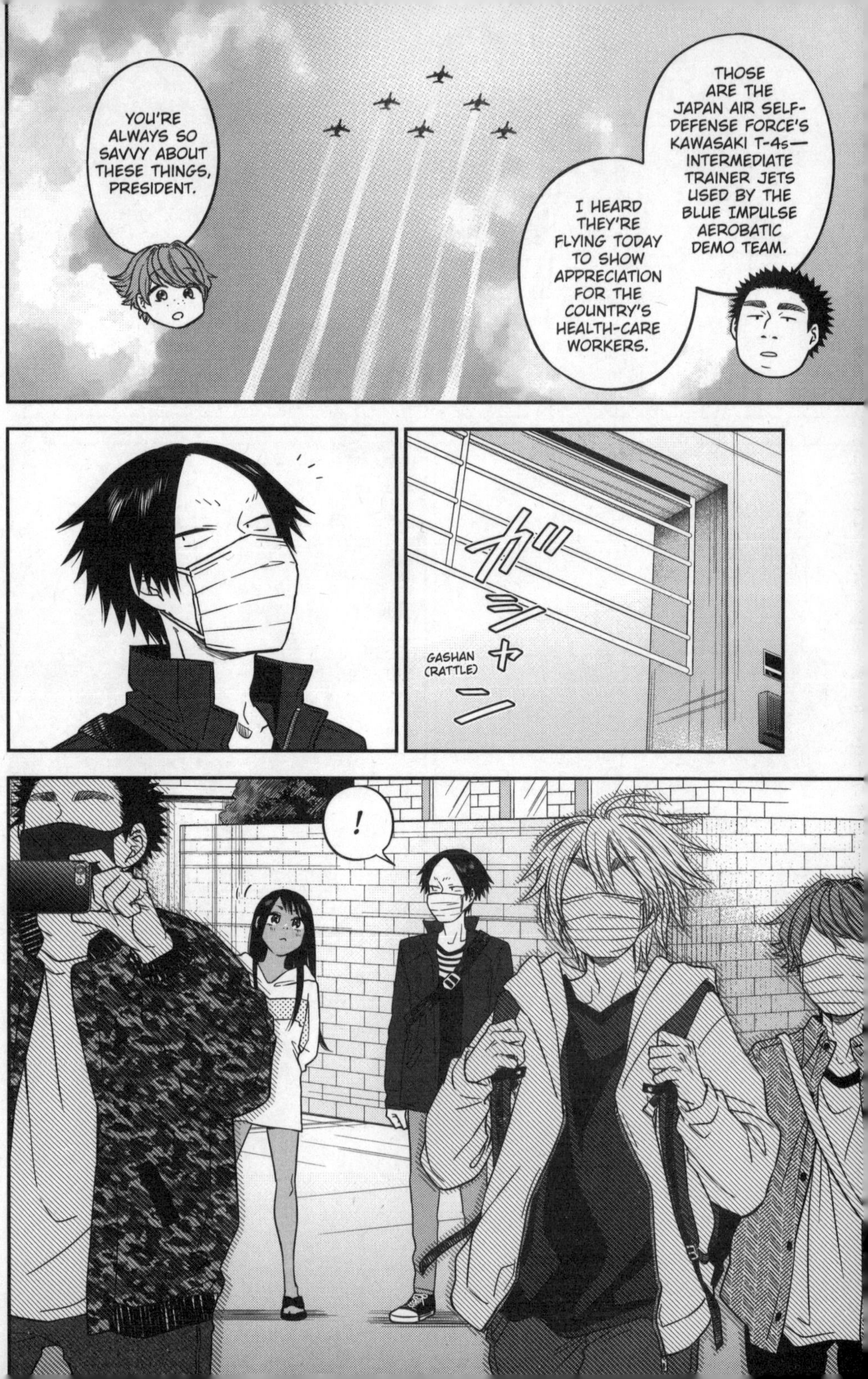
THOSE ARE THE JAPAN AIR SELF-DEFENSE FORCE'S KAWASAKI T-4s—INTERMEDIATE TRAINER JETS USED BY THE BLUE IMPULSE AEROBATIC DEMO TEAM.
I HEARD THEY'RE FLYING TODAY TO SHOW APPRECIATION FOR THE COUNTRY'S HEALTH-CARE WORKERS.
YOU'RE ALWAYS SO SAVVY ABOUT THESE THINGS, PRESIDENT.
ガシャーン
GASHAN (RATTLE)
!

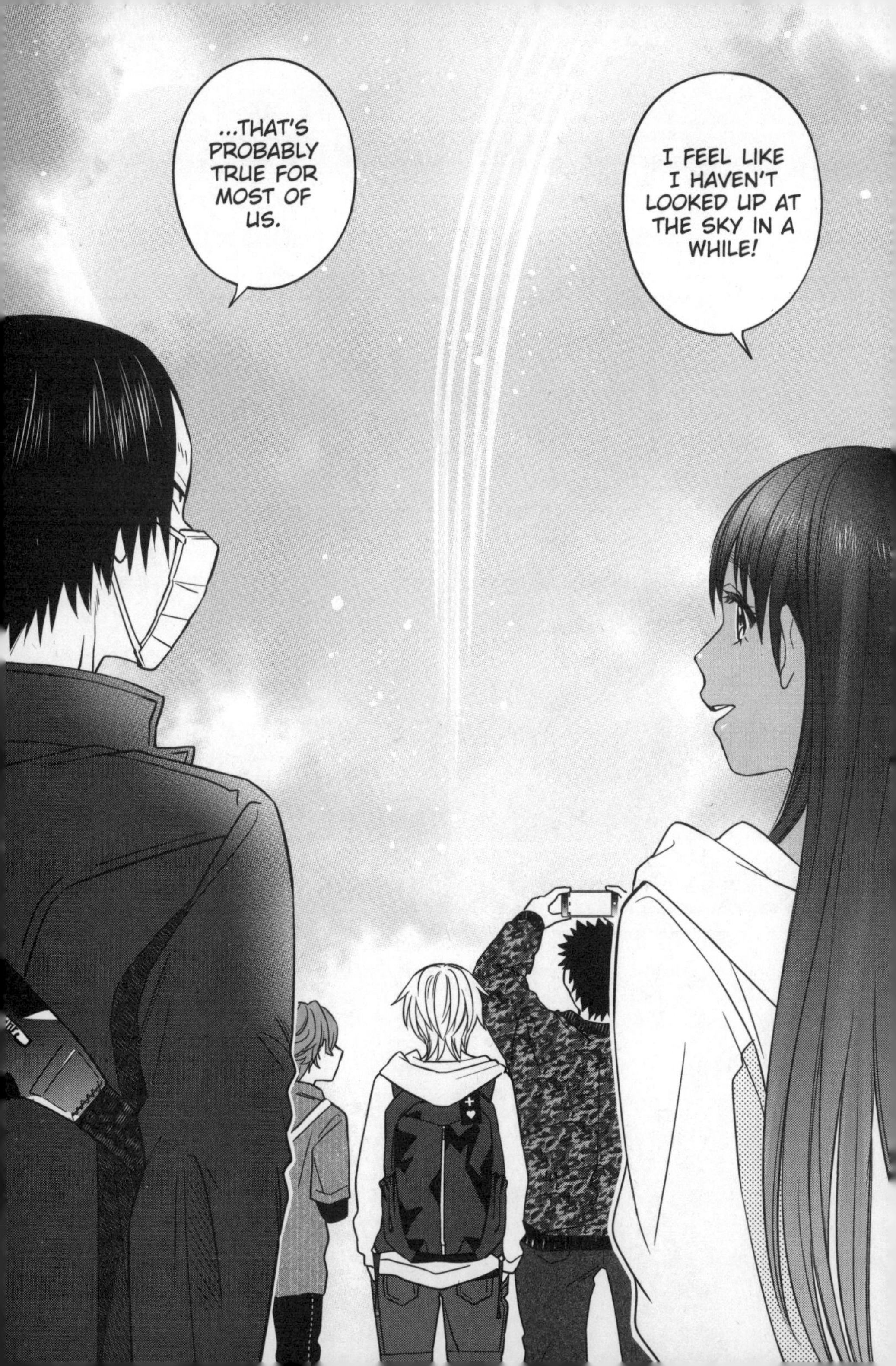
I FEEL LIKE I HAVEN'T LOOKED UP AT THE SKY IN A WHILE!
...THAT'S PROBABLY TRUE FOR MOST OF US.

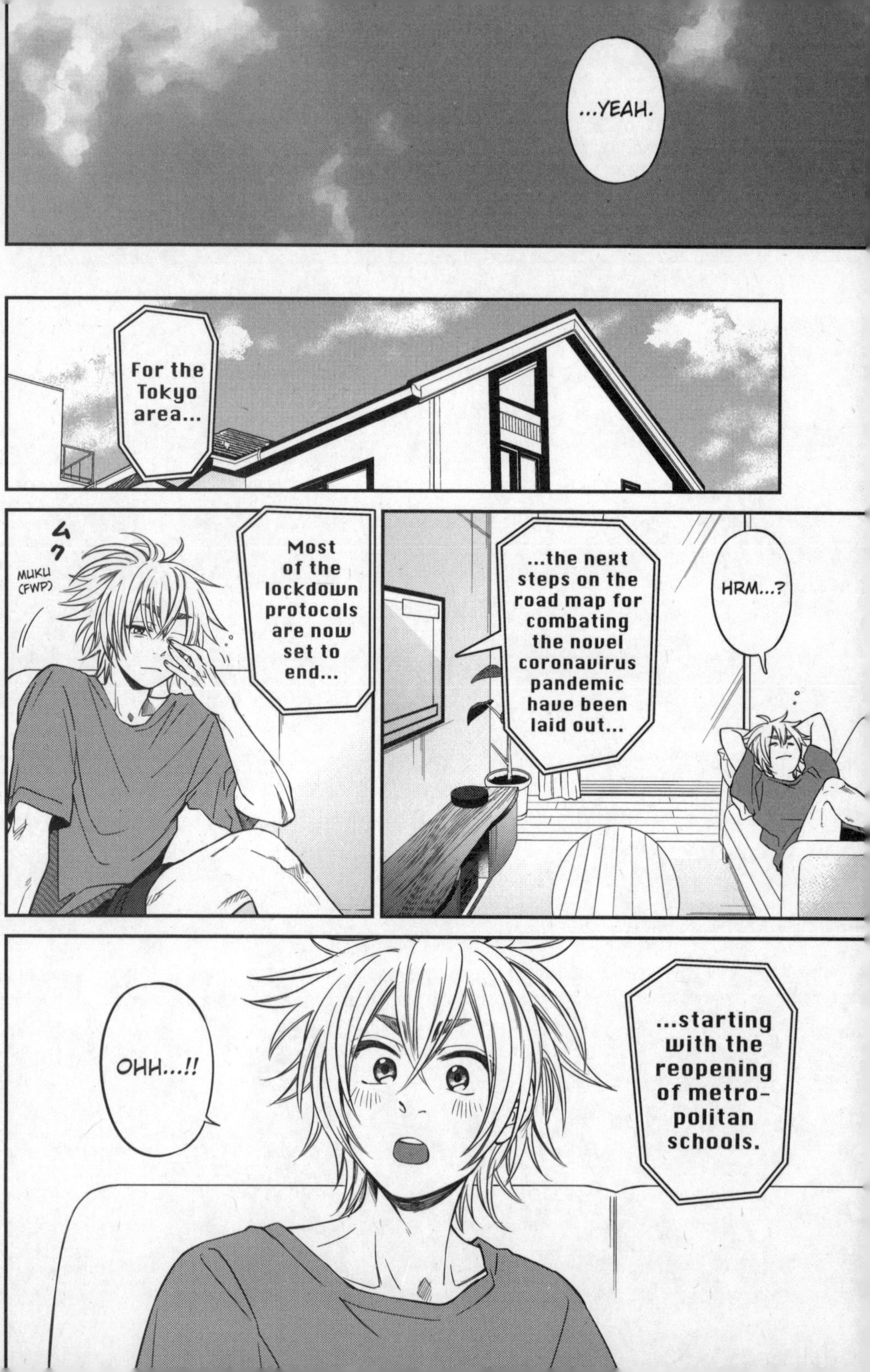

...YEAH.
For the Tokyo area...
HRM...?
...the next steps on the road map for combating the novel coronavirus pandemic have been laid out...
Most of the lockdown protocols are now set to end...
ムク
MUKU (FWP)
...starting with the reopening of metro-politan schools.
OHH...!!

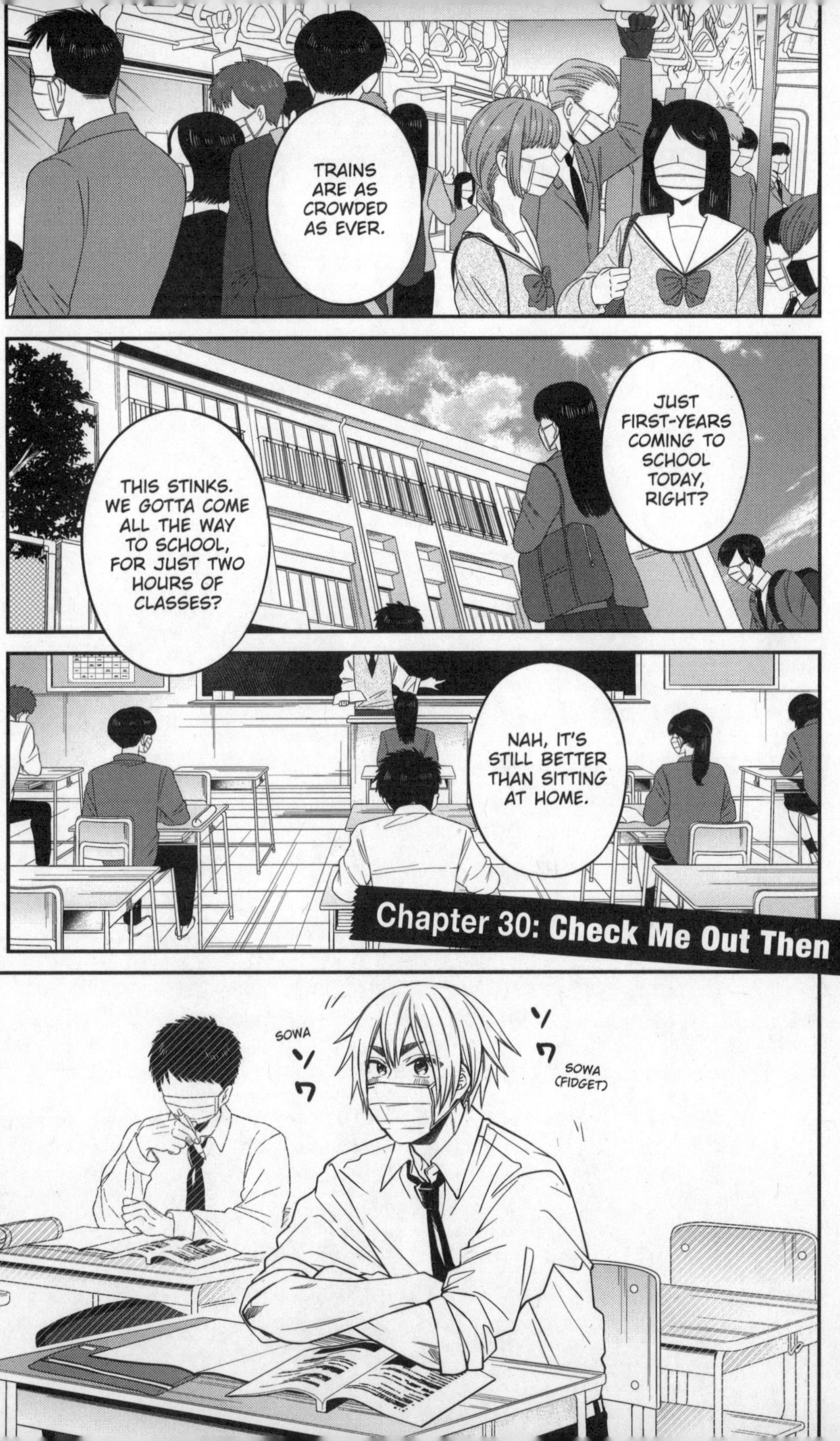
TRAINS ARE AS CROWDED AS EVER.
JUST FIRST-YEARS COMING TO SCHOOL TODAY, RIGHT?
THIS STINKS. WE GOTTA COME ALL THE WAY TO SCHOOL, FOR JUST TWO HOURS OF CLASSES?
NAH, IT'S STILL BETTER THAN SITTING AT HOME.
Chapter 30: Check Me Out Then
ソワ
SOWA (FIDGET)
ソワ
SOWA

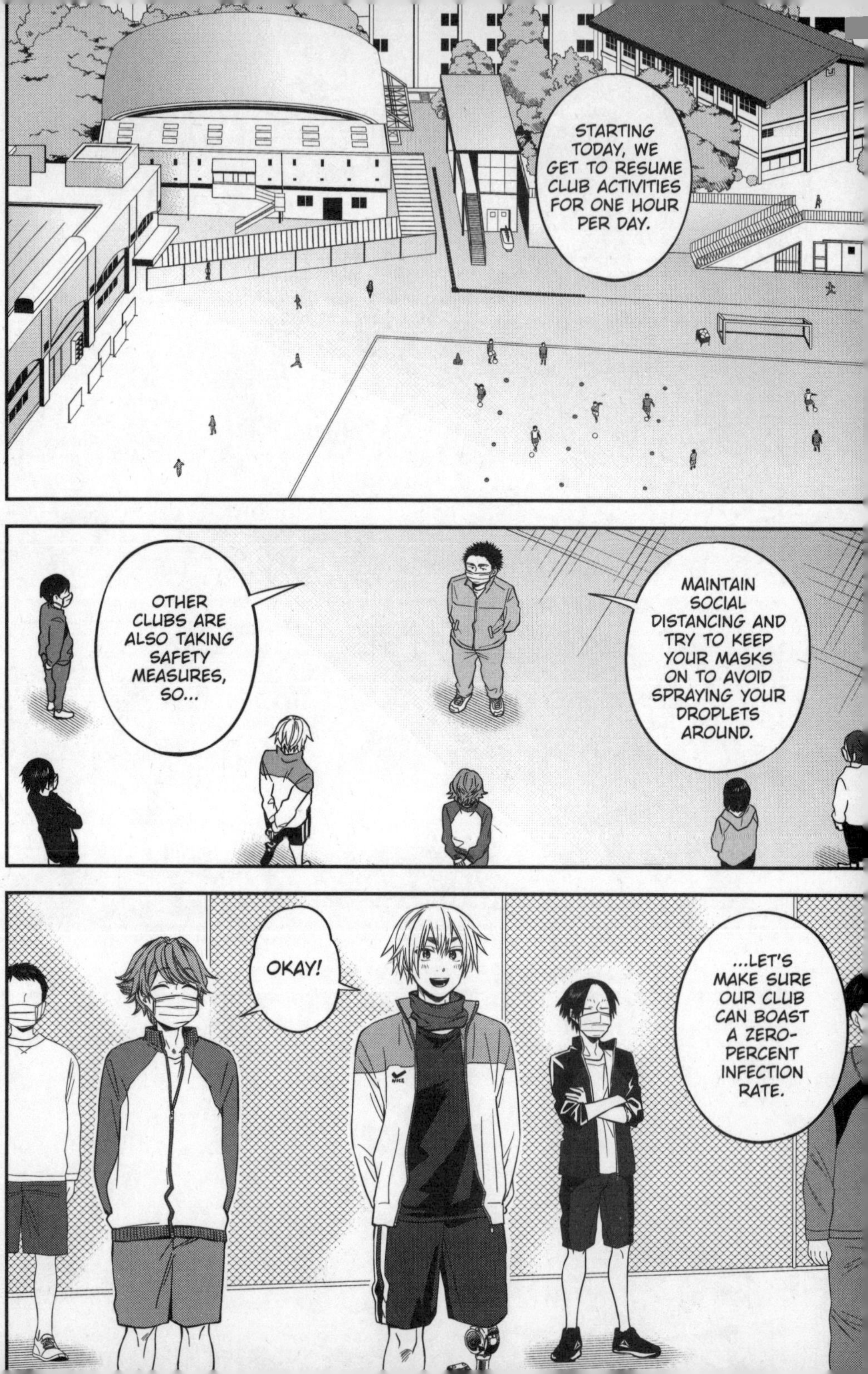
STARTING TODAY, WE GET TO RESUME CLUB ACTIVITIES FOR ONE HOUR PER DAY.
MAINTAIN SOCIAL DISTANCING AND TRY TO KEEP YOUR MASKS ON TO AVOID SPRAYING YOUR DROPLETS AROUND.
OTHER CLUBS ARE ALSO TAKING SAFETY MEASURES, SO...
...LET'S MAKE SURE OUR CLUB CAN BOAST A ZERO-PERCENT INFECTION RATE.
OKAY!

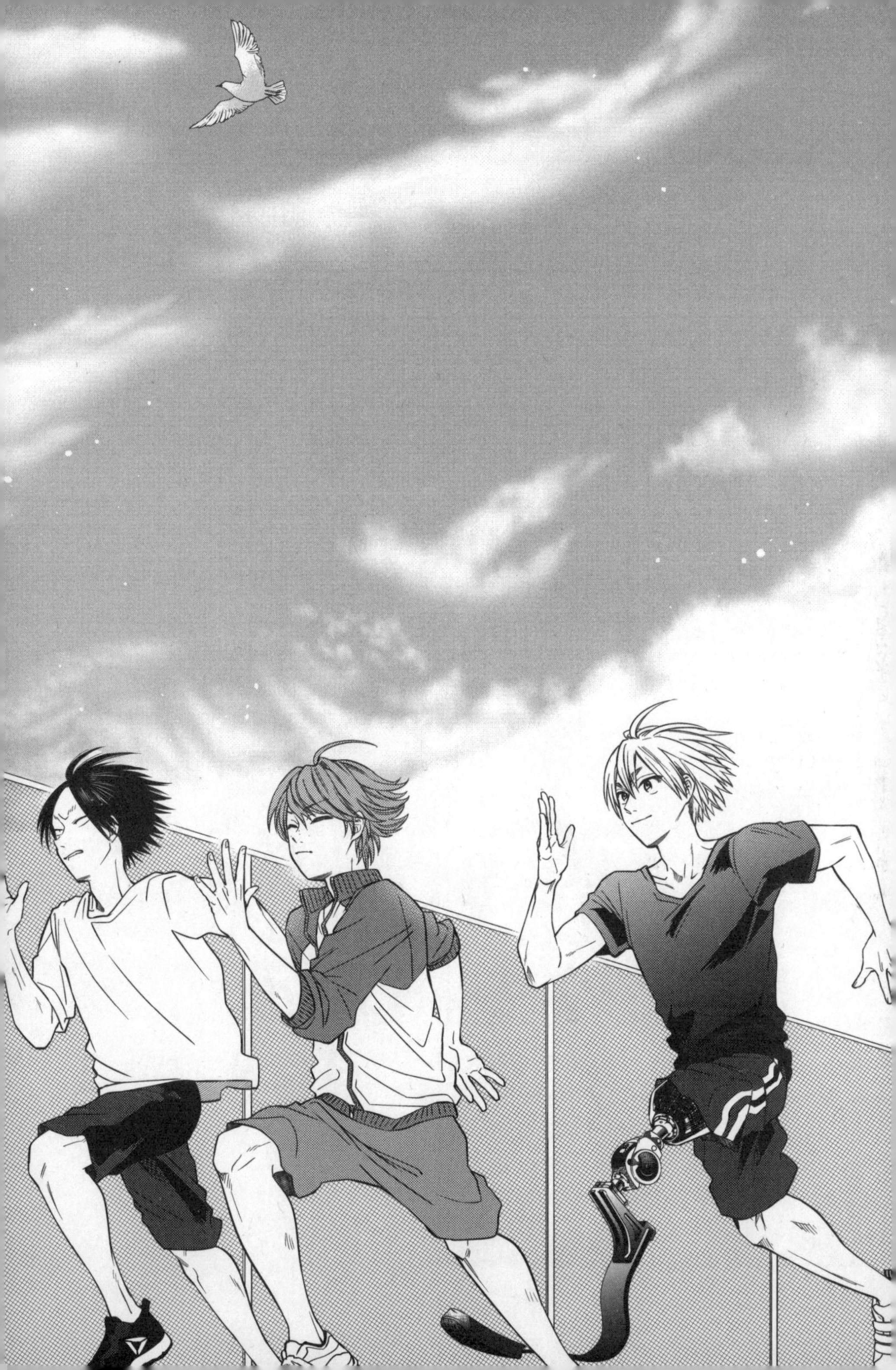

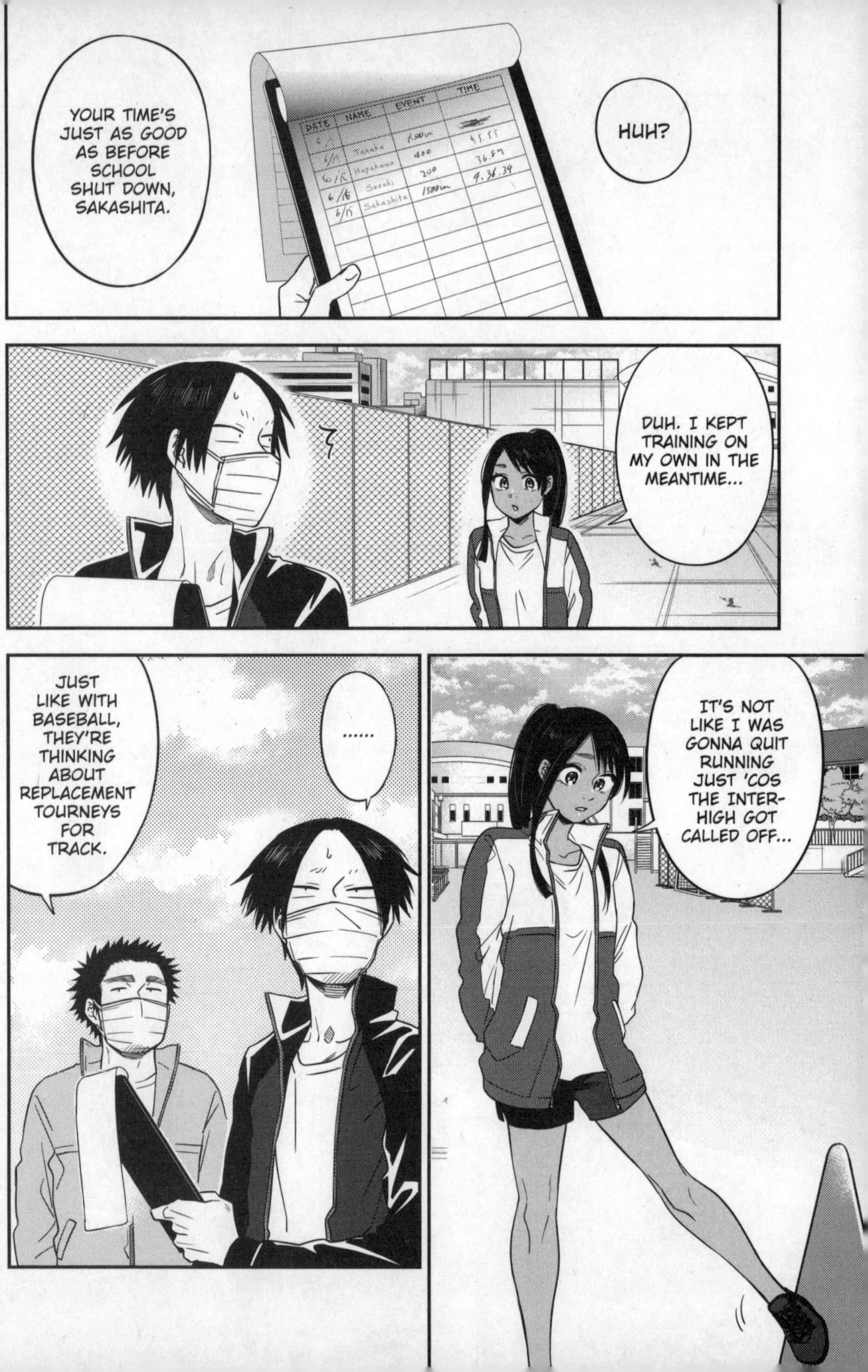
YOUR TIME'S JUST AS GOOD AS BEFORE SCHOOL SHUT DOWN, SAKASHITA.
HUH?
DUH. I KEPT TRAINING ON MY OWN IN THE MEANTIME...
IT'S NOT LIKE I WAS GONNA QUIT RUNNING JUST 'COS THE INTER-HIGH GOT CALLED OFF...
......
JUST LIKE WITH BASEBALL, THEY'RE THINKING ABOUT REPLACEMENT TOURNEYS FOR TRACK.

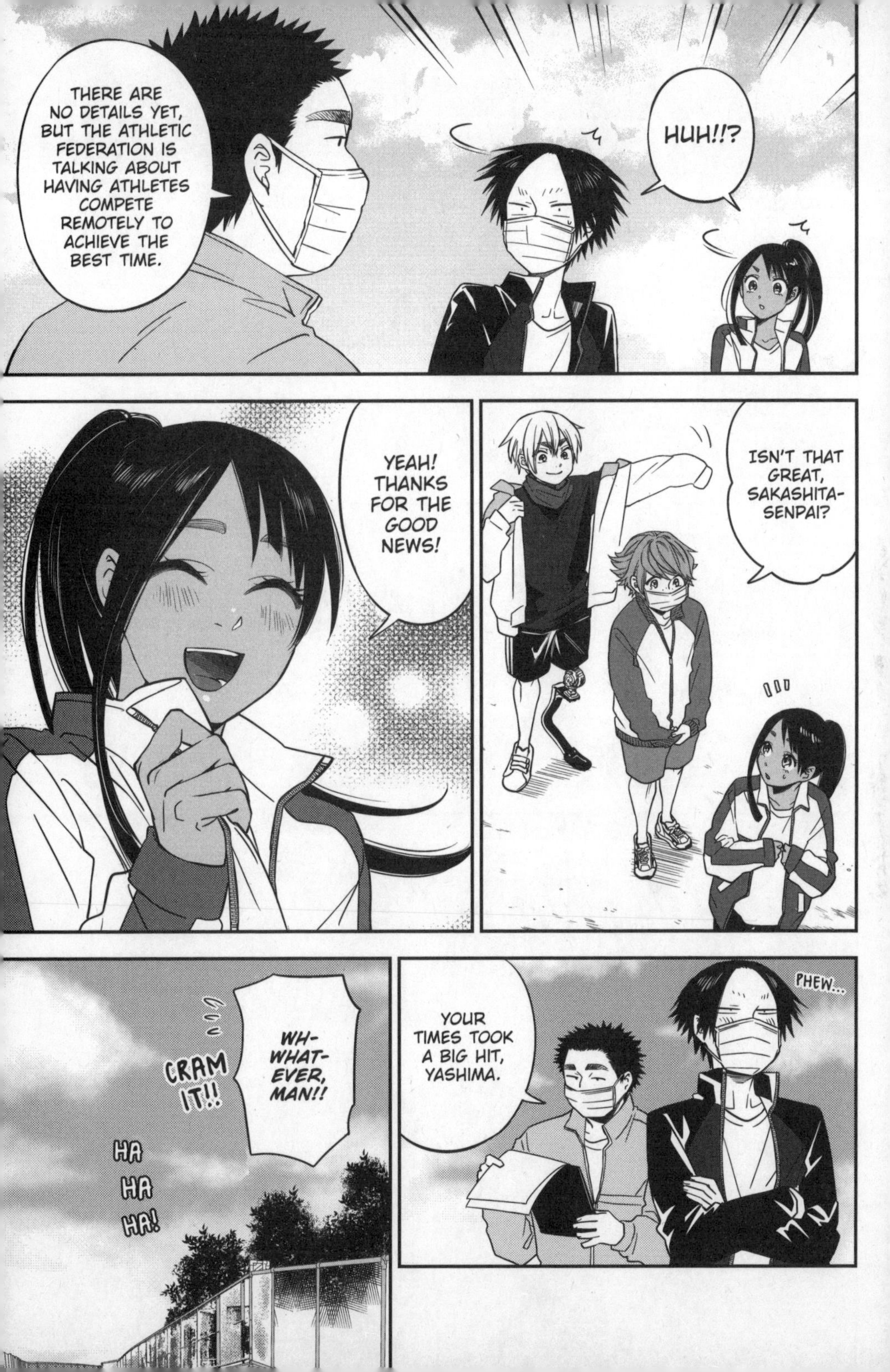
THERE ARE NO DETAILS YET, BUT THE ATHLETIC FEDERATION IS TALKING ABOUT HAVING ATHLETES COMPETE REMOTELY TO ACHIEVE THE BEST TIME.
HUH!!?
ISN'T THAT GREAT, SAKASHITA-SENPAI?
YEAH! THANKS FOR THE GOOD NEWS!
PHEW...
YOUR TIMES TOOK A BIG HIT, YASHIMA.
WH-WHATEVER, MAN!!
CRAM IT!!
HA HA HA!

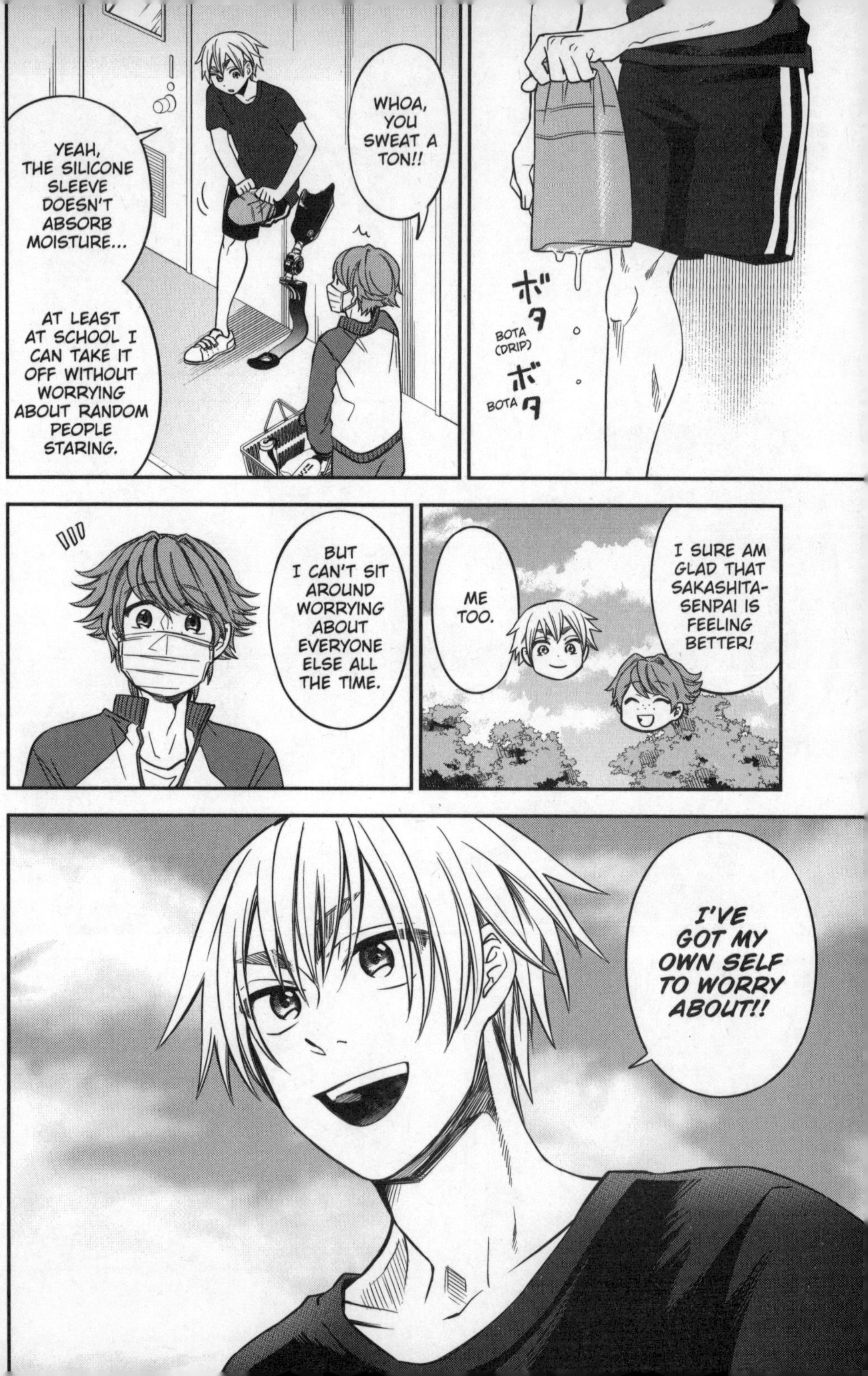
ボタ
BOTA (DRIP)
ボタ
BOTA
WHOA, YOU SWEAT A TON!!
YEAH, THE SILICONE SLEEVE DOESN'T ABSORB MOISTURE...
AT LEAST AT SCHOOL I CAN TAKE IT OFF WITHOUT WORRYING ABOUT RANDOM PEOPLE STARING.
I SURE AM GLAD THAT SAKASHITA-SENPAI IS FEELING BETTER!
ME TOO.
BUT I CAN'T SIT AROUND WORRYING ABOUT EVERYONE ELSE ALL THE TIME.
I'VE GOT MY OWN SELF TO WORRY ABOUT!!

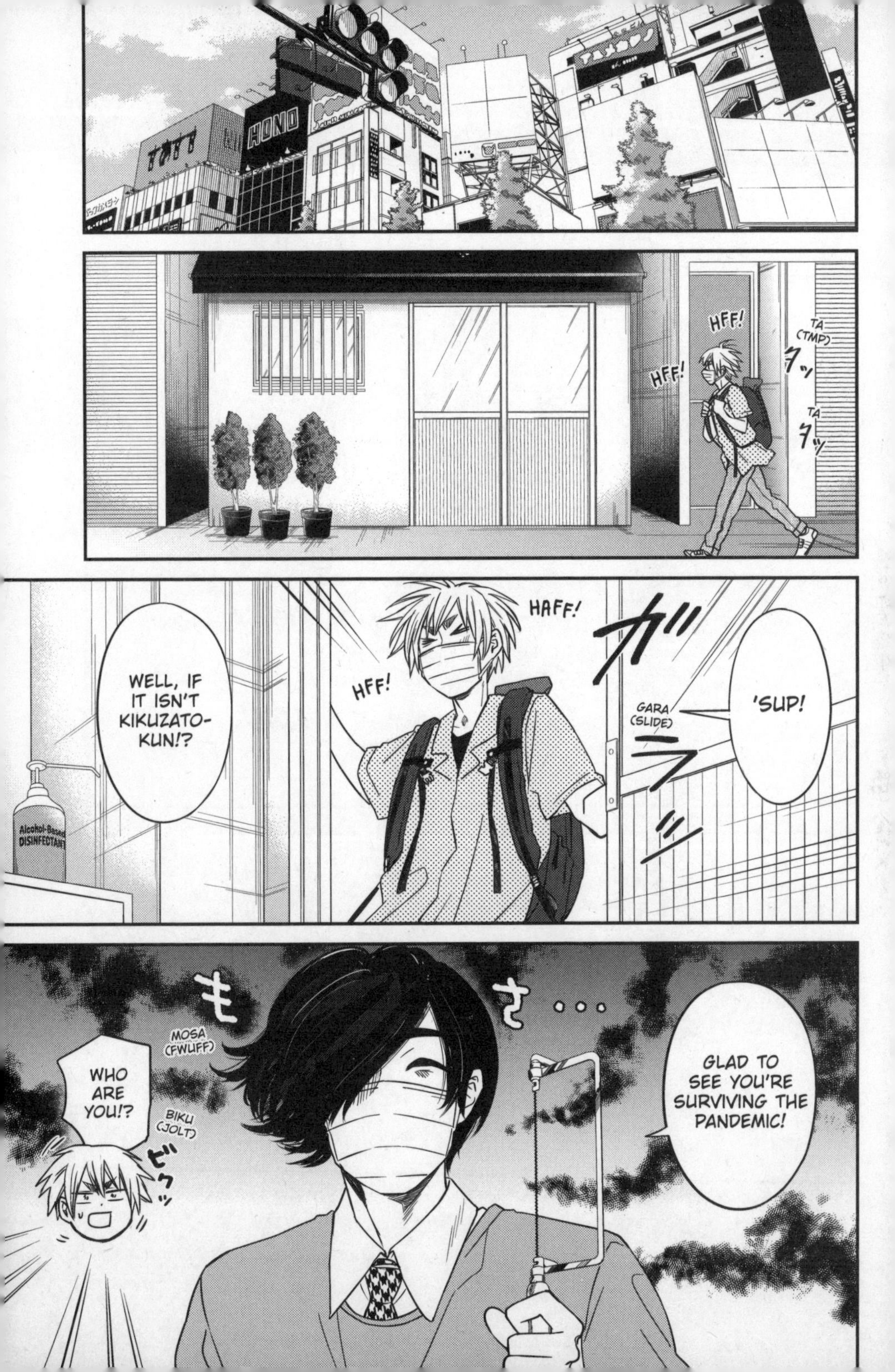
HONO
TA (TMP)
TA
HFF!
HFF!
'SUP!
GARA (SLIDE)
HAFF!
HFF!
WELL, IF IT ISN'T KIKUZATO-KUN!?
Alcohol-Based DISINFECTANT
GLAD TO SEE YOU'RE SURVIVING THE PANDEMIC!
MOSA (FWUFF)
WHO ARE YOU!?
BIKU (JOLT)

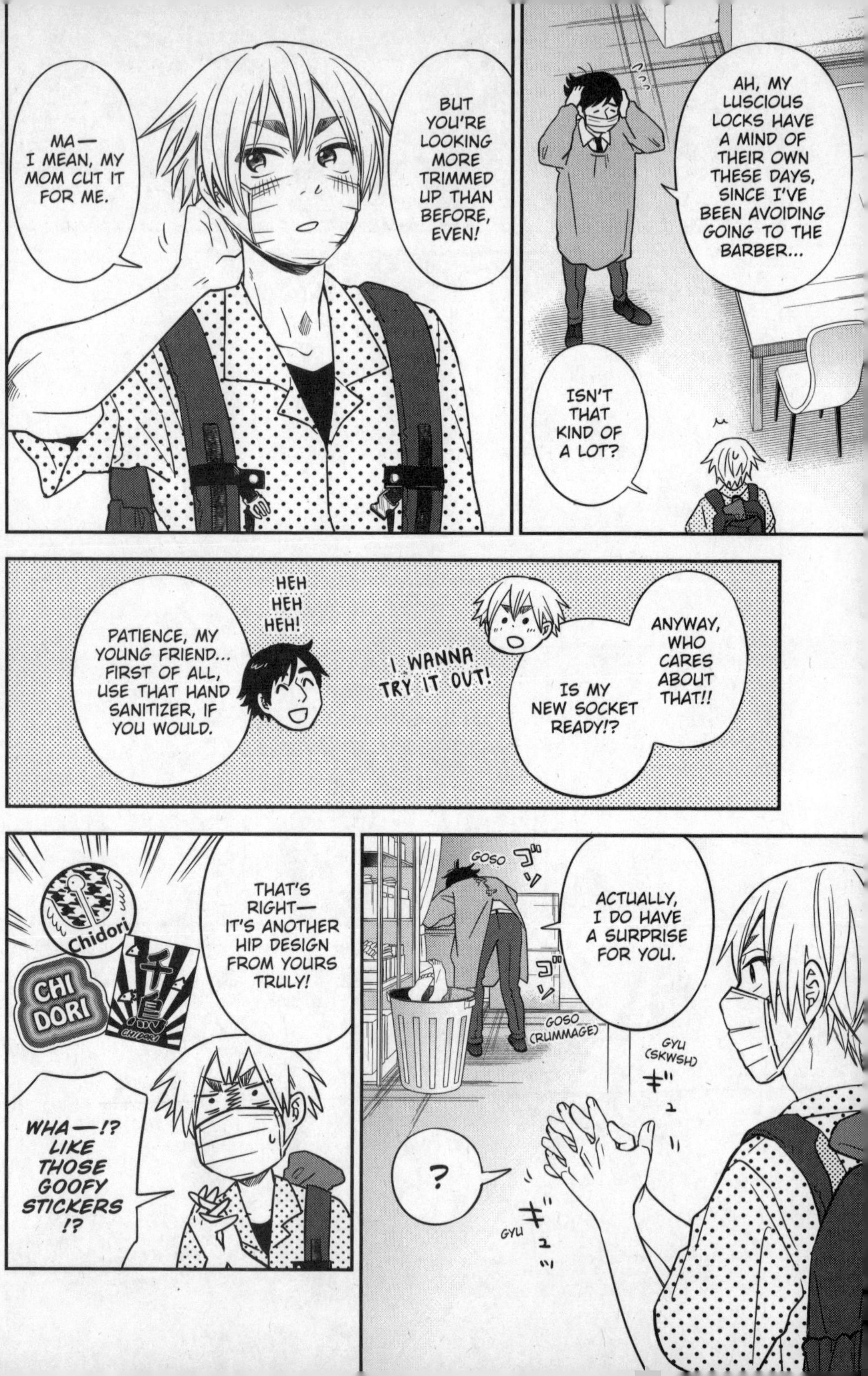
AH, MY LUSCIOUS LOCKS HAVE A MIND OF THEIR OWN THESE DAYS, SINCE I'VE BEEN AVOIDING GOING TO THE BARBER...
ISN'T THAT KIND OF A LOT?
BUT YOU'RE LOOKING MORE TRIMMED UP THAN BEFORE, EVEN!
MA— I MEAN, MY MOM CUT IT FOR ME.
ANYWAY, WHO CARES ABOUT THAT!!
IS MY NEW SOCKET READY!?
I WANNA TRY IT OUT!
HEH HEH HEH!
PATIENCE, MY YOUNG FRIEND... FIRST OF ALL, USE THAT HAND SANITIZER, IF YOU WOULD.
GOSO
ACTUALLY, I DO HAVE A SURPRISE FOR YOU.
GOSO (RUMMAGE)
GYU (SKWSH)
?
GYU
THAT'S RIGHT— IT'S ANOTHER HIP DESIGN FROM YOURS TRULY!
Chidori
CHI DORI
WHA—!? LIKE THOSE GOOFY STICKERS !?

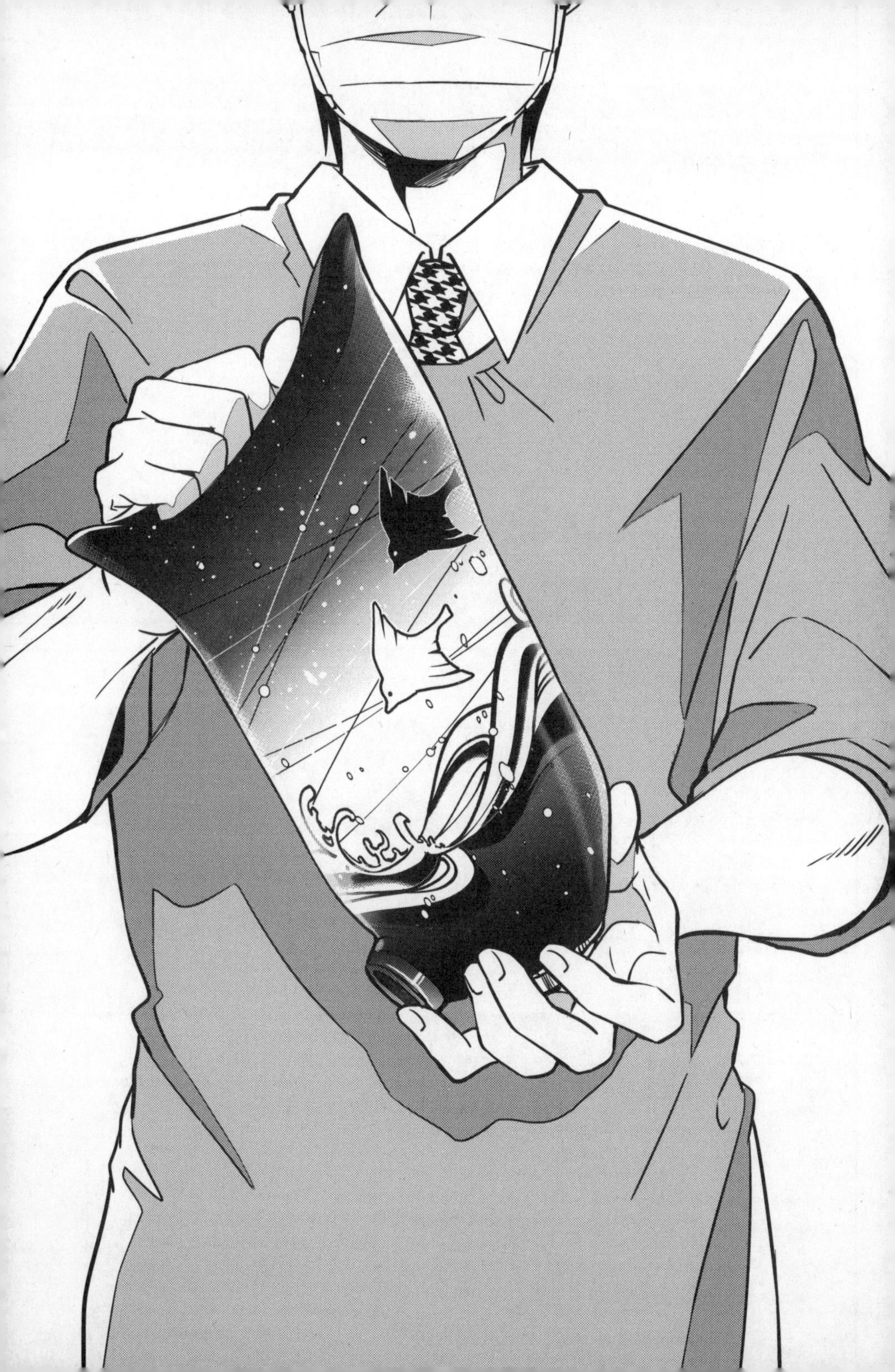

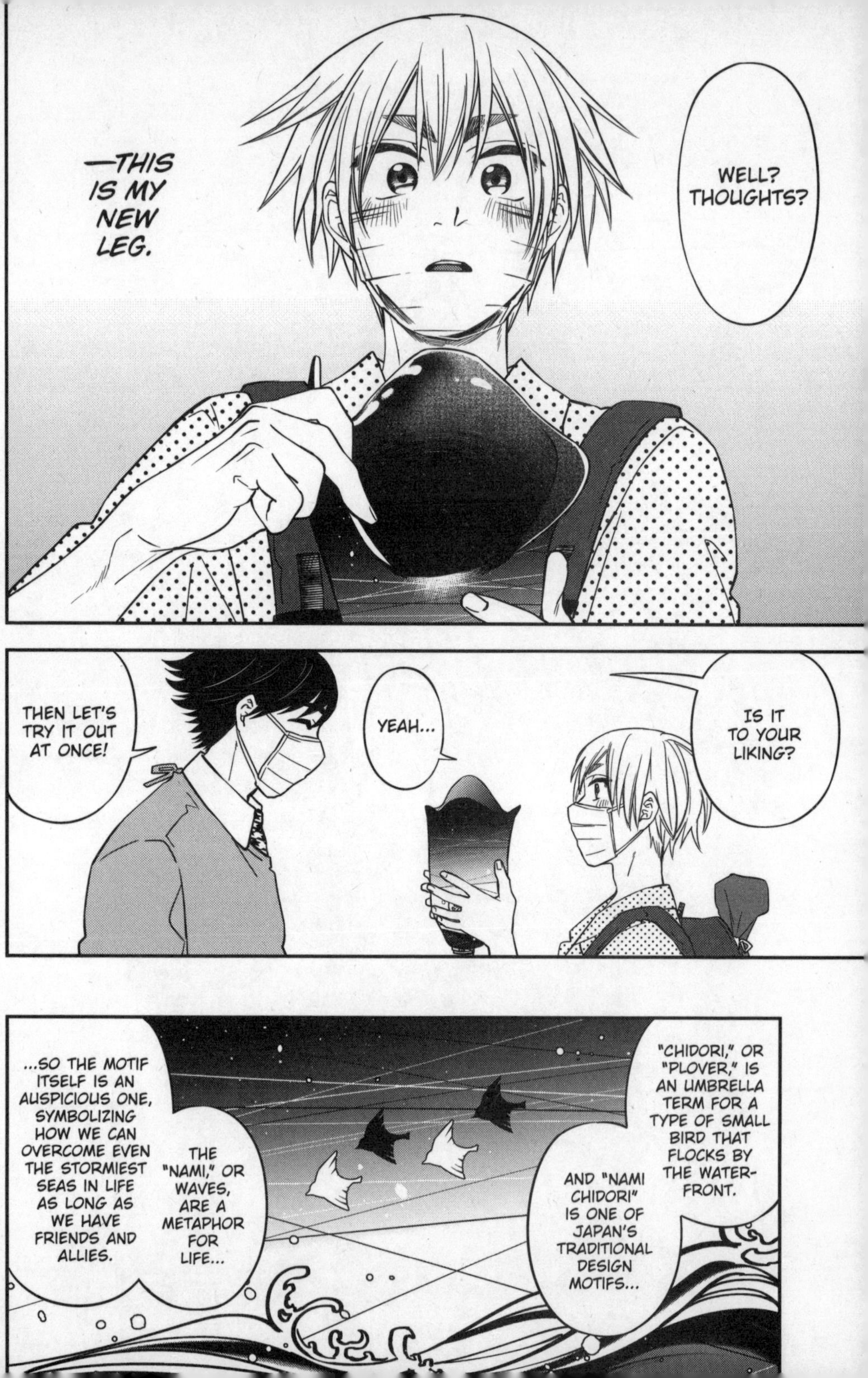
WELL? THOUGHTS?
—THIS IS MY NEW LEG.
IS IT TO YOUR LIKING?
YEAH...
THEN LET'S TRY IT OUT AT ONCE!
"CHIDORI," OR "PLOVER," IS AN UMBRELLA TERM FOR A TYPE OF SMALL BIRD THAT FLOCKS BY THE WATER-FRONT.
AND "NAMI CHIDORI" IS ONE OF JAPAN'S TRADITIONAL DESIGN MOTIFS...
THE "NAMI," OR WAVES, ARE A METAPHOR FOR LIFE...
...SO THE MOTIF ITSELF IS AN AUSPICIOUS ONE, SYMBOLIZING HOW WE CAN OVERCOME EVEN THE STORMIEST SEAS IN LIFE AS LONG AS WE HAVE FRIENDS AND ALLIES.

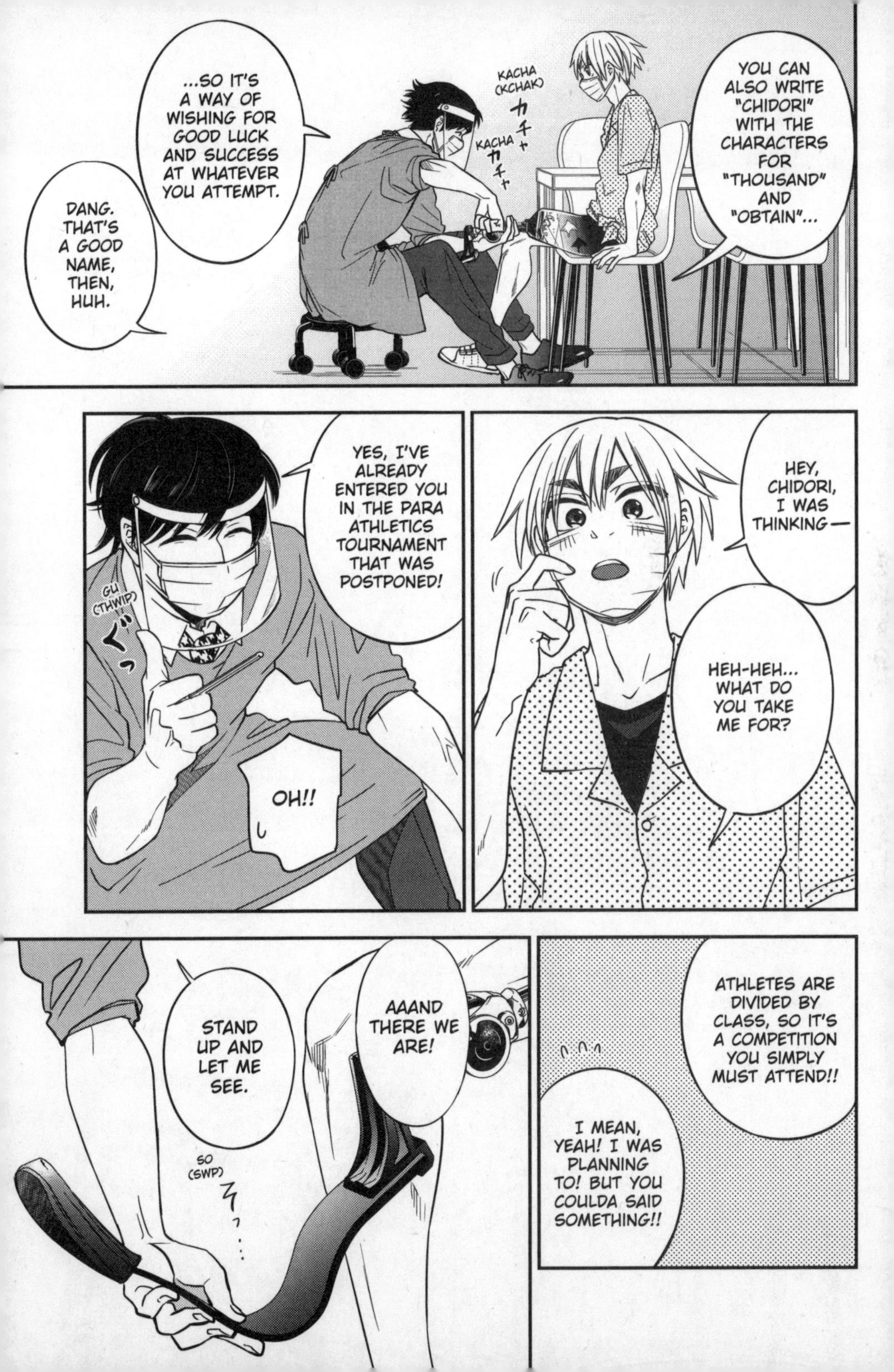
YOU CAN ALSO WRITE "CHIDORI" WITH THE CHARACTERS FOR "THOUSAND" AND "OBTAIN"...
KACHA (KCHAK)
KACHA
...SO IT'S A WAY OF WISHING FOR GOOD LUCK AND SUCCESS AT WHATEVER YOU ATTEMPT.
DANG. THAT'S A GOOD NAME, THEN, HUH.
HEY, CHIDORI, I WAS THINKING—
HEH-HEH... WHAT DO YOU TAKE ME FOR?
YES, I'VE ALREADY ENTERED YOU IN THE PARA ATHLETICS TOURNAMENT THAT WAS POSTPONED!
GU (THWIP)
OH!!
ATHLETES ARE DIVIDED BY CLASS, SO IT'S A COMPETITION YOU SIMPLY MUST ATTEND!!
I MEAN, YEAH! I WAS PLANNING TO! BUT YOU COULDA SAID SOMETHING!!
AAAND THERE WE ARE!
STAND UP AND LET ME SEE.
SO (SWP)

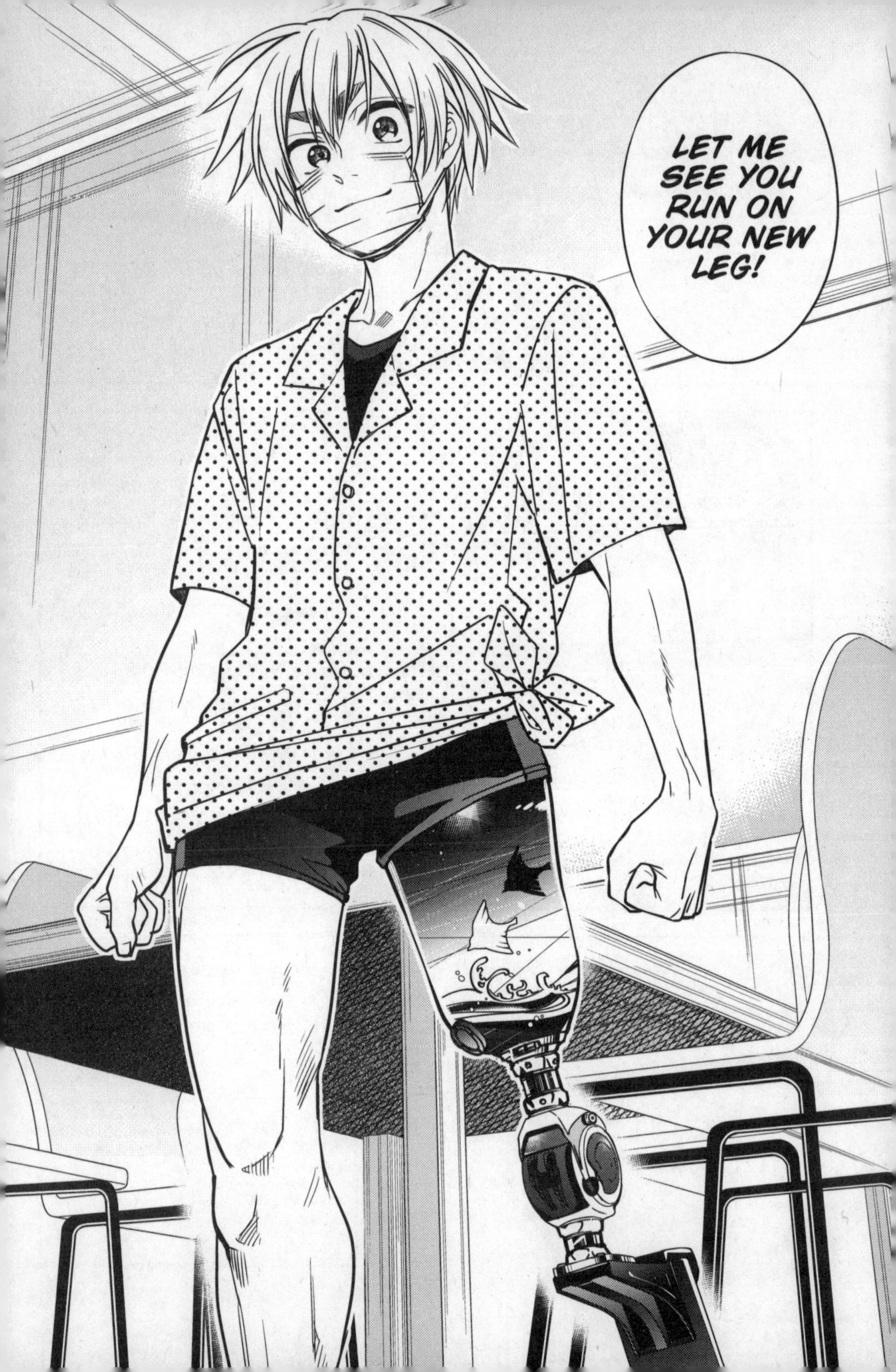
LET ME SEE YOU RUN ON YOUR NEW LEG!

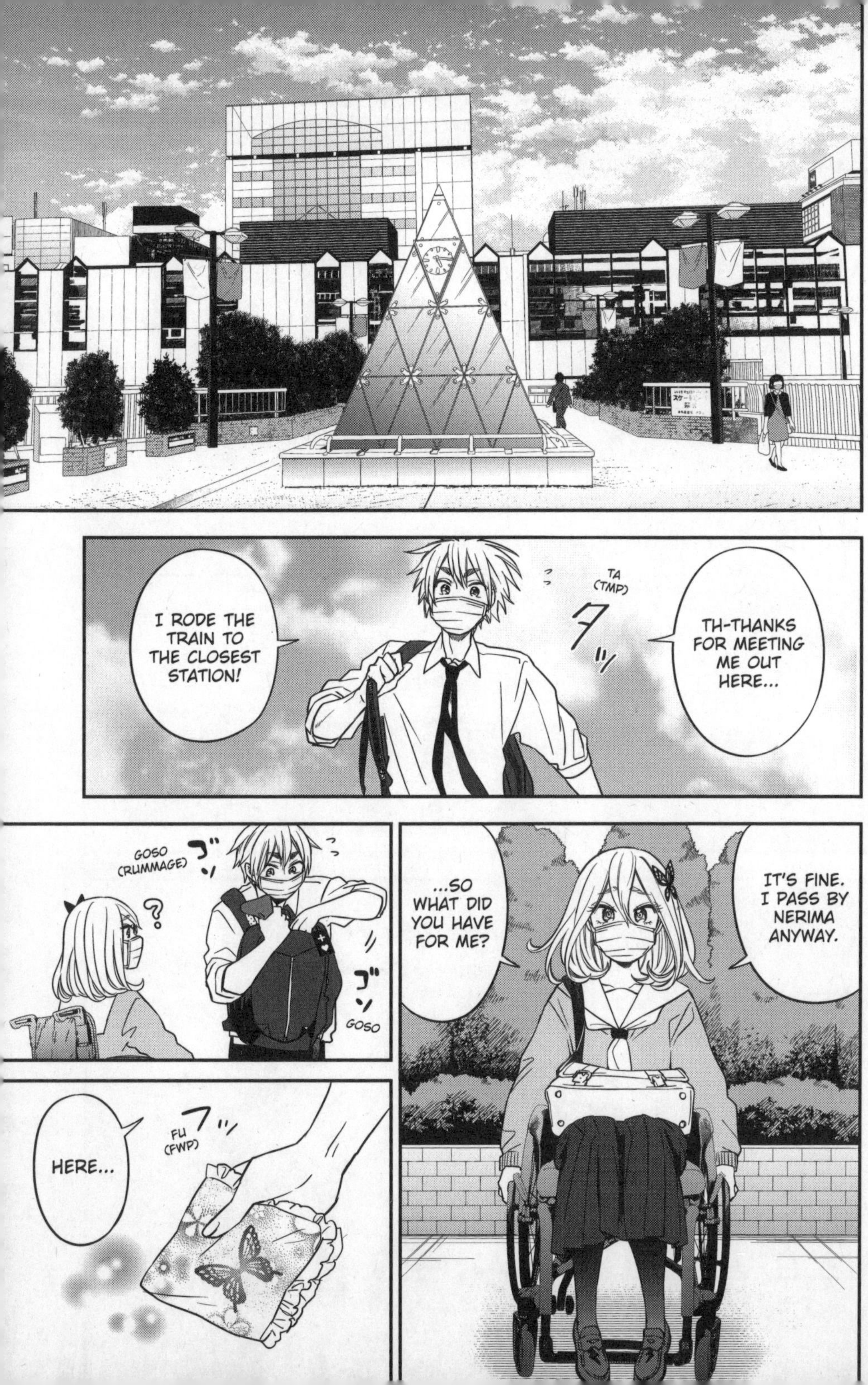
TH-THANKS FOR MEETING ME OUT HERE...
TA (TMP)
I RODE THE TRAIN TO THE CLOSEST STATION!
IT'S FINE. I PASS BY NERIMA ANYWAY.
...SO WHAT DID YOU HAVE FOR ME?
GOSO (RUMMAGE)
?
GOSO
FU (FWP)
HERE...

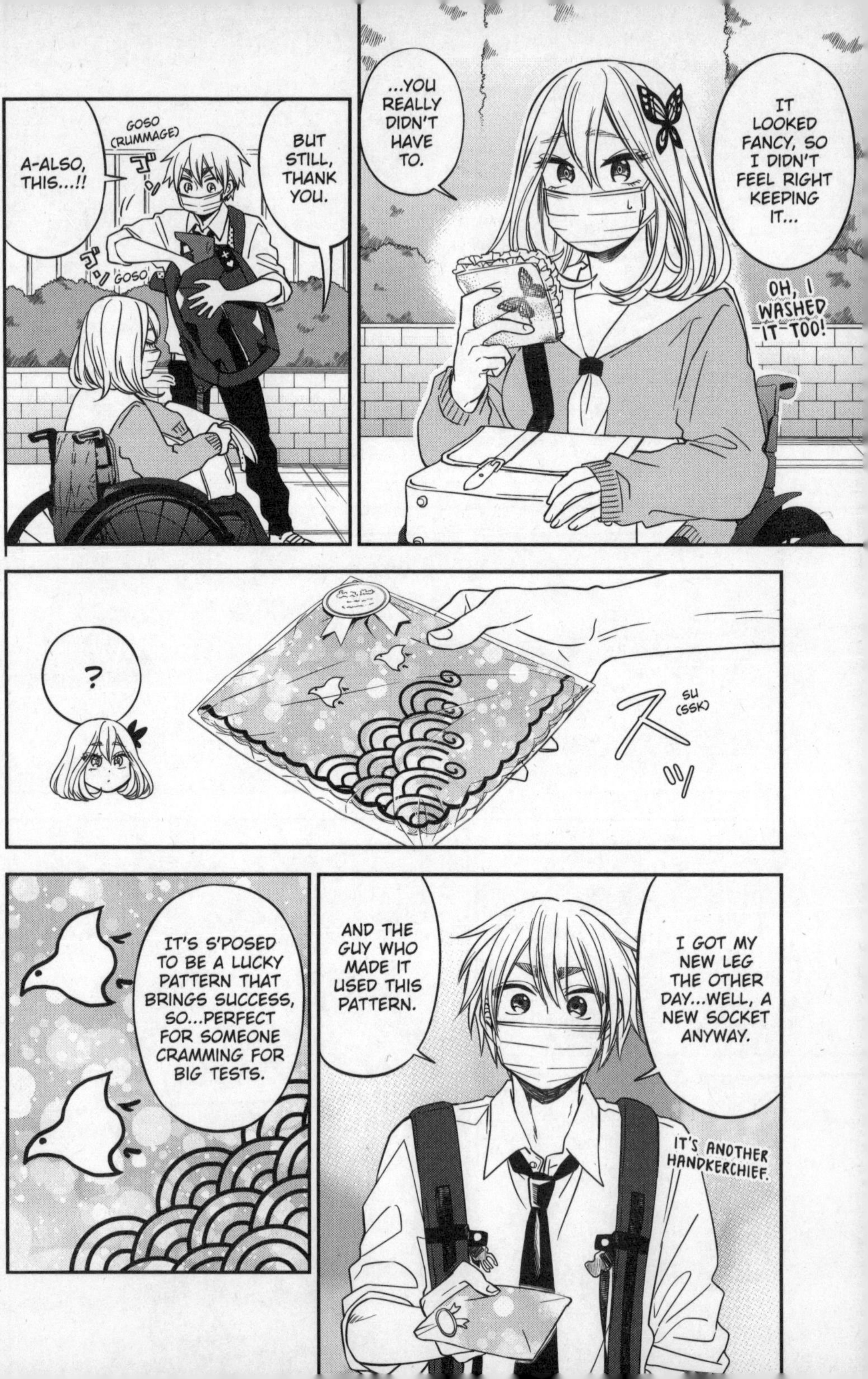
IT LOOKED FANCY, SO I DIDN'T FEEL RIGHT KEEPING IT...
OH, I WASHED IT TOO!
...YOU REALLY DIDN'T HAVE TO.
BUT STILL, THANK YOU.
GOSO (RUMMAGE)
A-ALSO, THIS...!!
GOSO
SU (SSK)
?
I GOT MY NEW LEG THE OTHER DAY...WELL, A NEW SOCKET ANYWAY.
AND THE GUY WHO MADE IT USED THIS PATTERN.
IT'S ANOTHER HANDKERCHIEF.
IT'S S'POSED TO BE A LUCKY PATTERN THAT BRINGS SUCCESS, SO...PERFECT FOR SOMEONE CRAMMING FOR BIG TESTS.

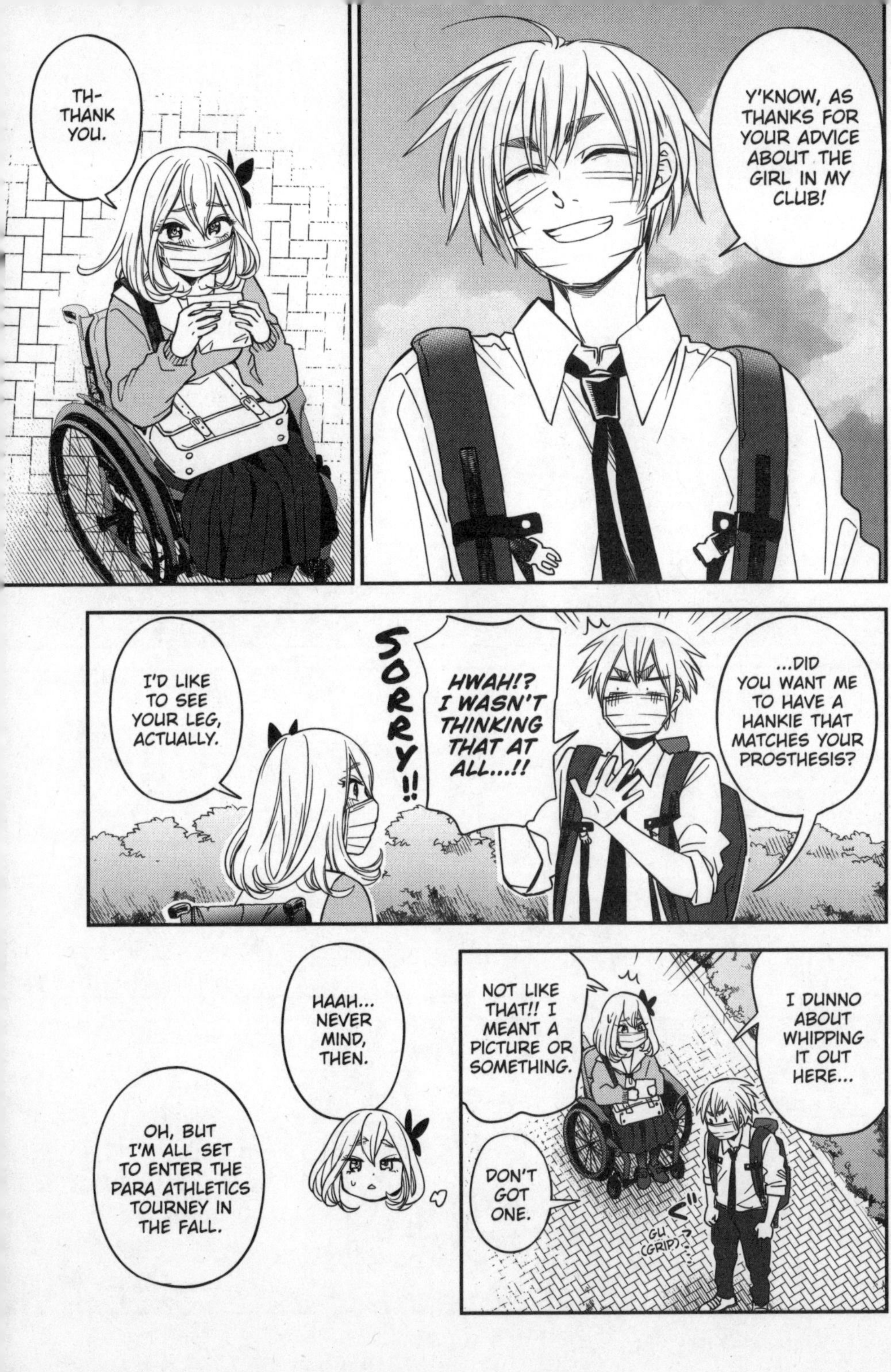

Y'KNOW, AS THANKS FOR YOUR ADVICE ABOUT THE GIRL IN MY CLUB!
TH-THANK YOU.
...DID YOU WANT ME TO HAVE A HANKIE THAT MATCHES YOUR PROSTHESIS?
HWAH!? I WASN'T THINKING THAT AT ALL...!!
SORRY!!
I'D LIKE TO SEE YOUR LEG, ACTUALLY.
I DUNNO ABOUT WHIPPING IT OUT HERE...
NOT LIKE THAT!! I MEANT A PICTURE OR SOMETHING.
DON'T GOT ONE.
GU (GRIP)
HAAH... NEVER MIND, THEN.
OH, BUT I'M ALL SET TO ENTER THE PARA ATHLETICS TOURNEY IN THE FALL.

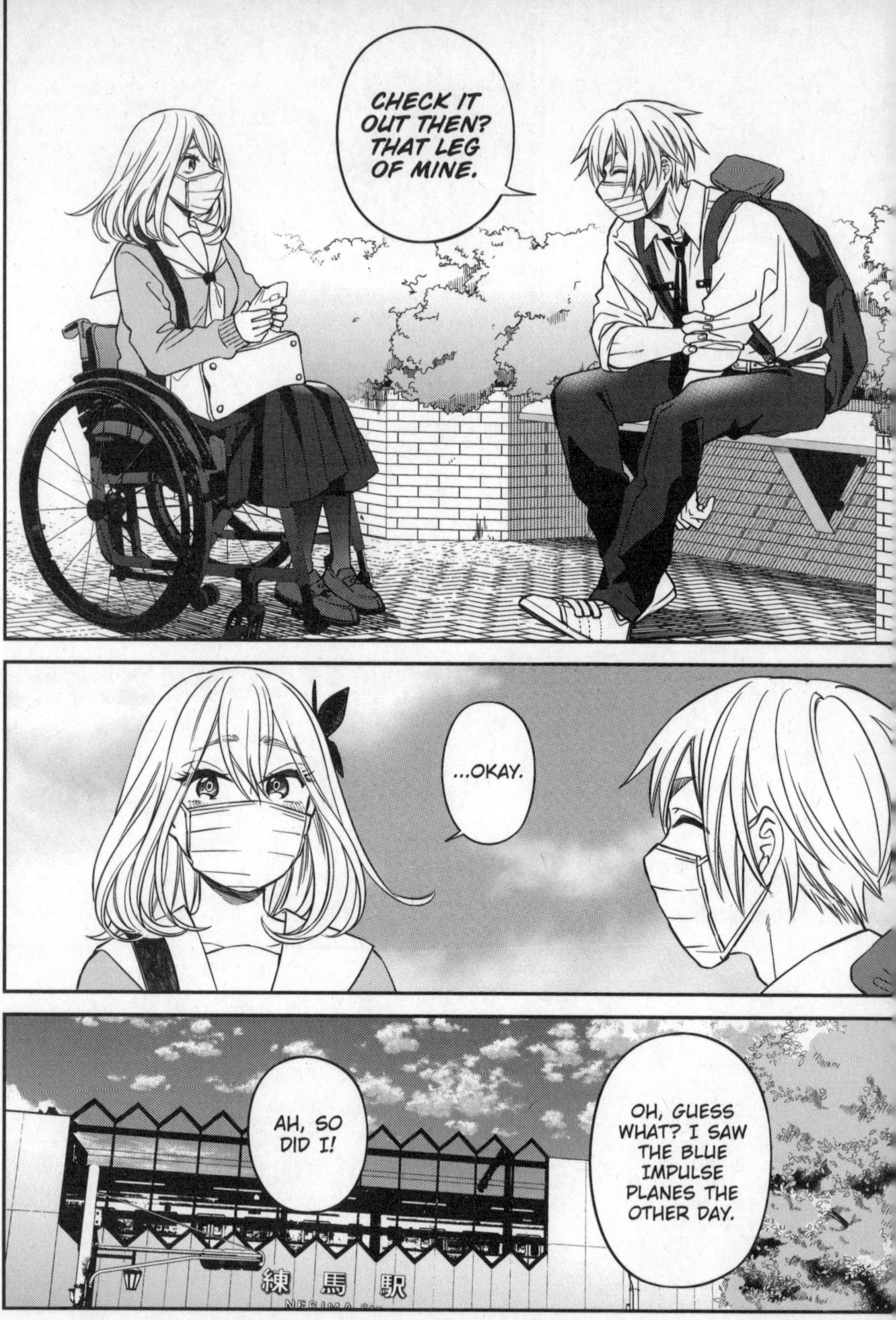
CHECK IT OUT THEN? THAT LEG OF MINE.
...OKAY.
OH, GUESS WHAT? I SAW THE BLUE IMPULSE PLANES THE OTHER DAY.
AH, SO DID I!
練馬駅

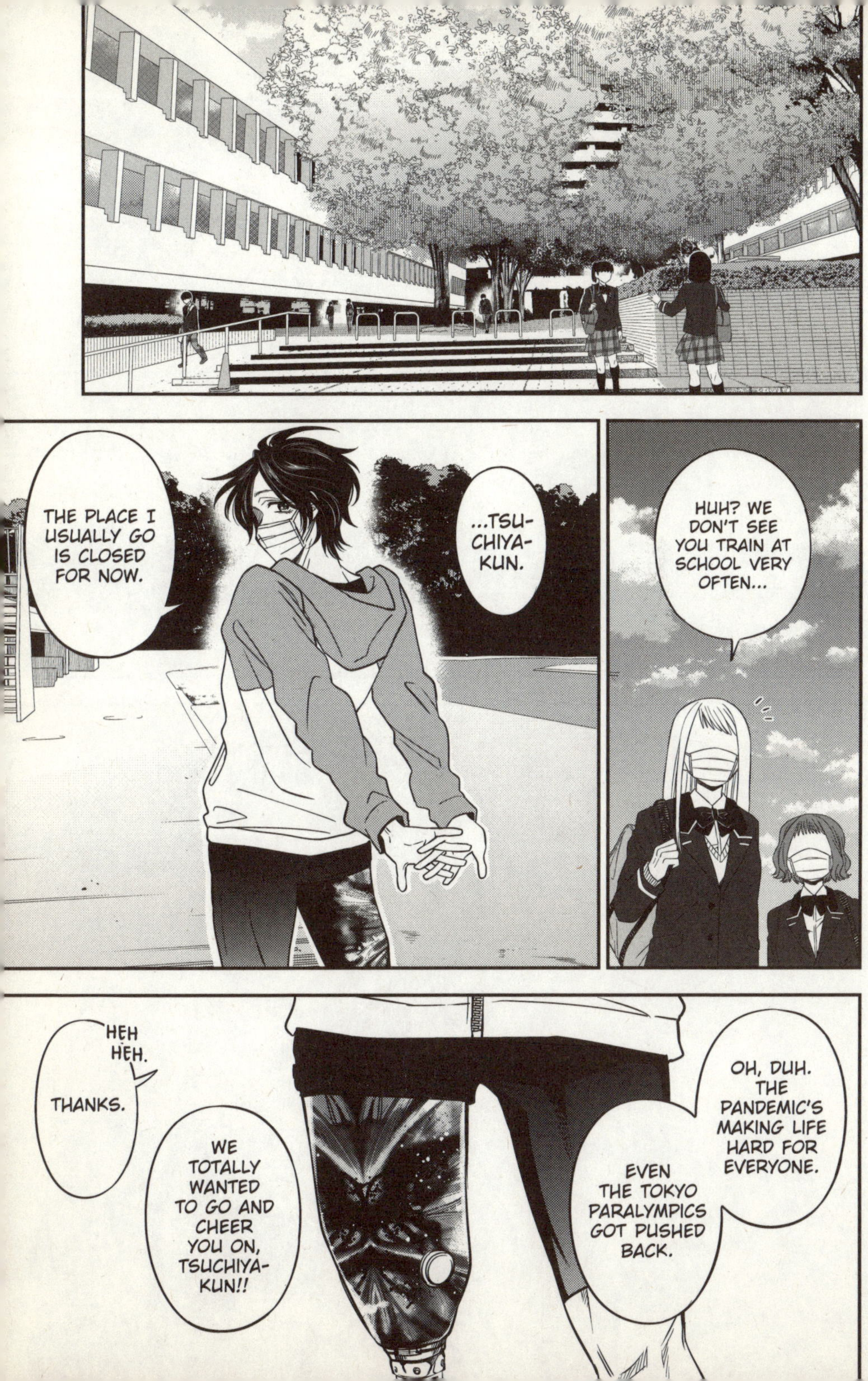
HUH? WE DON'T SEE YOU TRAIN AT SCHOOL VERY OFTEN...
...TSU-CHIYA-KUN.
THE PLACE I USUALLY GO IS CLOSED FOR NOW.
OH, DUH. THE PANDEMIC'S MAKING LIFE HARD FOR EVERYONE.
EVEN THE TOKYO PARALYMPICS GOT PUSHED BACK.
WE TOTALLY WANTED TO GO AND CHEER YOU ON, TSUCHIYA-KUN!!
HEH HEH.
THANKS.

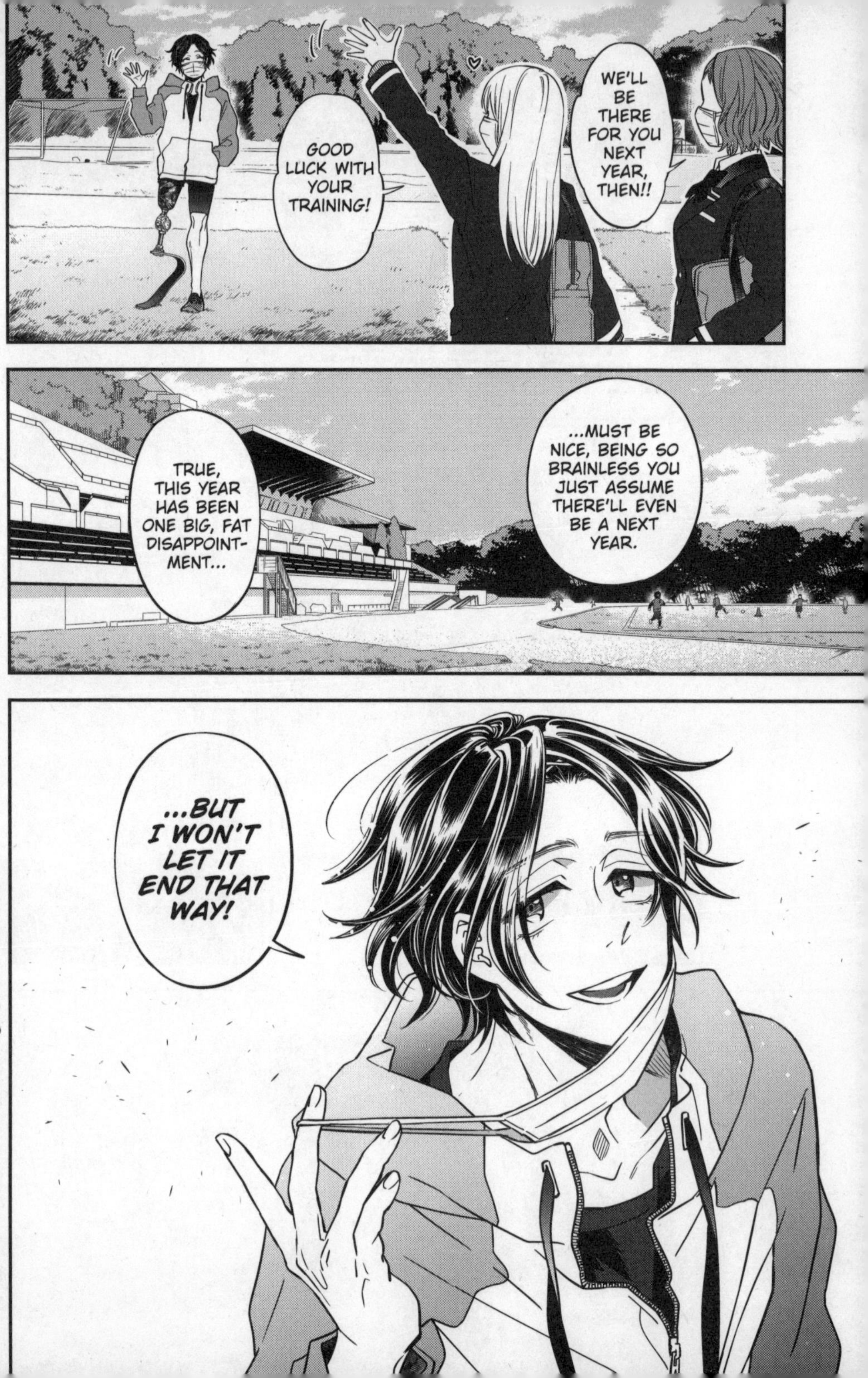
WE'LL BE THERE FOR YOU NEXT YEAR, THEN!!
GOOD LUCK WITH YOUR TRAINING!
...MUST BE NICE, BEING SO BRAINLESS YOU JUST ASSUME THERE'LL EVEN BE A NEXT YEAR.
TRUE, THIS YEAR HAS BEEN ONE BIG, FAT DISAPPOINTMENT...
...BUT I WON'T LET IT END THAT WAY!

Run on Your New Legs, Vol. 4 : **END**

TRANSLATION NOTES

COMMON HONORIFICS
no honorific: Indicates familiarity or closeness; if used without permission or reason, addressing someone in this manner would constitute an insult.
-*san*: The Japanese equivalent of Mr./Mrs./Ms. This is the fail-safe honorific if politeness is required.
-*kun*: Used most often when referring to boys, this honorific indicates affection or familiarity. Occasionally used by older men among their peers, but it may also be used by anyone referring to a person of lower standing.
-*chan*: Affectionate honorific indicating familiarity used mostly in reference to girls; also used in reference to cute persons or animals of any gender.
-*senpai*: A suffix used when addressing upperclassmen or more senior coworkers.
-*sensei*: A respectful term for teachers, artists, or high-level professionals.
-*sama*: An honorific conveying great respect.

CURRENCY CONVERSION
While exchange rates fluctuate daily, a good approximation is ¥100 to 1 USD.

Page 4: A *bento* is a Japanese lunch box, often with partitions like a lunch tray to separate the various dishes.

Page 7: No, the students aren't planning an international voyage during the pandemic! Tokyo **Disneyland** was the first official Disney theme park to open outside the US, and it shares many similarities with California's Disneyland and Florida's Magic Kingdom.

Page 33: *Katsudon*, literally "pork cutlet bowl," is a deep-fried pork cutlet served over rice with egg and vegetables.

Page 89: Koshien Stadium was built near Kobe, Japan, in 1924 to host national high school baseball tournaments and seats 55,000 spectators. Playing at Koshien is a major aim of many high school players.

Page 145: Japanese employs **Chinese characters**, called *kanji*, in writing to help distinguish between words that may be pronounced the same. As Chidori explains, the same Japanese word or name can be written with different characters that sound the same but provide a different meaning.

Special thanks to all my consultants

Atsushi Yamamoto (Shin Nihon Jusetsu)
Junta Kosuda (Open House)
Mikio Ikeda (Digital Advertising Consortium)
Tomoki Yoshida

Xiborg
Otto Bock Japan
Okino Sports Prosthetics & Orthotics (Atsuo Okino)
D'ACTION (Shuji Miyake)
Naoto Yoshida (Writer)

Cramer Japan: Hideaki Daiya/Seiji Nonaka/Everyone Else
National Research and Development Agency
National Institute of Advanced Industrial Science and Technology
Hobara Hiroaki

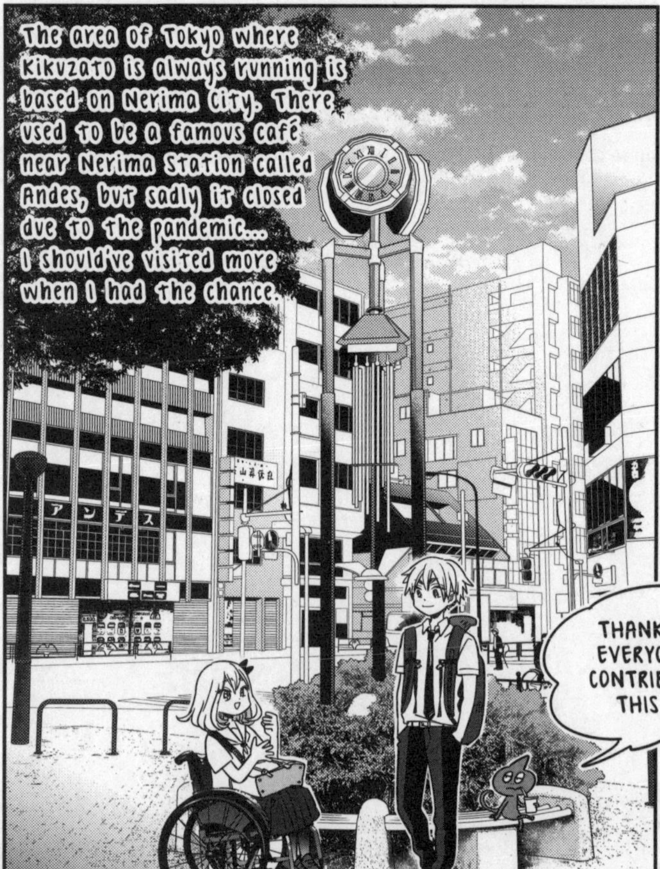
The area of Tokyo where Kikuzato is always running is based on Nerima City. There used to be a famous café near Nerima Station called Andes, but sadly it closed due to the pandemic... I should've visited more when I had the chance.
アンデス
THANK YOU TO EVERYONE WHO CONTRIBUTED TO THIS BOOK!

BONUS

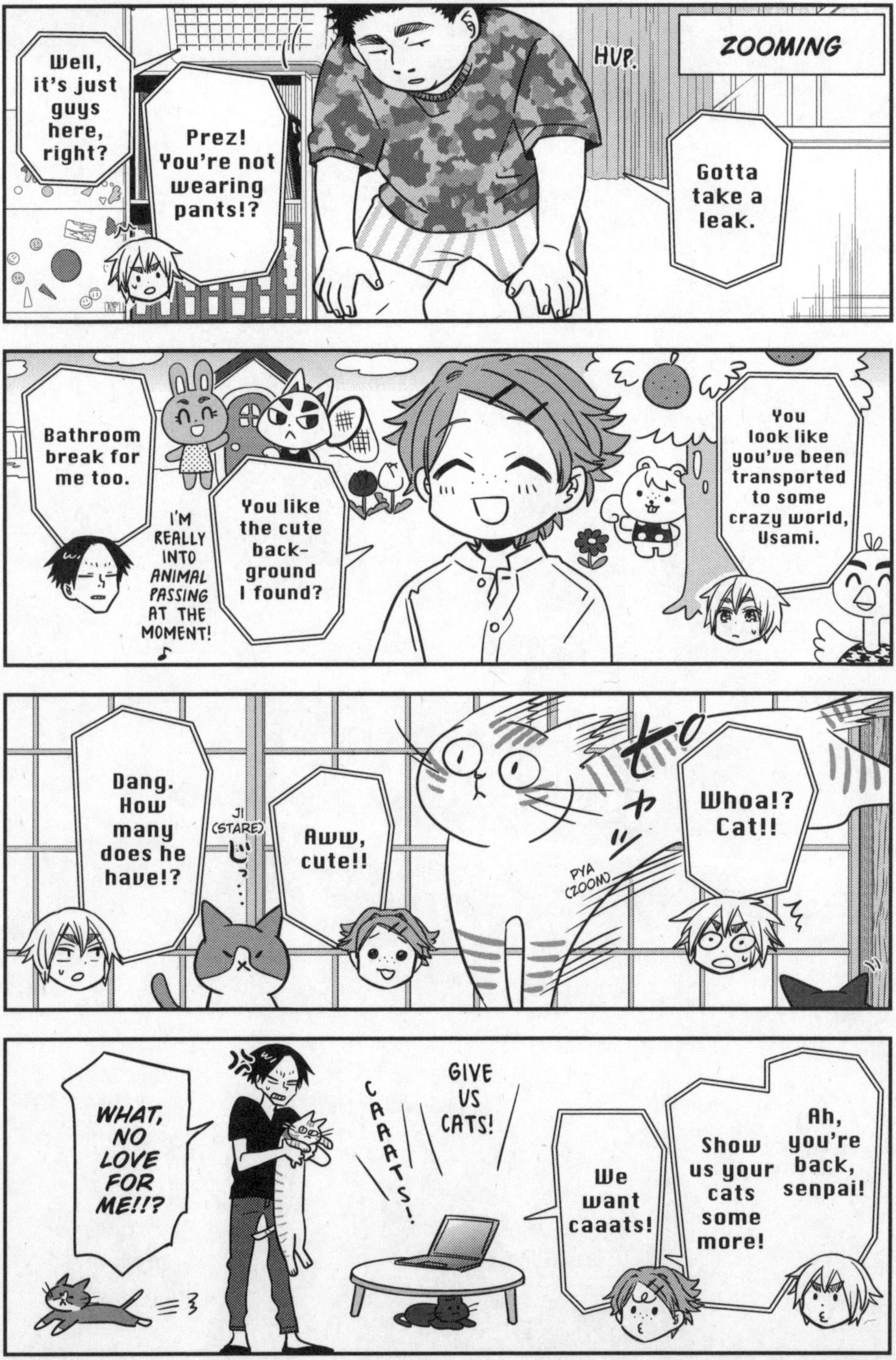
ZOOMING
HUP.
Gotta take a leak.
Prez! You're not wearing pants!?
Well, it's just guys here, right?
You look like you've been transported to some crazy world, Usami.
You like the cute back-ground I found?
I'M REALLY INTO ANIMAL PASSING AT THE MOMENT!
Bathroom break for me too.
Whoa!? Cat!!
PYA (ZOOM)
Aww, cute!!
JI (STARE)
Dang. How many does he have!?
Ah, you're back, senpai!
Show us your cats some more!
We want caaats!
GIVE US CATS!
CAAATS!
WHAT, NO LOVE FOR ME!!?

STORYBOARD BY: ART BY: NAKAJIMA-SAN (ASSISTANT)

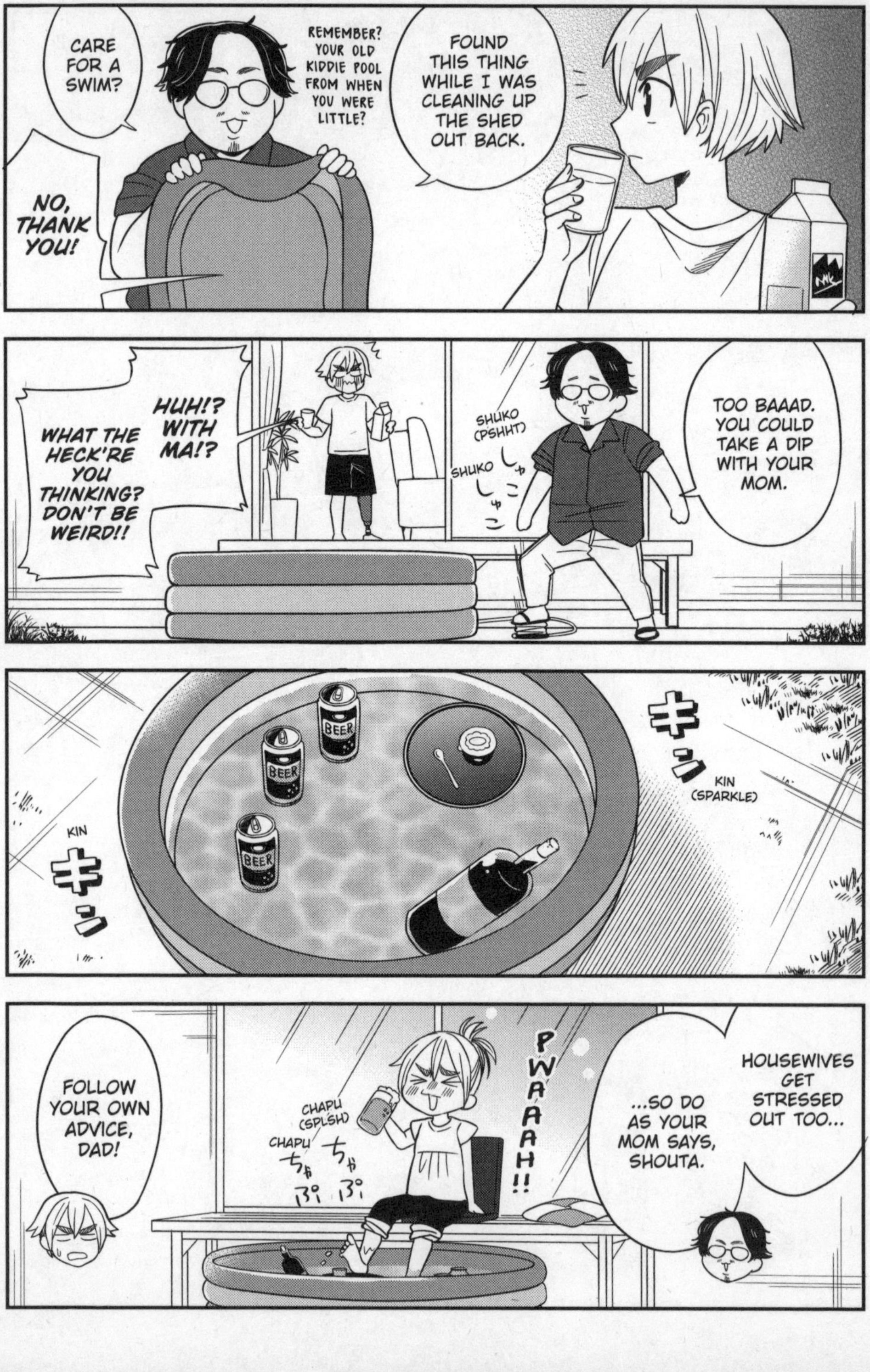
FOUND THIS THING WHILE I WAS CLEANING UP THE SHED OUT BACK.
REMEMBER? YOUR OLD KIDDIE POOL FROM WHEN YOU WERE LITTLE?
CARE FOR A SWIM?
NO, THANK YOU!
TOO BAAAD. YOU COULD TAKE A DIP WITH YOUR MOM.
SHUKO (PSHHT)
しゅこ
SHUKO
しゅこ
HUH!? WITH MA!?
WHAT THE HECK'RE YOU THINKING? DON'T BE WEIRD!!
キン
KIN (SPARKLE)
BEER
BEER
BEER
KIN
キン
HOUSEWIVES GET STRESSED OUT TOO...
...SO DO AS YOUR MOM SAYS, SHOUTA.
PWAAAAH!!
CHAPU (SPLSH)
ちゃぷ
CHAPU
ちゃぷ
FOLLOW YOUR OWN ADVICE, DAD!

STORYBOARD BY: ART BY: MORUNGA-SAN (ASSISTANT)

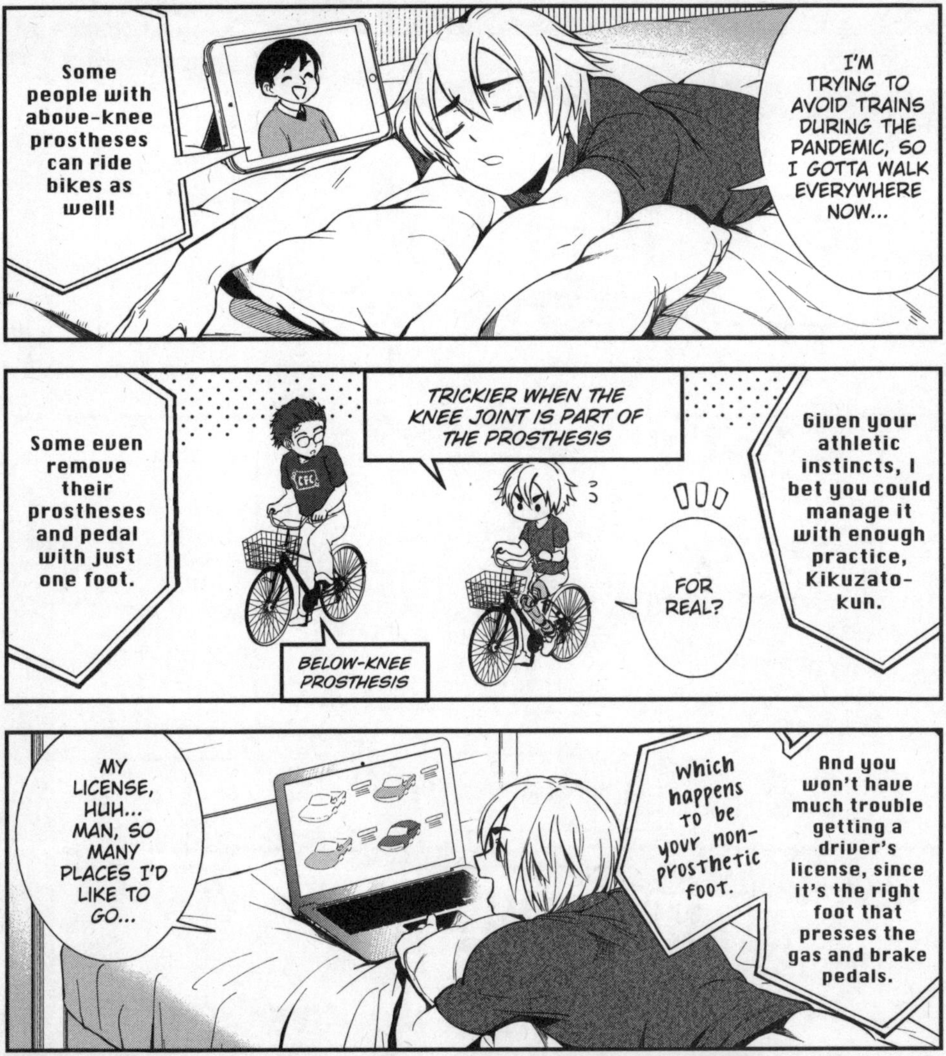
I'M TRYING TO AVOID TRAINS DURING THE PANDEMIC, SO I GOTTA WALK EVERYWHERE NOW...
Some people with above-knee prostheses can ride bikes as well!
Given your athletic instincts, I bet you could manage it with enough practice, Kikuzato-kun.
TRICKIER WHEN THE KNEE JOINT IS PART OF THE PROSTHESIS
FOR REAL?
Some even remove their prostheses and pedal with just one foot.
BELOW-KNEE PROSTHESIS
And you won't have much trouble getting a driver's license, since it's the right foot that presses the gas and brake pedals.
Which happens to be your non-prosthetic foot.
MY LICENSE, HUH... MAN, SO MANY PLACES I'D LIKE TO GO...

*CARS CAN BE MODIFIED WITH PEDALS ON THE LEFT TO ASSIST THOSE WITH A PROSTHESIS ON THEIR RIGHT LEG

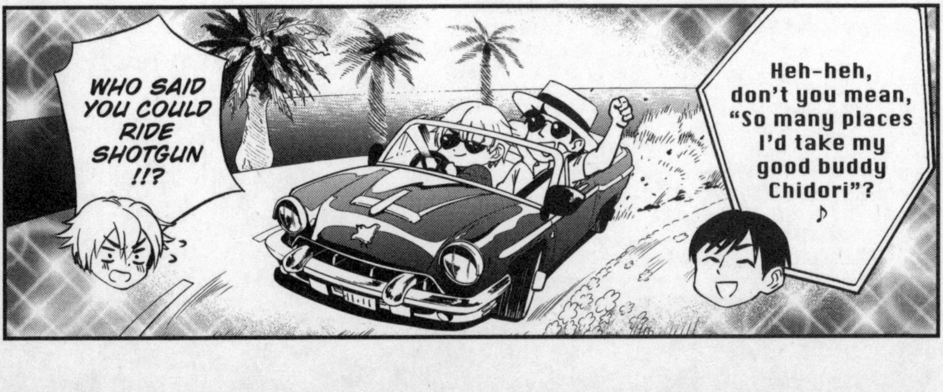
Heh-heh, don't you mean, "So many places I'd take my good buddy Chidori"? ♪
WHO SAID YOU COULD RIDE SHOTGUN !!?

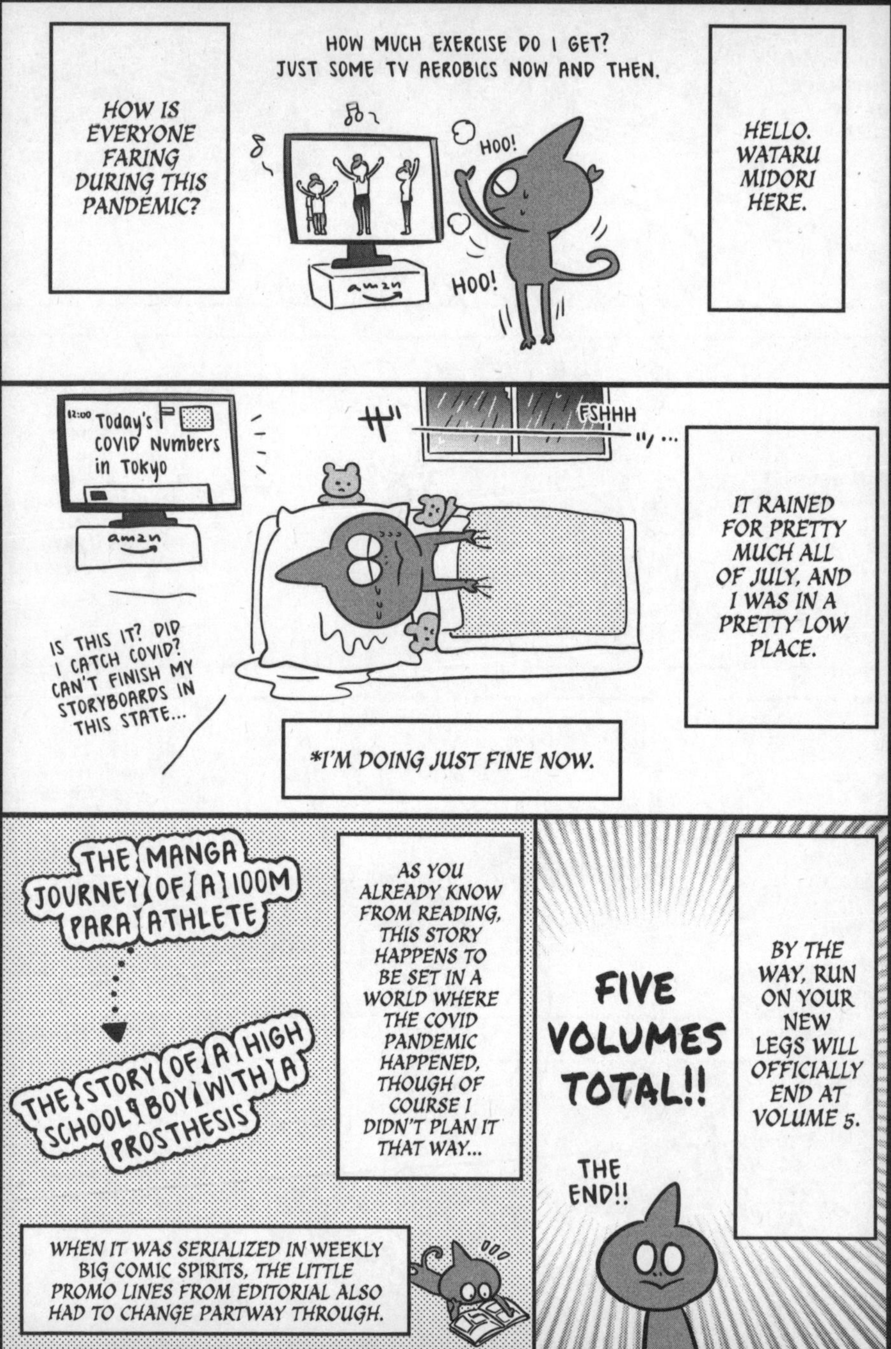
HELLO. WATARU MIDORI HERE.
HOW MUCH EXERCISE DO I GET? JUST SOME TV AEROBICS NOW AND THEN.
HOO!
HOO!
HOW IS EVERYONE FARING DURING THIS PANDEMIC?
IT RAINED FOR PRETTY MUCH ALL OF JULY, AND I WAS IN A PRETTY LOW PLACE.
FSHHH
12:00 Today's COVID Numbers in Tokyo
IS THIS IT? DID I CATCH COVID? CAN'T FINISH MY STORYBOARDS IN THIS STATE...
*I'M DOING JUST FINE NOW.
BY THE WAY, RUN ON YOUR NEW LEGS WILL OFFICIALLY END AT VOLUME 5.
FIVE VOLUMES TOTAL!!
THE END!!
AS YOU ALREADY KNOW FROM READING, THIS STORY HAPPENS TO BE SET IN A WORLD WHERE THE COVID PANDEMIC HAPPENED, THOUGH OF COURSE I DIDN'T PLAN IT THAT WAY...
THE MANGA JOURNEY OF A 100M PARA ATHLETE
THE STORY OF A HIGH SCHOOL BOY WITH A PROSTHESIS
WHEN IT WAS SERIALIZED IN WEEKLY BIG COMIC SPIRITS, THE LITTLE PROMO LINES FROM EDITORIAL ALSO HAD TO CHANGE PARTWAY THROUGH.

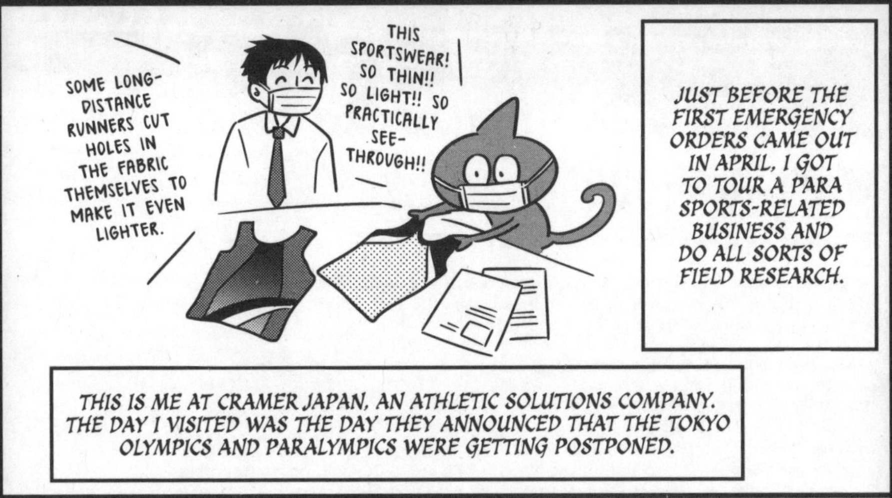
JUST BEFORE THE FIRST EMERGENCY ORDERS CAME OUT IN APRIL, I GOT TO TOUR A PARA SPORTS-RELATED BUSINESS AND DO ALL SORTS OF FIELD RESEARCH.
THIS SPORTSWEAR! SO THIN!! SO LIGHT!! SO PRACTICALLY SEE-THROUGH!!
SOME LONG-DISTANCE RUNNERS CUT HOLES IN THE FABRIC THEMSELVES TO MAKE IT EVEN LIGHTER.
THIS IS ME AT CRAMER JAPAN, AN ATHLETIC SOLUTIONS COMPANY. THE DAY I VISITED WAS THE DAY THEY ANNOUNCED THAT THE TOKYO OLYMPICS AND PARALYMPICS WERE GETTING POSTPONED.
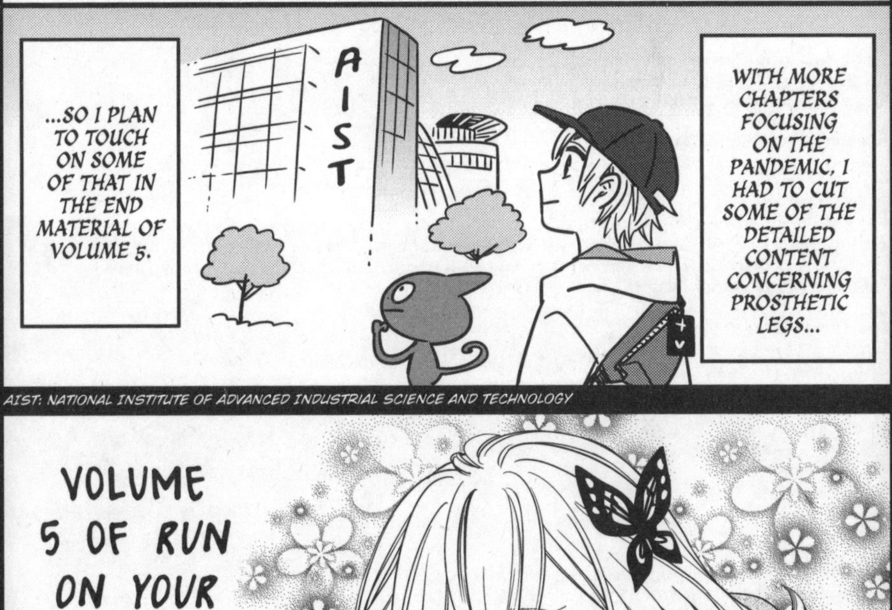
WITH MORE CHAPTERS FOCUSING ON THE PANDEMIC, I HAD TO CUT SOME OF THE DETAILED CONTENT CONCERNING PROSTHETIC LEGS...
AIST
...SO I PLAN TO TOUCH ON SOME OF THAT IN THE END MATERIAL OF VOLUME 5.
AIST: NATIONAL INSTITUTE OF ADVANCED INDUSTRIAL SCIENCE AND TECHNOLOGY
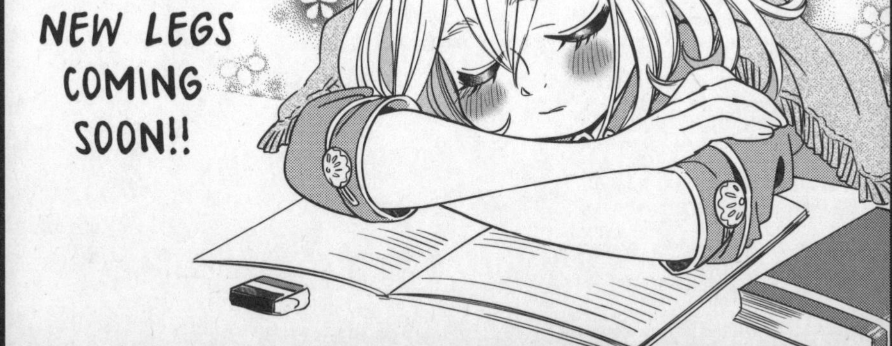
VOLUME 5 OF RUN ON YOUR NEW LEGS COMING SOON!!

RUN ON YOUR NEW LEGS 4

WATARU MIDORI

TRANSLATION: Caleb Cook • **LETTERING:** Abigail Blackman

This book is a work of fiction. Names, characters, places, and incidents are the product of the author's imagination or are used fictitiously. Any resemblance to actual events, locales, or persons, living or dead, is coincidental.

ATARASHII ASHI DE KAKENUKERO. Vol. 4
by Wataru MIDORI
© 2020 Wataru MIDORI
All rights reserved.
Original Japanese edition published by SHOGAKUKAN.
English translation rights in the United States of America, Canada, the United Kingdom, Ireland, Australia and New Zealand arranged with SHOGAKUKAN through Tuttle-Mori Agency, Inc.

Original Cover Design: Yoko AKUTA

English translation © 2023 by Yen Press, LLC

Yen Press, LLC supports the right to free expression and the value of copyright. The purpose of copyright is to encourage writers and artists to produce the creative works that enrich our culture.

The scanning, uploading, and distribution of this book without permission is a theft of the author's intellectual property. If you would like permission to use material from the book (other than for review purposes), please contact the publisher. Thank you for your support of the author's rights.

Yen Press
150 West 30th Street, 19th Floor
New York, NY 10001

Visit us at yenpress.com
facebook.com/yenpress
twitter.com/yenpress
yenpress.tumblr.com
instagram.com/yenpress

First Yen Press Edition: April 2023
Edited by Abigail Blackman & Yen Press Editorial: Carl Li
Designed by Yen Press Design: Liz Parlett, Wendy Chan

Yen Press is an imprint of Yen Press, LLC.
The Yen Press name and logo are trademarks of Yen Press, LLC.

The publisher is not responsible for websites (or their content) that are not owned by the publisher.

Library of Congress Control Number: 2021951359

ISBNs: 978-1-9753-3903-6 (paperback)
      978-1-9753-4572-3 (ebook)

10 9 8 7 6 5 4 3 2 1

WOR

Printed in the United States of America